D0331463

The Red Goves Collection

GIDEON'S GIFT
MAGGIE'S MIRACLE
SARAH'S SONG
HANNAH'S HOPE

FOUR NOVELS BY

KAREN KINGSBURY

WARNER
Faith®

NEW YORK   BOSTON   NASHVILLE

Warner Faith

Time Warner Book Group
1271 Avenue of the Americas, New York, NY 10020
Visit our Web site at www.twbookmark.com.

Warner Faith® and the Warner Faith logo are trademarks of Time Warner Book Group Inc.

Printed in the United States of America

First Edition: October 2005
10 9 8 7 6 5 4 3 2 1

ISBN: 0-446-57966-1 (Christian Book Distributors Edition)

GIDEON'S GIFT

To my parents, Anne and Ted Kingsbury, on the celebration of their fortieth wedding anniversary. Thank you for defining that elusive, "forever" kind of love the world needs so badly. You have been and continue to be an inspiration to each of us five kids, and to our families.

And a special thanks to Dad for creating a rich and poignant memory for me when I was a little girl, something I have never forgotten—something that inspired the writing of *Gideon's Gift*. The memory goes something like this:

> It is Thanksgiving and after the meal you heap leftovers on a sturdy paper plate. We pile into the van and drive around until you find one of the local street people. With tears in your eyes, you step out of the car and hand over the food. "Happy Thanksgiving," you say, your voice choked.
>
> When you climb back behind the wheel, you look at Mom and shrug, your chin quivering. And then you say it, the thing you say still today:
>
> "There, but for the grace of God, go I."

GIDEON'S GIFT

PROLOGUE

The gift that changed them all had led to this: a Christmas wedding.

Nothing could have been more appropriate. Gideon was an angel, after all. Not the haloed, holy kind. But the type that once in a while—when the chance presented itself—made you stare a little harder at her upper back. In case she was sprouting wings.

From his seat in the back of the church, Earl Badgett's tired old eyes grew moist. A Christmas wedding was the only kind for Gideon. Because if ever angels shone it was in December. This was the season when Gideon's gift had mattered most.

Gideon's gift.

A million memories called to him. Had it been thirteen years? Earl stared at the vision she made, sur-

I

rounded by white satin and lace. The greatest miracle was that Gideon had survived.

He brushed the back of his hand over his damp cheeks. *She actually survived.*

But that wasn't the only miracle.

Earl watched Gideon smile at her father—the glowing, unforgettable smile of a young woman on the brink of becoming. The two of them linked arms and began a graceful walk down the aisle. It was a simple wedding, really. A church full of family and friends, there to witness a most tender moment for a girl who deserved it more than any other. A girl whose love, whose very presence, lit the room and caused people to feel grateful for one reason alone: They had been given the privilege of knowing Gideon Mercer. God had lent her a little while longer to the mere mortals who made up her world. And in that they were all blessed.

Gideon and her father were halfway down the aisle when it happened. Gideon hesitated, glanced over her shoulder, and found Earl. Her eyes had that haunting look that spoke straight to his soul, the same as they always had. They shared the briefest smile, a smile that told him he wasn't the only one. She, too, was remembering the miracle of that Christmas.

The corners of Earl's mouth worked their way up his worn face. *You did it, angel. You got your dream.* His heart danced with joy. It was all he could do to stay seated, when everything in him wanted to stand and cheer.

Go get 'em, Gideon!

As they rarely did anymore, the memories came like long lost friends. Filling Earl's mind, flooding his senses, linking hands with his heart and leading him back. Back thirteen years to that wondrous time when heaven orchestrated an event no less miraculous than Christmas itself. An event that changed both their lives.

An event that saved them.

Time flew . . . back to the winter when Earl first met Gideon Mercer.

CHAPTER ONE

The red gloves were all that mattered.

If living on the streets of Portland was a prison, the red gloves were the key. The key that—for a few brief hours—set him free from the lingering stench and hopeless isolation, free from the relentless rain and the tarp-covered shanty.

The key that freed him to relive the life he'd once had. A life he could never have again.

Something about the red gloves took him back and made it all real—their voices, their touch, their warmth as they sat with him around the dinner table each night. Their love. It was as though he'd never lost a bit of it.

As long as he wore the gloves.

Otherwise, the prison would have been unbearable. Because the truth was Earl had lost everything. His life, his hope, his will to live. But when he slipped on the gloves . . . Ah, when he felt the finely knit wool surround his fingers, Earl still had the one thing that mattered. He still had a family. If only for a few dark hours.

It was the first of November, and the gloves were put away, hidden in the lining of his damp parka. Earl never wore them until after dinner, when he was tucked beneath his plastic roof, anxious to rid himself of another day. He would've loved to wear them all the time, but he didn't dare. They were nice gloves. Handmade. The kind most street people would snatch from a corpse.

Dead or alive, Earl had no intention of losing them.

He shuffled along Martin Luther King Boulevard, staring at the faces that sped past him. He was invisible to them. Completely invisible. He'd figured that much out his first year on the streets. Oh, once in a while they'd toss him a quarter or shout at him: "Get a job, old man!" or "Go back to California!"

But mostly they just ignored him.

The people who passed him were still in the race, still making decisions and meeting deadlines, still believing it could never happen to them. They carried themselves with a sense of self-reliance—a certainty that they were somehow better than him. For most of them, Earl was little more than a nuisance. An unsightly blemish on the streets of their nice city.

Rain began to fall. Small, icy droplets found their way through his hooded parka and danced across his balding head. He didn't mind. He was used to the rain; it fit his mood. The longer he was on the street the more true that became.

He moved along.

"Big Earl!"

The slurred words carried over the traffic. Earl looked up. A black man was weaving along the opposite sidewalk, shouting and waving a bottle of Crown Royal. He was headed for the same place as Earl: the mission.

Rain or shine, there were meals at the mission. All the street people knew it. Earl had seen the black man there a hundred times before, but he couldn't remember his name. Couldn't remember most of their names. They didn't matter to him. Nothing did. Nothing except the red gloves.

The black man waved the bottle again and shot him a toothless grin. "God loves ya, Big Earl!"

Earl looked away. "Leave me alone," he muttered, and pulled his parka tighter around his neck and face.

The mission director had given him the coat two years ago. It had served its purpose. The dark-green nylon was brown now, putrid-smelling and sticky with dirt. Earl's whiskers caught in the fibers and made his face itch.

He couldn't remember the last time he'd shaved.

Across the street the black man gave up. He raised his bottle to a group of three animated women with fancy clothes and new umbrellas. "Dinner bell's a callin' me home, ladies!"

The women stopped chatting and formed a tight, nervous cluster. They squeezed by the man, creating as much distance between them as they could. After they'd passed, the black man raised his bottle again. "God loves ya!"

The mission was two blocks up on the right. Behind him, Earl could hear the black man singing, his words running together like gutter water. Earl's cool response hadn't bothered him at all.

"Amazing grace, how sweet da sound . . ."

Earl narrowed his gaze. Street people wore thick skins. Layers, Earl called it—years of living so far deep inside yourself, nothing could really touch you. Not the weather, not the nervous stares from passersby, not the callous comments from the occasional motorist.

And certainly not anything another street person might say or do.

The mission doors were open. A hapless stream of people mingled among the regulars. Earl rolled his eyes and stared at his boots. When temperatures dropped below fifty, indigents flooded the place. The regulars could barely get a table.

He squeezed his way past the milling newcomers, all of them trying to figure out where the line started and the quickest way to get a hot plate. Up ahead were two empty-eyed drifters—young guys with long hair and years of drug use written on their faces. Earl slid between them, grabbed a plate of food, and headed for his table, a forgotten two-seater off by itself in the far corner of the room.

"Hey, Earl."

He looked up and saw D. J. Grange, mission director for the past decade. The man was bundled in his red-plaid jacket, same as always. His eyes were blue. Too blue. And piercing. As though he could see things Earl didn't tell anyone. D. J. was always talking God this and God that. It was amazing, really. After all these years, D. J. still didn't get it.

Earl looked back down at his plate. "I don't come

for a sermon. You know that," he mumbled into his instant mashed potatoes.

"We got people praying, Earl." D.J. gripped the nearest chair and leaned closer. Earl could feel the man's smile without looking. "Any requests? Just between us?"

"Yes." Earl set his fork down and shot D.J. the hardest look he could muster. "Leave me alone."

"Fine." D.J. grinned like a shopping-mall Santa Claus. "Let me know if you change your mind." Still smiling, he moved on to the next table.

There was one other chair at Earl's table, but no one took it. There was an unspoken code among street people—sober ones, anyway: "Eyes cast down, don't come around." Earl kept his eyes on his plate, and on this night the code worked. The others would rather stand than share a meal with a man who needed his space.

Besides his appearance would easily detract even the most hardened street people. He didn't look in the mirror often, but when he did, he understood why they kept their distance. It wasn't his scraggly, gray hair or the foul-smelling parka. It was his eyes.

Cold, dead eyes.

The only time he figured his eyes might possibly show signs of life or loneliness was at night. When he wore the red gloves. But then, no one ever saw his eyes during those hours.

He finished his plate, pushed back from the table and headed for the exit. D.J. watched him go, standing guard at the front of the food line. "See you tomorrow, Earl." He waved big. "I'll be praying for you."

Earl didn't turn around. He walked hard and fast out the door into the dark, rainy night. It was colder than before. It worried him a little. Some years, when the first cold night had hit, another street person had swiped his bed or taken off with his tarp. His current tarp hung like a curtain across the outside wall of his home. It was easily the most important part of his physical survival. Small wonder they were taken so often.

He narrowed his eyes and picked up his pace. His back hurt and he felt more miserable than usual. He was anxious for sleep, anxious to shut out the world and everything bad about it.

Anxious for the red gloves.

He'd spent this day like every other day, wandering the alleyways and staring at his feet. He always took his meals at the mission and waited. For sundown, for sleep, for death. Years ago, when he'd first hit the streets, his emotions had been closer to the surface. Sorrow and grief and guilt, fear and loneliness and anxiety. Hourly these would seize him, strangling his battered heart like a vice grip.

But each day on the streets had built in him another layer, separating him from everything he'd ever felt, everything about the man he used to be and the life he used to lead. His emotions were buried deep now, and Earl was sure they'd never surface again. He was a shell—a meaningless, unfeeling shell.

His existence was centered in nothingness and nightfall.

He rounded the corner and through the wet darkness he saw his home. It was barely noticeable, tucked beneath an old wrought-iron stairwell deep in the heart of a forgotten alley. Hanging from seven rusty bolts along the underside of the stairs was the plastic tarp. He lifted the bottom of it off the ground and crawled inside. No matter how wet it was, rain almost never found its way beyond the tarp. His pillow and pile of old blankets were still dry.

He'd been waiting for this moment all day.

His fingers found the zipper in the lining of his parka and lowered it several inches. He tucked his hand inside and found them, right where he'd left them this morning. As soon as he made contact with the soft wool, the layers began to fall away, exposing what was left of his heart.

Carefully he pulled the gloves out and slipped them onto his fingers, one at a time. He stared at them, studied them, remembering the hands that had knit them a lifetime ago. Then he did something that had become part of his routine, something he did every night at this time. He brought his hands to his face and kissed first one woolen palm and then the other.

"Good night, girls." He muttered the words out loud. Then he lay down and covered himself with the tattered blankets. When he was buried far beneath, when the warmth of his body had served to sufficiently warm the place where he slept, he laced his gloved fingers together and drifted off to sleep.

❧

The next morning he was still half given to a wonderful dream when he felt rain on his face. Rain and a stream of light much brighter than usual. With eyes closed, he turned his head from side to side. What was it? Where was the water coming from and why wasn't his tarp working?

He rubbed his fingers together—

—and sat straight up.

"No!" His voice ricocheted off the brick walls of the empty alley.

"Noooo!" He stood up and yelled as loudly as he could—a gut-wrenching, painful cry of the type he hadn't uttered since that awful afternoon five years ago.

His head was spinning. He grabbed at his hair, pulled it until his scalp hurt. It wasn't possible. Yet . . .

He'd been robbed. In the middle of the night someone had found him sleeping and taken most of what made up his home. His tarp was gone. Most of his blankets, too.

But that wasn't all. They had stolen everything left of his will to live, everything he had to look forward to. Nothing this bad had happened to him since he took to the streets. He shook his head in absolute misery as a driving rain pelted his skin, washing away all that remained of his sleep.

He stared at his hands, his body trembling. The thing he'd feared most of all had finally happened.

The red gloves were gone.

CHAPTER TWO

The hardest part was pretending every-thing was okay.

Brian Mercer held tightly to Gideon's small hand and kept his steps short so she could keep up. With all his heart he hoped this would be the day the doctors looked him in the eye and told him the good news: that his precious eight-year-old daughter was in remission.

It was a possibility. Gideon seemed stronger than last week at this time. But Brian had felt that way more than once and each time the report had been the same. The cancer wasn't advancing, but it wasn't backing off, either.

Brian stifled a sigh as they made their way from the car to Doernbecher's Children's Hospital. If only Tish were here with them. Tish was wonderful at raising Gideon's spirits. Optimism and laughter rang out in every conversation between them. It was something the two of them brought out in each other.

Tish would have found a way to make the doctor appointment fun. But she couldn't miss even a day of work. Not with Gideon's medical bills piling up. Not with his boss threatening layoffs and more hourly cuts at the lumber mill. No, Tish couldn't possibly be here. Her two cashier jobs were sometimes all they could depend on.

At least the neighbors took little Dustin whenever Gideon had an appointment.

They stepped into the elevator and Gideon looked up at him, her head cocked to one side. "What's wrong, Daddy?"

"Nothing." Brian gave Gideon's hand a light squeeze. "I was wishing Mommy could be here."

"Me, too." A shadow fell across Gideon's face and her eyes took on that soulful, deep look—the look that had become a permanent part of her expression since her diagnosis six months ago. They fell silent for a moment. "Do you think I'll be better today?"

"Well . . ." Brian bit the inside of his lip. There was

no point getting her hopes up, but at the same time he had a feeling. *Maybe . . . just maybe . . .* "How do you feel?"

Her eyes lit up. "Better."

"Okay." He leaned down and kissed the top of her woolen beret. "Then, yes. I think today might be the day."

The routine was the same every time. Once they reached the right floor, they checked in at the lab and a technician drew a vial of Gideon's blood. In the beginning——when she'd first gotten sick——the needles had scared her. But she was used to them now, poor girl.

After the blood draw they made their way down a long, glassed-in catwalk, fifteen floors above Portland's hilly downtown. Halfway across, they found their bench and stopped. At first they had used the bench as a resting point, because Gideon tired so easily. Now it was just something they did. Besides, Gideon's test results always took awhile, so there was no hurry.

The bench was placed at a point where the view was breathtaking. There were still sailboats on the Columbia and Willamette, and the sun glistening off a dozen tributaries that crisscrossed the city. And, on a clear day like this one, the towering white presence of Mt. Hood.

"Pretty, isn't it?" Brian slipped his arm around Gideon's shoulders.

Gideon's eyes narrowed. "Sometimes I feel like a bird up here. Like I could fly over the city and down along the rivers." She looked up at him. "And never, ever be sick again."

Brian swallowed hard. Something about this part of their routine always made Gideon pensive. It was the hardest part for Brian. The time when he wanted to cry out to God and ask "Why?" Why an eight-year-old little girl? Why his daughter? How was it he and Tish could help strangers, but do nothing for their own child?

All he wanted was his family back. Tish and Gideon and Dustin and him. Laughing and loving and taking walks on crisp winter mornings like this one. Just a series of days where none of them had to wonder whether Gideon was getting better. Whether she'd live to see the following Christmas.

There was nothing Brian could say to his daughter, no promises he could make. Instead he hugged her and cleared his throat. It was time to pick a topic. Since her first doctor visit, the two of them had always chosen this time to discuss special things. So far they'd covered a dozen subjects: how mountains were formed, why rivers flowed, and where exactly was heaven. But today, the second of December, Brian had a specific topic in mind. A happy one. One he and Tish had talked about the night before.

"Let's talk about Christmas, Gideon." He took her hand once more and they continued down the catwalk toward the doctor's office.

"Yeah." A slow smile lifted the corners of her mouth. "Let's do that."

They checked in and found their usual spot, on a sofa near the back of the waiting room. Brian angled his body so he could see her, study her wispy brown hair and unforgettable eyes. She was a miniature of Tish. A more serious, ethereal miniature. She'd been that way even before the cancer. As though she carried something deep in her heart—an innocent wisdom, an ability to see straight to the soul of a person. It was what set her apart from other children.

And what he and Tish would miss most if—

Brian blinked. He had ordered himself never to think such things. Nothing could be gained by worrying and dreading the future, borrowing tomorrow's pain for today. Still, there were times when fear didn't bother knocking. Times when it kicked in the door and tramped right in. Times like these.

"Okay." He exhaled slowly. "Christmas." He reached

for Gideon's hand once more. "Where should we start?"

Her eyes danced like the twinkling lights on the hospital's Christmas tree. "Let's talk about the *perfect* Christmas."

"Hmmm . . . The perfect Christmas." Brian leaned into the sofa and gazed out the glass-panel window at the brilliant blue sky beyond. The answer was an easy one. They would find enough money to get Gideon a bone-marrow transplant. She would recover quickly and find her place once more among her little friends at school. And they'd never, ever again have to talk about Christmas from the corner of a cancer doctor's office.

He shifted his eyes to Gideon. "You go first."

"Okay." The twinkle in her eyes dimmed somewhat. She suddenly looked a million miles away, lost in a world of imagination. "We would have a real tree, a tall one that almost touches the ceiling. With lights and decorations and a star on top for you and Mom." She released his hand and stretched her arms over her head. "A big turkey. And a fire truck for Dustin."

Brian could feel his heart breaking. Gideon's perfect Christmas was the kind most kids expected. But money had never come easily for him and Tish. This Christmas—like so many others—they would assemble a four-foot green-plastic tree and cover it with a seventy-cent box of tinsel. Toys would be secondhand and maybe missing parts. Dinner would be chicken and mashed potatoes.

But it was more than many people had, and he and Tish were grateful. Christmas was always wonderful, despite the lack of material trappings. And the children never complained, never made mention of the fact that their Christmases were any different from that of other children.

Until now.

Of course, Gideon was hardly complaining. She was just playing along, talking about the topic he'd suggested. Brian clenched his jaw. If there'd been a way to find the money, he would have done just that—found the biggest, best, most fragrant, Christmas tree and all the trinkets and toys to go with it. But the mill had cut his hours down to twelve a week. It was barely a job. And Gideon's medical bills—

Brian pushed the thought from his mind. He met his daughter's eyes. "Didn't you forget someone?"

Her expression was open, unpretentious. Then it hit her and she giggled. "You mean me?"

"Yes, you." Brian twirled a lock of her hair around

his finger. "What would you get on this perfect Christmas?"

She lowered her chin. "Really?"

"Really."

"Well . . ." She let her gaze fall to her hands for a beat. When she looked up, the twinkle was back. Brighter than ever. "In my *perfect* Christmas my gift would be a brand-new dolly. The kind with pretty hair and eyes that blink and a soft lacey dress."

"A new doll, huh?" Brian tried to sound surprised, but he wasn't. "How come?"

"A doll never gets sad when you're sick." She looked up and smiled. Her knowing expression spoke volumes. "Sometimes a friend like that would be nice."

From the time she was old enough to talk Gideon had wanted a new doll. A few years ago she'd even cut a doll photo from a catalog and taped it to the wall beside her bed. The clipping still hung there today. From time to time Brian had come across a used doll and brought it home for Gideon. It always smelled funny or was missing its dress or shoes. But Gideon didn't mind that. No, the problem was that in very little time she always loved the doll into nonexistence. A leg would fall off, or an arm, or the doll's head.

And Gideon would talk about her new doll again.

Each year Brian and Tish considered the possibility, and each year it was out of the question. New dolls like the one Gideon wanted were expensive. As much as a week's worth of groceries.

Gideon seemed to sense his thoughts. "It's just pretend, Daddy. No big deal." She leaned closer and let her head rest on his shoulder. "What's your perfect Christmas?"

The answers that had come to mind earlier returned. "That's easy." He kissed her forehead. "In the perfect Christmas we never have to come back here again."

Brian felt Gideon nod against his arm. "Know what my teacher said last week?"

"What, baby?" He stayed close, his face nuzzled against the top of her beret.

"She said Christmas miracles happen to those who believe."

The words played over again in Brian's mind. "I like it."

"Me, too." Gideon sat a bit straighter and stared at the doctor's office door. "I believe, Daddy."

"We all do."

"Then maybe that's what we'll get this Christmas. A

miracle." She turned to him. "That would be better than anything, wouldn't it?"

"You mean like finding out that you're better today?"

"Well, that." She giggled. "But I mean something really big. Something so big it could only be a Christmas miracle."

A lump formed in Brian's throat as he studied his daughter. *She has no idea how sick she is, God. No idea.* He struggled to find his voice. "Then that's what we'll pray for."

"Let's pray now, Daddy. Right here."

He gave her a slow smile. "Thata' girl, Gideon. That's the way to believe."

Then, with cancer patients coming and going around them, Brian took hold of Gideon's hands, bowed his head, and prayed for something so big, it could only be a Christmas miracle.

An hour later Brian had the answer that mattered most to him.

Gideon was in remission!

Her blood results were better than they'd been since she was diagnosed with leukemia. The doctor was cautious. Remission was a tricky thing. It could last weeks or years, depending on the patient. There was no way to know. And a person with her type of leukemia was never really cured until they'd had a successful bone-marrow transplant.

Still, it was the answer Brian and Tish had been praying for since Gideon got sick. Brian blinked back tears as they walked back to the car.

"I can't wait to tell Mom." Gideon skipped a few steps and then stopped and faced him. "If I'm not sick, it's going to be a great Christmas!"

"Yes, it is." Brian stopped and held out his hands. Gideon knew the sign well. She took a running jump and he caught her, sweeping her into his arms and holding her close. "We even got our miracle."

Gideon giggled. "Daddy, that's not the miracle." She rubbed her nose against his. "Remember? We asked God for something *really* big."

"Oh, that's right." Brian chuckled as he set her back down. They had reached the parking lot, and he took hold of her hand. "Something tells me Mom will think it's pretty big."

On the way home, Gideon fell asleep and Brian turned off the radio. Traffic moved along slowly. *God, you're so good. Gideon asked for a miracle and we got one. Just like that.*

Memories of Gideon filled his mind. The time when she was two and shared her pacifier with the neighbor's cat. Her kindergarten year when a little boy didn't bring a snack for two months straight and Gideon gave him hers. The way her perfect Christmas involved a fire truck for Dustin before anything for herself.

The loss of any child would be devastating. But Gideon—

Tears clouded his eyes once more. *Thank you, God. Thank you a million times over.* He was consumed with gratefulness the whole way home. But as he neared their apartment building, a passing thought hit him.

If this wasn't the miracle Gideon had prayed for, what was? What could possibly be bigger than the news that she was in remission?

Without warning, a chill passed over Brian.

If Christmas miracles truly happened to those who believed, then maybe God wasn't finished handing out miracles to the Mercer family. Somehow, someway,

Brian had the uncanny certainty that some other amazing thing was about to happen. Some sort of direct response to Gideon's prayer.

Something so big it could only be a Christmas miracle.

CHAPTER THREE

The hardest part about being sick was this: Her parents thought she was help-less.

As Gideon played cards with Dustin and waited for her mother to come home that afternoon, she hoped the doctor's news would help change their feelings. After six months of hardly ever going to school, and of sleeping all the time, she was ready for a change. Ready to join her parents in the thing their family loved most.

Their helping work.

As far back as Gideon could remember, she and Dustin had been part of their parents' helping work. Sometimes they met with other people from church and visited hospitals or homes where old people with gray hair lived. Lots of times they painted a church or picked up dirty pop cans and hamburger wrappers along busy roads. Other days they knocked on doors and collected canned food for hungry people.

She couldn't explain it to her friends at school. But working with her parents and helping people was the happiest thing Gideon ever did.

Right before she got sick her parents had talked about serving dinner at someplace called "the mission." Then she'd started getting bruises and colds, and every time she brushed her teeth there was blood in her spit.

After that she had to see the doctor a bunch of times and finally they told her she had leukemia. Gideon still wasn't exactly sure what that was, but it was very bad. Worse than a cold or a flu or even chicken pox. Leukemia didn't always hurt like those things, but it lasted longer. Sometimes it lasted forever. Gideon knew that because she'd heard her mom and dad talking about it.

But now she was better. That's what the doctor said. Maybe not better all the way, but better than she had been. And that had to be a good thing.

The card game ended, and an hour later she was sitting by the window waiting when her mother came home. Gideon raced to the door and flung it open.

"I'm better, Mommy. The doctor said so." She wrapped her arms around her mother's waist and held on tight.

"Gideon." Her mother dropped to her knees. Gideon felt her hair move with her mom's warm breath. "Are you sure?"

"Yes. Daddy can tell you about it."

Usually her mom's hugs lasted just a little while. But this one went on for a long time. When her mother let go and stood up, she was wiping her cheeks.

"You're sad."

A big smile filled her mother's face. "No, honey. I'm happy."

Gideon nodded just as her father and Dustin came around the corner.

"Gideon's better, Mommy! Gideon's better!" Dustin jumped three times and raised a fist in the air.

"You heard the news?" Her dad came up and hugged her mom. They looked so happy it made glad tears in Gideon's eyes.

"Is she . . . is it really in remission?"

"Yes." Her father tousled Gideon's hair and patted Dustin's head. "It's going to be the best Christmas ever."

Gideon waited until they were finished talking. Then

she stood before them and caught their attention. "Can I ask you something?"

"Sure." Her mother leaned against her father's shoulder. They were still in a half hug with their arms around each other's waists.

Gideon hesitated while Dustin ran off to play. "There's something I want to do. I've wanted to do it ever since I got sick. And now that I'm better . . ."

Her parents gave each other a funny look. Like even though the doctor said so, they weren't sure she was really that much better. "Okay, Gideon." Her father's eyes looked softer than before. "What do you want to do?"

She took hold of her mom's hand and looked at them both. "I want to serve dinner at the mission." She started to smile. "Remember? We were going to do that before I got sick and you said we had to wait?"

Once more her parents looked at each other, but this time her father lifted one shoulder. "D. J. called yesterday and asked about it. The holiday season gets pretty busy, I guess."

Her mom's forehead wrinkled up a little and her mouth stayed in a straight line. But after a moment she nodded. "I guess we could give it a try. As long as Gideon doesn't get too tired."

"Yes!" Gideon threw her arms around her parents. "When can we go?"

"They need someone tomorrow night." Her father bent down and kissed the top of her head. Her parents always did that. It was one of the reasons Gideon knew they loved her so much. "I'll call D. J. and make the plans."

Before she went to bed that night, her dad warned her about the mission.

"Some of the people might seem scary, Gideon. But most of them just look that way from living on the streets."

"On the streets?" Gideon pulled the covers up to her chin and studied her father. She couldn't tell if he was teasing her. "No one lives on the streets, Daddy. There're too many cars."

"Not right on the street, honey. But on the sidewalk. In doorways and under stairs. Sometimes in alleys or under bridges."

Gideon could feel her eyes get big. Her father wasn't teasing at all. He was serious. "Under bridges?"

"Yes."

"That's sad, Daddy." A scared feeling came up in Gideon's heart. "How come?"

"Well . . ." He reached for her hand and immediately she felt safe again. "Some people don't have a place to live. Those are the people who go to the mission for dinner."

"So the mission is sort of like their home?"

"It's where they eat. But most of the people who take meals at the mission don't have a home."

Gideon thought about that. About being outside without her blankets and warm pillow, without her mom and dad. If the people at the mission didn't have a home, then maybe— "Don't they have a family, either?"

"No." Her dad took a long breath. "Most of them don't, baby."

Tears filled Gideon's eyes and she had to blink to see her father clearly. "That's the saddest thing. Isn't there someone they could live with?"

Her father looked like he was thinking very hard. "It's not that easy, Gideon. You'll see." He squeezed her hand. "The best thing we can do is serve them dinner and pray for them."

Gideon's heart felt like a wet towel: heavy and full of tears.

Then she got an idea. "They probably aren't very happy people."

"No. Probably not."

Gideon wiped her fingers across her eyes and sniffed. "Then maybe . . . maybe we can make them smile."

For a moment her father said nothing, and Gideon thought his eyes looked wet. Then the corners of his mouth lifted just a little. "That's my girl." His voice was quieter than before. "Let's get the whole place smiling."

CHAPTER FOUR

Edith Badgett's heart had ached for her missing son since the day he disappeared.

The fact that she was an old woman and her son a man in his fifties did nothing to ease Edith's pain.

It made it worse.

Life didn't wait forever. She knew that better than most people. If Earl didn't come home soon, if he didn't call or leave a message or write a letter, she and Paul might not be around when he did. They were pushing eighty now, and neither of them in good health.

Edith lowered herself into a chair by the window and stared out, the same way she did every morning. It was December already. Five years since that awful day when their family had changed forever. She drew a shaky breath and dismissed the memories; they were not welcome, not now or ever. She and Paul had spent enough time grieving. There was precious little time left, and she refused to spend it dwelling on a moment in time she could do nothing about.

She reached for her leather journal and the blue pen she kept tucked inside. The book held hundreds of lined pages, but after nearly five years most of them were written on, filled with letters she'd penned to Earl. At first the letters had been about the tragedy of that long-ago afternoon. But eventually Edith wrote about other things—Earl's childhood, his high school days, the feelings she had for him and wasn't sure she'd told him.

The times he had lost since leaving.

Earl's brother and sister still lived in Redding, still came by every few weeks for Sunday dinner or a game of Hearts. There were nieces and nephews and whole seasons of life that Earl was missing.

But . . . maybe he wasn't missing them. Maybe he was delusional or drugged or even dead.

Edith found the first blank page and began to write. Today she wanted to talk about Christmas. Christmas had been Earl's favorite time of year, after all. The time when he had always seemed most like the little boy he'd once been.

Dear Earl. She paused and gazed out the window once more. *Where is he? How is he getting along?* For a moment she closed her eyes and remembered him the way he'd been before he left. *Come home, son. Please. Before it's too late.*

She blinked her eyes open and returned her attention to the matter at hand. Slowly her pen began to move across the page.

It's December again and I must tell you, son, my hope is strongest at this time of the year. I picture you, somewhere out there, and know that wherever you are you know this much: Special things happen at Christmas. I hope—wherever you are—you're still thinking of us, Earl. We're still here—your father and I. Still waiting for your return.

Still watching the door.

A single tear fell on the page and Edith gave it a delicate brush of her fingers. She had never been a praying woman; she didn't figure it mattered much whether some sort of silent words went up to a God who maybe didn't exist. But days like this she almost wished she did believe.

She reached for a tissue and wiped it beneath her eyes. As she did, Paul entered the room and quietly took the seat beside her.

"Writing to Earl?"

She nodded and met his eyes. No matter how much time passed, she and Paul had promised each other they would not forget their youngest son. They would continue to hope for his well-being, and most of all for his return. They would keep watch for him and believe with each passing season that one day he would come home.

Paul stroked his wrinkled chin and turned to the front walkway. "It's Christmastime again."

"Yes." Edith closed the journal. "I was thinking the same thing."

"Every Christmas since he left—" Paul took a quick breath. He was winded more often now, weaker than he'd been even a year ago. "—I tell myself this is the year. He'll find his way home. Walk up the sidewalk and make Christmas perfect. Like it used to be."

This was what she loved about Paul. He shared his heart with her. So many men couldn't, wouldn't do that. But not Paul. They had cherished each of their fifty-seven years of marriage because they were first and always friends. Best friends.

She reached over and laid her hand on Paul's. "Maybe this is the Christmas."

Normally, when she made a statement like that, Paul would smile and agree with her. After all, they had nothing if they didn't have hope. But this morning Paul's eyes narrowed. After a long pause, he gave a shake of his head. "I don't think so, Edith. Not this time."

The corners of Edith's mouth dropped. "What?"

He stared at her and what she saw in his eyes left a pit in her stomach. Paul didn't have to answer her. His eyes told her exactly what he didn't want to say.

After five Decembers without Earl—without hearing from him or having any idea where he was—Paul had given up. The thought grieved Edith deeply. Because Paul's hopelessness could only mean one thing. He no longer expected Earl to come home. Not this Christmas or next.

Not ever.

CHAPTER FIVE

The red gloves had been gone for five weeks, and Earl no longer recognized himself.

Always before there had been a remnant deep within him, a small shadowy bit of the man he'd once been. But not now.

He glanced around the mission, grabbed a plate, and headed for his corner table. His hair was wet and his bones ached more than usual. In the days since he'd been robbed, Earl hadn't been able to find a tarp. Instead he'd ripped apart an old cardboard box and used that to shield himself from the rain and ice. He was fighting a cold, and a cough that seemed worse every day. But he didn't care. So what if his lungs filled with fluid? If he was lucky, it would kill him in his sleep. Then he wouldn't have to look for a way to die.

That's what his life had come to: looking for a way to end it. He could beg a few dollars, buy a bottle of wine, and throw himself in front of a bus. Or hole up beneath his stairwell and never come out, not for food or water or anything.

But neither plan seemed like a sure thing.

The only certainty was that he would never see his girls again.

Though he had long ago given up on life, Earl had still harbored a thought that somehow his family was in heaven. And that if he came around at some point and let D.J. pray for him, maybe, just maybe, he'd wind up there, too. Then they could spend eternity together. Not that he'd ever regularly entertained the thought of eternity, even before he was robbed. Still, it had been there. Lying dormant in the shallow soil of his heart.

But not anymore.

The red gloves were all he'd had, the only thing that had mattered. What kind of God would take his family and then his will to live? No, the whole God thing was a pipe dream—a crutch that helped people through the frightening valley of death.

Well, that was fine for other people, but not Earl. He didn't need any help. He *wanted* to find death. Wanted it so badly it was all he thought about anymore. How he could do it . . . where . . . when . . .

He stared at his plate. Stew again. There was a stale roll beside the mound of mushy meat and potatoes, but only one. The mission must be losing money. Usually they gave two rolls. Maybe he should go back and get another one, before they ran out.

He looked up. And there, standing beside his table, was a young girl whose soulful eyes took his breath away. "Hello, sir." A smile lifted the corners of her mouth. "Can I get you anything?"

She was small—underweight, even—and she wore a woolen beret. Her brown hair was thin and scraggly, and her clothing was faded. She was definitely not the most beautiful child Earl had ever seen.

But there was something about her eyes. Something almost angelic.

Don't look at me that way, kid.

Earl kept the words to himself and let his gaze fall to his plate again. Kids worked at the mission now and then, but they always left him alone. He expected this girl to back away, but instead she took a step closer.

"Sir?" The child stood there, unmoving. "I said, is there anything I can get you?"

Earl planted his fork into a piece of meat and lifted his eyes to hers once more. "They only gave me one roll."

Again she smiled. "That's easy. I'll get you another one."

She walked off, slower than most children. He watched her approach the line, take an empty plate, and slip two dinner rolls onto it. Then she carried the plate back to him, set it down, and waited.

"Aren't you going to say thank you?" Her voice was gentle, like a summer breeze.

"Leave me alone, kid."

The girl hesitated for a moment, then pulled out the chair opposite Earl and sat down. "My name's Gideon." She scooted her chair in. "What's yours?"

Earl didn't know whether to yell at the kid or get up and find a new table. Maybe if he answered her question, she'd go away. "Earl."

"It's only three weeks till Christmas, Earl. Did you know that?"

Christmas? Why was the girl here? There had to be a dozen old ladies in the room who would enjoy a conversation with her. Why him? He swallowed a bite of stew and let his eyes meet hers for a brief moment. "I hate Christmas."

He expected that would do the trick. Tell most kids you hate Christmas and they'd get the hint. But not this girl. She clasped her hands neatly on top of the table and stared at him. "My daddy and I were talking about the perfect Christmas. You know—if you could have the perfect Christmas, what it would be like." She waited. "Wanna know mine?"

His meal was half finished, so there was no point looking for a new table. Maybe she'd leave if he said nothing. He took a bite of the roll and lowered his eyes.

The child was undaunted. She took a quick breath and continued. "A perfect Christmas would have a real tree that reached almost to the ceiling, with twinkly lights and a star that lit up the room. And a fire truck for my brother, Dustin, and a brand-new doll with golden hair and a lacey dress . . . for me." She drummed her fingers lightly along the edge of the table, completely at ease. "How 'bout you, Earl? What's your perfect Christmas?"

The girl's question did unexpected things to his heart. His throat grew thick. He had to set his roll down and take a swig of water. The perfect Christmas . . . For the briefest instant he could see it all the way it had been, year after year after year. Him and his family around the Christmas tree, celebrating and—

A burning anger rose up and stopped the memory short. Earl stared at the girl one more time. Who was she, anyway, and what right did she have asking him questions? "Get lost, kid."

The child blinked, but her eyes remained the same. Deeper than the river that ran through downtown.

"Daddy and I prayed for a Christmas miracle. My teacher says Christmas miracles happen to those who believe. If I can't have a new dolly, a miracle would be pretty good, don't you think?"

"Listen." A stale sigh eased between Earl's weathered lips. "I eat my meals alone."

"Oh." The child pushed her chair back and stood. "I'll leave." There was a sorrow in her expression that hadn't been there before. Something about it gave Earl a pinprick of guilt. Like he owed the child an apology.

The feeling passed as quickly as it came.

As she turned to leave, the girl tried one last time. "Maybe if you believed, God would give you a Christmas miracle, too."

This time Earl raised his voice. "I don't believe in anything." He slammed his cup down. "Now leave me alone."

❧❧

From across the mission mess hall, Brian Mercer worked the food line and kept an eye on Gideon. She had lived up to her promise, finding ways to make the tired, weary street people smile as she moved from one table to the next.

But not the old man.

Brian had watched Gideon as she got the man a few dinner rolls and then as she sat down across from him. Clearly the man didn't want Gideon's company. But how dare he shout at her? Brian had to fight back his own anger. *What type of miserable man could do that to a child? A child who's only trying to help?*

Brian was about to go find out when D. J. came up beside him. The two of them had gone to high school together and been friends as far back as Brian could remember.

D. J. pointed in the old man's direction. "That's Earl."

"Oh, yeah?" The frustration in his friend's voice told Brian everything he needed to know about the man. "He yelled at Gideon."

"I know." D. J. frowned. "I saw it."

Brian shifted his attention to his daughter. She had crossed the room and was working beside Tish. Her energy seemed half what it had been before. "She wanted to make him smile."

D. J. pursed his lips and exhaled hard. "No one ever reaches old Earl."

"If he can yell at a kid like Gideon, no one ever will."

Gideon crossed the room and came toward them. Brian wanted to shake the old man for taking the bounce out of her step.

"I tried, Daddy." She pointed at the man in the corner. He was hunched over his food, shoveling it in as though the table had a time limit. "But I can't make Earl smile."

Brian clenched his jaw and waited until his anger subsided. "Forget about him, Gideon. Look at all the people who did smile." He lowered himself to her level. "You were great out there. Those people came for a plate of food and instead they got a cup of happiness."

Gideon's dimples deepened and her sorrow lifted somewhat. "Earl needs a whole bucketful."

D. J. took a step closer. "Don't worry about him, Gideon. We've all tried to reach old Earl. He's not a

happy man, honey. Believe me, it would take a miracle to make him smile."

Gideon's mouth hung open for a moment, her eyes wider than before. She turned to her father, her voice filled with awe. "What did he say?"

Clanging came from the kitchen as volunteers washed the dishes. Brian moved closer to his daughter so she could hear him. "He said it would take a miracle."

"Good." Gideon's eyes lit up and she turned to look at Earl again. He had dropped his plate in the tub of dirty dishes and was making his way out into the cold, dark night. "That's what I thought."

And with that, she skipped off toward another table of street people. Her energy seemed to have returned as quickly as it had left. Brian wondered why. Whatever thoughts were going through Gideon's head, he hoped they had nothing to do with old Earl.

A bitter man like that didn't deserve the attention of anyone.

Least of all his precious Gideon.

Gideon waited until Dustin was asleep before she did it.

When she could hear his soft breathing and she was sure he wasn't going to wake up, she slipped out of bed and dropped to her knees. The floor felt bumpy through her worn nightgown, and her knees hurt. They'd done that ever since she got sick. But right now the hurt didn't matter.

She'd been planning this since they left the mission.

The idea had come when she'd heard her father's friend talking about Earl. What was it he'd said? *It would take a miracle to make Earl smile.* Yes, that was it. It would take a miracle. Gideon had thought about that ever since.

At first when Earl yelled at her, she'd been sad. Like maybe she had said something to make him angry. But that wasn't it at all.

The old man was worse than a person who didn't smile, and Gideon knew why: Earl didn't believe.

And her dad's friend said it would take a miracle to change that.

Gideon's heart bumped around inside her the same way it did on the first day of school. She folded her hands and bowed her head. Sometimes she prayed quietly, in her own heart. But not tonight. This was a big prayer—one of the biggest she'd ever prayed. That's why she'd had to wait for Dustin to fall asleep. So she could whisper the words out loud.

"Dear God. Hi. It's me. Gideon."

She waited, just in case God wanted to talk.

"Daddy and I asked you for something so big it could only be a Christmas miracle." The air was cold around her legs, and she began to shiver. "Well, God, I think I found something. You see, there's a man at the mission named Earl. He's old and mad and he doesn't remember how to smile. Worse than that, he forgot how to believe."

She shifted position so her knees wouldn't hurt. "My teacher says Christmas miracles happen to those who believe. If that's true—if it's really true—then please, God, please help Earl believe again. That's something very big, but I know you can do it. And when you do, it will really be the best Christmas miracle of all."

CHAPTER SIX

It was time to face reality.

Christmas was only twelve days away and Brian Mercer had no choice but to admit the obvious: There simply wasn't enough money to make this Christmas the perfect one Gideon dreamed of. There would be no real tree, no shiny new fire truck for Dustin, and no new doll for Gideon.

D. J. had found a bag of donated items—a well-loved stuffed cow for Gideon, a bag full of Matchbox cars for Dustin, and a stack of books that looked barely read. And he and Tish had saved up and bought the kids new shoes and socks. It would be a more extravagant Christmas than some. But far from perfect.

Tish had tried to comfort him about that fact. After all, Gideon was in remission. What more could they ask for? Gideon's illness had cost them every spare dime. If she stayed well, if work at the mill picked up, then maybe they could pull off that kind of Christmas next year or the year after that.

He made his way through the front door and slung his coat over an old chair. He felt tired and defeated. "Tish?" He dropped to the old sofa as Tish and Dustin bounded down the stairs.

"Hi, Daddy! Guess what?" Dustin jumped on his lap. He was small for six, but he had enough energy for two boys his age. "Me and Mommy are making Christmas strings."

Christmas strings. Brian hid his frustration. Every year Tish saved up junk mail and old magazines so the kids could cut them apart, twist them into colorful wads of paper, and sew them onto long pieces of string. Christmas strings, they called them. They draped the strings around the apartment as a way of preparing for the holidays.

Couldn't they have real decorations? Just once? Brian kissed Dustin on the cheek. "Good for you, buddy. I'll bet they're the best yet."

Tish leaned down and hugged Brian. She was so beautiful, so happy despite their means. He breathed in her optimism and smiled. "Where's Gideon?"

"Stacking newspapers for Mrs. Jones in 2D."

"Again?" He slid to the edge of the sofa. "Didn't she do that last week?"

"Hmmm." Tish lowered her chin. "I'd say someone's been a little preoccupied."

Brian's mind went blank. "What do you mean?"

Dustin slid down and ran upstairs to play. When he was gone, Tish sat on one of Brian's knees and wove her arms around his neck. "I mean Gideon's been working for the neighbors ever since that first night at the mission."

"What? How come I didn't know about this?" *Why is Gideon working for the neighbors?*

"I think she wants it to be a surprise." Tish nuzzled her face against his. "She makes a quarter every time she brings the mail up for Mrs. Jones and fifty cents for stacking newspapers or dusting."

Brian's frustration doubled. "She's only eight years old, for heaven's sake, Tish. We can't have her out working like that. What's she trying to do?"

"She must need money for something." Tish gave the end of his nose a light tap. "Don't worry about her, Brian. She wants to do this. Whatever she's up to, I figure let's let her do it. She probably wants to buy a present for someone. If it matters to Gideon, it should matter to us."

The following Monday, Gideon brought a tattered paper bag of change to Brian and made an announcement.

"I need to go to the store."

Brian kept his expression neutral. "What for, honey?"

"I wanna buy a Christmas present for Earl."

A strange mix of awe and frustration shot through Brian. "Old Earl, the man at the mission?"

"Yes." Resolve was written across Gideon's earnest face. Her excitement was palpable. "For the Christmas dinner at the mission tomorrow. I asked God to make Earl believe again and I decided maybe he needs a present. Maybe no one's ever given him something for Christmas."

"Okay." Brian hesitated. The old man didn't deserve a gift from Gideon, but how could he tell that to his daughter? "How much money do you have?"

Gideon's eyes sparkled. "Five dollars and fifteen cents."

Five dollars and fifteen cents. The amount was barely enough for a greeting card. Still, Tish was right. If this gift mattered to Gideon that much—no matter what he thought—he could hardly stand in her way. He pulled Gideon into a hug and whispered in her ear, "Alright, sweetie. I think I know just the place."

Two hours later they were walking out of the second-hand store arm in arm. Swinging from Gideon's elbow was a gift that had cost every last dime she'd saved. Everything she'd worked for those past two weeks.

When they got home, Gideon asked Tish to help her.

"I wanna sew something inside the gift."

Tish's smile was tender and understanding. Brian watched, frustrated. *Better her than me. Too much time and money on the old man.* Gideon's love was far too precious.

Gideon spent another half hour coloring a picture for Earl. She slipped the gift into a brown paper bag, dropped the picture inside, and tied it shut with a piece of string. Then she decorated the outside with Christmas trees and angels. Smack in the middle she wrote the old man's name.

Brian and Tish admired it when she was done. "It's perfect, honey."

"Think he'll like it?" Her hopeful eyes searched theirs.

"Like it?" Tish hugged Gideon to her side. "He'll love it."

❧

The next night at the mission, after they finished serving dinner, Brian and Tish anchored themselves at a table not far from Earl's and waited. Since the night included a Christmas concert and figured to last longer than the others, Dustin had stayed with a neighbor. The concert had come first, then dinner. Now, with everyone eating, Gideon found the place where she'd hidden her gift, raised it so Brian and Tish could see it, and flashed them a thumbs-up.

Carrying the decorated brown paper sack in front of her, she approached Earl's table and sat down. "Merry Christmas, Earl."

Brian could hear their conversation perfectly. *Make him smile. Please.*

Earl's fork froze halfway to his mouth and he lifted his eyes to Gideon. "Get lost."

Gideon shot Brian and Tish a weak look. Tish motioned to her, encouraging her to go ahead. Gideon stood a little straighter, nodded, and turned back to Earl. Then she lifted the decorated brown bag and set it in front of his plate. "I brought you a Christmas present."

Earl stared at it. For a long moment Brian actually thought the gift had worked. Then the old man set his fork down. "I hate Christmas. Didn't I tell you that?"

"Yes." Gideon's eyes were fixed on his. "You told me you didn't believe. But believing is the best gift of all and I thought maybe if I gave you a—"

"You thought wrong." Earl's voice boomed across the table.

Brian made a move toward the man, but Tish grabbed his arm. "Don't, Brian." She shifted her gaze to Gideon. "This is her thing."

"But she spent all her money on that stupid gift." His teeth were clenched, his anger so strong it choked him.

"She *wanted* to do this."

Brian sighed. "You're right." He felt the fight simmering within him. They watched Gideon and Earl. Their daughter hadn't said anything since Earl's rude interruption.

Now she leaned forward and clasped her hands on the table. "Aren't you going to open it?"

Earl dropped his gaze. "I'll probably throw it away."

Again Brian's muscles tensed. *How dare he.* Even from their spot a few tables away they could see tears building in Gideon's eyes.

"You can't throw it away. It's a Christmas gift. I . . . I bought it for you."

Something in their daughter's voice must have caused the old man to look up. When he saw her sad face he huffed hard. "Fine." He jerked the bag from the table and stuffed it into his coat pocket. "Happy?"

It took every ounce of Brian's resolve not to go after the old man and knock him to the floor.

Gideon blinked back the tears. She was trying so hard to be brave. "I-I want you to open it, Earl."

This time he snarled at her. "I'm not opening it, okay? Now, leave me alone." The old man's eyes looked dead as he lowered his voice. "I hate Christmas, kid. And I hate people like you."

The shock on Gideon's face must have startled Earl, as though even he couldn't believe what he'd just said. He tossed his fork down, pushed back and stood. Then without saying a word, he took five angry strides toward the door and disappeared into the night.

Gideon watched him, her mouth open. When he was gone, she cast a desperate look at Brian and Tish.

The pain in her eyes hurt Brian more than anything ever had. They went to her and together wrapped her in a hug.

"Oh, honey, I'm sorry." Tish kissed her cheek and wiped one of her tears.

Brian held Gideon tightly, unable to speak. *God? How could you let this happen? After all her hard work?* He closed his eyes and rested his head on her smaller one.

"He didn't even open it." Gideon's tears were under control. No hysteria or loud sobbing. Just the quiet pain of a little girl whose heart had been broken. It was only then that Brian was struck by something he hadn't wanted to see before. The dark circles under Gideon's eyes were back. She looked tired and weak and when he felt her head, his breath caught in his throat.

She was burning up.

Oh, God, no! Don't let her be sick now. Brian worked to focus. "It wasn't your fault, sweetheart." He ran his hand along the back of her head. "You did everything you could."

"But, Daddy, I asked God for a miracle. I thought if I gave Earl a Christmas gift he'd believe again." She pulled back and searched his eyes, then Tish's. "How come it didn't work?"

It was a question that hung in the air all that night and threatened to darken everything about the coming Christmas. But Earl's rudeness paled in comparison with the news they got two days later.

"I'm sorry." The doctor had asked Gideon to wait in the examination room while he talked to Brian and Tish in his office. Gideon had been so sick that morning, Tish had taken the day off. "Her cancer's back. Worse than before, more aggressive. I'm going to have to admit her."

Admit her? Brian could barely breathe. *No!* It wasn't fair. *Not Gideon!* His hands and feet felt numb, and the room tilted. Beside him, Tish began to cry.

The doctor looked at an open chart on his desk. "Her younger brother is a perfect match for a bone-marrow transplant." The doctor's voice dropped. "At the rate the disease is moving, I think it's time to do the procedure."

Brian huffed. "Sure." He stood and paced to the office window. "How are we supposed to pay for it?" He turned and met the doctor's eyes. "We don't have insurance; you know that."

"Yes." The doctor crossed his arms. "I've gotten the okay from the hospital. We can do it for twenty-five thousand. That's below cost, Mr. Mercer." He hesitated. "We could get started with half that much."

"Twenty-five thousand dollars?" A sound that was more sob than laugh came from his throat. "Sir, I don't have twenty-five *dollars.*"

"Is there any other way?" Tish folded her arms tight around her waist. "Anything we can do to raise the money?"

"Yes." The doctor reached for a brochure and handed it to her. "You can hold a fund-raiser. Many families do that as a way of paying for the transplant."

"And if we don't get enough?" Brian's body trembled, battling an onslaught of fear and anger, confusion and heartache.

"We'll start chemotherapy immediately, just like before." The doctor grimaced. "If we're lucky she might slip back into remission."

"If that happens, Doctor, luck won't have anything to do with it." Tish clutched the fund-raising information tightly to her chest. There was a determination in her eyes Brian had never seen before. She stood and moved toward the door. "I need to be with Gideon."

When Tish was gone, Brian locked eyes with the doctor. "Be straight with me, Doc. How bad is it?"

"She needs a transplant, Mr. Mercer." The man blinked and Brian could see he was considering how much to say. Finally he sighed and shook his head. "She doesn't have much time."

Gideon was quiet while they set her up in a room. A stream of nurses came to draw blood, hook up monitors, and start an IV line. Thirty minutes later a drip bag was hooked to her other arm. This one contained the chemicals that would ravage her small body and maybe—if God smiled down on them—leave her cancer free one more time. But God had let the cancer come back. And he hadn't done much to help Gideon's surprise with Earl.

Why ask him for help now?

When the nurses were gone, Brian and Tish moved to Gideon's side. Tish leaned over the bed and kissed her on the forehead. "How're you feeling, honey?"

Gideon's eyes were flat. "I don't wanna be here." She looked at the monitors stationed around her. "Can't they do this stuff at home like last time?"

Brian wanted to rip out the needles and tell her it'd all been a mistake. That she had a cold, nothing more. He gritted his teeth and willed himself to smile. "You won't be in long, Gideon. A few days maybe." He took her delicate fingers in his. "One of us will be here until you come home, okay?"

"Okay." Her voice was slow and tired. "But there's one thing I wish I knew."

"What's that, honey?" Brian could only imagine the questions that had to be running through her head. Why her? Why now? Why, when it had looked like everything was going to work out? Of course even those would be nothing to the one burning question that had shouted at him every moment since their meeting with the doctor: How were they going to find the money?

Tish brushed her fingers lightly over Gideon's hair. "What, sweetheart? Tell us."

"I wish I knew . . ." Gideon stared out the window. ". . . if Earl opened my gift."

CHAPTER SEVEN

Earl must have passed a hundred trash cans since the Christmas dinner.

Each time he told himself to take the kid's bag and throw it out—toss it in with the rotting food and wet pieces of paper and empty beer bottles. Forget about it the same way he'd forgotten everything else.

But each time he couldn't do it.

Stupid kid. Why'd she have to give him a present, anyway? He was past that, past the need for caring or being cared for. He was supposed to be planning his death, not worrying about what to do with some Christmas gift.

He wandered down the alley. It was Sunday, three days before Christmas. If he hadn't been so preoccupied he might already have been dead by now. Instead—against every bit of his will—the gift had come to mean something to him. Maybe it was the child's drawings, the crooked way she'd colored a Christmas tree on the bag or the wobbly letters of his name scrawled across the middle.

Somehow it reminded him of the life he used to lead. And that was the most frustrating part of all. Earl didn't want to remember the past. Without the red gloves, it was over. Dead. There was no hope, no history, no family to conjure up in the cold of the night.

There was nothing.

Until he took the girl's gift.

He felt in his jacket. It was still there, the scrunched-up package tucked into a deep pocket of his parka. He hadn't opened it—didn't plan to. Especially not three days before Christmas.

He leaned against a damp brick wall and stared at a slew of trash cans across the alleyway. The rain had let up, but it was colder than before. Icy, even. Back when he'd had the red gloves he would have been asleep by now, savoring the hours until daybreak. But without them, time ran together. One meaningless hour after another.

A breeze whistled between the buildings and made the cans rattle. Earl barely heard it, barely felt the cold against his grizzled face.

December 22.

No matter how distant he became, how changed he was from the man he'd once been, he would never forget this date. It was hard to believe five years had gone by.

He narrowed his eyelids and there in the shadows of the alleyway he could see them. The people he'd once loved. His mother and father, his sister and brother and their children. But most of all his girls: Anne and Molly. The women who had been everything to him.

Memories played out before him, the way they had constantly played out since he'd received the child's present. A dozen Christmas Eves during which Anne had wanted only one thing: for Earl to join them at the annual church service.

"Come on, honey. Please?" She'd smile that guileless smile of hers and weave her fingers between his. "Your family won't go with us. Please?"

But Earl wouldn't hear of it. "I won't be a hypocrite, Anne. You know how I feel about church. I wasn't raised that way."

"Think about Molly." She'd wait, holding her breath, probably praying he'd change his mind. "She's going to grow up without a single memory of her daddy sitting beside her in church."

"That's better than having her grow up knowing I'm a hypocrite."

Anne would sigh. "Okay, Earl." She'd plant a kiss on his cheek. "But one of these days, God's going to blow the roof off your safe little box and you won't have any choice but to believe."

The memory faded.

Yes, Anne had known how he felt about church. His whole family knew, because they felt the same way. If a person didn't believe in God, they shouldn't go. And Earl's people didn't believe. It was that simple. He bit his lip and pulled his jacket tight around his neck.

If only he'd gone with her. Just once. What had he been thinking, denying her that simple pleasure? His belief system wasn't the most important thing.

Anne was. Anne and Molly and the rest of his family.

Earl stared at his boots. Memories like that one came all the time these days. Morning, noon, night. It didn't matter. Ever since he'd shoved the kid's gift in his jacket there'd been one memory after another.

He reached into his pocket and pulled out the brown bag. It was flatter than before, more wrinkled. Earl studied it—the trees, the angels, his name. He gave the contents a few gentle squeezes. What would a little girl buy for a mean old man like himself? Probably something homemade, like cookies or a tree ornament. Something childish like that. Whatever was inside certainly couldn't make a difference in his life, couldn't change him.

So why was he hanging onto it?

Open it, Earl. Open it.

The voice sliced through Earl's consciousness. It sounded like Anne. But that was impossible. Who else could . . .

He spun around, staring first one direction, then the other. The damp alleyway glistened beneath the city streetlights, but it was completely empty. Where had the voice come from? And why now? It had been years since Earl had heard Anne's voice that clearly. Certainly he'd never heard it over the cold winter breeze of a deserted back alley.

The words played again in his mind. *Open it, Earl.*

This was ridiculous. He was obviously delusional. Maybe the cold was getting to him. Or his constant thoughts of death. Maybe he was fighting a virus. Whatever it was, he had no intention of standing there waiting for more voices. If the child's gift was causing him that much grief, then fine. He would open the bag, and get it over with. Then he could toss it in the nearest bin and get on with dying.

He started to pierce the brown paper with his fingers, but the girl's drawings stopped him. A burst of air escaped his pursed lips. Dratted child. Why'd she have to give him the gift in the first place? He fumbled with the string around the mouth of the bag and finally worked out the knot.

Leaning against the brick wall once more, he angled the bag toward the streetlight and peered inside. The darkness made it difficult to see, but it looked like a scarf, maybe. Or a wooly hat. He reached inside and felt a piece of paper. Earl's hands were big and awkward, and the paper wrinkled as he pulled it out.

What was this? He unfolded it and found a colored picture of an old wooden stable and a manger that glowed like the sun. Around it stood different crayoned characters Earl couldn't quite make out. But the most striking part was the girl's message, scrawled across the bottom of the page:

Christmas miracles happen to those who believe. Love, Gideon

Earl's heart hesitated. They were the same words the girl had shared with him that first night when she worked at the mission. He blinked and read the words again. What was he supposed to feel? Sadness? Truth? Hope? Those things had died from his life years ago. Yet, something strange and unfamiliar stirred in his soul. Hadn't Molly drawn a picture like that the Christmas before she—

That was enough. He had promised himself he wouldn't let the gift get to him. He folded the picture, careful not to add any creases. Then he tucked it carefully into his pocket and reached inside the bag for the gift.

The moment his fingers made contact with the soft material of whatever lay inside, Earl knew it wasn't a scarf or a hat. The feeling was almost familiar. And it wasn't one thing; it was two. He peered inside again and this time pulled out the contents.

As he did, as he stared at the matching items, the ground beneath him gave way. His head felt disconnected from his body, and he dropped to his knees.

I'm dreaming. He blinked hard several times, but still the gift was there. How could it be? It was completely out of the question. *Impossible.*

The child had never met him before that first mission dinner. She couldn't possibly have known. Besides, how had she found them? They'd been stolen seven weeks ago. He shook his head, trying to clear his thoughts. Nothing made sense.

But still there was no disputing the evidence in his hands. The child had given him a pair of handmade red gloves. Gloves that looked exactly the same as those he'd lost.

They . . . they couldn't be. Could they? How could she have found them? Earl leaned back on his heels, his body trembling. He peeled back the cuff of one of the gloves . . . and his heart sank. Anne's initials weren't there. Instead, stitched inside was this message: *Believe*.

He blinked three times, but still the words remained. What was this? These gloves were exactly like his gloves. His red gloves. There couldn't have been two pairs like this. They were Anne's very own creation, the work of her hands. And yet, where were her initials?

He reminded himself to breathe. And then he brought the gloves to his face and breathed them in. They were his; they had to be. They hadn't changed since the last time he'd worn them.

A sudden downpour of memories overtook him as he buried his face into the red wool. What was it Anne had prayed for him? That God would blow the roof off his safe little box and leave him no choice but to believe? Yes, that was it. That's exactly what Anne had prayed all those years ago.

He peeked at the inside of the glove once more. *Believe.* It was still there. With a sudden thought, he pulled back the cuff on the other glove. It was the same as the last. Anne's initials were gone, but the single word was there—in clean, new white thread.

Believe.

A chill worked its way down his spine.

Oh, Anne.

No wonder he could hear her voice as plain as the hum of nearby traffic. God had blown the roof off. Somehow this God he hadn't wanted to believe in had done the one thing that left him no choice but to believe.

"God?"

He opened his eyes and stared toward heaven. No matter that the sky above Portland was flat and utterly dark. In that moment he could see beyond it to a place that wasn't a figment of other people's imagination. It was real. As real as God and miracles and life itself.

As real as Christmas.

Tears spilled from his eyes and he covered his face with the gloves once more. Suddenly he remembered the little girl. Gideon. He pictured her face, her piercing, innocent eyes. She'd spoken to him when most people would have avoided the idea, cared for him even after he'd shouted at her. And bought him the greatest gift of all, without receiving either a thank-you or even a smile.

What had he told her? That he didn't like people and he didn't like her. His insides tightened at the memory. What a wretched man he'd become. Anne wouldn't even recognize him. Neither would Molly.

He clutched the red gloves in his fists and slipped them onto his hands, one finger at a time. Next he carefully folded the brown bag and found a pocket where it would stay dry. Poor little girl. She'd worked so hard on the gift. How could he have been so mean hearted?

His tears became sobs and he looked up once more. He had been terrible to the child, his behavior unconscionable. He'd told her to get lost. And when she'd wished him a Merry Christmas, he'd barked at her that he hated the holiday.

As though even God was grieved by his terrible behavior, a steady rain began to fall, splattering on his face and mingling with his tears.

"What have I done, God?" His words echoed down the alley. "Forgive me. Please, forgive me!"

The rain fell harder, but he didn't care. He stayed there, his gloved hands tucked deep inside his jacket, allowing himself to be drenched by the downpour, washed clean from all he'd once been. The wetter he grew, the more layers melted away. "I believe in you, God! I do!"

God was real. The red gloves proved it. No matter how badly he had messed up, God wasn't finished with him. Not yet. Right there and then, in the middle of a freezing downpour, a burst of sunshine exploded in his heart. He didn't want to die; he wanted to live—to make his life good and wonderful and true, something Anne and Molly would have been proud of. The flame of their faith hadn't gone out that terrible afternoon. It lived. First in the memory of how they'd loved him, and now in the burst of life deep within his soul. No wonder he had felt compelled to open Gideon's gift. Look what it had done to him.

The rain continued, but he no longer cried. His face felt strange, pinched almost, and in a burst of understanding he realized why.

He was smiling.

A smile so big and bold it stretched into uncharted areas of his face, places that had forgotten the feeling. He had his red gloves back! They had to be his; he was determined to believe it. The unfathomable had happened. Somewhere in the city of Portland that little sprite of a girl had found his gloves. Maybe in a bin of old clothing or at the mission or maybe from a second-hand store. However it had happened, she'd found them. Then—not knowing what they meant to him— she'd made a decision to take them home, wrap them, and give them to him for Christmas.

What were the odds of that? How could such a thing be anything but an act of God?

God *was* real after all. Watching over Earl as surely as somewhere he was watching over Anne and Molly. He struggled to his feet and he realized something else. He felt different—lighter, more alive. Gideon's generosity had changed him, changed everything. It had brought about a miracle amidst the stench and emptiness.

Because of a child's generosity, Earl was no longer a hopeless street person. He was a believer whose life was about to change. And the place where he stood was not the freezing wet pavement of a neglected alleyway.

It was holy ground.

A hundred ideas raced through his mind. Things he wanted to do. Things he needed to do . . . now that he believed. He made a mental list, almost bursting with excitement at what the days ahead might bring.

Then another thought occurred to him. All of this had happened three days before Christmas! The same day that he'd lost everything five years ago.

His knees shook. Without waiting another minute, he strode toward his shanty home. This time he kept his eyes up, soaking in everything about the city. The damp air and bare maple trees, the cold stone walls and fancy Adidas billboard. The blanket of lights that marked the hills around downtown. Even the trash cans behind Tara's Diner, the place where he scrounged soggy French bread and leftover lasagna when the mission wasn't serving.

He wanted to remember it all. Because with God's help, in a very few days he would leave the streets for good. And he never wanted to forget the place where God had found him.

But there was one thing he had to do before leaving. Tomorrow he would find D. J. at the mission and ask him about the child. He owed her his life, after all. Her gift had given him more than he could ever repay. But at least he could apologize, and certainly he could thank her.

The way he should have when the child handed him the gift.

That night after Earl had tucked himself beneath his new tarp, after he'd kissed the woolen palms of his gloves and bid his girls good night, he didn't dream about the past. Neither did he sleep. Rather, he stayed awake, wide-eyed, and dreamed of something he hadn't thought about in five years: his future. A future he believed in. One that was suddenly as real as God himself.

And as possible as a Christmas miracle.

CHAPTER EIGHT

Gideon lay as still as she could.

Not just because it hurt too much to move. But because the doctor said she should rest if she wanted to get better. And she wanted that very much. If she was even a little better the doctor said she could go home tomorrow—Christmas Eve—and spend a few days with her family.

She angled her head and stared out the window. The rain was gone, but the clouds were still there. Snow clouds, maybe. Dustin had said the kids at school were talking about snow. Lots of snow. Everyone wanted a white Christmas.

She sank deeper into the pillow. Snow didn't matter. She couldn't play outside anyway. But if the weather got that cold, where would Earl go? Where did people without homes sleep when the ground was covered with snow?

If only he'd opened the gift. Then at least his hands would be warm.

She thought back to that day at the secondhand store. She'd wanted the gift to be perfect, but until she saw the red gloves she hadn't been sure what to get him. She had walked the aisles with her father looking at socks and a flashlight and an old blanket. The socks hadn't seemed thick enough and the flashlight had needed batteries. The old blanket cost too much. Daddy said lots of stuff at the secondhand store wasn't practical for a man like Earl.

Then she'd found the gloves.

They were soft and thick and red like Christmas. Her father had said they were long enough for a man's hands. Even a big man like Earl. Gideon figured they'd help Earl stay warm on the streets. She also figured they'd make him believe again.

That's why she'd asked her mom to help her sew the word inside both of them. *Believe.* Because that's what she wanted for Earl more than warm hands. That he might believe again.

If he had only opened the gift that night at the mission. Maybe then it would have happened. And she would have had her Christmas miracle. The one she'd prayed for.

But it was too late now. Christmas was almost here. D. J. from the mission had told her dad last night that Earl wasn't wearing the gloves when he came for dinner. No one knew what he'd done with her gift, or if he'd ever opened it.

So there'd been no miracle after all, even though she'd believed with her whole heart. A tear rolled onto her cheek and she brushed it away with her fingertips. Her teacher must have been wrong. Christmas miracles didn't happen to those who believed. They didn't happen at all. Maybe they were just part of the olden days, like in the Bible.

She breathed out and it sounded sad in the quiet room. She was pretty sure she was sicker than before, because her parents cried all the time. When she'd first come to stay in the hospital one of them was always with her. But after a few days they'd had to go to work and Dustin had to go to school. Now they came every night. They would hold her hands, play with what was left of her hair, and turn their backs when they had to cry. She pretended not to notice. They had cried a lot last time she got sick, too. When she let their tears worry her, it only made them sadder.

There was a pain in her leg. She moved it. Sometimes sliding it to another spot on the sheets made it feel better. Not today, though. She made a face and watched a bird land on her windowsill.

"Hi, little birdie." Her words were slow and quiet. "Hi." The bird hopped two times and flew away.

She stared at the clouds again. The pain wasn't so bad when she didn't think about it.

The thing was this time it hurt worse. Not in one spot, but all over. Sort of like a flu bug. And things her parents had said lately made her think maybe this time she was sicker. Once in a while when they thought she wasn't listening, the doctor would talk to her mom and dad about something called a transplant. She had heard that word before, but she didn't know what it was.

Maybe a medicine or a special tool that would make her better.

She wasn't sure, but whatever it was it cost too much. Otherwise the doctor would have already given it to her. That was okay. God was with her, and he would take care of her no matter what happened.

But God, whatever happens to me, please let me go home for Christmas.

Of course, she might not get better. Kids died from

cancer sometimes. Once when she and her dad had gone over for a treatment, a man and woman were crying in the waiting room. She hadn't meant to stare, but she couldn't help it. Later she asked her nurse why the people were sad.

"Their daughter died this morning," the nurse told her.

"Died?"

"Yes. She'd been fighting cancer for three years." There were lines on the nurse's forehead and her eyes looked tired. "Today she lost the battle."

After that Gideon had had a different way of thinking about cancer. It wasn't just a bad sickness, like a long cold or an ear infection. It was a battle. And if you lost the battle, you could die.

She yawned.

Death would be sad because she would miss her mom and dad and Dustin. But it wouldn't be scary. Her parents had always talked about heaven and in the secret places of her heart, she was sort of excited to go there. Streets of gold. No more pain. No more tears. Besides, one day her family would be there, too.

After she knew the truth about cancer and how bad it could be, she wanted her parents to know she wasn't afraid. She'd told them a few days ago when she was first put in the hospital.

"Heaven will be wonderful, don't you think?" She'd looked straight up, first at her mother, then at her father.

Her dad squeezed her hand. "Sure, honey, it'll be great." His eyes were red and wet, and when he smiled his chin moved up and down. "But not for a long time, okay?"

"So we can all go together, you mean?"

"That's right, sweetheart."

As good as heaven seemed, her dad was probably right. It'd be better to wait until they were all old. That way they could be there together without having to wait.

She yawned again and turned onto her side. She was tired all the time lately, but that was a good thing. When she slept she had the most wonderful dreams. She felt her body relax. The sounds and lights and even the pain began to go away.

Gradually she fell asleep and a glorious city appeared before her eyes. Sparkling gold buildings and bright blue streams that ran along either side of the street. Up ahead was a man she didn't quite recognize. She took a few steps forward, then a few more, and suddenly she could see the man's face. It was Earl! Only his clothes weren't tattered and his face was smooth. He wasn't angry, either. In fact . . . Yes! She took a step closer and she could see it was true. He was smiling! And there was something different in his eyes. She tried to think of what it was . . .

Earl believed! That was it, she was sure. His eyes looked all glowing and clean.

Then Earl turned around and started to leave.

"Wait! Don't go!" she called after him, but he didn't hear her.

"You will stay, Gideon."

"Who said that?" She spun around and there, beside her, was a tall man with shining hair.

He reached for her hand. "You'll like it. We have a palace ready for you."

What was this place? And why weren't her parents here? What about Earl? If he could leave, why couldn't she?

Then she realized where she was. Of course. She was in heaven. Cancer had won the battle and now she was here. It wasn't supposed to feel sad, but it did. Just a little. Not because it wasn't wonderful, but because her mom and dad and Dustin weren't here. And that meant somewhere they were crying and missing her.

Just like she missed them.

"Earl!" she called after him once more and this time he turned around.

"Gideon. I thought that was you." He stayed in his spot, far away. But she could still see his face. He looked like maybe he was crying. "Thank you, Gideon. Thank you so much. Thank you . . . thank you . . . thank you . . ."

His voice got quieter with each word. Gideon shook her head, confused. She looked up at the tall man beside her. "Why's he telling me thank you?"

The man said nothing. A smile moved across his face and he pointed back at Earl.

This time when she looked she saw something she hadn't before and she breathed in sharp and quick.

He was wearing the gloves! The red gloves she'd given him for Christmas!

She tugged on the hand of the man beside her. "Look at his hands!" Her happy heart lifted her and she began to fly around the golden city like an angel.

Earl was wearing the red gloves!

From her place in the clouds she looked at Earl once more to make sure it was true. It was. Earl waved at her with both arms and smiled again as he disappeared through a gate in the city. Gideon came down from the clouds and landed near the tall man, but his voice began to fade. In fact, everything was fading. The man with the shining hair, the golden city, and even the road she was standing on.

Bit by bit the light returned and Gideon opened her eyes. A nurse stood beside her with a fresh bag of medicine. She wasn't in heaven; she was in the hospital. Earl hadn't changed. He'd probably never even opened her gift.

It had all been a dream. But that fact didn't leave her sad like after other dreams. Because this time she had a feeling God was trying to tell her something very special.

Christmas miracles weren't just for the old days.

They were for now. For anyone with faith enough to look for them. Gideon smiled to herself as the nurse hooked the medicine bag to a tube in her arm. Yes, Christmas miracles still happened. God had let her see Earl, after all.

The way he still could be, still might be.

If only he would believe.

CHAPTER NINE

This time Earl didn't take them off.

When sunup came, Earl wore the red gloves as he made his way a block south to an old gas station. There, for two dollars, a man could shower, shave, and run a clean comb through his hair. Earl scrounged up the money from his knapsack and did all three.

Then he headed for the mission.

D. J. was in his office looking at his computer when Earl knocked on the door.

"Yes." The mission director looked up, his expression blank.

Earl resisted a smile. "You don't recognize me?"

The man narrowed his piercing blue eyes. "Earl?" His eyebrows lifted so far they looked like part of his hairline. He stood, came around his desk, and shook Earl's hand. The man's smile was as much a part of his face as his eyes and nose. "I can't believe it! You look twenty years younger. I guess I've never seen you without a beard. It's a nice change."

"It's not the only one."

D. J. leaned against his desk. "Really?"

"Yes." Earl's heart ricocheted off the insides of his chest like a pool ball. "God found me last night, D. J. He found me good."

He saw a dozen questions flash in D. J.'s eyes. "It wasn't a church service or anything like that." He paused. The shame of how he'd treated the child was still painfully fresh. "It was the kid. That little girl."

"Girl?"

Earl dropped his gaze to the floor. What was her name? Why couldn't he remember it? He couldn't afford to sound delusional, not now. "You know, the girl. Brown hair, deep eyes. Wooly hat. She was here with her family at the Christmas dinner. Gave me a gift."

"Oh." A knowing look filled the man's face. "You mean Gideon."

"Gideon. Yes, that's it." Earl swallowed hard. "I need to thank her. Today. Before another hour goes by."

D. J.'s eyes bunched up and he took a step backwards. "Earl, I don't think—"

Earl waved his hand and cut him off. "I know there's privacy rules, but I don't need her last name or phone number. You can make the call." Earl's fingers began to shake. "You don't understand." He licked his lips and grabbed two quick breaths. "I was terrible to her, rude and mean and . . . and just awful."

The muscles in D. J.'s jaw flexed. For the first time since Earl had met him, the man wasn't smiling. "You want to apologize to her? Is that it?"

"Yes. Her and her parents. And I want to thank Gideon." Earl's heartbeat sped up. "You have no idea . . ." His voice drifted. "That little girl changed my life."

"Oh, I have an idea." This time D. J.'s smile barely lifted the corners of his mouth. "I've known Gideon for a long time. She's a special little girl."

Earl's stomach hurt with the thought of the child going another minute without knowing how sorry he was—how much he appreciated her gift. "Call her, then, will you? So I can tell her what I need to say. Apologize to her and her parents. Make things right. Please?"

D. J. opened his mouth but no words came out. From somewhere deep within him came a sigh that seemed to last a minute. It was the kind of sigh one might expect from a man who'd spent his life working with street people, a man who probably had very little in the way of worldly success.

But not D. J.

In years of taking meals at the mission, Earl had never heard the man sigh.

He knew what was coming. D. J. would politely send him on his way and he'd never see the girl again. Never apologize to her or tell her parents how wrong he'd been. That couldn't happen. He couldn't bear it! "Please. I need to talk to her."

"You can't." D. J. locked eyes with Earl. "Gideon's sick. She's in the hospital." His gaze fell and with it, Earl's heart. "They don't know if she can be home for Christmas."

The child was sick? Hadn't she been healthy a week ago at the mission dinner? "You mean like the flu or something?"

"No." D. J. looked up. His face was pale. "She has cancer, Earl. Leukemia."

"What?" Earl grabbed the door frame to keep from falling. "Since when?"

"She was in remission a week ago." He bit his lip. "But she's worse now. A lot worse."

A pit the size of a bowling ball filled Earl's gut. His head was spinning and he shuffled across D. J.'s office to the nearest chair. "I did this." His words were barely more than a mumble. "It's all my fault."

"No, Earl." D. J. took a few steps closer and put his hand on Earl's shoulder. "Gideon's been sick for a long time. The doctors knew her cancer would come back eventually. They just hoped it wouldn't be this soon."

Earl squeezed his forehead between his thumb and forefinger. Now the poor child was lying in a hospital bed, knowing that one of her last acts of kindness had been rejected. Since last night, he'd wanted to pick up the phone and tell her how sorry he was, how thankful. But it was too late. He could hardly call her at the hospital if she was that sick.

"It's not your fault, Earl." D. J. cleared his throat. "These things happen."

Earl felt a hundred years old as he struggled to his feet. He locked eyes with D. J. "Is there anything I can do?"

"We can pray." D. J.'s eyes grew watery. "She needs a bone marrow transplant but her family can't afford it. Without that, her chances . . . well, they aren't good."

The seedling of an idea sprouted in Earl's mind. "How expensive is it?"

"The transplant?"

"Yes." Earl's heartbeat doubled. "How much does it cost?"

"Tens of thousands of dollars, Earl. More than you and I will ever have."

"Actually . . ." Earl considered his words carefully. He didn't want to sound like a lunatic. "I have some money put away."

"What?" D. J. uttered a curious chuckle and studied Earl. "How much do you have?"

Earl didn't blink. "How much does she need?"

The mission director stared at Earl for a long time. "Maybe it's time you told me your story."

"Maybe it is." Earl settled back in the chair and looked hard at D. J. "I wasn't always like this."

"Most street people aren't." D. J. cast him a kind smile. "Something happens: a death, an addiction, a lost job, a bout of depression. You'd be surprised at the stories behind some of the regulars at the mission."

Earl was quiet. "I guess I never thought about it. They're just like me."

"That's normal. It's hard to see past the dirty clothes and haggard faces, hard to imagine anything other than the vacant eyes and familiar stench. But bottom line is this: Everyone has a story."

Dirty clothes and familiar stench? Earl let the words play again in his mind. What would Anne and Molly think about the way he'd let himself become? Shame wrapped its arms around him and squeezed until he could barely breathe. *Help me, God. Let me see beyond this meaningless life I've created.*

"Okay." The mission director motioned to him. "So tell me yours."

Tears welled up in Earl's eyes as for the first time in five years he allowed himself to go back to that December five years ago—allowed himself to remember the events that had led him to a life on the streets. As they had in the alleyway the night before, layers began falling from Earl's heart until he knew exactly where to start. Back at the beginning. In the days when he'd first fallen in love.

When the images were clear, they formed words. And finally, after years of silence, Earl began to speak.

CHAPTER TEN

Her name was Anne." Earl's vision grew cloudy as he drifted back in time. "We grew up across the street from each other. Down south in Redding, California."

D. J. crossed one leg over the other and listened.

"She was the prettiest kindergarten girl I'd ever seen, and even though I was two years older, I told my mother she was the one. Some day I was going to marry her."

The mission director chuckled softly as Earl's story tumbled out.

At first his parents had smiled the way parents do when their children say something cute and innocent. They'd patted him on the head. "Sure, son. Marry the girl across the street." Right.

As the years passed, Earl never wavered in his plan. But there was one problem.

Anne didn't know he was alive.

Outgoing and social, she was surrounded by friends and only waved at him occasionally when they passed in the street outside their respective homes. But all that changed the summer Anne turned sixteen. That year, Earl's first out of high school, she and her friends took to tanning in the front yard. One afternoon, an hour after Earl got home from work, Anne knocked at his door.

"Hi, Earl." Her smile outshone the sun. "My friend wants to meet you. Why don't you come over and hang out with us for a while?"

Earl had finished work at three that day. With his heart knocking about and his hands sweaty, he changed into shorts, jogged across the street, and took his place with the girls. Long after her friends went home, Anne stayed and chatted with him.

"How come we never did this before?" She angled her face, her eyes dancing.

"Busy, maybe." Earl could feel his face growing hot. Now that they were alone he was terrified she would see the truth. That he'd been in love with her since before she could write her name.

She leaned back, and the breeze played in her hair. "Know what my friend said about you?"

"What?" Earl relaxed some.

"She said I'm lucky you live across the street." Anne batted her eyelashes at him. "And that you're the best-looking guy she's seen all year."

"That's good, I guess." Earl shrugged. "Of course, does she get out much?"

Ripples of laughter spilled from Anne's slender throat and she fell back against the grass. When she regained control she locked eyes with him. "So . . . you dating anyone serious?"

"Nope. You?"

Anne shook her head, her expression achingly innocent. "I'm too young."

"Yeah."

She bit her lip. "I turned sixteen last month."

Earl's mind raced. Why was she telling him this? "Really?"

"Really." She hesitated. "That means I can date. But only guys I trust. You know, guys I've hung out with before. Guys my parents have met."

The lining of Earl's mouth felt like paper. He swallowed. "Right." Again he had no idea where the conversation was headed.

"So . . ." Anne's smile grew suddenly shy. "Maybe you and I can hang out this summer."

"Yeah." Earl's heart exploded in fireworks, but he kept his tone level. "Maybe we could."

❧

The memory faded and Earl blinked at the mission director. "After that we were inseparable. Spent the summer swimming and fishing at Lake Shasta. Every moment I wasn't working, I was with Anne."

"She sounds like a wonderful girl."

Earl nodded. "She— She was." Even now the past tense hurt—hurt as bad as the parts of the story yet ahead.

The pieces of yesterday came into focus once more, and Earl continued.

At the end of the summer, Earl and Anne took a walk through their neighborhood.

"I've been thinking." He kicked at a smattering of loose gravel on the sidewalk.

"That's good." She elbowed him in the ribs and gave him an easy grin. "I wonder sometimes."

He chuckled and slowed his pace. "Actually," his eyes met hers, "I was thinking how we've hung out all summer."

She stopped and faced him. Earl was certain she had never looked more beautiful. "We have, haven't we?"

"Mm-hmm." He smothered a lopsided grin. "And I've met your parents."

"Several times."

"So maybe the two of us ought to . . ."

Anne took a step closer. "I'm listening."

Earl exhaled and it sounded like a weary laugh. "What I'm trying to say is, Anne, would you go out with me Saturday night? Please?"

As long as he lived, Earl would never forget the way her eyes lit up. "You know what, Earl?"

"What?"

"I thought you'd never ask."

Their first date was sheer magic. A picnic dinner along the shores of Lake Shasta and afterwards milk shakes at the A&W. They got home early and sat in the porch swing at her house. Before Earl crossed the street and went back home they shared the briefest kiss. With their faces still inches apart, Earl searched her eyes and brushed a lock of hair gently off her forehead.

"When I was seven I thought you were the most beautiful girl in the world."

She giggled. "When you were seven?"

"Yep." He brushed his lips against hers again. "I used

to tell my dad that one day I was going to marry you."

Anne's face softened. "Really?"

"I was just a kid." He drew back so he could see her better. "But, yeah, that was my dream."

"Well . . ." The moonlight reflected in her eyes, and Earl could see the depth of her soul. "My daddy used to tell me the best thing about dreams was this."

He waited, wanting to kiss her again.

Her voice fell to a whisper. "Every once in a while they come true."

In many ways that night marked the beginning. Because after that there was no turning back for either of them. By the time Anne was a senior in high school and Earl into his second year as an electrician, no one doubted Earl's intentions.

Two years later, he proposed.

Anne happily accepted and they were married that summer.

Earl blinked as the images faded from his mind. His eyes met D. J.'s again. "Being married to Anne was . . . it was like all my dreams had finally come true."

"Yes." The mission director shot an understanding smile at Earl. "Marriage is like that."

"I didn't think I could be happier." Earl held his breath. "Until two years later when Molly was born."

Earl settled back into his story. At first, Anne had struggled to get pregnant. For that reason, they were thrilled beyond hope that fall when Anne delivered a healthy baby girl. Earl spent hours standing over their daughter's crib, staring at her. The perfect features and scant feathering of dark hair. Her precious lips. Even as an infant she was the mirror image of Anne, and Earl used to fall asleep feeling like the luckiest man in the world.

In the following years Anne lost two babies and then began having severe bouts of abdominal pain. The doctors found her uterus scarred and diseased; a hysterectomy was her only option. The day after Molly's fifth birthday, Anne underwent the surgery. Molly didn't understand the implications, so Anne and Earl did their grieving in private.

"I'm so sorry, Earl." Anne buried her face against Earl's shoulder that night in the hospital room. "I wanted to give you a houseful of babies."

Earl silenced her with a kiss. "No, sweetheart, don't

ever say that. It isn't your fault. And besides, I'd rather have Molly than a dozen other children. With her, our family is complete."

It was true, and after Anne's surgery it became even more so. The three of them were together constantly. They shared meals and conversation and storytime when Molly was little. As she grew, they took weekend drives to Medford and Grant's Pass.

They were only apart on Sunday mornings. Anne would take Molly to service, but she never pushed the idea on Earl. Never even asked him to come. Except on Christmas Eve. Earl was adamant about not attending.

A decision he would regret until he drew his last breath.

Molly was blessed with a voice that moved people to tears. From an early age she sang at church and took piano lessons. As she got older, she spent many evenings entertaining her parents.

Sometime after Molly reached middle school, Anne took a job teaching first grade. It was the perfect supplement to Earl's modest living and it allowed them to spend a week each summer traveling to exotic places— the south of France, the Caribbean, or Bermuda.

But though they cherished their summer vacations, Christmas was easily the family's favorite time of year.

From early on, Earl and Anne and Molly had en-

joyed a tradition. The three of them would each exchange one homemade present. A card or a poem or
sometimes a framed piece of artwork. Something Anne
had knit or sewn, or a special craft. One year Molly even
sang her parents a song she'd written. Each Christmas
these were the gifts they looked forward to most. The
gifts they remembered.

That was true even up until their last year together.

That spring Earl was laid off and times were
rougher than they'd ever been. In June, instead of traveling, they sold their house and furniture and moved in
with Earl's parents. Anne's folks had sold their house by
then, but Earl's still lived right where he'd grown up. It
was a sprawling place with six bedrooms and three
baths. Plenty of room for Earl and his family.

But Earl was discouraged.

"I promise I'll make it up to you, Anne," he told her
as they turned in that first night in his parents' house.
"This is only temporary."

"Silly man." Anne leaned over and gave him a linger-
ing kiss. Her smile shimmered in the muted moonlight.
"It doesn't matter where we live. You'll get work again.
And when you do, I'm sure we'll have another house."
She brushed her nose against his. "All that matters is
that we have each other. Me and you and Molly."

They settled into a routine. That fall, Earl found a job. Despite their housing situation, it was one of the happiest Thanksgivings Earl could remember. They shared warm conversations with his parents and ate pumpkin pie late into the night.

None of them could wait for Christmas.

Earl's story stopped short. He blinked and his gaze fell to his weathered hands. This was the hard part, the part that didn't make sense. Earl and his family had been halfway to forever, enjoying the kind of life and love most people only dreamed of.

Bad times weren't supposed to fall on people like Earl and Anne and Molly.

Across from him, D.J. inhaled sharply. "Something happened to them?"

"Yes." Slowly, painfully, Earl allowed a handful of stubborn layers to join the others in a heap on the floor beside him. If he was going to tell the story, he couldn't stop now. "Yes, something happened to them."

CHAPTER ELEVEN

Earl hadn't talked about this to anyone. Not ever. But there, with the kindly mission director listening, it was time. He drew a slow breath and let the details come.

On December 22 that year, most of their gifts had been wrapped and placed beneath the tree. Anne and Earl still had shopping to do, but Molly was adamant about going out to dinner and taking a drive to see Christmas lights. Usually the three of them waited until after Christmas to check out local displays.

Earl cast Anne a questioning glance and shrugged.

"Why not?" She grinned at their daughter. "Shopping can wait. Maybe your grandpa and grandma would like to come."

"That's okay." Earl's father grinned at them. "You young people go and have a good time."

At six o'clock that evening they set out. The night was cool and clear; a million stars fanned out across the winter sky. They were two blocks away from home when it happened.

One moment Earl was driving his family through an intersection. They were all talking at once, pointing at lights and laughing about something Molly had said. When suddenly, in the blink of an eye, Earl saw a truck the size of a freight train barreling toward them.

"Noooo!" Earl's piercing shout stilled the laughter just as the truck made impact. For what felt like minutes, they were surrounded by the deafening sound of twisting metal and breaking glass. Their car was spinning, flying through the air. Then, finally, it jolted to a stop, leaving a bone-chilling silence.

Earl's legs were pinned beneath the dash. His breathing was shallow and choppy and at first he couldn't find the wind to speak.

"Anne . . . Molly . . ." His words were the dimmest of whispers. Inch by inch, he forced himself to turn until he could see Anne beside him. Her head was hanging strangely to one side. Blood trickled from her mouth and ear. "Anne!" This time his voice shook the car. "Anne, honey, wake up!"

There was a moaning in the backseat and Earl fought the pain to twist around. "Molly? Sweetheart, are you okay?"

She was silent. Then Earl noticed something that turned his stomach. Her head wasn't right. The entire right side was flatter than before. "Somebody, help us! Please!"

Sirens sounded in the distance and Earl heard people running toward them. A man's voice shouted at him. "Hang on, in there. Help'll be here any minute. Everything's going to be okay."

Earl wanted to shout at the man that no, it wasn't okay. His girls were hurt. He needed to check on Anne, make sure she was breathing. But black dots clouded his vision. The man outside the car began to fade and Earl realized he was fainting.

No, he ordered himself. *Not now. The girls need me.* Then with a final burst of strength he reached out and took hold of Anne's fingers. "Anne . . ."

It was the last word he said before blacking out. When he woke up the next day he was in a hospital, desperate to find his family. Within an hour he knew the awful truth.

Anne had died on impact, and Molly was on life support. Her brain waves were completely gone, but doctors wanted to wait. In case Earl woke up in time to say good-bye.

His own injuries were life threatening, but he insisted they wheel him in to see his daughter. He was holding her hand when her heart stopped beating, and with it, every reason Earl had to live . . .

Again the memories lifted.

Tears spilled from Earl's eyes onto his old parka as he searched D. J.'s face. "I buried them the day after Christmas."

The mission director placed his hand on Earl's shoulder and said nothing. For a long while they stayed that way, while Earl quietly cried. "I'm sorry. It still hurts like it was yesterday."

"Take your time."

Earl closed his eyes and finished the story.

The night after the funeral, despite his breaking heart, Earl had opened his presents. He did so in the quiet of the night, long after his parents were asleep. Among the practical store-bought things were two gifts wrapped in white tissue paper—the symbol he and the girls had used over the years to designate the gifts that were homemade. He opened the one from Molly first.

It was a framed painting she'd worked on at school, a picture of the manger scene that was eerily similar to the one Gideon had drawn for him. Above it was scribbled this message: "Daddy . . . you make every Christmas beautiful."

Earl had stared at it, run his fingers over the glassed drawing, and wept as he hadn't since the accident. All of his hopes and dreams for the future had been caught up in that one girl. How was he supposed to live without her?

Finally, he opened the package from Anne.

Inside were the red gloves—lovingly knit with heavy wool and tiny stitches. They were lined for warmth, and Earl held them like they were made of glass. How had she found time? Another wave of tears filled his eyes and he ached for her, ached for one last chance to tell her he loved her. One last day together.

When he could summon the strength, Earl lifted the gloves and studied her handiwork and attention to detail. Sweet Anne. How careful she'd been to keep them a secret. Slowly, carefully, he buried his face in the red softness, and deep within the fibers of the wool he could smell her. Smell the woman he'd loved since he was a boy.

The woman he had lost forever.

Earl had hidden the gloves beneath his pillow. Every night after that he nestled his face against them as he fell asleep. Breathing in the smell of her, dreaming she was still there beside him.

In the weeks after the accident details began to surface. The truck had experienced brake failure. The driver had done everything he could to keep from hitting Earl's car, but the accident was inevitable. A week later an attorney contacted Earl about a class-action lawsuit.

"The truck was owned by a multimillion-dollar company. This is the tenth accident where one of their fleet lost its brakes. Each time the brass has looked the other way and done nothing." The man hesitated. "The company deserves to be punished."

Earl agreed, but he was hardly interested. Over the next four months the attorney built his case against the company, carefully contacting each of the other victims and their families. Earl paid no attention; he was hurting too badly, caught up in a pain he had never experienced before. Each morning he would shower, dress, and look for work. But every step, each breath, was an effort. The tragedy of what had happened to Anne and Molly was so agonizing that at times Earl came back to his parents' house after lunch, unable to last another hour.

Finally, in June, the suit against the truck company wrapped up. A verdict was handed down: The corporation was guilty as sin. It was ordered not to operate until a brake inspection and all necessary repairs had been performed on the entire fleet.

"What this company allowed was an abhorrent act of negligence," the judge said at the verdict.

The judgment was more than the attorney hoped for. After everything had been divided between the plaintiffs, Earl received two million dollars for the unnecessary deaths of Anne and Molly.

With the legal victory, Earl had expected to feel relief from the constant hurt of missing his girls. Their deaths were not in vain, after all—no one else's mother or daughter or wife would die as a result of that company's negligence.

But there was no relief whatsoever.

When the check for Earl's money arrived in the mail, he drove to the bank, opened a savings account, and deposited the entire amount. He wanted nothing to do with it. The check was blood money—money bought and paid for with the lives of Anne and Molly.

That night back at his parents' house he knew it was over.

He could no longer play the game, no longer get up each morning pretending there was a reason to live, a reason to come home at the end of the day. If not for his parents he would have bought a gun and ended his life. Certainly he wanted to die. Wanted it more than anything. But he was afraid to kill himself, afraid such a move might hurt his chances at getting into heaven.

And getting into heaven was his only hope of seeing Anne and Molly again.

But if he couldn't kill himself, at least he could stop living. Stop pretending.

As his parents slept that night he reached under his pillow and pulled out the red gloves. He still slept with them near his face, pretending he could smell Anne within the fibers, though her gentle scent had long since faded. In the closet he found an old duffel bag and filled it with a few jeans and T-shirts, a raincoat, a pair of boots, and the red gloves. Then he opened his wallet, slipped a photograph of Anne and Molly inside, and shoved it in his pocket.

For the next hour he took a final look at the house he'd grown up in, the box of artwork Molly had made for him, the photographs that lined the walls. It was over, all of it. Earl's injuries had healed by then, but the man he'd been had died right there on the street beside Anne and Molly.

He scribbled a note to his parents telling them not to look for him. "I can't do this anymore," he wrote them. "Forgive me. I love you both."

An hour later he was at the train station and by the next morning he was halfway to Portland.

"I had planned to find a quiet place where no one knew me, sit down, and wait for death." Earl stared out the window of the mission. "But it didn't work that way."

D. J.'s voice was kind. "It usually doesn't."

"It took me a while to get smart about the streets. They stole my wallet, my clothes, my sack. Over time I lost just about everything from my old life. But not the red gloves. Never them." Earl shifted his gaze back to the mission director. "Until this past November. Someone found me under a tarp and took them off my hands while I slept."

"Ah, Earl. I'm sorry. I had no idea."

Earl fumbled in his pockets, his eyes locked on D.J.'s. Then he pulled out the red gloves and held them up. "These are the gloves. At least I think they are. They look . . . exactly the same."

The mission director stared at them for a moment. "I don't understand."

"Me, either." Earl lifted the gloves higher. "This is the gift I got from Gideon."

Confusion spread across D.J.'s face. "The gloves your wife made?"

"I think so. They don't have her initials, but they're the same in every other way." Earl let the gloves fall slowly to his lap. "That child couldn't have possibly known what they would mean to me. I still can't imagine where she found them. But I know this: Her gift saved my life. She made me want to live again."

"And now? Now you want to help Gideon? Is that right?"

Earl could feel the sorrow lining his face. "That little girl loved me. For no reason at all she loved me." He swallowed, searching for the right words. "The gift she gave— I can't explain it but it was a miracle."

D. J. nodded. "I have no doubt."

"You know what she said?" Earl's tone was filled with awe. "She told me Christmas miracles happen to those who believe."

A smile eased the sadness in D. J.'s eyes.

"She told me about her perfect Christmas, and then she said none of that would matter if she could get a Christmas miracle."

"That's Gideon."

"Well." Earl drew a deep breath. "Sounds like Gideon could use a miracle about now."

The mission director was choked up, touched by Earl's story. "Your money—is it still in the bank?"

"All of it." Earl reached down, untied his boot, and lifted the insole. From underneath he pulled out a worn bankbook and tossed it onto the desk. "I haven't looked at it since I left home." He leaned back. "I couldn't bear to spend it. Not when it was Anne and Molly's blood money. Not for anything in the world." Earl shrugged, the pain in his soul deeper than the ocean. "Besides, what good was money with my family gone?"

"Unbelievable. I never would have guessed."

"The point is, now I know how I can use it."

For the next two hours the men worked out a plan. When they were finished, D.J. helped Earl find clean clothes and shoes. Before lunchtime they set out with two activities in mind.

Banking. And shopping.

CHAPTER TWELVE

Gideon wasn't getting better.

Brian hated to admit it, but the truth was obvious. Gideon was pale and weak and it seemed she grew worse by the hour. It was the day before Christmas and they were gathered in her hospital room, searching desperately for a way to make the moment feel happy.

Dustin watched television as Gideon received constant treatment. Nobody said much. Every time Brian looked at Tish she was wiping her eyes, filled with the terror that Gideon was slipping away from them.

And she was. The doctors had told them so earlier that morning. Her blood levels were not responding to the chemotherapy like they'd hoped. A transplant was critically necessary.

When Brian wasn't leaning over Gideon, holding her

hand or stroking her thin arm, he dreamed of ways he might get the money. Bizarre, outlandish ways. Like selling his organs or spending a season on a crabbing boat in the icy seas of Alaska. He'd heard on television once that a crew member could earn twenty-five thousand dollars in eleven weeks.

He wondered if he'd have time to work a season and return with the money before Gideon died. He wondered if anyone might be interested in purchasing his lung or a kidney.

He wondered if he was losing his mind.

The only good news of the day came just after two o'clock. One of Gideon's doctors entered the room and approached her bedside. "I have a surprise for you."

Gideon raised her eyes. She looked so frail, her body wasting away before their eyes. "I'm getting better?"

A flicker of sadness crossed the doctor's face. "We're working on that part." He smiled first at Tish, then Brian. "We've reviewed her chart and decided she can go home this afternoon." He looked down at Gideon again and patted her hand. "You get to be with your family for Christmas, Miss Gideon."

Tish took a step closer to the doctor. "Does she have to come back?"

"Yes." The doctor shot her a sympathetic look. "First thing on the twenty-sixth. A few days away won't hurt. We'll have a nurse stop by twice a day with her medication. But after that she needs to be back here."

When the doctor was gone, there was silence. Then Dustin flicked off the television and popped up from his chair. "Why's everyone so sad?" He looked around the room at each of them. "At least we'll be together for Christmas."

Brian forced a smile, though he was certain it didn't reach his eyes. "Dustin's right. If we have this time, let's make the most of it. In fact"—he met Gideon's eyes and winked—"let's stop for ice cream on the way home."

An hour later they were making their way along the hallway toward their apartment when Brian stopped a few feet from the front door. Gideon was in his arms, Tish and Dustin in front of him, but even then he could see something wasn't right.

The door was open half an inch.

"Wait." He set Gideon down and moved past his family. He had locked the door that morning; he was sure of it. So why was it open? Had someone broken in and torn the place up? On the day before Christmas?

Brian looked back at Tish and motioned for her to keep the kids. Then he pushed the door open and slammed on the light, ready for the worst.

What he saw took his breath away. His mouth fell open as his eyes circled the living room and kitchen. How in the world . . . Who had done this? And how had they gotten in?

From behind him, Tish sounded impatient. "What is it, Brian? Let us see."

He stepped back into the hallway, swept Gideon into his arms once more, and took three steps into the apartment. Tish and Dustin fell in beside him. For a moment they stood there in stunned silence.

The place had been completely transformed.

In the middle of the living room stood a towering Christmas tree laden with twinkling lights and dozens of colorful ornaments. Beneath the tree were wrapped presents piled so high they spilled over onto the matted gray carpeting. A brand-new toy fire truck was parked against one wall. Leaning against the other were four stockings stuffed with gifts and labeled with each of their names.

"Daddy?" Gideon tightened her grip around his neck and stared at him. "How did you do this?"

"I didn't do anything, honey. Not a thing."

"But the tree is alive and it reaches to the ceiling just . . . just like the one in my perfect Christmas."

"Come on, Brian. You didn't plan this?" Tish wandered about the room, her mouth open. "You must have. Where did all this stuff come from?"

"Santa Claus brought it!" Dustin was still frozen in place. He looked like he was afraid to blink, lest the entire scene disappear like some sort of wonderful dream.

Lined along the kitchen floor were bags of food, one after the other. Brian opened the refrigerator and found it full to overflowing. Milk and fruit and cheese and bread. And on the center shelf was a turkey twice the size of anything Tish had ever cooked.

"Hey!" Gideon shifted in his arms, and pointed to the kitchen counter. "What's that?"

All of them gathered round and stared at the thing Gideon was pointing at. It was a golden bag, three feet high with tissue paper bursting from the opening at the top. Scrawled across the front of the bag was this message:

For Gideon. Open this first.

"It's for me?" Gideon's voice sounded stronger than it had in days.

"That's what it says." Brian eased Gideon from his arms so she could stand against the counter. "Go ahead, honey. Open it."

Gideon looked first at Brian, then at Tish. "Really?"

"Yes, honey. It has your name on it."

With gentle fingers, Gideon took hold of the bag and lay it sideways. Then she pulled out the tissue, one piece at a time until she could just make out the top of a box. "It can't be . . ."

"What is it? What is it?" Dustin jumped up and down, barely able to contain himself.

"Just a minute, son." Brian tried to peer into the bag, equally anxious to see what was inside. "Give her a chance to open it."

Carefully Gideon pulled the box out, gasping at what was inside. "She-she's perfect. Just like the one in the catalog."

Brian felt his stomach drop. It was a brand-new doll, the kind with shiny hair and eyes that opened and shut, and a beautiful dress with tiny lace trim. It was the exact doll Gideon had always wanted. Brian stared at Tish and shook his head. She did the same, tears in her eyes.

There was nothing he could say. *God, where did this come from?* It wasn't possible. No one knew about Gideon's perfect Christmas except the people in her immediate family.

Gideon opened the cardboard and pulled the doll out. There in the doll's hands was an envelope. Gideon wrinkled her nose and stared at it. "What's this, Daddy?"

Brian took the envelope, his hands shaking. Maybe the person had signed the card. Maybe they would finally know where this amazing abundance had come from. He slid his finger beneath the flap and pulled out a folded piece of paper. As he did, something fell onto the counter.

"Brian, look at that." Tish sounded almost frightened.

"What is it? Someone tell me?" Dustin tugged at Brian's sleeve.

"Wait, son." He lifted the smaller piece of paper from the counter. It was an official cashier's check from a bank in Redding, California, made out to Gideon. Brian's eyes darted over to the amount and his heart stopped.

It was for fifty thousand dollars.

Fifty thousand dollars! *God, what have you done? How did you do this?* Fifty thousand dollars? Brian blinked, but the number remained the same. It was more money than he could make in two years. Three even. His entire body shook and he had to remind himself to breathe. His heartbeat raced like it might tear through his chest. "Tish? Do you see this?"

He looked at her. She nodded, but she was weeping too hard to speak. Her arms clutched Gideon and Dustin.

"Is it money, Daddy?" Gideon stared at the check, her innocent eyes not understanding the zeroes.

"Yes, honey." There was nothing Brian could do to stop the tears. They filled his eyes and spilled onto his cheeks. "Enough money for your transplant."

"Really?" Gideon's eyes were brighter than before. "You mean I can get better now?"

"Yes, honey." Brian's voice cracked and he circled his arms around the others, too shaken to speak.

They stayed that way a long time, until Dustin poked his head up near Brian's side. "Is it a lot of money, Daddy?"

"Yes, son, it is." Brian wiped his eyes on the sleeve of his shirt and stared at Tish. How was it possible? Who could have done this? The unanswered questions in his own heart were mirrored in her expression.

"Can we open our stockings?" Dustin's eyes were wide and he took three quick steps toward them. "Please, can we?"

Tish nodded. "Go ahead. You can both open them."

Dustin raced into the living room. Gideon followed more slowly. Her color looked better than it had all day. She cradled her new doll in her arms and settled into the chair closest to the tree. "Go ahead, Dustin. Me and my dolly need a rest."

When the kids were out of earshot, Brian set the check carefully on the counter and took Tish in his arms. "It's a miracle," Brian whispered against the side of her face. "She's going to be okay, honey. I can feel it."

Tish was trembling, her body still jerking every few seconds from the sobs that racked her body. "But where did it come from, Brian? Money like that doesn't just show up."

"Right now I don't know, and I really don't care." Brian stepped back and stared at the check once more. "It's here. And because of that Gideon's going to get better."

"Wait." Tish searched the counter. "Wasn't there a note in the envelope?"

"There was." Brian reached inside the doll box and

picked up the folded piece of paper. He opened it and as he read the message, chills flashed up and down the length of his spine.

Dear Gideon, Christmas miracles happen to those who believe.

It was the same sentiment Gideon had shared with him that day at the doctor's office. Other than those words, the page was blank. There was no name, no signature. The gifts, the tree, the money—all of it was from someone who remained completely anonymous.

"Hey, Gideon."

She looked up from her doll. "Yes, Daddy."

"There was something written in there with the money." Brian's eyes welled up, and he blinked so he could see. "'Dear Gideon, Christmas miracles happen to those who believe.' Does that mean anything to you?"

Across the room Gideon gasped. "It's from Earl! Earl at the mission!"

Earl? The old man who had been so cruel to Gideon? Brian and Tish exchanged a knowing look. There was no way Earl was behind the gifts that surrounded them. He was a street person, after all. And a mean one at that. Brian cleared his throat. "Uh, Gideon, I don't think so."

She sat up straighter in her chair, her doll clutched to her chest. "But it is, Daddy. That's what I wrote on his Christmas picture. And he's the only one besides you and Mommy who knew about my perfect Christmas." Her eyes got dreamy. "That means he opened my gift. And this is his way of telling me thank you!"

"Hmm," Brian answered noncommittally. He shrugged in Tish's direction. The doctors had asked them to keep Gideon as calm as possible, and this discussion was only exciting her.

"Really, Daddy." Her expression was nearly frantic. "I know it's from Earl."

"Okay, sweetheart." Tish moved to her side and felt her head. In the corner of the room, Dustin played with his fire truck, surrounded by a dozen new toys. Tish looked at him for a moment then back at Gideon. "Don't get worked up."

"God did it, Mommy. He really did it!" Gideon settled back into the chair. "This is exactly what I prayed for."

"Yes, honey." Tish smiled, her eyes red and swollen.

Brian joined them, placing his arm around Tish as they studied their daughter. "A tree. A doll. Presents. It's the perfect Christmas."

"No." Gideon looked up, and Brian was struck by the wisdom in his daughter's eyes. A wisdom that went years beyond her age. "That's not what I prayed for."

Suddenly Brian knew what was coming. After all, he had been there with Gideon that afternoon in the doctor's waiting room when she'd prayed.

"Well? What did you pray for?" Tish sniffed, her cheeks still wet.

"Daddy knows." Gideon shot a glance at Brian. "Right?"

"Right." He loved the sparkle in Gideon's eyes. It was still hard to believe she might live. That God had used the generosity of someone they didn't know to bring them a gift they could never repay.

"Okay, guys." There was life in Tish's eyes again, too. "I'm the only one in the dark here."

"Well." Gideon drew a slow breath. "I prayed God would do something really amazing. Not like a dolly or a fire truck or money. I prayed he would make Earl believe again." Her smile took up most of her face. "And that's just what happened."

"Something big like that, huh?" Tish looked at Brian and shook her head, clearly struck by Gideon's tender heart.

"Yes, Mommy." Gideon hugged her doll. "Something so big it could only be a Christmas miracle."

Earl caught a late flight that afternoon and by five o'clock a taxi was dropping him off in front of the old house. There were several cars parked in the driveway.

For a moment he stood there and stared at it—the place where he'd grown up, the yard where he and Anne had once sat and talked and fallen in love. Not once during his time on the streets of Portland had he ever thought he'd be here again.

But here he was. And all because of one special little girl.

Okay, God. Give me the words.

He'd checked the mirror in the airport and knew he looked presentable. In fact, he barely recognized himself. That was just as well. It would have killed his parents to see the way he'd looked a few days ago. This new look—clean clothes, neatly shaven—was much better for a reunion.

Not that he knew whether they were home or not.

There'd been no time to call. The idea was too last

minute. He had no idea what he'd find, no way of knowing whether his parents would even *want* to see him after so many years. Or whether they were still alive. Shame kicked at him again. How wrong he'd been not to call, not to make some attempt at communicating with them before this.

He stood a little straighter. Either way, he was a fifty-one-year-old prodigal son, and it was Christmas Eve. Whatever had happened to his parents in the past years, there was no better time to find out.

He strode up the walkway to the front door. Then, without waiting another moment, he knocked.

Nearly five seconds passed. Suddenly the door opened and his mother appeared. Christmas music filled the house, and the voices of people laughing and talking rang in the background. His mother stared at him strangely. "Can I help—"

"Mom." Earl saw the flash of recognition in her eyes. She hadn't known it was him at first, but now . . . now she knew. "Mom, I'm home."

"Earl?" Her voice was broken and weak—almost childlike. He stepped into the house and took her in his arms. She was shaking, and for a moment Earl thought she might pass out. "Thank God. Oh, thank

God. I knew you'd come home at Christmastime."

All he could do was hold her.

After a moment of silence, she leaned back and framed his face in her hands. Then, with a smile, she linked arms with him and headed into the living room.

At one end sat his father. He looked older, more frail than the last time Earl had seen him. Seated around the room were Earl's brother and sister, their spouses, and kids. Conversations stopped and the room fell silent as Earl and his mother walked into view.

His sister gasped and then covered her mouth.

For a moment, no one spoke. Earl knew it was his move, his turn to apologize. But his throat was thick and he knew if he tried to talk he would break down and cry.

Almost as though he could sense Earl's discomfort, his father stood and moved slowly across the room. Their eyes met and held, then his father engulfed him in a desperate hug that erased the years. "Welcome home, son."

"I'm—I'm so sorry, Dad." Earl's voice broke and he buried his face in his father's shoulder.

One by one the others rose and joined in the embrace. Earl stood utterly still, his tears splashing against his new shoes. What was this? How could they so quickly forgive him? And why would they still love him after all his years of silence?

It was a moment that defined their love, a moment that told Earl everything he needed to know: He was going to be okay. No, he would not have Anne and Molly. Not for a long while. But he had the love of his family. And a faith in God that had never been there before.

"Oh, Earl." His mother clung to him even more tightly than before. "You're really here!"

Then, as briefly as he could, he told them about Gideon and her gift and how it had changed his mind about life and love. Even God's love.

His mother still looked at him as though he might disappear at any moment. Then she said something Earl had never expected her to say. "How fitting—that God would use a child to make the miracle happen. Especially at Christmas."

Earl's legs trembled. The love from his parents, his family, was almost more than he could take. He was so undeserving. What if he hadn't opened the child's gift? What if he'd tossed it in the trash can like he'd planned? Neither of them would have found life—neither him nor her.

With a shudder, he shook his head and cast a pleading look at his father. "We've lost so much time."

"Yes," his father wrapped his arm around him once more. "But think how much time we have left."

POSTSCRIPT

The wedding was over and Earl slipped into the foyer. He needed to find Gideon, needed to give her something.

How good God had been to them over the years. Gideon had figured out that their Christmas surprises were from him, and he had flown back to Portland and spent time with the Mercer family. He'd stayed in touch throughout Gideon's transplant process. And when she came home two months later with a healthy report, Earl was the first one she called.

She had become something of a granddaughter to him. Someone he loved as dearly as he'd loved his own girl.

He had flown out for the wedding. He still lived in Redding. His parents had both died years ago, so he had the old house to himself now. Just him, alone with the Lord, celebrating life and anxious for heaven.

He maneuvered himself past the milling crowd and peered over the heads of a group of men. There she was. Surrounded by guests in the far corner of the church foyer. He made his way closer and motioned to her. "Can I talk to you for a minute, Gideon?"

Her face lit up, those unforgettable eyes shining. She excused herself and followed him to a quiet spot around the corner.

"Earl." She took his hands in hers. "I'm so glad you made it."

A blush warmed his face and he stared at his shoes for a moment. "I have a plane to catch in a few hours." He handed her a package. "I wanted you to open this before I go."

"Earl, you shouldn't have. It's enough that you're here." She slid her finger into a seam in the wrapping paper and pulled out a framed painting. For a long moment she merely stared at it. Then two delicate tears trickled down her cheeks. "Oh . . . It's beautiful, Earl. I can't believe it."

It was an original painting, one he had commissioned from an artist friend he knew at church. Earl had found an old photograph of Gideon as an eight-year-old, a picture she'd given him long ago. Then he'd asked the artist to duplicate it on canvas. The man had done a stunning job of capturing Gideon's soulful eyes and the emotion she carried in her heart at that young age.

But that wasn't what made Gideon stare in wonder.

There was something else—something Earl had asked the artist to add to the painting. On the left side it read, "Christmas miracles happen to those who believe." And beneath that was a perfect illustration of the gift that had started it all.

The gift that had both changed them . . . and saved them.

A pair of bright red, woolen gloves.

AUTHOR'S NOTE

Dear Reader,

Many of you know me as a best-selling fiction author. Others think of me as the writer who brings you collections of true miracle stories. *Gideon's Gift* is a combination of both these passions. Whereas other miracle stories I write about are rooted in truth, this one grew from the soil of my heart.

I hope you enjoyed traveling the pages of *Gideon's Gift,* walking the streets of Portland with Earl, and standing by as a very special little girl longed for a miracle. Perhaps you've read a chapter a night for each of the twelve days of Christmas. Or maybe you found time to curl up in a chair and read Gideon's story in one sitting. Either way, my prayer for you is this: that like Gideon you would believe in miracles this Christmas season.

Maybe for you that means trusting God in a dark time. Or maybe it means making a phone call and mending ties between you and someone you love. Maybe it's a new doll for your daughter or a fire truck for your son. Whatever your situation, please, look for God's presence this holiday season.

Because, like Gideon said, Christmas miracles do happen to those who believe. On the following pages I've included a list of Red Gloves Projects for you and your friends or family, or maybe your office or church group. Last year our children took on a Red Gloves Project—by raising money to feed fifteen homeless people on Christmas Day. My challenge to you is to take on a Red Gloves Project of your own. So that the type of miracle love spread by little Gideon might be spread in our own towns and communities as well.

As always, I would love to hear from you. Please contact me at my email address, rtnbykk@aol.com, or at my website, www.karenkingsbury.com.

May God grant you and yours the wonder and beauty of a miraculous and memorable Christmas.

Karen Kingsbury
www.karenkingsbury.com

RED GLOVES PROJECTS

A Red Gloves Project is a way of giving something back during the Christmas season. Each project idea involves red gloves. I invite you and your family to take part in one of them—or to create one of your own.

Remember, Christmas miracles happen to those who believe.

🌺 Start saving your pennies. The week before Christmas, purchase a pair of red gloves, wrap them, and stick a card or drawing inside. Then deliver it to the first needy person you see—whether he or she is standing at the end of a freeway ramp or eating dinner at your local homeless shelter. Do this with a group of people and impact an entire group of street people.

- Use your extra money to buy food for street people. As you distribute meals, include pairs of red gloves. Again, if you're bagging the food, you can put the gloves inside where they can find them.

- Sing Christmas carols at a local homeless shelter or retirement center. Wear red gloves during the performance. When the singing is over, you and your group can walk around and give away your red gloves to those in attendance.

- Organize your church, school, or office, to have a Red Gloves Drive. Collect toys and food for needy families in your area. When you deliver the gifts, have everyone in the group wear a pair of red gloves. Then leave the gloves with the people who need them more.

Maggie's Miracle

Maggie's Miracle

A Novel

KAREN KINGSBURY

A Division of AOL Time Warner Book Group

Copyright © 2003 by Karen Kingsbury
All rights reserved.

Warner Books, Inc., 1271 Avenue of the Americas, New York, NY 10020
Visit our Web site at www.twbookmark.com.

WARNER *Faith* A Division of AOL Time Warner Book Group
The Warner Faith name and logo are registered trademarks of Warner Books, Inc.

Printed in the United States of America

First Printing: October 2003
10 9 8 7 6 5 4 3 2

Library of Congress Cataloging-in-Publication Data
Kingsbury, Karen.
    Maggie's miracle / Karen Kingsbury.
        p. cm.
    "Warner faith."
    ISBN 0-446-53230-4
    1. Single mothers—Fiction. 2. Father figures—Fiction. 3. Portland (Or.)—
Fiction. 4. Women lawyers—Fiction. 5. Widows—Fiction. I. Title.
    PS3561.I4873M34 2003
    813'.54—dc21   2003049699

Book Design by Fearn Cutler de Vicq

dedicated to...

Donald, my forever prince
Kelsey, my beautiful laughter
Tyler, my favorite song
Sean, my indefinable joy
Josh, my gentle giant
EJ, my chosen one
Austin, my miracle boy

And to God Almighty, the author of life,
who has—for now—blessed me with these.

Maggie's Miracle

PROLOGUE

The letter was his best idea yet.

Jordan Wright had already talked to God about getting his wish, and so far nothing had happened. But a letter . . . a letter would definitely get God's attention. Not the crayoned pictures he liked to send Grandpa in California. But a real letter. On his mom's fancy paper with his best spelling and slow hands, so his a's and e's would sit straight on the line the way a second grader's a's and e's should.

That way, God would read it for sure.

Grandma Terri was watching her yucky grown-up show on TV. People kissing and crying and yelling at each other. Every day his grandma picked him up from St. Andrews, brought him home to their Upper East Side apartment in Manhattan, got him a snack, and put in the video of her grown-up show. Jordan could make his own milk shakes or accidentally color on the walls or jump on his bed for an hour when Grandma watched her grown-up show. As long as he wasn't too loud, she didn't notice anything.

"This is my time, Jordan," she'd tell him, and her eyes would get that in-charge kind of look. "Keep yourself busy."

But when the show was over she'd find him and make a loud, huffy sound. "Jordan," she'd say, "what are you into now? Why can't you read quietly like other children?" Her voice would be slow and tired, and Jordan wouldn't know what to do next.

She never yelled at him or sent him to his room, but one thing was sure. She didn't like baby-sitting him because yesterday Jordan heard her tell his mom that.

"I can't handle the boy forever, Megan. It's been two years since George died. You need a nanny." She did a different kind of breathy noise. "The boy's wearing me out."

Jordan had been in his room listening. He felt bad because maybe it was his fault his grandma couldn't handle him. But then he heard his mom say, "I can't handle him, either, so that makes two of us."

After that Jordan felt too sick to eat dinner.

Ever since then he'd known it was time. He had to do whatever it took to get God's attention because if he didn't get his wish pretty soon, well, maybe his mom and his grandma might not like him anymore.

It wasn't that he tried to get into trouble. But sometimes it was boring looking for things to do, and he'd get curious and wonder what would happen if he made a milk shake with ice cubes. But how was he supposed to know the milk-shake maker had a lid? And using paper and a red crayon to trace the tiger on the wall calendar probably wasn't a good idea in the first place, because of course sometimes crayons slip.

He took the last swallow from his milk and waited until the cookie crumbs slid down the glass into his mouth. Cookies were the best snack of all. He set the cup on the counter, climbed off the barstool, and walked with tiptoe feet into his mom's office. He wasn't allowed in there except if his mom was working on her lawyer stuff and he had to ask her a serious question.

But she'd understand today because a letter to God was very serious business.

The room was big and clean and full of wood stuff. His mom was the kind of lawyer who put bad guys in jail. That's why sometimes she had to work late at night and on Sundays. Jordan pulled open a drawer near his mother's computer and took out two pieces of paper and two envelopes. In case he messed up and had to start over. Then he snuck real quiet out the door, down the hall, and into his room. He had a desk and pencils in there, only he never used them because second graders at St. Andrews didn't get homework till after Christmas.

One time he asked his mommy what would happen if he couldn't do the homework when he got it, what if the stuff he had to do was too hard.

"It won't be too hard, Jordan." His mother's eyebrows had lifted up the way they did when she didn't want any more questions.

"Are you sure?"

"Yes, I'm completely sure."

"How come?"

"Because, Jordan, I've been through second grade and I know all the answers. If you have trouble, I'll help you."

His heart felt a little less scared after that. Not every second grader's mommy had *all* the answers. If she knew everything, then he could never really get in too much trouble with his homework, and that was a good thing because Christmas wasn't too far away.

He sat down at his desk, took a pencil from the box, and spread out the piece of paper. The white space looked very empty. Jordan stared at it for a long time. If God was going to read the letter, it had to be his best work ever. Big words would be a good thing. He worked himself a little taller in the chair, sucked in a long breath through his teeth, and began to write.

Dear God, my name is Jordan Wright and I am 8 years old. I hav somthing to ask you. I tride to ask you befor but I think you wer bizy. So I am riting you a letter insted.

Jordan's hand hurt by the time he finished, and he could hear music playing on Grandma's grown-up show. That meant it was almost done, and any minute Grandma would come looking for him. He quickly folded the letter in half, ran his finger along the edge, and folded it again. Then he stuck it in the envelope and licked the lid shut. With careful fingers he wrote "God" across the front, then his pencil moved down a bit and froze. He'd forgotten something.

He didn't know God's address.

His heart felt extra jumpy. God lived in heaven, so that had to be part of it. But what about the numbers? Jordan could hear footsteps coming closer. He didn't want Grandma to see the letter. She might want to read it, and that would ruin everything because it was a secret.

Just between him and God. He looked around his room and saw his backpack near his bed. He ran fast to it and slipped the letter inside. He could give it to his mother on the way to school tomorrow. She would know God's address.

She knew everything.

CHAPTER ONE

Megan Wright tucked her blouse into her navy skirt as she rounded the corner into the kitchen. Her biggest opening argument of the month was in less than an hour. "Let's go, Jordan. Two minutes."

"Just a sec."

"Not just a sec." She blew at a wisp of hair as she grabbed a cold piece of toast from the kitchen counter. These were the times she missed George more than any other because the morning routine had been his deal. As long as he was at work by eight-thirty he'd been happy. But she had briefings and depositions that started earlier than that.

"*Now*, Jordan. I have a hearing today."

She poured two glasses of orange juice, snatched one and spun toward the vitamin cupboard. Two C's, one A,

7

one E, a B-complex, a CoQ_{10}, and two garlics. She popped the pills into her mouth and swallowed them with a single swig of juice. George had been more than twenty years older than her, a man she respected and tried to love. But the fortress surrounding George's deepest emotions was unyielding stone and razor wire, and in his presence, Megan never felt like more than an amicable business partner. When the love she'd dreamed of never materialized, Megan allowed herself to become like him. Married to her job.

Neither of them had figured Jordan into the plans.

But surprise gave way to possibility, and for a time Megan believed that maybe George would come around, spend less time at work, and get caught up in fatherhood. They would have quiet moments together, watching their baby sleep and dreaming of his future. Laughter and passion would finally find them, and her life would be all she'd ever hoped it to be. But the dream never quite materialized. George was nearly fifty by then, and thrilled with the idea of a son, a child to carry on his name, but he was as distant as ever with Megan.

"You treat me like part of the furniture, George." Megan whispered the words to him one night after they climbed into bed. "Don't you want more?"

His eyes had been steely cold. "You have all you could

ever want, Megan. Don't ask more of me than I can give."

George had been a bond trader, a financial wizard with a spacious office in Midtown. For two weeks straight he'd complained about a stiff neck, but neither of them saw the signs. When his secretary found him that October morning, arms spread across his desk, his head resting on a pile of client files, she'd thought he was merely resting. An hour later a client call came in and she tried to wake him. Her scream brought most of the office staff and fifteen minutes later paramedics gave them the truth.

He was dead, the victim of a massive coronary.

Megan lifted the juice to her lips once more and downed it in four swallows. It had been two years now. Her grieving period had lasted only a few months. The two of them had never loved the way Megan had hoped, the way she'd once, a long time ago, believed possible. She and George were business partners, friends who ran a common household. She missed George in a functionary sense—especially on mornings like this—but he'd taken none of her heart with him when he died.

The problem was Jordan.

The boy was the one person George had truly loved, and what little free time and sparse emotions he was able to give had been completely reserved for their only child. Megan never admitted it, but more than once she'd found herself feeling jealous of George's love for Jordan. Because it was a love he'd never had for her. When George died, Jordan was devastated. In the two years since his death, the level of Jordan's behavior in school and at home had plummeted.

Grief and anger, his doctor had called it. A passing phase. Megan and Jordan met with a counselor after George's death, but the sessions were costly and time-consuming, and Megan didn't notice any improvement in Jordan's behavior. She'd asked her doctor about medication for the boy. Ritalin or one of the other drugs kids were using.

"Let's wait." The pediatrician had angled his head thoughtfully. "I still think his behavior is related to the loss of his father."

That was three months ago, and Megan was tired of waiting.

Her mother had lived with them since just after George's death, an arrangement Megan had thought would be best for all of them. Her mom had retired from teaching in Florida that year and lived on a limited income. They could share expenses, and her mother could help her with Jordan after school and on the weekends.

But Jordan was too much for her mother, especially now that the weather was cooler and they were inside more.

She set the juice glass in the dishwasher. "Jordan!"

Her son's tennis shoes sounded on the hardwood hallway as he ran into view. "Sorry, Mom."

Megan looked at the boy and felt her patience waning. "Jordan, orange and green?"

"Miss Hanson says October is orange month."

"Miss Hanson isn't your mother." Megan pointed down the hallway. "Find something that matches, and do it now. We have to go."

"Okay." Jordan ran back down the hall, his steps a bit slower this time.

Megan glanced at the clock on the microwave oven. 7:16 A.M. They'd have to catch every green light along Madison Avenue to make it on time. She darted into her bathroom, brushed her teeth, and checked her look. Trim and professional, dark hair swept into a conservative knot, makeup applied just so. She still turned heads, but not because she was pretty.

Because she was powerful.

At thirty-two she was one of the youngest prosecutors in the borough, and she had no intention of getting sidetracked. Not until the D.A.'s office was hers alone. That hadn't been her goal before George's heart attack, but now—now that she was their single source of income, things would always be tight if she didn't keep climbing.

"Jordan . . ." She grabbed her leather jacket and flung her bag over her shoulder. "Now!"

He was waiting for her near the door. "Beat ya!"

His crooked grin caught her off guard, and for half a second she smiled. "Very funny."

"Big hearing?" Jordan opened the door for her.

Megan shut and locked it. "The biggest."

They hurried down the stairs and out onto the street. It was raining, and Megan hailed the first cab she saw. "Get in, Jordan. Hurry."

He tossed his backpack in and slid over. She didn't have the door shut before she said, "Fifth and 102nd. Fast."

The routine was the same every morning, but sometimes—days like today—they had less room for error. They were a block away from school when Jordan pulled something from his backpack and stuck it in Megan's bag. "Hey, Mom. Could you mail this? Please?"

Megan jerked a folder from her purse and opened it. The hearing notes were in there somewhere. She'd stayed up until after midnight studying them, but she wouldn't be prepared without going over them one more time.

"Mom?"

The folder settled on Megan's lap and she looked at Jordan. "What is it, honey? Mommy's busy with her court notes."

"I'm sorry." His eyes fell to his hands for a moment. "I put something in your bag."

"Right . . ." Megan concentrated. What had the boy said? Something about the mail? "What was it again?"

Jordan reached into her bag and lifted a white envelope from the side pocket. "It's a letter. Could you put the 'dress on it and mail it this morning? It's important."

"*Address*." Megan raised her eyebrows at him. Whatever they taught kids at St. Andrews, it wasn't enough. Her son's academic abilities were nowhere near Megan's expectations for an eight-year-old child. Yes, he could hit a ball over the fence and throw it to home plate. But that wouldn't help him get into college. She patted his cheek. "The word is *address*. Not 'dress."

"Address." Jordan didn't skip a beat. "Could ya, Mom? Please?"

She dropped her eyes back to the folder and lifted it closer to her face. "Sure, yes." She cast him a brief smile. "Definitely." The letter was probably for his grandpa Howard in California. But usually he addressed them.

The cab rumbled along, inching its way through a sea of early-morning yellow, but Megan barely noticed as she

13

studied her notes. Getting a conviction on the case was a sure thing. The defendant was a nineteen-year-old up for murder one, the ringleader of a gang of teens who'd spent a week that past summer lying in wait for late-night female victims in Central Park. In each case, the young men studied their prey for days, watching them enough to know their walking pattern, the direction they came from, and what time of night.

At an opportune moment, they'd grab the victim, strangle her with fishing wire, and rob her clean. They dumped the bodies in the brush and made their escape through back trails out to the street. The first two times, the gang pulled off their deed without a hitch. The third time, an off-duty police officer happened by and heard someone struggling in the bushes. He darted off the path into the bramble, and a gun battle ensued. The victim escaped with bruises on her neck, but the police officer and one of the gang members were killed in the fight.

Megan wanted the death penalty.

The cab jarred to a stop. "St. Andrews." The cabbie put the car in park and didn't turn around.

"We're here, honey." Megan leaned over and gave Jordan a peck on his cheek. "Get your bag."

Jordan grabbed his backpack, climbed out of the cab, and looked back at her. "Don't forget, okay?"

Megan's mind was blank. "Forget what?"

"Mom!" Jordan's shoulders slumped some. "My letter. Don't forget to mail my letter."

"Right . . . sorry." Megan gave a firm nod of her head. "I won't forget."

"Promise?"

Something desperate shone in his little-boy eyes, and Megan felt as if she were seeing him for the first time that morning. He was a great kid, really, and she loved him in a way that sometimes scared her. But then why didn't she spend more time with him? She had no answers for herself, and suddenly she needed to hug him more than she needed air. Even if she missed her hearing.

She slid out of the car and went to him, pulling him into her arms and ignoring the surprise in his eyes. Her answer was quiet, whispered against the top of his head. "Promise." For the briefest moment she savored the way he smelled, the way he felt in her arms—like a little boy again. "Have a good day, okay?"

His arms tightened some, and he pressed his face against her. "I'm sorry I'm so much trouble."

Megan shot a quick look at the cabbie. "You're not so much trouble, honey. We'll figure everything out somehow." She glanced at her watch. "Okay, buddy. Mom can't be late. Love you."

"Love you." Jordan gave her one last look, then darted up the sidewalk to St. Andrews. Megan climbed back into the cab and watched until he was safely through the front door, then she turned to the driver and raised her voice a notch. "Supreme Court on Centre." She straightened her notes and slipped them back in the folder. "Fast."

It was nightfall before Megan had a chance to grab a cup of coffee, sit down, and go over the cases she'd worked on that day. The hearing had gone brilliantly. The jury—made up of married women and retired men—was bound to be more conservative than most in Manhattan, and her opening remarks had been right on. By the time she sat down, half the jurors were nodding in agreement. The trial would take two weeks of formalities, and she'd have her conviction.

She liked to call Jordan after school, but the morning hearing had blended into an afternoon briefing and two late depositions. Now it was seven o'clock, and she still hadn't gone over her files, five of them spread out across her desk. One at a time she worked her way through each document, checking the facts, going over witness lists, looking for loopholes. Trying to think like a defense attorney in case some small detail had slipped her mind. By seven-thirty she was convinced none had.

She was loading the files into a cabinet when the phone on her desk rang. Megan grabbed the receiver and kept filing. "Hello?"

"Megan, I can't take it. The boy made a racetrack in the bathroom and flushed a Mustang down the toilet. We have an inch of water on the floor, and the supe's on his way up because Mrs. Paisley in 204 has a wet ceiling." Her mother paused only long enough to refuel. "I fixed chicken for dinner, but by then he didn't want to eat, so I sent him to his room to read. He's been crying for the past half hour."

Megan shut the file drawer and fell back into her chair. "A wet ceiling? Mom . . . how long was it flooded?"

"Not long, and don't have that tone with me."

"You were watching your soap, weren't you? No wonder he was playing in the toilet."

"Megan, the boy's crying. Come home. We'll talk about it here."

Traffic was a nightmare, and Megan used the time to think about her life. Tears were nothing new for Jordan, not lately. She thought about her options, but none of them brought her peace. Her mother was right, the boy needed a friend—someone to take walks with and play sports with. But where would she find someone like that?

A fragment of a conversation played in Megan's mind. A couple had been talking in the halls outside Megan's office.

"Child support is fine, but he needs more than that." The woman kept her voice to a low hiss.

"It's not my problem. I'm writing the checks; that's all the court asked me to do."

"We wouldn't be here if you spent even a few days a month with him, can't you see that? Kids need more than food and a roof over their heads."

Megan stared out the window of the cab at the dark, wet streets of New York City. *More than food and a roof over their heads* . . . The words echoed in the most solitary part of her heart, the part she'd closed off the spring of her thirteenth year.

That was the problem with Jordan, of course. He was lonely, left with only a tired old woman far too often. The truth made Megan's eyes sting and it roughed up the surface of her perfect plans. She'd have time for Jordan later, when she made a name for herself as a prosecutor, when she was making big money and able to choose her hours. Wasn't that what she always told herself? For now, Jordan had to know she loved him. She told him all the time.

It took Megan half an hour to get home. She rarely felt tired after a full day in court; exhilarated but not tired. Today, though, she wanted only to bypass the situation with Jordan and go straight to bed. The three flights of stairs felt like five, and Jordan met her at the door.

"Did you do it?"

Megan locked eyes with him as she walked in and closed the door behind her. "Do what?"

"Mail the letter." Hope shone in his expression. "Did you?"

Her heart skipped a beat, and she resisted the urge to blink. "Of course."

"Really? You found the address?"

The lie came easier the second time. She brushed at a wisp of his hair and kissed his forehead. "Definitely."

Jordan flung his arms around her. "Thanks, Mom . . . you're the best."

Guilt found its way to her throat and put down roots. "Enough about that." She swallowed hard and pulled back. "What happened in the bathroom?"

It was an hour later before they got through the story and she tucked him into bed. By then her mother was asleep, and finally Megan took her bag and retreated to her bedroom. The letter was still tucked inside. As she pulled it out her heart stumbled. Jordan had scribbled just one word across the front of the envelope:

God.

Suddenly she remembered. Jordan had asked her to address it before dropping it in the mail. Megan closed her eyes, clutched the letter to her heart, and exhaled hard. Then, afraid of what she'd find, she dropped to her bed and opened it. Inside was a single page, filled with Jordan's neatest handwriting.

Megan narrowed her eyes and began to read.

> *Dear God, my name is Jordan Wright and I am 8 years old. I hav somthing to ask you. I tride to ask you befor but I think you wer bizy. So I am riting you a letter insted.*

A sad, aching sort of pain ignited in the basement of Megan's soul, the place where she had assigned all feelings about God and prayers and miracles. Jordan had said it perfectly. God had always been too busy to hear the prayers of a lonely, forgotten woman, and now He was too busy for her son. She gritted her teeth and kept reading.

I hav a wish to ask you abot, and here it is: Plese God, send me a Daddy. My daddy died wen his heart stopped pumping, and now its just my mom and gramma and me.

Tears filled Megan's eyes and made the words blurry. She blinked and forced herself to continue.

My frend Keith has a daddy who plays baseball with him and takes him on Saterday trips to the park and helps him with his plusses and minuses evry day after scool. Mommy is too bizy to do that stuff, so plese God, plese send me a Daddy like that. Chrismas would be a good time. Thank you very much. Love, Jordan.

Megan wiped her tears. She read the letter again and again, and finally a fourth time as the sobs welled within her. Deep, gut-wrenching sobs of the type she hadn't allowed herself since she was a little girl. She could give Jordan everything he needed, but never the one thing he wanted. A daddy—a man to play with him and love him and call him his own.

And the fact grieved her as it hadn't since George died.

Megan slipped the letter back inside the envelope and eased it under her pillow. Then, with her work clothes still

21

on, she lay down, slid beneath the comforter, and covered her face with her hands. Suddenly she was thirteen again, alone on the sandy shores of Lake Tahoe, devastated by her own losses and desperate for answers.

The boy had been fifteen, tall and wiry with sun-drenched hair and freckles, and they met each other near the water every day for a week. What was his name? Kade something? The memory was dimmer than it had once been, and she could barely picture his face. But Maggie had never forgotten something the boy told her that summer.

Hold out for real love, Maggie, because real love never fails.

Megan had gazed out across the chilly lake and shook her head. It would take a miracle for that kind of love, she'd told him. Nothing short of a miracle.

"Then that," the boy had said as he grinned at her, "is what I'll pray for. A miracle for Maggie."

Megan rolled onto her side and let the full brunt of the sobs come. For years she'd held on to the boy's definition of love—a love that would never fail. But the boy on the beach had been wrong. Love—whatever love was—certainly failed. And miracles? Well, they didn't happen for her, and they certainly weren't about to happen for Jordan.

The sooner he understood that, the better off he'd be.

CHAPTER TWO

Year-round, Saturday mornings were busy at Casey's Corner in Midtown Manhattan. The smell of hot blueberry pancakes and sizzling bacon drenched the air, while the clamor of clattering trays and a dozen conversations served as a backdrop for customers lined up at the door. The café was a hot spot for tourists from Texas to Tokyo and extremely popular among Midtown's business elite. With a menu that was "healthy eclectic," ripe avocado and alfalfa sprout sandwiches were served up alongside a half dozen styles of homemade cheesecake. The food was fresh and fast, and the atmosphere as diverse and dynamic as New York City itself. In the six years since Casey Cummins opened the café, it had practically become a local landmark.

One of the regulars was telling him a joke, and Casey

had to remind himself to laugh. His mind was a million miles away, stranded on an island of memories and secrets he would share with no one.

Especially today.

Most days, Casey jogged to work. He wore his trademark blue nylon sweats and white Nikes, same as always, so that when the morning was behind him he could run the twenty blocks through Central Park back to his apartment. His routine was the same as it had always been, but these days Casey logged more miles and rarely ran the straight path to his front door. Not because he needed the exercise, but because he wanted to be anywhere but back at the lonely set of walls he called home.

It was the third Saturday in October, and Casey easily drifted from one conversation to another as he made the rounds. "Joey . . . how's the new job at the bank?" or "Hey, Mrs. Jackson, another Saturday closer to Christmas," or "Marvin, my man, how 'bout those Nets? Jason Kidd'll tear 'em up this season."

Hours passed, and Casey kept himself in the moment. Never mind that his thoughts were somewhere else, the café routine was as familiar as putting one foot in front of the other. Even on a day like this.

The crowd began thinning around noon, and Casey found a seat at the counter. "Long morning, Billy-G."

The old black chef peered out from his position in front of the kitchen stove. "Okay . . ." He studied Casey for a moment. "Give it up."

Casey blinked and kept his gaze on the man's face. Billy Gaynor was a quiet family man from Nigeria who'd worked for Casey since the café opened. Billy's culinary magic was as much a part of the success of Casey's Corner as the quirky New York street signs and Broadway memorabilia that hung on the hand-painted walls. Casey and Billy-G were colleagues and friends—even more so since Amy died. They were both widowers now, and despite the thirty years between them, there was no one Casey would rather spend an hour with.

Billy-G was waiting, and Casey grabbed a nearby pitcher, poured himself a cup of coffee, and took a slow drink.

"Yes, sir." Casey peered over the top of his steaming mug. "Another great Saturday morning in the Big Apple, eh Billy-G."

His friend's eyebrows forged a slow path through the thick skin that made up his forehead. "Ya ain't fooling me, Casey." He lumbered around the corner and leaned against the counter opposite Casey. "Ya gotta talk about it." Customers still filled most of the seats, so Billy-G kept his voice low. "You can't fake it with me, Casey. I already know."

Casey set down his coffee and lowered his chin. He thought about smiling again, but changed his mind. "What ya know, Billy-G?"

"It's your anniversary." The man leaned closer. "One month after mine, remember?"

A brief burning nipped at Casey's eyes. "That." He sniffed hard and sat up straighter on the stool. "No big deal, Billy-G. Life moves on."

"Yes." The old man leaned against the counter, his eyes still locked on Casey's. "But only a fool would forget a girl like Amy." He hesitated and took a step back toward the kitchen. "And you ain't no fool."

"Yeah, well . . ." Casey narrowed his eyes some and sucked in a quick breath. He set down his cup and gave the counter a light slap. "Time for my jog."

Billy-G stopped and leveled his gaze at Casey once more. "I'm here. Anytime you wanna talk, I'm here."

"Thanks." Casey glanced over his shoulder and mentally mapped out a course for the door. His throat was thick, and memories were drawing close to the surface. Some days he could talk about Amy for hours and never feel the tears. Times like those he liked nothing more than to hang out with Billy-G after closing time and talk about a thousand yesterdays. But not today.

He flashed a smile at Billy-G. "See ya tomorrow."

The pavement felt like ice beneath his feet, and Casey ran faster than usual. Some of the regulars had waved him down, hoping for a conversation or a laugh, but he couldn't pretend for another minute. Billy-G was right.

Casey Cummins was no fool, and today he could keep up the happy-guy act only for so long. It was his eighth wedding anniversary, and if Amy and the baby had lived, they would've spent the day together, celebrating life and love and cherishing that special something they'd had between them, the kind of love so few people shared.

He headed north on Broadway and cut across the street toward Central Park. The thing of it was, no one wanted to hear about his loss. Not really. People had their own tragedies, lost jobs and children in the Armed Forces, broken relationships and bankruptcies. At Casey's Corner everyone wanted a sympathetic ear, and he made it his job to listen.

But rarely did he talk.

Casey slowed his pace some and headed into the park on a paved path. He'd heard people question God after a tragedy, wondering how a loving Creator could allow a world filled with devastation and loss. Some of his customers were so angry with God after September 11, they'd stopped believing.

Casey didn't feel that way at all.

Bad things happened in the world, it was that simple. A fifteen-year-old rape victim, the mother of a toddler killed by a drunk driver, the wife of a police officer shot in the line of duty—each of them had their own September 11, a day when they'd been forced to realize that without faith, life didn't make sense.

Not a single minute of it.

Casey's had happened a week after the terrorist attacks, on September 18. That was the day Amy went into labor and began bleeding. He rushed her to Mount Sinai Hospital, and even after the doctors ushered him into a private waiting room, Casey thought Amy and the baby were going to be fine. It wasn't until almost an hour later, when a weary doctor shuffled up to Casey, that he realized something was wrong.

"We lost them both, Mr. Cummins." The doctor had tears in his eyes. "I'm sorry."

Amy had begun hemorrhaging when she went into labor. The blood loss was too much, and there'd been no way to save either of them.

Casey was breathing harder now. He rounded a corner and saw the familiar green and tan plastic play equipment and the giant slide to the right. The East Meadow play area wasn't the largest or most popular in Central Park, but it was the place where Casey and Amy had come after they'd moved to New York. Normally, he would run past the area with only a quick glance and a flash of memories. Past the worn-out bench anchored near the back by the big slide, past the place where he had given Amy a ring, the place where she'd told him she was going to have a baby. The quiet spot where they'd held each other and wept once the dust settled after the collapse of the Twin Towers.

He slowed his steps and came to a stop, his sides heaving. The place, the bench, was a graveyard of memories, and most days he was better off not to stop.

But today . . .

Today, there was suddenly nowhere else he wanted to be.

A chill hung in the air, and the bushes rustled with a strong fall breeze. Casey gripped his knees and bent over, waiting for his lungs to fill. After a few seconds, he straightened and linked his hands behind his head. For half a minute he moved his feet in small circles, until his breathing was normal again. A dozen children were scattered amid the swings and slides, and not far away their parents stood in clusters or sat on other benches, chatting and sometimes yelling out at the little ones, warning them not to walk in front of swings or promising to play with them in a few minutes.

The voices faded, and Casey headed toward the back of the play area. Their bench was empty, like always. It was smaller, older than the others, and partially hidden by an overgrown bush. Only half the play equipment could be seen from that bench, so most of the parents didn't bother with it.

He sat down and stretched out his legs. The ground was damp, carpeted with a layer of month-old fallen leaves. Casey kicked at a dark, wet clump and crossed his feet.

Eight years.

If Amy had lived they would've been close to celebrating a decade together. He let his head fall back a few inches and stared into the gray. *Come on, let me see her . . . just once.* He narrowed his eyes, willing himself to look beyond the clouds to the place where Amy still lived, still loved him and waited for him.

But all he could see was the swirl of late-autumn sky, and his heart settled deeper in his chest. He closed his eyes.

The pain is worse now than ever. I— He held his breath, determined to keep his emotions at bay. *I miss her so much.*

His eyes opened, and a robin caught his attention. It hopped along the sidewalk a few feet away, studying the ground, pecking at it. Then it stopped and tilted its head toward the trees, and in a rush of motion, flapped its wings and lifted into the air.

Casey watched until it disappeared. If Amy were here, she'd slip her arm around his shoulders and tell him to learn a thing or two from the robin. What good ever came from muddling around on the ground? It had been two years and Amy would've wanted him to fly again. Live again . . . love again. Amy, with her wheat-colored blonde hair and light brown eyes, her easy laugh and tender heart. The unaffected way she said exactly what was on her mind.

Come on, Casey . . . He could almost hear her, see the sparks flying in her eyes. *What're you going to do . . . stop breathing? Get out there and live.*

But where would he start? And with whom? And how—after loving and losing the woman of his dreams— was he supposed to fly again? So what if two years had passed. He didn't want to fly yet, didn't want to move on. Better to be alone with her memories than find someone to replace her.

The very idea made his stomach hurt.

"Jordan, not so high." A woman's voice broke the moment, and Casey's eyes followed the sound. She was a brunette, pretty in a professional sort of way, and she stood a few feet from the play equipment. "Jordan . . . did you hear me?"

Casey shifted his gaze to the big slide and saw a young boy, seven or eight years old. For a moment he looked as though he might disobey her, but then he stopped, turned around, and headed back down the ladder. Casey blinked, and he was back in the hospital room again, hearing the news about his wife and child for the first time.

The baby had been a boy.

The doctor had said so right after telling him the awful news. A boy who would've had Amy's eyes and Casey's sense of adventure. A boy like the one climbing on the play equipment. He would've been two years old, and he would've loved the East Meadow, where the carpet of green gave way to a view of the reservoir. Yes, this would've been his favorite place. Amy would've been by his side, holding his hand, and together they would've watched their son run and skip and jump across the play bridge.

Casey shifted his gaze, and the invisible picture disappeared. He sucked in a quick breath and slid a bit lower on the bench. Why was he letting his thoughts run wild? What good did daydreaming do him now? So what if it was their anniversary. Amy was gone—and with her every hope he'd ever had for the future. There was no hand to hold, no happy ending, and no towheaded little boy to play with.

He stood and turned around, using the back of the bench to stretch his legs behind him one at a time, loosening his arches and calves for the run home. No reason to stay another moment. The bench was nothing but a tombstone now. A tombstone marking Amy's easy grin, and a baby boy's unheard cry, and every other good thing about life and living, all of which had died on the operating table right alongside Amy and their infant son.

CHAPTER THREE

Megan had caught glimpses of the man ever since she and Jordan arrived.

The park had been Jordan's idea, the least she could do after reading his letter to God. She couldn't take the place of a father, but she loved the boy, and the letter had done nothing but underline the fact. Jordan needed more time with her, and now she would do whatever she could to be there for him. If that meant giving up a Saturday at the office, she would find another way to get the work done.

She'd been pushing Jordan on the swing, laughing at something he'd said, when the man jogged up, cooled down a bit, and sat on a bench at the far back near the big slide. Megan met his eyes only briefly as he walked past, but immediately she knew something was wrong. Megan was an attorney, after all. She could read body language and facial expressions as easily as she could read a court paper.

And she was an expert at reading eyes.

The man's were haunting, filled with the kind of private pain you saw in theater seats and restaurants and office places, a pain that was commonplace in New York City. At least in the last two years. For a moment, Megan wondered about the man's story. He looked nice enough, and the way he held himself stirred something vaguely familiar in her. For a moment she wondered. Had he lost a parent or a child? A lover, maybe. Or was he merely struggling with a rough workweek?

Ten minutes passed, and Megan considered the solitary man. Maybe she should go to him, find out why he was here and what made his eyes look that way. Maybe he wanted to talk. Megan turned her attention to Jordan and the idea passed. Crazy thoughts like that didn't flit across her mind very often. The man was obviously sitting alone for a reason, and Megan wasn't about to interrupt him.

"Time me, Mom." Jordan waved at her. His eyes danced as they hadn't in months, and Megan felt a ripple of hope. Everything would be all right. She could do this—this playtime thing. And eventually, Jordan would see that he didn't need a father, not with how much she loved him.

"Time you?" She looked at her watch. "For what?"

"See how long it takes me to run around the swings, climb the ladder, and drop down the slide, okay?"

"Okay." Megan did a salute in Jordan's direction. "Whenever you're ready."

For the longest time, the two of them played the game, and when Jordan was finally too tired to make another go at it, Megan noticed that the man was gone. Gone home to whatever family waited for him, whatever it was that caused his eyes so much sorrow.

Jordan jumped off the slide and jogged over to her. "Ready?"

"Yep." Megan pushed up the sleeves of her sweater and rose to her feet. "Ready if you are."

He walked alongside her and yawned. "That was way fun."

"*Way* fun?"

"Come on, Mom . . ." Jordan grinned at her. "You know, like really, *really* fun."

"Oh . . ." Megan tilted her head back and shot him a teasing look. "All right, then I *way* liked being with you today."

"Yeah . . ." The silliness faded from Jordan's eyes, and

he gave her the type of adoring smile she hadn't seen for years. "Me, too."

See, Jordan, she wanted to say. *You don't need a dad.* "Wanna get lunch?"

"Don't you have to work?" Jordan stopped walking and turned to her. His mouth was open.

"Nope." She tickled him in the ribs. "I'm yours all day."

"Really?"

"Really."

Jordan jumped and raised his fist in the air the way he did when his favorite football team scored a touchdown. "Yes!"

Megan laughed, and the sound of it stuck in her heart. Like a favorite song she hadn't heard in far too long. She lowered her chin and grinned at Jordan. "Does that mean pizza or hot dogs?"

"Hot dogs near the Conservatory. Definitely." They started walking again, and this time Jordan tucked his hand in hers. "Hey, Mom . . ."

"Yes." Megan ran her thumb along the side of Jordan's hand and realized something. She'd told Jordan the truth. Spending the day with him had been wonderful and refreshing, the perfect break after a long week.

"You look pretty today."

Megan angled her head and gave a single nod in Jordan's direction. "Why, thank you, kind sir." She ran her fingers through her short dark hair. "Must be my new haircut."

"No . . ." Jordan shook his head. "It's the jeans. Mommies look nice in jeans."

The conversation veered from jeans to the zoo animals at the far end of the park to the open house at school the coming week to the one thing Megan had desperately hoped he wouldn't talk about.

The God letter.

It happened when they were twenty yards from the hot-dog vendor. Jordan let go of her hand and pivoted to a standstill. "Mom!" Concern flashed in his eyes. "You mailed my letter, right?"

Megan's heart skipped a beat. "Letter?"

Jordan knit his eyebrows together. "The one I put inside your purse. Yesterday, before school?"

"Oh, that." Megan urged herself to smile. "Of course I mailed it." She started walking again and he fell in beside her. "I already told you that."

"When did you?"

It took all of Megan's effort to spit out the lie. "Just

after lunch." She kept her eyes straight ahead, moving along as though nothing were wrong.

"But you found the address?"

Megan felt two inches high. "Yes, Jordan." She pointed at the vendor. "How 'bout hot dogs and chips?"

Jordan skipped a bit in front of her and tossed a smile over his shoulder. "I knew you'd know the address for God, you know why?"

Megan ordered herself to look relaxed. "Why?"

"Because you know everything, Mom. Even God's address." He glanced ahead at the vendor. "Hot dogs are perfect."

They were in line when Megan found her voice again. "Uh . . . Jordan . . . about the letter . . ."

"Yeah?"

"What . . . what exactly did you tell God?"

Jordan lifted his shoulders twice. "I just sort of asked Him something." He squinted his eyes and looked toward the sky. The clouds had burned off, and blue patches were showing above them. "It's a secret. Between me and God."

Megan could kick herself for pushing the issue, but she'd hoped he might tell her what it held. That way she could break the news to him gently—that God wouldn't be hand-delivering a daddy anytime soon. But if Jordan wouldn't tell her what the letter said, she could hardly let on that she knew.

They moved up a bit in line, and Jordan looked at her once more. "Mom . . . are you ever gonna get married again?"

The question shot darts at Megan's soul. "No." Her answer was quick and pointed. "Not ever."

Jordan let his gaze fall to his feet, and he kicked up a bit of loose gravel. When he looked up again, his eyes were flatter than before. "How come?"

A sigh filtered through Megan's tight throat. "Because . . ." She took Jordan's hands in hers and faced him, ignoring the people in line on either side of them. "I'll never find anyone who loves me as much as you do, buddy. Okay?"

"You still believe in love, though, right?"

Megan felt his words like so many rocks. "Of course." She squeezed Jordan's hands and managed a curious smile. "Why would you ask?"

"Because one time—" Jordan hesitated. "One time I heard you tell Grandma that you didn't believe in love anymore."

"Well . . ." They were next in line, and Megan couldn't let her surprise show. She would have to be more careful about what she said around the apartment. "Sometimes I get sad about Daddy being gone, and I feel that way. But not most of the time, okay?"

"Okay." He smiled at her, but the spark from earlier was gone.

They bought their hot dogs, and for the rest of the afternoon Megan grieved the fact that Jordan had heard her say such a thing about love. Worse, she grieved that what she had said was true. She didn't believe in love, not for a minute. How far had she come since that long-ago summer when—in the midst of the worst days of her life—she'd been given the gift of hope by a boy she hadn't seen before or since?

And that night as she drifted off to sleep, she didn't think about court cases or Jordan's loneliness or how a person could wake up one morning with neck pain and be dead of a coronary by noon. Rather, she allowed twenty-year-old memories to surface like seaweed, memories she'd buried long ago. And as she did, she felt herself drift back in time, back to a Lake Tahoe beach, and a boy named Kade, and a kind of love that lasted forever.

A kind of love she no longer believed in.

CHAPTER FOUR

Once Megan allowed the memories, they came like old friends and took her back to a place when she was barely more than a child.

She and her younger brother had lived a life that seemed idyllic to everyone, especially Megan. They had a home with a swimming pool in West Palm Beach, and every summer they took family vacations. After work her father would come in from the garage, drop his keys in the apple jar by the telephone, and clap his hands. "Where's the best kids in the world?" he'd ask.

When she was a little girl, Megan would wait for him by the front window and at the sound of his voice she would run and jump into his arms. Her father wasn't very tall, but to her he was strong and bigger than life. Once when Megan was six years old, her father had been teaching her how to ride a bike at Farlane Park. He jogged alongside her, and when she grazed a tree and began to fall, he caught her by the waist and kept her from hitting the ground.

Caught her in midair.

It was something Megan never forgot. When she was older, her brother did the running and jumping, and Megan would call from the next room, "Hey, Dad, how was your day?"

And every evening he'd find her and kiss the top of her head.

When he was home, that was.

Now she knew that her parents had often been fighting, arguing over whether her dad was sleeping with other women or stepping out secretly without her mother knowing it. But Megan and her brother had no idea.

Not until the day their father walked out.

She could still hear her parents' voices, the way they sounded that awful day. Hear them as clearly as if they were standing beside her bed. At first Megan hadn't believed the loud noises could be coming from her parents. She figured her father must've been watching something on television. Her brother was only seven that spring, and he played in his room, unaware that the story of their lives was being rewritten in the kitchen below.

Megan had gone to the top of the stairs and listened. That's when she realized the loud, angry words weren't coming from the TV at all, but from her parents. Her parents, who never yelled at each other. Megan had felt the blood drain from her face. She sat down, hugged her knees to her chest, and concentrated on what they were saying.

"Walk out now, and don't bother coming back!" The words had belonged to her mother, and they terrified Megan. *Walk out? What was that supposed to mean?* Daddy had just come home from work, and they hadn't eaten dinner yet. He would never have gone back out now.

"I didn't want it like this." Her father's voice hadn't been as loud, but it was filled with fury. "You're the one who made the phone call."

"Of course I made the call." Her mother's tone rose a notch. "I find a receipt for roses in your coat pocket? When you haven't given me flowers in five years? The phone call was a natural, Paul. The florist was more than willing to give me your girlfriend's name, so blame him."

"Okay, I've got a girlfriend. What're you gonna do about it?"

"No, Paul, what're *you* going to do?" Her mother sounded half crazy, desperate.

"Nothing." The word was an explosion in the kitchen below. "There's nothing I can do now."

"Yes, you can! You can tell her it's over, tell her we're going to get counseling and try to work things out. Tell her you have a family."

"No, Terri. *You* have a family. I have a job and a mortgage and bills to pay. The kids barely know me."

Megan gripped the staircase and closed her eyes. Her head spun and she felt sick to her stomach. What was her father talking about? Of course they knew him. Whenever he was home they read books together and went for walks and . . .

That's when she'd realized something. Her father hadn't been home much since Christmas, really. Once in a while she'd heard her mother comment about the fact, but never with so much shouting. Megan hadn't thought anything of his absences. Her father was a banker, a busy man, and sometimes his work kept him out late. That was all it was. Right?

Her mother began to weep, a loud, wailing cry Megan had never heard before. "Forget the girl, Paul. I can if you can." She was shrieking, panicking, and the sound of her voice made Megan's heart race. "Don't leave us now, please, Paul. Think about the kids!"

That's when the shouting and crying and angry words had suddenly stopped. Her father's voice was calm once again, and he said only two words, the last words Megan ever heard him say.

"Good-bye, Terri."

That was it. Nothing about even hearing her mother's plea or possibly breaking up with the girlfriend, whoever she was. No final words of love passed on to the kids, no words of concern for Megan and her brother. Just "Good-bye, Terri."

Megan had held her breath as she peered down into the foyer and watched her father leave. She could still see him, the way he stood by the door with a single suitcase in one hand, a briefcase in the other, dressed in his business clothes. He gave one last look around the living room, then he turned and walked out, shutting the door behind him.

At first Megan had figured it was some kind of bad joke, or maybe even an awful nightmare. A girl in Megan's third-grade class had a father who left them on New Year's Day, and a few years later Sheila Wagner's mother ran off with the assistant principal.

But never, in all her imaginings, had Megan considered such a thing could happen to her family. After all, her family went to church on Sundays and prayed before every dinner and kept a Bible on the coffee table downstairs.

Fathers didn't run out on families like that, did they?

Megan had swallowed her fears, and for the first two days she said nothing about what she'd seen and heard at the top of the stairs that night. But on the third day, her mother pulled her aside and choked out the truth. Her father was gone, and until he came home they'd have to fend for themselves. Her brother was too young to understand what had happened, and their mother told them only that Daddy wouldn't be home for a while.

Looking back, Megan figured her mother held on to that idea—that her father would come home one day—for the next two months. Then in June, something happened and Megan's mother no longer peered out the window after dark looking for their father's car to pull up in the driveway.

The day school was out, they set off in the station wagon for Lake Tahoe—where Aunt Peggy lived. The only explanation Megan and her brother got was that they all needed some time away.

Four days later they arrived at Aunt Peggy's house on the lake. Her brother was in the pool before they unpacked. That entire first day, Megan did nothing but sit at the far end of the living room and pretend she was reading a book. Really, she was listening to her mom and Aunt Peggy talk about her father. Something about the money he was sending and some kind of papers he'd had delivered to her.

"At least the jerk's sending you support," Aunt Peggy said, and then she shot Megan a glance. "Megan, honey, why don't you go out and play with your brother?"

By that point, Megan had felt sick to her stomach going on two months straight, and when her aunt suggested she leave the house, Megan was more than happy to go. She didn't understand exactly what her aunt and her mother were talking about, but it was something bad, something about her father. And Megan knew deep in her heart that her daddy wasn't coming home, maybe not ever.

She wandered outside, past her brother splashing in the pool, and through a thicket of pine trees out onto the beach. It was a private stretch of sand shared by only the houses in Aunt Peggy's neighborhood. Megan kicked off her shoes and walked along the shore about a hundred yards until she spotted a fallen tree trunk. She sat at one end, stared out at the water, and wondered.

Why had her father left, anyway, and where was love? Was it real? If people like her parents could split up, how could it be? And what about her and her brother? Since he'd been gone, their dad hadn't called or visited. Not once. So what was the point of growing up and getting married if it all fell apart in the end?

If only her father would come home. Then she would know love was real after all, and that God answered prayers.

"Where are you, Daddy?" Her whispered question mixed with the breeze rolling off the south end of the lake and sifted through the tree branches behind her. But she heard no answer.

Tears filled her eyes, and she blinked them back. She'd always done her crying in private, and this wasn't the time for tears. *I miss you.* She gazed up at the sky to a place she wasn't quite sure existed. *I want him to come home and kiss the top of my head like he used to. God, you can make miracles happen, so please make one happen now for me.*

As she sat there a little while longer she realized something. Her father's routine—the way he came home each day and showered Megan and her brother with attention—had been something that made her feel safe and protected. Now, without him, Megan felt unattached, like she was falling without a parachute.

She was about to head back to her aunt's house when something in the opposite direction caught her eye. A boy, about her age, was walking a white Lab along the beach. He noticed her, and before she could escape, the boy waved and headed over.

"Hi." He came up and stood in front of her. "You must be new."

Megan shrugged and tried not to feel interested. The boy had clear, blue eyes and something about the way he looked at her made her feel as though he'd known her forever. She struggled to find her voice. "Just visiting."

"Us, too. My grandpa lives here. We come up each June." He sat down a few feet from her on the fallen log. "I'm Kade."

"I'm Maggie."

He hesitated a minute, and a smile played on his lips. "Okay, Maggie, tell me this. If you're on vacation, why're you sitting here looking like it's the end of the world?"

For some reason, Megan felt safe with the boy. She tilted her head and felt the pretense fade from her expression. "Because it is."

Kade's smile dropped off like the bottom of the lake. "Ya wanna talk about it?"

And Megan had.

For the next week, she and Kade met out on the shoreline and talked about everything from the meaning of life to Kade's passion for baseball and his dream of playing in the big leagues. But whenever the topic would turn to Megan's father and her situation, Kade would tell her the same thing: Real love never fails, and where there is that type of love, there is hope. Always.

Kade's father was a minister at a small church in Henderson, Nevada, just outside Las Vegas. His daddy had told him that in a town nicknamed "Sin City" it was important to know what real love was.

"But what about when love dies? Like it did for my parents?" They were walking along the beach, their arms occasionally brushing against each other.

"Maybe they never understood real love." Kade stopped and picked up a flat rock from the sand. He skipped it across the water and turned to her. "You know, the kind of love in the Bible. The love that Jesus talks about."

That was another thing. Megan had never met anyone her age so versed in Scripture. Not that he talked about it all the time. In fact, they spent most of their hours playing Frisbee or swimming in her aunt's pool or splashing in the lake. One day she found a dozen pale purple azaleas growing wild near a clump of bushes just off the beach.

"Here." She picked the prettiest one and handed it to Kade. "So you'll remember me."

"Okay." The hint of a smile played on his mouth, and his eyes sparkled. "I'll put it in my Bible and save it forever."

They teased and laughed and played hide and seek among the pine trees that lined the beach. But each afternoon as the sun made its way down toward the mountains, she and Kade would find their place on the fallen log and he'd say something profound about love or God's plan for her life. Something that didn't make him seem anything like a fifteen-year-old boy.

Late one afternoon, she narrowed her eyes and studied him for a minute. "You sure you're not an angel or something?"

"Yep, that's me." He let his head roll back, and his laugh filled the air around her. "An angel with a mean fastball and a .350 batting average."

She breathed hard through her nose. "I'm serious, Kade. What kind of kid knows about love like that?"

"I told you." His cheeks were tanned from the week in the sun, and his eyes danced as the laughter eased from his voice. "My dad's a preacher, Maggie. The Bible's like, well . . ." He gazed out across the water. "It's like the air in our house. It's all around us."

"And the Bible talks about love?"

Megan hadn't known anything about the Bible, really.

Sure it sat on the coffee table, and she and her family had gone to church once in a while when they were little. But never in the past few years. Especially not since her father left.

Kade pulled one leg up and looked at her. "The Bible talks all about love. How it's kind and how it never fails."

On their last afternoon together, Megan admitted something to him, something she hadn't really understood until then. "I want to believe, Kade. In love . . . in God . . . in all of it." She let her gaze fall to her hands. "But I don't think I know how anymore."

Kade slid closer to her on the fallen log and took her fingers in his. "Then what you need, Maggie, is a miracle. So that one day everything we've talked about will really happen in your life."

"A miracle?"

"Yep." He scooted closer still and tightened the grip he had on her hand. "Close your eyes, and I'll pray."

Then, while a funny, tingling sort of feeling worked its way down Maggie's spine, she and Kade held hands, and he asked God for a miracle for her, that her father would come home and that no matter what else happened or didn't happen, one day she would know the type of love that never failed.

They made a plan then, that they'd meet there on the

fallen log every June, so long as their families came to Lake Tahoe. Before she left, Kade hugged her and gave her the briefest kiss on the cheek. "I'll pray for you, Maggie. Every day. That you'll get your miracle." He gave her a sad smile. "See ya around sometime."

When she and her mother and brother left for home the next day, Megan couldn't decide what to feel. She hated leaving Kade, but her heart soared with a hope she hadn't felt before the trip, and she found herself convinced of several things. First, that God was real, and second, that He was going to give her the miracle they'd prayed for. That one day she'd know for herself a kind of love that didn't walk out the front door one night before dinner. A love that never failed.

CHAPTER FIVE

Casey pulled open the blinds and stared up between the buildings that surrounded his apartment. Rain, again. Cold, driving rain. He pulled away from the window, padded across the living room, and found his running shoes. Rain was good. Clean and honest and simple, reducing the moment to nothing but Casey and the air he breathed. Besides, the café wouldn't open for another hour and now, while it was still dark, there was nowhere he'd rather be than running the streets of New York City.

Rain, sleet, or snow, he would run.

Three days had passed since his anniversary, and still Casey couldn't pull himself from the past. Crazy, really, that a calendar day could send him into a tailspin of memories and longing. Anniversaries, birthdays, Valentine's Day, Christmas. The trigger was any day the two of them would've been together.

Freedom was out on the pavement, where it always was. Running gave Casey a chance to think about life the way he couldn't at his crowded café or in the confines of an apartment where every square inch held memories of Amy.

He laced up his shoes and noticed that his shoulders felt lighter, as though the mountain of sorrow and regret he lived under couldn't follow him out onto the streets. Three flights down the ancient stairs that ran through the core of the apartment building and he was outside. A wind gust slapped him in the face and sprayed his cheeks with rain. The air was colder than it looked, but it was clean, and Casey sucked in three mouthfuls as he set off.

Five minutes later it happened, the same thing that happened every time he ran. The early-morning commuters and sounds of the waking city faded to nothing, and Casey gained entrance to a world where Amy was still alive and memories of her came easily. A world where he could catch a glimpse of the place where she and their son still lived, where the pain of existence was dimmed—if only for an hour.

He'd run enough over the past two years that come spring he was going to do a marathon. Why not? He would put in the miles one way or another. It gave him a reason to run more, something to tell Billy-G and the regulars at the café. He was training. Not that he needed the time to relive his past or sort through how he could've done something different that awful day, how he could've helped save Amy and the baby.

He had to run to be ready for the race.

Since Saturday, he'd used his running time to indulge himself in the rarest luxury of all. The luxury of going back to the beginning, back to the days when he and Amy first met. Casey brushed his gloved hand over his face and wiped the rain off his brow. He had to be careful how often he did this, this going back to the beginning thing. Because each time he allowed himself, the sound of her voice, the feel of her hand in his were more vivid. Intoxicatingly vivid.

And each time it was harder to find his way back to real life.

But here, on this rainy Tuesday morning, Casey didn't care. One more time wouldn't hurt. Besides, memories were all he had left, all he'd ever have. And they were worthless if he didn't spend time with them every now and then.

He turned right and headed toward Central Park, no longer seeing steamy manholes and cabdrivers vying for early riders. Instead he was in Port-au-Prince, Haiti, his sleeves rolled up and sweat beading on his forehead.

From the time he started high school, Casey had known what he wanted to do in life. He had no intention of becoming a preacher or a doctor or any of the things his parents had figured for him. He would get his MBA and do something different, something where he could keep his own hours and be his own boss, work around all types of people. Then he'd meet a nice girl, get married, and have the kind of life his parents had shared.

But first, he would travel.

A month after he graduated from high school, he turned down three track-and-field scholarships for a one-year position working as a driver for an orphanage in Haiti. The job paid nothing but food and expenses, but it taught him more about life than he could've learned in a dozen college courses.

He drove a twenty-year-old pickup truck with boarded sides and an engine that started only half the time. At first the road conditions terrified him. Traffic ran in multiple directions without any clear sense of right-of-way, and people honked their horns as often as they hit their gas pedals. Vendors littered the roadways, and children darted into traffic at every intersection waving rags and squirt bottles, hoping to make a dime or two by cleaning a dirty car window.

The food was rice and beans and an occasional skimpy chicken leg. Meat wasn't refrigerated in Haiti, showers were scarce, and hot water unheard of. Every mosquito bite carried the threat of malaria. During the day, when Casey was driving the streets of Port-au-Prince, not only was he an oddity because he was American, but he was often the only white person amid hundreds of thousands of teeming people on the main thoroughfare. Casey knew enough Creole to say, "I'm here for the supplies," and "I'll be back next week," and a few other key words, but the language barrier felt like the Great Wall of China. Rats ran the floor of the orphanage at night, and at times the adjustment period felt as if it would stretch on forever.

But after a month in Port-au-Prince, Casey felt more comfortable. He no longer noticed the strange looks he got from people he passed on the streets, and the traffic was somehow invigorating. When he took the time to smile, people treated him kindly. He spent his days getting supplies, shuttling children to various appointments, and helping the ministry team when they staged outreaches on the street corners.

At the end of the first year, Casey signed up for a second.

"What about college?" His father had been worried, but not nearly as much as his mother.

"Have you gone mad?" Her voice was pinched with fear. "Universities won't wait forever."

Casey figured they would. He was still in great shape and ran the hilly side streets at the far end of Port-au-Prince four times a week.

Halfway through his second year, a group of high school youth-group students came to the orphanage for spring break. Casey had been in the driveway on his back, working on the muffler of the old pickup truck, when the students filed through the high security gate. He paused, taking in the group of them as they made their way into the complex.

That's when he saw her.

She was at the end of the line, listening to one of the counselors point out details about the orphanage, and Casey did a double take. Even looking at her upside down, he could feel his breath catch in his throat. She wasn't striking in the typical sense. Her hair wasn't streaked with blonde, and she wore no makeup. She was a simple kind of beautiful, like wildflowers scattered across an untouched mountain pasture. Casey's hand froze in place, the wrench poised a few inches above his sweaty forehead. She didn't yet know he was alive, and already something in her light brown eyes had worked its way into his heart.

Casey picked up his pace, ignoring the way his legs screamed for relief. The pain of running felt good, especially now. He blinked and allowed the memories to continue.

Her name was Amy Bedford. By that evening Casey had found out enough about her to know that his first impression had been right on. She held no pretense and spoke with a wisdom that was far beyond her sixteen years. The youngest of five girls from central Oregon, her father was a science teacher for a small public high school, her mother a homemaker. Amy's sisters were in college, anxious to get degrees in something other than education and move on to anything more lucrative than a teacher's salary.

Not so Amy.

"My dad's the best man I know," she told Casey that night. "He's touched a thousand hearts in his lifetime, and I want to do the same." She rested her elbows on the old wooden table. "How 'bout you?"

"Well . . ." He gripped the bench he was sitting on and straightened his back. "I want to open a café."

"A café, huh?"

"Yeah." He gave a few thoughtful nods. "I can be my own boss, make my own hours, and meet new people every day." His heart felt light at the prospect. "I've been thinking about it for a while."

"Wow. I never met anyone who wanted to open a café."

Quiet filled the space between them for a moment. "My parents aren't real thrilled about the idea."

She smiled then and said something Casey would remember for the rest of his life. "Someday I want to eat there, okay? At your café."

Casey wasn't sure if it was her faith in his dreams or the sincerity in her voice or the way her skin glistened in the hot, humid night, but with every passing hour he felt himself falling for her. The week passed in a blur of painting the orphanage kitchen and talking late into the night. Three years separated them, but Casey didn't notice a minute of it. Amy was as true as an orphan's smile, guileless and able to speak her mind. Something about her made Casey want to wrap his arms around her and protect her from anything cold or cynical, anything that would dim the warmth in her smile.

They finished the kitchen and moved into the room where twenty-two orphans slept on eleven small wire cots.

"Let's paint the door red," Amy told him.

"Red?" Casey made a face and flicked his paintbrush at her. "Why red?"

"Because." She tapped her brush on the tip of his nose. "Red is the color of giving."

And so they painted the orphans' bedroom door red.

On Amy's last night in Port-au-Prince, Casey asked if he could write to her.

"Yes." They were sitting on a bench in the orphanage courtyard just before midnight and the air around them was stagnant, silent but for the sound of a distant drumbeat. She lowered her chin and locked eyes with him. "I'd like that."

He wanted to kiss her, but he didn't dare. He was on staff, and she was a student, a minor. Instead he swallowed and tried not to notice the way their shoulders brushed against each other. He dropped his voice a notch. "Know something, Amy?"

"What?" She leaned back against the crumbling façade of the orphanage wall and met his eyes again.

"I had fun this week."

"Me, too."

"I'm . . . well, I'm gonna miss you."

She nodded, and her eyes glistened, hinting at tears. "I have to go. The counselors want us in bed by twelve."

"I know." He smiled so she wouldn't see how hard it was to say good-bye. They'd be gone in the morning before sunup, and chances were he'd never see her again. "Be safe."

"And get that café going." Her chin quivered, and she hesitated just long enough to draw another breath. Then she reached into the pocket of her jean shorts and pulled out a folded piece of paper. "Here." She tucked it into his hand. "I've been practicing my Creole."

He started to open it, but she closed his fingers around the paper before he had a chance. "After I go." She took a few steps back and then turned and ran lightly up the steps. When the door closed behind her, Casey opened the piece of paper and saw that she'd written only three words.

Me reme ou. . . . I love you.

CHAPTER SIX

Casey had already run four miles—more than his usual route. But today the memories were crisp and vivid. He would've run to California if it meant giving them a reason to continue.

And so he kept running, his strides long and even, eyes straight ahead.

Me reme ou.

He could still see the words, the way she'd scrawled them on that piece of paper. The truth of what she'd written had dropped his heart to his knees and made him certain that somehow, someway, he would see her again. They wrote to each other for the next six months, and by the following summer Casey had enrolled at Oregon State University and made plans to move to Corvallis.

He'd visited the campus just once and met with the

track-and-field coaches. Running the hills of Port-au-Prince had paid off, and he was offered a full scholarship. Casey was thrilled, but by then he was convinced of one thing. His future wasn't in running or jumping or throwing a javelin.

It was in business.

And OSU had exactly what he was looking for. An excellent business school and a full-ride scholarship. And something else.

A twenty-minute drive to Amy Bedford's house.

His parents knew nothing about Casey's attraction to Amy because Casey wasn't sure about it himself. In some ways, even with their letter-writing—the week he'd shared with Amy in Haiti felt like a wonderful dream, as surreal as nearly everything about his time there.

After he enrolled at OSU, he returned home to his parents, sat them down one night after dinner, and broke the news.

"I . . . I thought you'd go to a Christian college, Casey." His mother's lips drew together. "You've been gone so long, and now, well, you'll be gone again."

His father crossed his arms. "Your mother's right, son. You can't learn much about God at a place like OSU."

It was a moment of truth, and Casey gripped his

knees. "Dad . . ." He met his father's gaze. "I already know about God." Silence stood between them for a moment. "Maybe it's time I learn something about people."

In the end, his parents agreed. Where better to practice his faith than out in the real world? Despite their reservations, they sent Casey off with their full support.

"Be careful," his mother warned him the night before he left. "The Northwest is a liberal place, and the girls . . . well . . . they don't have the same standards you're used to."

Casey had to stifle a smile. "Okay, Mom."

He had only one girl in mind, and they met up again that September, a couple of hours after his first day of classes, at a coffee shop just off campus. Amy was seventeen by then, a high school senior. The moment she walked through the door of the shop, Casey knew his feelings for her weren't some sort of strange dream.

She moved across the room, past the other tables. Even from ten yards away Casey could see how her eyes danced. When she sat down, he took her hands in his and struggled to find his voice. "There's something I have to tell you, something I couldn't say in a letter."

Curiosity mingled with hesitation and took some of the sparkle from her eyes. "Okay." She studied him. "Tell me."

He waited until he could find his voice. *"Me reme ou."*

Turning back wasn't an option for either one of them. The next fall, Amy joined him at OSU, and four years later they married and left the Northwest for a small apartment in Manhattan and the chance for Casey to open the café he'd always dreamed about.

"It's perfect, Casey." Her eyes would light up every time they talked about it. "Let's make it happen."

Casey's Corner was still a crazy idea to his parents, but never to Amy. She took a job at a local preschool and stood by Casey as he got the loans he needed to open his shop. On the weekends, they worked side by side decorating and collecting memorabilia for the walls. At the grand opening, no one was prouder than Amy.

The years that followed blurred together like a kind of larger-than-life tapestry of brilliant reds and oranges and thoughtful shades of blue. She had been everything to him—his closest friend, his confidante, his greatest support. Losing her had been like losing his right arm, and the pain of it made every breath an effort.

Even after two years.

Casey slowed his pace to a walk. He had worked his way through five miles of trails—two more than usual—and he was only a few blocks from the café. The memories had been stronger than usual, more vivid, and he fought the urge to keep running.

What was wrong with him anyway? If he could feel like this after two years, maybe he'd never move on, never find a way to get through life without her. Maybe this hazy underwater feeling of going through the motions was how life would always be. His breathing settled back to a normal rate, and he locked his eyes on a narrow stretch of sky as he walked. She was up there somewhere, probably elbowing God in the ribs, bugging Him to give Casey a reason to live again.

His café was a diversion, for sure. He spent most of the week there—talking to customers, helping Billy-G behind the counter, fixing up the place so it never lost the look Amy had given it way back when. But nothing about it made him feel alive, the way Amy had made him feel.

He reached the café and stared at the front door. Someone had hung a fall wreath on it, plastic leaves of orange and red and yellow and a nervous-looking turkey at the center, poking his pinecone head out at everyone who walked by. Thanksgiving was in a month and after that, Christmas.

Amy's favorite time of the year.

Casey gritted his teeth and pushed the door open. He

zigzagged his way past a dozen tables, chatting with the regulars and saying hello to a few newcomers. It wasn't until the morning rush was gone that he sauntered over to the counter and dropped onto one of the barstools.

"Hey, Billy-G."

His friend wiped his hands on his apron, reached beneath the counter, and pulled out a section of newspaper. "Saved this for you." Billy-G took a few steps closer and spread the paper out in front of Casey. "Something you need to think about."

Casey kept his eyes on the old man. "Not another one." He was always telling Casey about a support group here or a Bible study there. "I'm fine, Billy-G, I don't need your help."

"Yeah, okay." The man tapped at the paper. "Everything's great." He began to walk away. "Just read it."

Billy-G was back in the kitchen again when Casey released a long, slow breath and let his eyes fall to the newspaper. It was a small, two-column story, buried deep in the *Times'* Metro Section. The headline read "New Program Pairs Willing Adults with Grieving Children."

Casey blinked and thought about that for a moment.

Grieving children? People were hurting all over the place, people who'd lost sisters or uncles or husbands or friends. But grieving children? It was something Casey hadn't considered.

The article was only five paragraphs, and he gave himself permission to read it. When he finished, he picked it up, held it closer, and read it again. After the third time, the idea began to sink in. It was both simple and profound, really. A children's group in Chelsea had designed a program called Healing Hearts, a way to pair up grieving children with single adults. Children who had suffered the death of one or more parent would be linked with single adults. The article provided a phone number for people to call if they were interested.

Casey imagined for a minute Amy sitting beside him, breathing the same air, sharing his every thought and knowing the things in his soul before they even came into focus.

"It's a perfect idea, Casey," he could almost hear her saying. "Let's make it happen."

There was a problem, of course.

He wasn't any other single adult; he'd suffered his own loss and maybe the program director would hold that against him, maybe his own grief would minimize his ability to help a hurting child. But he doubted the program organizers would turn him away. Somewhere out there in the big, vast city was a child who needed a mentor, someone to help bridge the gap between his old life and the life he'd been forced to live these past two years. A child who needed love and direction and a reason to live the same way Casey, himself, needed it.

He could make the call and go through the screening, let the organization set him up with a child, and find a way to bring a little light back into both their lives. There were a hundred places where he could take a child in Manhattan, places where the two of them could find an on-ramp back to the highway of the living. Yes, he could make the call, and in maybe only a month or so he could—

"Interesting, huh?"

Billy-G's gruff voice interrupted Casey's thoughts, and he dropped the paper to the counter. "Yeah."

"So?"

Casey folded the paper in half and slid it a few inches from him. "So what?"

"Whadya think?"

"I think you ask too many questions, Billy-G." Casey stood up and gave his friend a half smile. "I also think it's time I get going. I'll be back for a few hours around dinner."

"I knew it." Billy-G's smile held a knowing.

"Knew what?"

"You're gonna call."

Casey shrugged. "I'll think about it."

"Okay." Billy-G gave a few soft chuckles. "You do that."

Casey turned to leave, desperate to appear noncommittal. The idea was too fragile, too new, to expose it to the light of open conversation—even with someone like Billy-G. He needed to play it out in his mind first. Important decisions were always that way for him, taking root and growing in the hidden places of his heart before making their way out into the open.

Casey turned around before he left. "Great job today, Billy-G."

His friend peered at him over his shoulder through the small window that separated the kitchen from the front counter. "Make the call."

"See ya." Casey raised his hand and headed toward the front door.

Under his arm was a folded-up newspaper. And stirring across the barren plains of his heart was something he hadn't felt in a little more than two years.

The early-morning winds of hope.

CHAPTER SEVEN

The bad guys were getting the upper hand.

The first part of November was always this way, and Megan was suddenly too busy to worry about real love or long-ago summers or even her own lonely son. Crime was up 11 percent from a month ago, and Megan had two murder-one cases spread across her desk. Months like this could make or break a prosecutor, and Megan wouldn't be broken by anything.

Besides, things were okay at home. Jordan's behavior had improved some, and she was making a point of lying down with him for a few minutes every night before he fell asleep. Maybe that was all her son had needed, after all. A little more one-on-one time.

The idea was as comfortable as a bed of nails.

Who was she kidding? It was like her mother kept

saying. Jordan needed a man in his life, someone to wrestle with him and lift him onto his shoulders and take in a basketball game with him every now and then.

"You work too much," her mother had told her the night before. "You'll never find a father for Jordan with your schedule."

The comment had made Megan's cheeks hot, and Jordan's letter to God came to mind as it had nearly every day since she'd read it. "I'm not looking for a father for Jordan. Life doesn't work that way."

"It could, Megan." Her mother's voice was softly persistent. "It could if you'd look for it."

Megan huffed and planted her hands on her hips. "You didn't exactly go looking for a father when I needed one."

Her mother had been silent for a moment, and a handful of emotions flitted across her eyes. Shock and anger, shame and regret. "I was wrong, Megan." She stood and took a step toward her bedroom. "You're young. Don't make my mistakes all over again. It's not fair to Jordan . . . or yourself."

The conversation had played again in Megan's soul several times that day, even as she held conversations with judges and researched precedents for her current cases. *Don't make my mistakes all over again. It's not fair to Jordan . . . or yourself.*

Megan pushed back from her desk and drew in a sharp breath.

It was nearly six o'clock, and she had two more hours of going over briefs and depositions before she could go home. The office was quiet, most people gone except for a few evening clerks and an occasional assistant, finishing up whatever assignment had been passed down from one of the district attorneys.

She stood and headed down the hall to the break room. A cup of coffee would clear the cobwebs, stop her from thinking about her mother's words and her son's sad eyes and the letter he'd written to God. It wasn't her fault things were such a mess. She and George hadn't exactly been given a choice about how their lives had played out.

The break room was empty. Megan went to the coffeemaker, grabbed a tall Styrofoam cup, and poured herself some coffee. She opened the freezer door on the refrigerator, took two ice cubes, and dropped them into her cup. She liked her coffee black and lukewarm. Hot coffee took too much time to drink.

She was holding her cup, stirring the ice cubes with her little finger, when her eyes caught something on a folded section of the *New York Times*. Someone had placed the paper beneath the coffeemaker, and it had collected a circle of brown spots around the base of the pot. A headline showed near the top, and without meaning to, Megan read it.

"New Program Pairs Willing Adults with Grieving Children."

She stopped stirring and set down her cup. A program for grieving children?

The newspaper was stuck to the bottom of the coffeemaker, and Megan lifted the pot, careful not to tear the article. She slid it out and held it close as she read through it. A children's club in the city had set up a program called Healing Hearts that would pair adults with children who had experienced the death of one or both parents.

Suddenly Megan didn't need the coffee. Her hands were shaking as though she'd already had five cups. A program for grieving children? It was exactly what Jordan needed! Megan left her cup on the breakroom counter and took the newspaper back to her desk. The club was probably closed at this hour, but it was worth a try.

She picked up the phone and punched in the numbers. Someone answered on the first ring.

"Manhattan Children's Organization, may I help you?"

Megan opened her mouth, but no words came. Tears filled her eyes, and with her free hand she massaged the lump in her throat until she could speak. "I . . . I read about your program."

The woman on the other end identified herself as Mrs. Eccles. "We have quite a few programs, ma'am. Could you be more specific?"

"Yes . . ." Megan found the newspaper once more, and her eyes darted over the text. "It's the Healing Hearts program. My . . . my son is a child like that."

"I see." The woman's tone was noticeably softer. "Well, then, the first step is for you and your son to come down and fill out the paperwork, give us a chance to meet you and interview both of you. Then we'll try to pair your son up with one of our male volunteers as quickly as possible."

"You have . . . volunteers waiting for children?" The idea knocked the wind from Megan. Why hadn't she heard of this sooner? She glanced at the date on the newspaper and saw that the article was nearly two weeks old.

"Yes, ma'am. The program's quite popular." She paused, and Megan heard a rustling sound in the background. "Can I sign you and your son up for an appointment?"

Megan thought of all she had to do at work, the depositions and briefs and precedents that had to be studied. An appointment would take time, maybe an entire afternoon. Time she certainly didn't have. A single teardrop rolled down her cheek, and she dabbed at it with the sleeve of her silk jacket. "Yes." She sniffed quietly and closed her eyes to stave off any more. "Yes, I'd like that very much."

The appointment took place a week later, and four days after that Megan took the call at work. It was Mrs. Eccles, and her voice rang across the phone line like a kind of early Christmas carol. "I have good news for you, Ms. Wright. We've found a match for your son."

Megan leaned back in her office chair and held the phone more tightly to her ear. "You have?"

"Yes. I think you'll be quite happy with our choice."

"Is he . . . is he young or old?" Megan's voice was breathy, and she could see the buttons on her blouse trembling with every heartbeat. Jordan hadn't stopped talking about the program since they signed up. "Tell me about him, please. Did he . . . has he always wanted to help children?"

"Well . . ." The woman hesitated. "His story's a bit different than most."

Megan's shoulders fell a bit. Wasn't that the point of the program, pairing children with adults who had a strong desire to help a lonely boy or girl? "Then . . . why did you pick him?"

"His wife died a few years ago, delivering their first child. The baby didn't make it, either." Some of the cheerfulness faded from the woman's voice. "He saw the article about Healing Hearts and was very interested. Thought maybe it'd be good for both him and a hurting child."

Remorse tapped at the door of Megan's conscience. "Oh." She wanted to let excitement grow within her again, but it all seemed so sad. "I'm sorry." How could a man with that type of loss be any kind of positive influence on Jordan? She kicked her doubts back into the closet and pinched the bridge of her nose. "What else? Tell me about him."

The woman gave as thorough an overview as possible. The man's name was Casey Cummins. He was thirty-four and ran his own café in Midtown. He was interested in basketball, football, baseball, and anything outdoors, and, because of his job, his hours were flexible.

"He jogs three miles a day and has a master's in business administration. He'd be happy to help with homework."

Megan glanced at the murder files on her desk and felt the door to her closet of doubts creak back open. "What about the screening process?"

"We went over that at the interview."

Megan crossed her arms and pressed her fist into the hollow near her lower rib cage. "I know that, but tell me anyway. I'm a district attorney, remember?" She paused and forced a more polite tone. "Specifically . . . how did this Casey check out?"

"No record of any criminal behavior with either the FBI or the local police. He's never served time, never been arrested, no history of drug abuse. Never even had a speeding ticket, as far as we can see. He pays his bills on time and has an apartment about twenty blocks from his café. We spent several hours interviewing him here at the office, and of course we had a licensed social worker check out his residence."

"And . . ." Megan hated her suspicions, but after a week of waiting, the whole setup sounded too good to be true.

"We give our volunteers a rating, Ms. Wright. It's not something we usually share with the child's parent, but in this case—given your job—I think it might be okay to tell you. Mr. Cummins earned the highest possible marks in all categories. He's the kind of volunteer we're desperate for."

Megan exhaled and felt herself relax. "So, then. When do they meet?"

"Today's Monday. . . . The woman's voice drifted off, and Megan heard her flipping pages. "Fridays are good for him, so let's try for this Friday, November 14, say three o'clock?"

She shot a look at her own calendar. A hearing would take up most of the afternoon, and normally Megan would use early Friday evening to go over her notes from the past week. Still, maybe there was a way to make it work. "I have to be there, right?"

"Yes." Megan could feel the woman's disapproval. "Of course. You'll come in with Jordan, and the two of you will spend an hour or so getting to know his special friend. Then, if you're all comfortable with the idea, Mr. Cummins can spend another hour or so with your son either at the club or across the street at the park."

"Right." Megan pictured Jordan, the way his eyes would light up when he heard the news. He deserved this; she believed that with all her heart. Work would simply have to wait. "Okay, that'll be fine." She killed a heavy sigh before it could escape. "Three o'clock Friday."

As she hung up, Megan realized something. Already she was looking forward to Friday, to meeting this Casey man and watching the way he might interact with her son. It was a wonderful idea, one that didn't rely on her dating and coaxing someone into being a surrogate father for Jordan. Healing Hearts was a program based on honesty and need, where expectations and guidelines were spelled out from the beginning.

Jordan and Casey would get together once or twice a week and possibly speak on the phone. All of them would meet with the counselors at the Children's Organization every month to discuss how the relationship was progressing, and to give each of them a chance to ask questions or air concerns.

Of course it was a good thing, and it was worth every minute of work she might have to forfeit to see that the setup was successful. Megan had planned to wait until after work to tell Jordan about the phone call, but suddenly she couldn't think of anything else. She picked up the receiver again and dialed her home number. Jordan answered after only a few seconds.

"Hello?"

His young voice filled her heart, and her eyes felt watery. "Hi, honey. It's Mom."

"Hi! When're you coming home?"

"Soon." She gazed out her window and tried to picture his face. "Jordan, I got a call from the Children's Organization today. You know . . . the ones trying to find you a special friend?"

Jordan sucked in a loud breath, and his words were louder and faster than before. "You mean . . . they found him?"

"Yes . . . yes, they found him." A sound that was part laugh, part sob slipped from Megan's throat, and for a few seconds she covered her mouth with her fingertips. "In fact, I think they found someone just right for you, buddy."

The phone was ringing as Casey slipped through his apartment door and tossed his jacket on the chair. Work had been busy, but the wind gusts were worse than usual. At least once for each of the last ten blocks he'd thought about giving up and grabbing a taxi. But he'd pressed on, and now he was glad. He felt alive and awake, the same way he'd felt since doing the interview with the people at the Children's Organization.

He hadn't even been assigned a child yet, and already Healing Hearts was living up to its name.

He darted around the back of his old, worn sofa into the kitchen, and picked up the phone just as the answering machine clicked on. "Hello?" He cradled the receiver between his cheekbone and shoulder and tore the gloves from his hands. The moment his fingers were free, he punched the Off button on the answering machine. "Hello?"

"Yes, hi, this is Mrs. Eccles at the Manhattan Children's Organization. We've matched you up with an eight-year-old boy, and we were wondering if you were available to meet him this Friday?"

The room began to spin. Casey felt behind him for one of the kitchen chairs. He positioned it and sank to the seat. "This Friday?" His words were little more than a whisper, and he repeated them again. "This Friday, the fourteenth?"

"Yes." The woman gave a happy laugh. "If that works for you."

Mrs. Eccles had said it could take six weeks to make a match between volunteers and children, but Billy-G had disagreed. "Two weeks tops." He had given a wave of his favorite spatula. "I have a feelin'. Two weeks, Casey."

Indeed.

Casey switched the receiver to the other hand and leaned back in the chair. "Friday would be perfect. Tell me . . . tell me about the boy."

"Okay." Mrs. Eccles drew a quick breath. "Well, he's a darling little guy, eight years old and midway through second grade. He likes a lot of the things you like, and he lives with his mother and grandmother on the Upper East Side."

"His father?" Casey almost hated to ask because the answer was obvious. The boy wouldn't be in the program if his father were alive.

"The man was in his fifties, a bond trader who died of a massive heart attack a few years ago at work. Since then the boy's mother and teachers have noticed a change in his behavior, enough that he's had counseling and other help. He's responded lately to spending more time with his mother." Mrs. Eccles hesitated. "Unfortunately, his mother is a district attorney, and she can't be home with the boy as often as she'd like."

The picture was as clear as air. The boy's mother loved him enough to sign him up for the program. But on her own, she simply couldn't make up for all the boy had lost when his father died. Casey stood and poured a glass of water. He wasn't dizzy anymore, but a certain kind of giddiness had come over him.

A child needed him!

He was about to get involved in the life of an eight-year-old boy, something he was certain Amy would've wanted him to do.

Mrs. Eccles was going over some of the details, and

Casey tried to focus on what she was saying. Something about coming at three o'clock and expecting an hour-long meeting with the boy's mother, and possibly having another few hours with the boy after that. Then, if the first meeting went well, he'd be given the boy's phone number and address.

"If Friday's a success, you can take the boy out for pizza. Something to break the ice."

Casey wrote "pizza" across the top of a pad of paper.

The woman was about to hang up when Casey remembered something. "You didn't tell me his name."

"Oh . . . sorry." He could hear a smile in the woman's voice. "His name's Jordan."

It was all Casey could do to finish the phone call. The boy's name was Jordan? How was that possible? He hung up the phone and walked across his apartment to the bedroom he'd shared with Amy. Her journal still lay in the nightstand beside their bed, and now he opened the drawer and pulled it out.

The book was worn and flimsy, with a light tan leather binding. Amy had saved favorite sermon notes and Bible verses on pieces of paper that still stuck out every twenty pages or so. Casey held it carefully, as though any sudden movement might break it in half. Inside the front cover, Amy's name was barely visible, scrawled in blue ink across the center of the page.

It was the same journal she'd had with her in Haiti, the year Casey had first met her.

He ran his fingers across the letters of her name and flipped past the accounts of how the two of them had met and the detailed feelings she'd had for him even back then, past the entries she'd made when they were dating, past every other passage, all of which she'd shared with him many times.

Then, at the back of the journal, he found it.

A list of baby names, names Amy and he had discussed and agreed on for their first child. He already knew what he'd find on the list, but he had to look anyway, and as his eyes scanned the names he saw he'd been right.

Amy had thought she was having a boy, but they'd come up with names for both a boy and a girl—just in case. The list held ten names, five for a girl, and five for a boy. And next to the name they liked best, Amy had doodled a happy face.

Her favorites were written over several times and stood out in bold on the finely pressed piece of paper. Kaley for a girl, and for a boy they'd chosen the name they'd most easily agreed upon.

Jordan Matthew.

Casey stared at the name and imagined the odds that Mrs. Eccles would pair him up with a boy named Jordan. Seconds passed, and chill bumps rose on Casey's arms and across the back of his neck. What was it Amy liked to say? Something about Christmas miracles. Yes, that was it. She used to tell him that Christmas miracles happened to those who believed.

He would tease her and tell her she was wrong. With her in his life, miracles happened every day of the year. But she had been adamant, insisting that something special happened to people at Christmastime, and that Christmas miracles were there if only people looked for them.

Casey shifted his gaze to the picture of Amy that hung on the wall nearby. *Were you right? All this time . . . ?*

If Christmas miracles really were a special kind of something that happened once a year for those who believed, then Casey was certain that wherever Amy was at that very moment, she was smiling down at him, glowing with that special something that had won him over so easily the first day he met her.

Because here and now, six weeks before Christmas, Casey was suddenly convinced that a miracle was in the works, and that somehow it involved an eight-year-old boy named Jordan.

Even if the two of them wouldn't meet until that Friday afternoon.

CHAPTER EIGHT

God had finally read his letter.

That was the only way Jordan could explain the things that were happening to him. He and his mother had spent more time together the past month than all the months before as far back as Jordan could remember. And then she'd found out about the special program. Healy Hearts. At least that's what Jordan thought it was called, not that it mattered, really.

The important thing was, God had found him a daddy.

Well, not a daddy really, but a pretend daddy. Someone who would play with him every week and take him to the park and help him with his pluses and minuses the way Keith's daddy helped him.

Jordan was so excited about the whole thing, he could

barely sleep. He'd lie in bed and stare at the blue-and-white-striped wallpaper and the little row of baseball gloves and bats that went around the top of his room, and picture God getting his letter and opening it and knowing that the program, the Healy Hearts thing, would be the perfect way to give him a daddy.

He tried not to, but lots of times that week he asked his grandma questions about that coming Friday.

On Wednesday he found her and tugged on her sleeve. "How many days, Grandma?"

"Until what?"

"Until I meet him. How many days?"

His grandma let out another huffy breath and patted his head. "Two days, Jordan. One less than yesterday. Don't keep asking."

"Do you think he'll be nice?"

"Very nice."

"Should I tell him my knock-knock joke about the chicken and the bulldog?"

"Sure, Jordan, tell him the joke." His grandma turned her attention back to the television. "Most men like jokes."

"What if he wants to be my daddy, Grandma. What then?"

"Jordan . . ." His grandma put her hands over her face and sort of stretched out the skin on her forehead until the bunches disappeared. "Your mother already talked to you about that. The man's name is Casey, and he won't be your daddy. Just a special friend."

"But kind of like a pretend daddy, right, Grandma?"

"No, Jordan. Not like a pretend daddy. Like a special friend. That's what he is, a special friend."

"Oh." Jordan thought about that for a minute. "But if he wants to move in with us, can he sleep in my bedroom?"

Grandma took tight hold of the arms of her chair and her eyes got wide. "He won't be moving in with us, Jordan. You need to understand that. Not now and not ever."

"Okay." Jordan waited until his grandma turned back to the TV one more time. Then as soft as he could, he did one more tug on her sleeve.

"My goodness, child." Grandma's voice was louder than before, and her eyebrows disappeared into her forehead. "Can't you leave an old woman in peace?"

"Just one more question." Jordan made his voice nice and quiet, the way Grandma liked it. Then he smiled just in case she might say no.

"Oh, bother." Grandma slid down a little in her big chair, and her bones got smaller in her shoulders. "Go ahead."

"What if . . . what if he doesn't like me?"

Grandma sat up straight again, and her eyes got softer. "Of course he'll like you." She reached out one arm and gave him a half hug. "Just don't ask him a hundred questions."

By Friday morning, Jordan was so excited he couldn't eat breakfast. This time the questions went to his mother. How many hours until they could meet him? What would he look like? Where would they go and what would they do? And most of all, what if Casey didn't like him? His mommy was starting to breathe hard, and Jordan was sure she was going to get mad at him, when all of a sudden she did something really strange, something she never did when she was getting ready in the morning.

She laughed.

Then she messed up his hair and set a glass of orange juice down in front of him. "Jordan, I don't have all the answers this time. Besides, I should be the one asking how many hours until we meet him." She planted her hands on her hips. "Because then you'll finally have all the answers you need."

Jordan laughed, too, but after that he tried not to ask any more questions the rest of the morning. His mother was right. She didn't know all the answers, but God did. And a little while later, on the way to school, Jordan added a P.S. to his letter. A P.S. was when you wrote a letter and remembered one more special thing you forgot to say.

His mother was reading one of her files, so Jordan looked out the window of the cab and made his P.S. extra quiet. So only God could hear.

"P.S., God. Please make Casey like me."

Jordan hardly listened to Miss Hanson that day, and twice he had to sit at the back of the room for not paying attention. But that didn't matter because when the bell rang, his mother picked him up in a taxi, and off they went to the kids' club, the place where he was going to meet his pretend daddy.

Except he wasn't going to tell that to anyone else, just himself. Because other people would call Casey a special friend, and that was his 'ficial title. But Jordan knew the truth. They walked in, and the same lady they met before took them to a room, and just then his mommy's pager went off.

"Phone call," she said. She smiled at the lady and held up her finger. "Just a minute."

When his mommy hung up, she talked to the lady in private for a long time, and Jordan heard only a few of their words. Something about an emergency situation and how it would never happen again and that his mother was very sorry. Then the lady from the club gave Mommy a mean sort of look and did a frowny face for a long time and said just this once maybe.

Finally, Mommy and the lady came over to him.

"Sweetheart"—his mother scrunched down so they were the same size—"Mommy has a special meeting at work, and I can't stay to meet Casey. Not this time." She looked at the other lady. "But Mrs. Eccles will stay with you after Casey comes, and everything will be fine. I'll meet him next week, okay?"

Jordan had a hurt feeling in his heart, but he decided this wouldn't be a good time to cry. Besides, his mommy had special meetings all the time, and at least he was still going to meet Casey. "Okay."

His mom left, and after another minute, Mrs. Eccles came back, and this time she had a man with her. A man who looked tall and strong and happy like Brett Favre of the Green Bay Packers. He walked up and held out his hand and did a kind of smile that made Jordan feel all warm and safe inside. "Hi, Jordan. I'm Casey."

"Hi, Casey." Jordan shook the man's hand, and right then and there he knew for sure. Casey was a pretend daddy, not a special friend. Because sometimes Jordan dreamed about having a daddy again, and every time the daddy in his dream looked the same way.

Tall and strong and happy, and exactly like the man standing in front of him right now.

Casey had to wait five minutes before he could meet Jordan, all the while listening to Mrs. Eccles rail on about Jordan's mother leaving early.

"I mean, it's the first meeting!" The woman gave several short shakes of her head. "No one leaves early at the first meeting."

Casey didn't really care. He hadn't given much thought to Jordan's mother. It had been meeting the boy that had kept him up at night and put an extra spring in his step as he jogged to work and back each day that week. New York City was the prettiest place in the world at Christmastime, and already the transformation was taking place. The first snow had fallen, and Central Park was white except the paths and play areas. Police were making provisions for the Macy's Thanksgiving Day Parade, and lights were being wound into trees and along storefronts throughout Manhattan.

The closer Friday drew, the more Casey thought that Amy must've been right after all. Christmas miracles did happen to those who believed, and somehow, some kind of miracle was definitely coming together for him and Jordan.

Mrs. Eccles finished explaining that this time—against her better judgment—she was going to let Casey meet Jordan even though the boy's mother wasn't there, and finally Casey was ushered into the room where the child was waiting. The moment he saw the boy, he had the strangest sense. As though somehow he'd seen the child before, maybe at the café or at the park somewhere.

He took the boy's hand in his own and shook it, and in that instant Casey felt it. A bond, a connection so quick and immediate he could compare it to only one thing—the way he'd felt when he first met Amy.

They spent an hour talking with Mrs. Eccles, and by the time Jordan started telling knock-knock jokes, Casey and the social worker nodded at each other and knew it was time.

"Hey, Jordan, wanna go play at the park?"

The boy's eyes lit up like the tree in Rockefeller Center. He shot a look at Mrs. Eccles. "Can we?"

"Yes. Your mother said it was okay."

They set off, and Casey held Jordan's hand when they crossed the street. The feel of the child's small fingers protected inside his own did strange things to Casey's heart. Was this how it would've felt to hold the hand of his own son, his own Jordan, if the boy had survived?

Casey took the boy to the East Meadow play area, the one with the big slide where he and Amy had come so many times before. As they rounded the corner, Jordan spotted the play equipment and did a series of excited jumps.

"Hey, Casey, guess what? This is where my mom takes me to play sometimes."

"Really?"

"Really!" He pulled Casey toward the tall slide. "Only she doesn't go down the slide with me, but that's okay 'cause she's a girl."

Casey laughed. "I'll go." He followed Jordan up the ladder. "But don't make fun of me if I get stuck, okay?"

Jordan giggled, and the two of them went down the slide one after the other until Casey lost track of how many times. The bench Amy and he had shared was only a few feet away, but Casey refused to look at it. Finally, after half an hour, he sucked in a deep breath and pointed toward the swings. "How 'bout I push?"

"Would ya?" Jordan's eyes grew wide, his cheeks ruddy from the cold wind and excitement. "My mom doesn't do that a lot, either. Pushing can break the heels on her shoes."

"I'm sure." Casey stifled a laugh. After a few minutes of pushing Jordan he tried to picture the boy's mother, how hard it must be to have a demanding job and a son as lonely for attention as Jordan clearly was. "Tell me about your mom."

Jordan stretched out his legs and made the swing go a few feet higher. "What about her?"

"Well, like, does she go to parties or out on dates or stuff like that?"

"Nope." Jordan leaned back and stared at the sky as the swing moved him up and down. "She only works."

"Oh." Casey wasn't sure what else to ask. He didn't want to upset the boy on their first time out. "She must like her job."

"She's a district attorney. Megan Wright." Jordan looked over his shoulder at Casey. "She's in the newspapers a lot."

Casey let the woman's name swing from the rafters of his mind for a moment. It sounded familiar, in a distant sort of way, and then he remembered. One of the regulars at Casey's Corner had a son who'd been shot and killed in a robbery a year ago. Megan Wright was the prosecutor, Casey was almost sure. Yes, that was it. The boy's father had said Megan Wright was tough as nails, one of the reasons Manhattan was still a good place.

Casey gave the boy another push. "I think I've heard of her."

"Yeah." Jordan's tone was less than excited.

"So that's why she works so much, huh? Because she has so many cases?"

Jordan shrugged and dragged his feet along the sandy gravel beneath the swing. When he came to a stop, he turned to Casey and narrowed his eyes. His expression made him look years older. "She doesn't believe in love."

Casey's heart slipped several notches. He stuffed his hands in the pockets of his jeans and gave a few slow nods of his head. "Is that right?"

"Yeah." Jordan kicked at the gravel and looked across the play equipment to a couple walking hand in hand beside two small children. "She told Grandma that my daddy didn't know how to love her and now . . ." He raised his small shoulders again. "Now that Daddy's gone, she doesn't believe in love anymore."

"Oh." Casey felt a shudder pass over him. "That's too bad." What must the woman's life have been like for her to feel that way? To have lost all faith in love? His customer had figured out the woman perfectly. Tough as nails. Both in the courtroom and out, if Jordan's assessment was true. He pictured her, locking away criminals as deftly as she locked away her feelings.

No wonder Jordan needed a special friend.

"What time is it?" Jordan rose off the swing and cocked his head. He'd given Casey a glimpse of his heart, and Casey was grateful for it.

"Time to get going."

The two of them started back, and for a while they said nothing. Casey looked at his watch. "We have enough time for pizza, if you want."

Jordan's face lit up, and he did a few more quick jumps. "Pizza's my favorite. Extra cheese and pineapple, but not with those slimy black things, okay?"

"Olives?" Casey chuckled and took the boy's hand. "Okay, we'll skip those."

"Yeah, olives." Jordan pinched his face up in a knot. "Yuck! They look like chopped-up eyeballs."

Casey laughed again, and he was struck by something. He hadn't had this much fun since before Amy died. The two of them crossed the park and found a small pizza place Casey hadn't visited before. He ordered and they took a booth near an old, broken jukebox. Eventually, he'd take him to Casey's Corner but not yet. It was too soon in their friendship to have people asking questions and introducing themselves.

Midway through a large extra-cheese pizza with

pineapple, Casey leveled his gaze at Jordan and lowered his voice.

"I've been thinking about your mom."

"Yeah, I wish she coulda come. She said she'd meet you next week."

"Good." Casey caught his red plastic straw between his fingers, drew it close, and took a long swig of ice water. "But I meant something else."

Jordan looked up from his pizza, curious. "What?"

"Okay, here it is." Casey gave a slow look over first one of his shoulders, then the other, as though the information he was about to share with Jordan were top secret. "My wife used to say that Christmas miracles happen to those who believe."

"Christmas miracles?" Jordan's eyes got wide.

"Yes." Casey stroked his chin. "So, maybe this is a good chance to see if my wife was right. You know, if Christmas miracles really do happen."

Jordan tilted his head and set his slice of pizza down on his plate. "Do you think they happen?"

"Well—" Casey hesitated. "I didn't used to." He took his straw and downed another mouthful of water. His eyes never left Jordan's. "But now something tells me they're true, that Christmas miracles really *do* happen."

"Hey, I know what you mean! I wrote a letter to . . ."

Jordan's eyes lit up, but then his expression changed. He paused and changed his words. "What I mean is, I believe in Christmas miracles . . . if you do, Casey."

"Then that's what your mom needs. A very special Christmas miracle."

Jordan's chin dropped slowly to his chest. "I don't think she believes in miracles. Not any kind."

"Well, then . . ." Casey sat up straighter, the mock conspiracy over. He wanted to know about the boy's letter and a hundred other things, but those questions could come later. Ten or twelve pizzas into their friendship. "If she doesn't believe, then that's what you and I can pray for."

Jordan's eyes got wide. "That Mommy will believe in miracles?"

"How 'bout one thing at a time." Casey bit his lip. "Let's pray that she'll believe in love again. That's always a good thing to pray."

"Yeah . . ." Jordan gave him a lopsided smile. "Then if she believes in love, maybe one day she'll believe in miracles, too, right?"

"Right." Casey wanted to say that by the sounds of it, if Megan Wright believed in love again, she would have to, by default, believe in miracles. Because it would take one to accomplish the other. But instead he nodded to the pizza. "Let's wrap up the rest for your mom. We have to be back in ten minutes."

"Okay." Jordan bit off a mouthful of pizza and washed it down with a swig of root beer. "Thanks for taking me out, Casey. I had fun."

"Me, too." A strange feeling wrapped itself around Casey's heart, and he gave a little cough to clear his throat. "I think we'll be special friends for a long time."

An hour later when Casey was back at home, he did something he hadn't done in months. He went to the edge of his bed, dropped to his knees, and thanked God for bringing Jordan Wright into his life. And for the alive feeling that still stayed with him, coloring his thoughts and soul and everything about the coming days. When he was done thanking God, he bowed his head and prayed for something with an intensity he hadn't known since his days in Haiti.

That Megan Wright would believe in love again.

When he was finished, he changed clothes, brushed his teeth, and after an hour of watching ESPN, slipped into bed earlier than usual. He pictured Amy and tried to imagine what she would've thought of Jordan. She would've loved him, of course. And if she knew anything about the boy's mother, Casey was sure that somehow he and Jordan weren't the only ones praying for Ms. Wright.

Somewhere up in heaven, Amy was praying, too.

Jordan told his mommy about the pizza and the park and the swings and the twenty-three times they slid down the big slide together. He talked the whole way home and through dinner and even after he brushed his teeth and Mommy tucked him into bed.

That's when she put her finger against his lips. "Enough, Jordan. It's bedtime."

Jordan took a long breath. "He's the best special friend in the world, Mommy. Wait till you meet him and then the three of us can—"

"Jordan . . ." She smiled and kissed him on the tip of his nose. "I'm sure he's wonderful. It makes me happy to see you so excited, but right now you need to get to sleep. We can talk about it more tomorrow."

He watched her leave the room, and after she closed the door he sat straight up in bed and looked out the window next to his bookshelf. "God, it's me. Jordan." He smiled real big. "Casey's so cool, God. He's the best. I'm so glad You sent him for me." A little bit of the smile slipped off his mouth. "Casey says we need to pray for Mommy, that she'll believe in love again." Jordan tucked his legs up beneath him so he could see the stars better. "That's why I'm here, God. And if You want, I'll write You another letter. Because if You can send me someone like Casey, I know You can make this happen. Especially at Christmas.

"Because Casey says that's when You make the bestest miracles of all."

CHAPTER NINE

Megan had heard Casey's name so often in the past three weeks, he seemed like part of the family.

She splashed water on her face and dried her cheeks with a hand towel as the voices wafted in from the dining room.

"Then he took me to Chelsea Piers, Grandma, and we rode the roller coaster and that spinning ride, and after that we ate a big pile of blue cotton candy, and he played pinball with me for five straight games even after I beated him, and . . ."

It was Saturday morning, and the previous night had been Jordan's third with his special friend. No doubt the Healing Hearts program had been the perfect solution for Jordan, and Megan had been able to give more of her attention to work because of it. Her son was happier, more at ease, and doing better at obeying his grandmother after school. Besides, when was the last time she'd taken him to Chelsea Piers?

Jordan's special friend had even taken to calling a few times a week, chatting with her son and asking about his day at school. The man seemed every bit the perfect volunteer Mrs. Eccles had made him out to be.

But sometimes a fingernail of doubt scratched the surface of Megan's conscience.

The program held no guarantees, really. No binding contract that could keep a single man like this Casey from walking out of her son's life and breaking his heart. Megan studied her reflection in the mirror for a moment and liked what she saw. Without her makeup she looked younger than her thirty-two years, and with Jordan happy again, the tiny lines at the corner of her eyes had faded.

She shut off the light and headed to the dining room.

"There you are." Her mother tossed her a pointed look. "Your eggs are getting cold."

Saturday mornings Megan's mother made breakfast, and Megan used the opportunity to sleep a little later than usual. She smiled at Jordan. "Sounds like you had another fun Friday."

"Yeah, but how come you had to cancel again?"

"I told you." Megan took the chair between Jordan and her mother and unfolded her napkin across her lap. "Fridays are busy for me, Jordan. It's hard to get away."

"That's what you said last week." Jordan didn't sound rude, just disappointed. "Casey really wants to meet you."

Megan angled her head as she balanced a forkful of eggs. "Does *he* say that, or just you?"

"Well . . ." Jordan thought about that for a minute. "He doesn't actually say that, but he thinks it. I know he does, Mom. The lady at the club says all the other parents have met their child's special friend except you."

Megan made a mental note to contact Mrs. Eccles and ask her to keep her comments to herself. Her frustrations should not be vented at Jordan.

Next to her, Megan's mother finished a piece of toast and dabbed her lips with the corner of her napkin. Her voice was more pleasant than before. "So, dear, exactly how old is this Casey? Is he a college boy?"

Jordan's voice rose a notch, his face filled with enthusiasm. "He's thirty-four, and he owns his own restaurant." Jordan looked at Megan and then back at his grandmother. "Isn't that cool?"

"Very cool." Her mother's tone took on a new level of interest. She made a subtle look in Megan's direction.

"Thirty-four, single, and owns his own restaurant." She paused and the corners of her smile lifted a bit. "Sounds like you should make time for the meeting, Megan."

"Mother . . ." Megan leveled her gaze at the older woman and lowered her voice. "I'm not interested. And I hate when you push."

"Mommy?" Jordan sounded forlorn. He tapped her hand with the end of his fork until she looked at him. "You don't wanna meet Casey?"

Megan raised her eyebrows at her mother and then made a quick shift back to Jordan. "Of course I want to meet him, honey. Next Friday for sure, okay? I'll clear my schedule."

"Good, then I'll call Casey today and tell him."

"Tell him what?"

"That he should get three tickets for the Nets game, not just two."

"Hmmm." Megan's mother stood up with her empty plate and walked to the kitchen. Her voice still had that cheerful matchmaker tone Megan hated. "Sounds like a date to me."

"Wait a minute!" Jordan jumped up from the table and ran to the drawer near the telephone. "That lady from the kids' club gave me a letter for you. She said it was extra important that you read it." He grabbed an envelope from the drawer and jogged back to Megan. "Here." He hesitated. "Read it, Mom. What's it say?"

Megan slid a single sheet from the envelope, opened it, and read silently to herself. It was from Mrs. Eccles, and it was short and to the point.

Dear Ms. Wright: We have tried on several occasions to contact you and relay to you the importance of your presence at a meeting with your son and his special friend. Parental involvement in the program is absolutely essential. Because you missed three consecutive meetings here at the club, we are giving you the opportunity to set up a meeting with Jordan and Mr. Cummins outside the arranged Friday meeting time. Below you will find the man's home and cell-phone numbers so that the two of you can find a way to meet. If you do not follow through with this program stipulation, we will be forced to remove Jordan from the program and assign Mr. Cummins to another child. Sincerely, Mrs. Eccles.

"Well, Mommy, well . . ." Jordan gripped the edge of the table and did two little jumps. "What does it say?"

Megan stared at her son, not sure what to tell him. Her mother was in the kitchen washing the frying pan and mercifully wasn't there to add her own questions. The nerve of the social worker, threatening to remove Jordan from the program. So what if she hadn't met this . . . this Casey, whoever he was. He was Jordan's special friend, not hers. Why were the people at the Children's Organization so set on the fact that parents be involved?

Her questions dissolved like springtime snow.

It didn't matter if Megan agreed with the rules, she had no choice but to play by them. Jordan had lost one man in his life; she wouldn't stand by and watch him lose Casey, too. Not because she hadn't done her part to follow the program guidelines.

"Jordan . . ." She folded the letter and slipped it back in the envelope. If they had to meet, they might as well get it over with. "How would you like to have Casey over for dinner?"

"Yes!" Jordan ran in a tight circle and made his trademark jump straight into the air, his fist raised toward the ceiling. "That'd be the best thing in the world, Mom! When can he come?"

Megan thought for a minute. She could get her Sunday work done early and share a meal with the man tomorrow. That way, she could call Mrs. Eccles on Monday and tell her the requirement had been met. Besides, her mother had bridge on Sunday nights, so no one would be around to pressure Megan into anything more than a casual dinner meeting. She smiled at Jordan. "How about tomorrow?"

"Yes! Yes . . . yes . . . yes . . ." Jordan darted over to the phone, grabbed the receiver, and ran it back to Megan. "Here!" He was out of breath, his eyes vibrant and alive. "Here, Mommy. Call him now."

From the kitchen her mother had caught on to what was happening, and she had the knowing look of a Cheshire cat as she dried the frying pan. Megan clenched her teeth and managed a smile. "Your friend doesn't know me, honey. Why don't you call. Tell him six o'clock, okay?"

Jordan raised his shoulders a few times and grinned. "Okay. I'll call his cell phone." He punched in numbers that had become familiar to him over the past few weeks, and the following conversation was short. When Jordan hung up he smiled big at Megan.

"He was at work. He says he'll be here at six." Jordan set down the phone, wrapped his arms around Megan's legs, and squeezed. "Thanks, Mom. I just know you'll love him as much as I do."

Megan couldn't figure out why she was nervous.

It was a few minutes before six on Sunday evening. She'd made meat loaf and baked potatoes and everything was ready, but still she had a funny feeling. What if they clashed somehow? What if he'd read about her work in the paper and didn't like female prosecutors? What if the evening ahead of them made Casey care less for Jordan than before?

Megan banished her thoughts and turned off the oven just as the doorbell rang. She ran her fingers through her hair one last time and watched as Jordan tore out of his room and raced for the front door.

"Casey!" He opened it and shouted the man's name at the same time. "Come on, I'll show you my room!"

"Hold on a minute, buddy. I think I'd better meet your mom first." The door opened a bit more, and a man appeared in the entryway, holding hands with Jordan. He was tall and broad-shouldered, and he wore faded jeans and an NYC sweatshirt. His dark hair was cut close to his head, and his eyes were a kind of clear blue, like the water off the Florida Keys. And something else, something familiar Megan couldn't quite figure out.

She set a pair of pot holders down on the counter and joined them in the living room. "I'm Megan. Thanks for coming."

"Casey." He nodded once and shook her hand. "Thanks for having me."

An awkward silence planted itself between them, but only for a few seconds. After that, Jordan tugged at Casey's arm again. "Come on, I have to show you the transformer plane you gave me. It's all set up and everything!"

Casey and Megan chuckled and exchanged a quick smile. "I better take a look."

"Go ahead. We'll eat in a few minutes."

Megan had dinner on the table in no time, and with Jordan filling in every spare moment, there was no need for conversation between the two of them. Finally, Megan had to tell him to stop talking and eat. The moment Jordan was quiet, Casey turned to her, his expression polite and guarded.

"Jordan tells me you take him to the East Meadow, my favorite play area. The one with the big slide."

"Yes, we've always—" Megan stopped herself. "Wait . . . that's where I've seen you."

Casey set down his fork and cocked his head, confused. "I don't remember meeting."

"We didn't meet." Megan could see the moment clearly in her head now. "You jog, don't you?"

"Every day."

"A month ago I took Jordan out to play, and I think that was you sitting on a bench at the back of the play area by yourself." Megan could suddenly see the pain in the man's eyes that day, and she chose her words carefully. "Jogging suit, knit beanie. You seemed kind of pensive."

Casey looked from Megan to Jordan. "Okay, now it's coming together. This whole time Jordan was familiar to me, like I'd seen him somewhere before." He hesitated and shifted his attention back to Megan. "That was a long day for me, the day I stopped on the bench. At work, I mean. I saw Jordan playing, and I thought he looked like . . . like a nice boy."

Megan searched Casey's eyes and saw holes in his story big enough to drive a truck through. But they were none of her business. Besides, the dinner meeting was only a formality. She forced a polite smile. "Small world, then."

"Very small."

Jordan jumped back into the conversation, and they talked about the past baseball season and whether the Nets would have a good run this year or not.

Casey turned away from Jordan for a moment and caught her eye. "Jordan told me to get three tickets for Friday. Will you join us?"

Megan was trapped. She lowered her fork to her plate

and looked from Jordan to Casey. The man was only being polite, but Jordan was practically desperate for her to say yes. "Sure." A sigh stuck in her throat, and she swallowed it. "I'd love to go."

"Cool! We'll have the best time!" Jordan ate a bite of potatoes and looked at Casey again. "I got flash cards in my room for pluses and minuses. If you wanna do 'em after dinner."

"Sure, buddy, I love flash cards."

The easy conversation continued, and Megan did her best to stay out of it. That way she could watch this man, the man she'd seen at the East Meadow play area that day, and wonder about his past. He'd lost his wife and baby, she knew that much. And certainly that explained the look in his eyes that day at the park. But how had he and her son gotten so attached, so quickly—almost as though they'd known each other for years?

They finished dinner, and Megan cut off the flash card session at seven-thirty. "School tomorrow, Jordan. Sorry . . ."

She and Jordan walked Casey to the door, but Jordan turned around and ran back toward his room. "Don't go yet. I forgot something."

When Jordan was gone, Megan caught Casey's gaze and held it. Now that she'd met him and seen how wonderful he was with her son, she felt awful about not showing up the past three Fridays. "Casey, listen." She kept her voice low so Jordan wouldn't hear her. "I'm sorry about the other meetings. I should've made it a priority."

"No big deal. Tonight'll satisfy old Mrs. Eccles." Casey winked at Jordan as he raced up to them once more and thrust a drawing into Casey's hands. "Besides, we had a good time anyway, didn't we, sport?"

"Yep." Jordan gave Casey a high five and pointed to the drawing. "That's a picture I made for you."

"Wow." Casey admired it for a long moment. "It's perfect. I'll save it forever, okay?"

"Okay." Jordan's eyes danced a little more than usual. "Should we tell Mommy about the prayer?"

"No." Casey gave Megan an easy grin. "Let's make the prayer a secret for now."

"A secret prayer, huh?" Megan gave Jordan a teasing look. "I take it that's a good thing."

"Yes." Jordan gave a hard nod in Casey's direction. "Very good."

They agreed on where to meet for the basketball game that coming Friday and said their good-byes. When Casey was gone, Megan helped Jordan to bed and went to her office to work.

It was only then that she realized she'd forgotten to ask Jordan about the secret prayer. Whatever it was, no harm could come from the two of them praying for her. Even if it had been a lifetime since she'd put any faith in praying. She opened the notes she'd been working on and positioned her hands on the keyboard.

But nothing would come. Not then or any time in the next hour.

At half past nine that evening, she finally gave up trying to work and headed for bed. The last thought on her mind before she fell asleep wasn't about how to win the case on her desk, or expose a witness, or find a missing bit of evidence. It wasn't even about Jordan.

Rather, it was the dimpled smile of a man she'd only just met. A man she felt as though she'd known her entire life, all because of a chance encounter in Central Park.

Casey stayed up late that night, thinking about Amy.

She and Megan Wright had nothing in common. Where Amy was simple, Megan was cultured. Amy's lack of guile was in utter contrast to Megan's cunning in the courtroom. No question Jordan's mother was beautiful, but a woman with a walled-up heart was not someone Casey wanted to spend a lot of time with.

Still, he prayed for her that night, as he had every night since he and Jordan made the deal. A secret prayer, he'd called it earlier that evening. And it was. Because Casey guessed if Megan had any idea they were praying for her to believe in love again, she'd order the whole thing off and forbid it. She had that kind of commanding presence.

Casey was glad Megan had figured out where they'd known each other from. The park, of course. It made perfect sense. If they both frequented the East Meadow, they were bound to have run into each other that afternoon. But as Casey fell asleep in his recliner watching *SportsCenter* that night, he was baffled by a strange thought.

He must've seen the woman only briefly that day at the park. The moment she'd described with him on the bench wasn't one he could remember, because he'd been too caught up in his past to notice a strange woman staring at him from across the way.

But if he couldn't remember seeing her, then why in the world was she so familiar?

CHAPTER TEN

Megan wanted to know more about Casey Cummins, and she used the Nets game as her chance to find out.

It was halftime, and the two of them were anchored outside the men's room waiting for Jordan. "Casey . . ." She leaned against the wall and nudged him with her elbow. "I have a question for you."

"Shoot."

"Why was it such a long day?"

Casey couldn't have looked more confused if she'd asked him to fly down the stadium stairs. "What do you mean?"

"That day at the park, when I first saw you." Her tone wasn't flirtatious or pushy, just matter-of-fact. She hoped it would make him drop his defenses a little and talk to her. If her son was going to be crazy about the man, she wanted to know more than his name and job description. "Why was it a long day?"

The muscles in his face relaxed some, and the pain Megan had seen that afternoon at the park flashed once more in Casey's eyes. "It was my anniversary. Eight years."

"Oh." Megan let her gaze fall to the tiled floor. "I shouldn't have asked."

"It's okay." Casey slipped his hands into the pockets of his jacket and rested his shoulders against the same wall. "The reason I noticed Jordan was because he made me think of my little boy."

Megan wanted to crawl into a hole. Whatever Casey had shared with his wife, it had been far richer, far more meaningful than the marriage between George and her. She was about to apologize when he spoke up.

"Now it's your turn."

She gave him a sad smile. "That's fair."

He tilted his head back a bit, his eyes locked on hers. "Why don't you believe in love?"

Before Megan's heart had a chance to find a normal rhythm, Jordan skipped out of the rest room and found his place between them. "Mom, can we get a hot dog before the second half? Please?"

In the space above his head, she whispered, "Not now, okay?"

"Okay." Casey grinned, and his expression told her that he doubted she would have given him an answer anyway.

At the end of the night, Casey told them he had a couple of extra tickets to a football game that Sunday at Giants Stadium. This time when Casey asked her to come, Megan found herself agreeing more quickly.

When Sunday arrived, the game was a nail-biter, and by the end of the evening the three of them were yelling at the top of their lungs.

"Nothing like Giants football!" Casey shouted the words above the roar of the crowd.

"Nothing like it!"

By the end of the weekend, Megan felt even more strongly that she'd known Casey Cummins all her life. She kept waiting for his attention to die off, fade into nothing as she expected it to. They'd met the program requirement, after all. Casey's interest was in Jordan, not her. But a few nights later Casey called, and Megan answered the phone. "Hello?"

"Guess what?"

"What?" Megan had kept their friendship very simple and businesslike, despite her probing questions at the basketball game. But at times like this, she couldn't help but feel a little thrill at the sound of his voice.

"It's snowing!" Casey sounded not much older than Jordan.

"Yes." She giggled. "And it's seven o'clock."

"That's the perfect time for skating at the park." He hesitated. "Wollman Rink, Megan. What do you say? You and Jordan get ready, and we'll surprise him, okay?"

"Well . . ." The whole thing made her wonder what was happening to her resolve, her steely determination. But she didn't dare voice her feelings. She'd kept them from her mother so far, and if she had any sense, she'd keep them from herself. After all, the man wasn't looking for a relationship. He was still in love with his dead wife. Besides, nothing smart could come from letting herself fall for Jordan's special friend. She was too busy, her heart too closed, for a man like Casey.

She glanced at the clock on the microwave. "Right now?"

"Ah, come on, Megan. You only live once."

"I don't know . . ." Megan hesitated just long enough for him to pounce.

"Good! I'll pick you both up in twenty minutes."

Jordan was thrilled with the surprise, and he didn't stop talking until, halfway around the rink the first time, Megan fell smack on her backside.

Jordan's face twisted in concern, but Casey stifled a

laugh as he held out his hand and helped her up. "If the judges could see you now."

"Stop." Megan made a sound that was more laugh than moan. When she did, Jordan relaxed and joined in. She winced as she made her way to her feet and brushed the ice off her woolen slacks. But she didn't fall again the rest of the night, and at the end of the evening Jordan gave Casey a quick hug and ran into the apartment, leaving Casey and Megan at the door still breathless from the adventure.

Their eyes met and held for a moment, and Megan thought of a dozen things she wanted to ask him. What were they doing and where was it leading? And most of all, didn't it feel wonderful to laugh again? But she was certain questions like that would send Casey running. Besides, she was feeling this way only because skating at Central Park in December was somehow magical. And magic didn't always make sense.

The moment passed, and the days began to blend together. Every time she joined Casey and Jordan for an evening out or a few hours at the park, she figured it was the last time, that she was still out of place in their midst because now that she'd fulfilled the program requirement and met Casey, the arrangement was intended for the two of them.

Not the three of them.

But Casey kept inviting her, and she kept hearing herself say yes.

They saw a Christmas play at an off-Broadway theater, and a few nights later he took them to his café. It was warm and brightly decorated with Broadway posters and street signs. A big man behind the counter welcomed Megan and Jordan with a hearty handshake. "So, you're the reason old Casey hasn't been around much, huh?" His smile lit the room.

When Casey sat Megan and Jordan at one of the tables by the window, she watched him head through the café and make brief conversation with a few of the customers. He was obviously a successful businessman, liked by all types of people. She watched as he made his way back to the counter, and she saw the man behind the counter lean close and whisper something.

Casey only smiled in response and lifted his hands in the air. When he returned to the table, Megan asked him about it. "Okay, what's the story? You're in trouble with your staff because of us, right?"

"Hardly." Casey grinned. "Now, what're we having for dinner?"

As busy as November had been for Megan, December saw the court calendar grind to a halt. Most of the hearings were used only to gain continuations until after the holidays, and Megan found herself looking forward to the time she spent away from the office.

Still, she worried about what would happen come January, when the calendar got busy again and the newness of her friendship with Casey wore off. She had to keep reminding herself that he wasn't in their lives for her, but for Jordan. And she promised herself that after December, she'd let the two of them get back to meeting without her.

"He's falling for you, Megan." Her mother confronted her one day as she was heading off to work. "And you?"

"Don't be ridiculous, Mother. We're grown adults, and neither of us is falling anywhere. I'm only helping Jordan get to know him better."

"Yes, and I'm the Easter Bunny." Her mother clucked her tongue and narrowed her eyes in silence for a long while. "Don't you hurt that boy, Megan. I know you."

"Mother, my goodness. I'm the one who took Jordan down and signed him up for the program. The last thing I'd do is find a way to hurt him where Casey's concerned."

Her mother only lowered her chin and gave Megan a look that shot arrows at her soul. "I'm not talking about Jordan." She paused and dropped her voice. "If you're not falling for him, then don't lead him on."

Anger and frustration mingled and boiled near the surface of her heart. How could she tell her mother that yes, she was falling. Especially when she was almost convinced Casey didn't share her feelings? Besides, she didn't believe in love. Wasn't that her? Maybe her mother was right. Maybe it was time she reminded herself of that fact so neither of them got hurt.

She sniffed hard. "I'm not leading him on. He's a friend, Mother. Nothing more."

The days melted away, and still the three of them continued to find ways to be together. They walked through Central Park and had a snowball fight on the meadow between the tennis courts and the reservoir, and Casey's fingers nearly got frostbitten.

"Where's your gloves?" Megan dropped beside Casey on the closest park bench and watched Jordan as he pelted bushes with one snowball after another.

"Lost 'em at the café last week." Casey shrugged. "I'll live. I can always use my coat pockets."

They shopped at Macy's and saw the lights of the city from a horse-drawn carriage. After her mother's warning, Megan was careful never to so much as let her arm brush against Casey's so that he wouldn't get the wrong impression. And as wonderful as their evenings together were, he never gave her any hint that he was interested in her.

Two days before Christmas, Casey called and talked to Jordan for a few minutes. Then he asked to speak to her.

"Hello?"

"Hey . . . listen, I want to bring by a gift for Jordan. Would tomorrow be okay?"

Megan's heart ached at the sound of his voice. The month was almost over, and she had the strangest feeling that these were their last days together, that after the New Year everything would change. But for now she couldn't bear to miss an opportunity for the three of them to be together again. "That'd be perfect. Why don't you come for dinner? Mom and I make turkey on Christmas Eve."

"You don't mind?"

"Of course not." Megan kept her voice casual. "We'd love to see you."

Jordan was ecstatic about the idea, and Megan's mother promised to be on her best behavior. Casey arrived with a box of roasted almonds and a bouquet of white roses for Megan.

He handed them to her and rubbed his bare hands together. "I hope they're not frozen."

Megan took the flowers and for just the flash of a moment wondered if he'd chosen white over red on purpose. "They're beautiful, Casey. Thank you."

"I figured a New York City prosecutor probably didn't get flowers too often." He looked down at Jordan and handed him a wrapped box. "Besides, your son here wasn't much help with Christmas suggestions for his mom."

"Can I open it?" Jordan held his fingers poised near the crease in the wrapping paper, waiting for the go-ahead signal.

Megan and Casey laughed, and Casey nodded. "Sure, buddy."

Jordan tore off the paper, and inside was the kind of baseball glove he'd wanted for three months. "Wow . . . I can't believe it. Can we try it out; huh, can we?"

"Tell you what . . ." Casey dropped down to Jordan's level. He took the glove and folded it in half near the base of the thumb. "Keep it like this and tuck it beneath your mattress. By the time the snow melts, you'll be able to catch 'em better than McGwire."

The night passed in a pleasant blur of getting the meal ready and eating together. Afterward, Jordan gave Casey a framed photo of the two of them for his café wall, and Megan gave him a pair of gloves.

Red gloves.

"Jordan told me you said red was the color of giving." She tilted her head. "I figured there's no one more giving than you these past few months." Her tone changed and became more teasing. "Besides, without gloves you aren't worth much in a snowball fight."

A sad, distant sort of look worked its way across his expression but only for a moment. "Yep." Then he smiled and slipped the gloves on his hands. "Red's the color of giving, and with these"—he shot a look at Jordan—"I'll be giving some pretty mean snowballs."

When they finished with the gifts, they played Monopoly and watched *It's a Wonderful Life*. Long before the angel got his wings, Megan's mother excused herself for bed and Jordan fell asleep. When the movie ended the TV went dark, and the room was lit only by the glow from the nearby Christmas tree.

Megan was about to carry Jordan to his room, when Casey stood and held out his hands. "Let me."

She sat back down and watched him sweep her sleeping son into his arms and carry him toward the bedroom. *Don't do this to yourself, Megan. Nothing good can come from what you're feeling. It's a shadow, a trick, a hoax. Keep the walls in place, and no one'll get hurt.*

But when Casey walked back into the room, the sight of him made her heart skip a beat. She could hardly order herself to keep the walls standing when Casey's kindness had long since knocked them to the ground.

He poured two mugs of coffee and returned to the spot next to her on the sofa. "Here."

"Thanks." Her voice was softer than before, and she was glad for the shadowy light, glad he couldn't see the heat in her cheeks. "Jordan was tuckered out."

Casey chuckled and shook his head. "I've never known a kid so full of life."

Megan wanted to say that Jordan hadn't always been that way, but she felt suddenly shy, unable to think of the right words. With Casey so close she could smell his cologne, she couldn't decide whether to bid him good night or find a way to stretch the night for another hour.

"Okay." Casey took a swallow of coffee and lowered the mug to his knee. "You can't run from the question this time."

"What question?"

Casey hesitated, and his eyes found hers. She could feel his gentle heart, his concern, and the fact that he wasn't joking. "Why don't you believe in love?"

Megan took a moment to catch her breath. Then she did her best to give him a teasing look. "Why do you want to know?"

"Because . . ." Casey reached out and brushed a section of hair back from Megan's face. The touch of his fingers against her forehead made her ache for his kiss in a way that shocked her. He let his hand fall back to his lap, and his voice was barely more than a whisper. "Because sometimes I think you wouldn't recognize love if it sat next to you at a Giants game."

Megan tried not to read anything into his sentence. Instead she drew a long, slow breath and set her cup down on an end table. "You really want to know?"

Casey nodded. "Really."

"Okay, I'll tell you." Then with careful words sometimes soaked in sorrow, she did just that. She told him about her father and how he'd left their family without warning, and about meeting George and believing their lives together would be everything her parents' lives were not.

"But he didn't love me, either. Not really." She felt her lip quiver, and she bit it to keep from crying. "He wanted me to work, but a few days after I passed the bar exam, I found out I was pregnant."

"He loved Jordan." It was a statement, as though Casey knew more than Megan realized.

"Yes, he did. But it was different with me. I was never more than a business partner to George."

"And that's why? Why you don't believe in love?" Casey's voice was gentle, tender, and something about it made Megan want to tell this man everything, even the things she'd never told anyone before.

"I did believe once, a long time ago." She drew her legs up and angled herself so she could see Casey better. "I was thirteen, and my mother took us to Lake Tahoe, to a private part of the lake where my aunt owned a house." Megan rested her cheek against the sofa cushion. "The first day there I met this boy." She felt herself drift back again, the way she had a few months ago when she'd given herself permission to remember that time in her life.

"Lake Tahoe?" Casey leaned a little closer and sat up. He seemed more alert now, taking in every word Megan said.

"Yes." Megan smiled and felt a layer of tears fill her eyes. "The boy's name was Kade, and that's all I remember, really. Kade from Lake Tahoe. He was fifteen, and he told me something I'll never forget." Megan wiped at a single tear. "He told me real love was kind and good and came from the Bible. A sort of love that never ends." Megan gave a quiet sniff. "He told me he'd pray for me every day, that I'd get a miracle and wind up knowing that kind of love." She reached for her glass again and took a sip. "I never saw him after that. I guess I figured maybe he was an angel."

"Hmm." Casey stirred across from her, and Megan noticed that he didn't look as comfortable as before. What had she said to change his mood? Had the talk about love scared him? Or was he merely missing his wife on another Christmas Eve without her?

"Sorry . . ." Megan looked at her watch and gave a stiff little laugh. "I've bored you and now it's late."

"No . . . no, you didn't bore me, Megan." He slid to the edge of the sofa and moved closer so that their knees were touching. Then he lifted his hand to her face and framed it with his fingertips. "I think it's a beautiful story and one that . . . that doesn't have to have a tragic ending."

It took all Megan's effort to concentrate on finding an answer. The nearness of Casey made her emotions war within her in a way she couldn't sort out. "It . . . it already did. George died before we ever figured out a way to love like that."

Casey lifted Megan's chin so that their eyes met and held. "What was your name back then? Your maiden name?"

The question pulled her from the moment and made her want to laugh. "Why?"

"Because . . ." Casey searched her eyes, looking to the depths of her soul. "I want to picture everything about the way you were, back when you still wanted to believe in love."

"Howard was my maiden name." Megan lifted her shoulders. "And I wasn't Megan, I was Maggie. Maggie Howard."

Even in the dim glow of the Christmas tree, Casey's face seemed to grow a few shades paler. Again, Megan wasn't sure what she'd said, but the magic of the moment was gone. Casey stood and gathered his red gloves and the photo of him and Jordan. "I guess I better go."

"Yes." Megan chided herself for being so transparent. A man like Casey had his own ghosts to deal with on Christmas Eve.

They walked to the door, and before Casey left he cupped his hand along the side of her face once more, leaned close, and for a single instant brought his lips to hers. The kiss was over before Megan realized what had happened, and Casey whispered, "Merry Christmas, Megan."

Not until he was gone did Megan realize something. The glistening look in Casey's eyes hadn't been a reflection from the Christmas tree.

It had been tears.

CHAPTER ELEVEN

It was a miracle.

No other explanation existed, except that in His ever-lasting mercy, God had stepped into Casey Cummins's world and handed him a Christmas miracle. The kind Amy had always believed in.

But not the one he'd been praying for these past few weeks. And not one he was sure he wanted. Not yet, any-way.

Casey's head spun, and his heart wasn't sure whether to take wing or drop to his shoes. Under the circum-stances he couldn't possibly ride a taxi home, so when he reached the ground level of Megan's apartment he began to walk. Strong and hard and fast into the chilly night, and after less than a block he felt his eyes well up.

He hadn't asked for any of this. He'd wanted only to

befriend a young boy, to bring hope and light and healing to a heart that had grieved as much these past two years as Casey's had. If he'd known he would find love, he wouldn't have made the call. Amy deserved more than that. It had only been two years, after all. Two years. How dare he give his heart to someone else after so little time?

His feet pummeled the ground, carrying him south and taking him into Central Park. The lights were still lit, and couples strolled the paved walkways. Casey stayed on the less traveled paths and let the tears come.

He walked until he reached the bench at the back of the East Meadow play area, the place where he and Amy had come so many times before. Then he sat down and dropped the gifts from Megan and Jordan on the cold wood beside him. How was it possible? The whole time while he'd been taking Megan and her son out, God had been orchestrating the events to lead up to this one night, that one conversation with Megan.

And that was something else. What had he been thinking, kissing her?

Amy . . . Amy, if you can hear me, I'm sorry, honey. I love you, still. I'll always love you.

His tears came harder now, and he covered his face with his hands. The thing of it was, it had already happened. All of it. And there was nothing he could do about it. Being angry at God wouldn't change the truth. He loved Megan with a fierceness that scared him, loved her in a way he hadn't even realized until a few hours ago. Loved Jordan, too. And now . . . after what he'd just learned . . . he was certain he would share his life with them, love them and live with them forever.

As sure as Christmas, it was all about to play out.

Casey wished for just a moment that Amy could be there beside him again, to hold his hand and hug him, tell him it was all okay. That none of them could do a single thing about time or the way it marched on without respecting loss or feelings or memories.

That sometimes life could hurt as much as death.

His fingers were wet from his tears, and an occasional icy gust of wind burned against them. He sniffed and remembered the gift Megan had given him. The red gloves. He pulled them from their wrapping once more and slid them onto his fingers. Then . . . as he stared at his hands, he realized something.

Amy had told him that red was the color of giving. That had come from her, not him. And if there was one thing she would've wanted to give him this Christmas, it was the gift of freedom. Freedom from the pain of losing her, freedom from holding on.

Freedom to love again.

She'd given him so much in life, and now, in death, she would give him this. But if that was true, if he was going to let go and move on with life, he needed this time to tell her good-bye. He lifted his eyes to heaven and spoke in a voice that even he could barely hear. "Amy . . . I never wanted it this way, you know that. But . . . it happened. And the way it happened . . . well, it can't be anything but a miracle."

He dried his tears with the red gloves and thought back to the night with Megan. "I love her, Amy. I love her son. Even before I found out about the miracle. And I was wrong about the two of you. I think you would've liked her. Maybe a lot." He felt another tear spill onto his cheeks, and his voice grew tight. "I'll always hold you close inside, Amy. But for now . . . for now I have to let go."

For a long while he sat there, longing for a chance to see her again. Instead he closed his eyes and felt it. Something had released in his heart, and at the same instant, he felt as new and alive inside as the fresh fallen snow. He dried his eyes one last time and stood. Then, without looking back, he jogged to the closest street and hailed a cab.

The time for tears had passed, and Casey grasped the

reality at hand. It was December 24, and a miracle no less amazing than Christmas itself was about to occur. Carrying Jordan's gift under his arm, he raced up the stairs to his apartment and headed for his bedroom. The box was at the bottom of his closet near the back corner, tucked behind his clothes in a place where it had been all but forgotten.

Casey slid it out and tore through it until he found the old Bible.

The one he'd had as a fifteen-year-old boy.

Then, as carefully and quickly as he could, he thumbed his way to the back, to the thirteenth chapter of 1 Corinthians, to a place where he was convinced he'd find it. And sure enough, there it was. The pressed purple flower, the one Maggie had given him that week. And written in his own youthful handwriting was this simple sentence:

Pray for a miracle for Maggie Howard.

Casey stared at it until the words faded and became pine trees, tall and proud, anchored in the sandy shore of Lake Tahoe. He'd gone there every summer with his parents, even after he met Maggie. Every year until he graduated from high school he'd looked for her, but she never returned to the lake.

She had seemed so sad back then, so sure that love

was a fraud. And he, a preacher's boy, had been so sure otherwise. Love was good and kind and pure and true. Love never failed. Wasn't that the message of his boyhood days, the message his father preached from the pulpit every Sunday?

His name was Kade Cummins, and back then he'd gone by Kade.

But sometime during his freshman year on the baseball team, the players began calling him by his initials, K. C. And in time, it was the only name he knew. Casey Cummins. He'd kept his promise to Maggie, praying for her every time he opened his Bible until he left for Haiti. That year his father gave him a new Bible as a going-away present, and his old one was packed away in a box of baseball trophies and old high school mementos.

He still thought about Maggie often that first year in Port-au-Prince.

But after he met Amy, his thoughts took a different direction, and not until tonight, when Megan told the story, did the pieces all finally and completely fall together. He'd spent years praying for Maggie Howard, praying that she'd find real love one day. And then—when his life had been little more than a chance to remember the past—God had brought the two of them together so that he, he himself, could be the answer he'd prayed for all those years ago.

And it had all happened on Christmas Eve.

If that wasn't a Christmas miracle, Casey wasn't sure what was.

Of course, it wasn't a complete miracle, not yet. Not until he could look into Maggie's eyes, the eyes he'd first met as a boy, and know without a doubt that she believed in love again. The kind of love he'd taught her to believe in back on the sandy shores of Lake Tahoe.

It was nearly midnight, but Casey didn't care. He picked up the phone, punched in Megan's number, and waited. She answered on the third ring.

"Hello?"

"Megan, it's me, Casey. I'm sorry to call so late."

"No . . . no, it's fine. I was up." She hesitated. "Are you okay? You sound like something's wrong."

"Everything's just fine, actually, but I have a favor to ask you."

"Anything, Casey." He could hear the relief in her voice. "Whatever you want."

Casey kept his words as slow and calm as possible. "Have your mother watch Jordan tomorrow morning at ten o'clock. Meet me at the East Meadow, at the bench near the big slide." He stopped himself from saying anything more. "Please, Megan."

She paused. "Of course. I'll be there at ten."

After they hung up, Casey found a blank Christmas card and began to write. When he was finished, he searched his top dresser drawer until he found an old velvet box. His heart raced as he checked the contents. It might not be a perfect fit, but it would work for what he wanted to do.

Sleep came slowly, in fits and starts, but Casey didn't mind. He couldn't stop thinking about what had happened, and more than that, how the timing was so utterly fitting. Everything was coming together on the most beautiful day of the year, the day when miracles truly did happen all around them.

Christmas Day.

CHAPTER TWELVE

Megan arrived at ten o'clock exactly.

It was cold and windy, a Christmas morning when nearly everyone else was still opening gifts and enjoying the warmth of their families. Megan looked beyond the empty play area to the bench at the back near the big slide, the one nestled against the bushes. She pulled her long wool coat tight around her neck, and lifted the collar to ward off a gust coming off the reservoir.

Casey was nowhere.

She checked her watch and saw that it was a minute after ten. Strange . . . Casey wasn't usually late. Careful on the icy gravel, she slowly made her way toward the bench. She was ten feet away when she saw it.

Sitting squarely on the middle of it was a wrapped gift. Megan's heart beat faster, and again she glanced around, looking for Casey. Had he already come and left her this present? It seemed an odd thing to do. After all, he'd brought her roses the night before, and if he'd had another gift, he would've given it to her then.

She shivered and walked the remaining distance to the bench. The gift was large, about the size of a big book. On the top was a card with her name written across the front, and tucked beneath the ribbon was a small pressed azalea, pale purple and tinged brown around the edges of the petals. Megan brought it to her face and breathed in the faint musty smell. Something about the flower was strangely familiar. Where had she seen it before?

She lowered the gift and turned enough to scan the play area. "Casey?" She waited, but there was no response. He must've left the gift, but why? Why here, and why hadn't he waited for her?

She opened the card, pulled it from the envelope, and began to read.

I've prayed for you a thousand times, Maggie Howard. Open your present and turn to 1 Corinthians, chapter 13. Then you'll know what I mean.

Megan's hands began to shake, and once more she glanced around, looking for Casey. A wind gust played with her hair, and she brushed it away from her eyes. Whatever did he mean, he'd prayed for her a thousand times? And why had he referred to her by her maiden name, the name she'd used as a little girl? She took the delicate pressed flower and set it in the card, then slipped them both into her pocket.

Without waiting another moment, she slid her fingers into the seam in the paper, and pulled it off the gift. Beneath the wrapping was an old, worn Bible, cracked and faded from the years. And embossed at the lower right corner was the owner's name.

Kade Cummins.

Megan gasped and nearly dropped the Bible. With her free hand she brought her fingers to her mouth and stared at the cover as everything around her began to tilt. How had Casey gotten Kade's Bible? And what about the flower? Was that the one she'd picked twenty years ago, the one she'd asked Kade to hold on to so he wouldn't forget her? And what did Casey mean by having her open it here, now?

She tucked the Bible beneath her arm and checked the card once more. 1 Corinthians, chapter 13. Megan slid the card into the front part of the big book, and after a few frantic moments she found the place. There, written in fading ink, were words that made her heart stop.

Pray for a miracle for Maggie Howard.

Nothing made sense, and Megan wondered if she

might faint. If this was Kade's Bible, then how had Casey gotten it? And why had he said in the card the prayers had come from him, and not Kade? She was about to gather the Bible to her chest and sit down on the bench when she heard something behind her. Her heart jolted into an unfamiliar beat and she turned around.

"Merry Christmas, Maggie." Casey was coming toward her, his eyes sparkling as he made his way.

"Casey . . . what . . . how'd you get this?"

He stopped a few inches from her, lifted the Bible from her arms, and set it on the bench. Then he took her hands in his and spoke words that made the blood drain from her face. "Kade, Maggie. My name's Kade."

"No . . ." she shook her head. "That's . . . that's impossible. Kade was . . . he was blonde and skinny and freckled and . . . you're Casey . . . you couldn't be . . ." Her voice faded, and she could no longer find the words. As strong as Megan Wright could be in court, she was suddenly thirteen again, desperate to believe in a love that wouldn't fail.

"Maggie, it's me. I promise." Casey must've known she was about to fall. He pulled her closer, let her lean on him for support. "I lost the blonde hair and freckles when I turned twenty. And everyone's called me by my initials since high school."

An explosion of feelings went off in Megan's heart. Disbelief and shock and the overwhelming sense that she was dreaming. "You . . . filled out." She remembered to breathe.

"Yes." A low chuckle sounded in his chest and he stroked her hair.

"I can't . . . is . . . is it true? You're really him?"

"I am. And see, Maggie, I was right all those years ago, wasn't I?"

She was still too shocked to answer, too amazed that she was in the arms of a man who so long ago had given her a reason to hope, a reason to believe in love. And now . . . now he'd done that all over again before she'd even known it was him.

"Remember the secret prayer Jordan and I had for you?"

"Yes . . . yes, I remember." Strength was returning to Megan's knees, and now her shock was being replaced by an explosive joy and a hundred questions. "What did you pray?"

"We prayed for a Christmas miracle, that you'd believe in love again."

"You did?"

"Uh-huh. Not so different from the way I prayed for you every day back when I was a boy."

Megan peered into his soul. "Kade Cummins, is that really you?"

He didn't answer her with words. Instead, he took her face in his hands and kissed her. Not the momentary kiss from the night before, but a kiss that silenced her doubts and her questions as well. When he drew back, he whispered her name against her cheek. The name he'd known her by nearly two decades.

"Maggie, I have something else to tell you. Something about Jordan."

She was lost in his embrace, falling the way she hadn't believed it possible to fall. Still, she forced herself to find his eyes again, to search them for whatever he had to tell her. "Okay . . ."

"I can't be Jordan's special friend anymore." Casey pulled back and studied her face. "Because after all of this, I could never be just a special friend to him."

Megan stared at Casey, not sure what he was saying. Why had he kissed her if he wasn't planning to stay? "You . . . you mean you're leaving us?"

"No, silly." Casey took her hands and kissed her again. "I didn't say that."

"You said you couldn't be his special friend anymore."

"No. I can't be his special friend." Casey locked eyes

with her once more, and she felt her heart come to life within her. "Not when all I want . . . is to be his daddy." He let go of one of her hands, reached into his coat pocket, and pulled out something small and shiny. "This . . ." he held it out to her, "belonged to my grandmother."

It was a diamond solitaire, brilliant and set in band of exquisitely etched white gold.

Her gasp was soft, but loud enough for him to hear. He smiled at her, his eyes glazed with tears, and suddenly she knew what was coming, knew he was about to say the words that would change all their lives forever.

And rather than fear it or dread it or doubt it in the least, Megan could hardly wait to say yes. Casey held the ring to her finger and slipped it over her knuckle. Then he kissed her again and spoke the words she was dying to hear.

"Marry me, Maggie Howard. Marry me, and let me love you the way you've always wanted to be loved. Let me be a daddy to Jordan, and let me show you that real love never fails." He hesitated, and she felt tears in her own eyes now. "And together I promise we'll spend forever remembering this moment and believing that yes . . . Christmas miracles really do happen."

EPILOGUE

It was October again, a year since he'd written the first letter, and now he could hardly wait to write this one. Jordan's parents were in the next room, so he took a piece of paper from his desk drawer—the place where his third-grade homework lay stacked neatly inside. Then he picked his nicest pen from the box on his desk, and steadied his hand over the paper.

Dear God . . .

He smiled at the way his letters looked, then he sucked in a big breath and began again.

> *I've wanted to write you for a long time, but I wated so I could tell you how good everything is. Plus also my spelling is better so I can write more stuff now. I hope you get this letter, because the daddy you sent me is the best*

daddy in the whole wide world. And plus something else. My mommy believes in love again. I heard her tell that to Daddy the nite before they got married.

I got to ware my nisest clothes for the wedding, and everyone said they could feel you there with us. I could feel you, too, and not just because it was Valentines Day. Because your kind of love is there every day of the year.

I know it because Daddy says so, and Daddy knows a lot about love.

Anyway, I wanted to tell you thanks for reading my letter and making everthing turn out so great. I'll write you again next year. Love, Jordan.

P.S. Thanks for hearing my prayer about a baby sister. Mommy says she'll be here before Christmas.

THE RED GLOVES SERIES

Last year, many of you journeyed with me through the pages of my first Warner Christmas story, *Gideon's Gift*. In that book, I shared with you the miracle of a sick little girl and an angry, homeless man, and the gift that changed both their lives forever. And in honor of Gideon's precious gift, at the back of that book I suggested several Red Gloves Projects for you and your friends and families.

In the hundreds of letters you've written me since then, I've heard one theme resonate loudly. You love the idea of the red gloves. Red for Christmas, red for a heart full of love and hope and Christmas miracles.

Red, the color of giving.

And because of that, I've decided to let the red gloves of *Gideon's Gift* play a cameo role in each of my Warner

Christmas stories. The Red Gloves Series, we're calling it, and each book will have a new list of Red Gloves Projects. As one of you told me last year, "I bought fifty copies of *Gideon's Gift* to give to everyone I know. My prayer is that we'd see red gloves all around us in the coming years, that they'd grace the hands of the homeless and widowed, the children without parents and parents without hope. So that red gloves would forever be the symbol of Christ's love at Christmas."

In that light, I bring you this year's Red Gloves Projects.

More Red Gloves Projects

1. Adopt an orphan through WorldVision or another international organization you feel is trustworthy. For usually pennies a day, you can make a difference in the life of at least one child and be to that little boy or girl a Christmas miracle every day of the year. Once you've chosen your child, send him or her a pair of red gloves. Then cut out the child's picture and attach it to a red glove, which can hang in your home all year long.

2. Contact your local branch of Social Services and find out how many children in your area are awaiting fam-

ilies. Make a list of the names of those children and commit along with your friends or family to pray for each of them. Buy gifts for these children, along with several pairs of red gloves, and take the wrapped presents to the local Social Services office. Ask that they be delivered to the children waiting for families.

3. If you're single and able to be more involved, check if your area has an organization that pairs lonely children with willing adults. Make a yearlong commitment to a child, and make your first gift to him or her a pair of red gloves with an explanation that red is the color of giving.

4. Talk to your local public elementary school or contact your church leaders, and locate a needy family in your area. Purchase presents for the family, and deliver them while wearing red gloves. Adorn the packages with red gloves for each of the children in the family.

I pray this finds you and your family doing well this Christmas, determined to mend broken relationships and let fall the walls that have come between you and those you love. God gave us the greatest gift of all that first Christmas Day. How much richer we—like Casey Cummins—are when we follow His example and give something back.

Especially something to a child.

Please check out my Web site at www.KarenKingsbury.com for more information about the Red Gloves Projects that have happened since last year. And leave me a note in my guestbook. As always, I'd love to hear from you, and if you have a Red Gloves Project idea you'd like to share with me, please do. I'll add it to my Web site and perhaps suggest it in my Warner Christmas story next year.

Until then, may God's light and life be yours in the coming year.

In His love,

Karen Kingsbury

www.KarenKingsbury.com

Sarah's Song

Sarah's Song

A NOVEL

KAREN KINGSBURY

WARNER
Faith®

NEW YORK BOSTON NASHVILLE

The words to "Sarah's Song" are copyrighted by Karen Kingsbury and used by permission.

Scriptures are taken from the HOLY BIBLE: NEW INTERNATIONAL VERSION®. Copyright © 1973, 1978, 1984 by International Bible Society. Used by permission of Zondervan Publishing House. All rights reserved.

Warner Faith
Time Warner Book Group
1271 Avenue of the Americas, New York, NY 10020
Visit our Web site at www.twbookmark.com

The Warner Faith name and logo are registered trademarks of Warner Books.

Book design by Fearn Cutler de Vicq
Printed in the United States of America
First Warner Books printing: September 2004
10 9 8 7 6 5 4 3 2 1

Library of Congress Cataloging-in-Publication Data

Kingsbury, Karen.
    Sarah's song / Karen Kingsbury.
        p. cm. — (The red gloves series)
    ISBN 0-446-53235-5
    1. Older women—Fiction. 2. Nursing students—Fiction. 3. Female friendship—Fiction. 4. Nursing home patients—Fiction. 5. Reminiscing in old age—Fiction. I. Title.
    PS3561.I4873S27 2004
    813'.54—dc22   2004006484

To Donald, my prince charming—you know the words to my song and sing it with me whenever I forget.

To Kelsey, my only daughter—your heart is laced together with mine; I feel it even when I'm a world away.

To Tyler, my music lover—you dream of Broadway and sing the soundtrack in the fairy tale that is our life.

To Sean, my tender boy—look over your shoulder at how far you've come, and try to imagine the rainbows ahead.

To Josh, my gentle giant—your strength is surpassed only by your ability to love. How glad I am that God gave you to us.

To EJ, my wide-eyed wonder—you are becoming everything we knew you could be; the sunbeam of your life keeps me warm on the coldest days.

To Austin, my miracle boy—your every heartbeat is testimony to God's grace and mercy. I see your fist raised to the sky after a soccer goal, and I can only think that somewhere in heaven the angels are doing the same thing.

And to God Almighty, who has—for now—blessed me with these.

Sarah's Song

It's not too late for faith to find us.
Not too late for right to win.
Not too late, let love remind us.
Not too late to try again.

In my life the straight and narrow had a face, and
it was yours.
I took crooked paths around you, shut you out,
and locked the doors.
Long I wandered tired and aimless, seeking all the
world might hold.
There you waited, true and blameless, soul of
goodness, heart of gold.

Nothing lasting came of those days, months of bitter freezing rain.
I was blinded, couldn't see you, choosing sorrow,
living pain.

Then one day I looked behind me, at the way life
  could've been.
Suddenly I had to find you, had to see your face
  again.

Somewhere in my mind I see a place for me and
  you.
A place where faith might find a future, give us
  both a life brand new.
Together in God's mighty grip is where we both be-
  long.
Find me, know me, teach your heart the words to
  Sarah's Song.

  It's not too late for faith to find us.
  Not too late for right to win.
  Not too late for love to bind us.
  Not too late to try again.

Sarah's Song

THE RITUAL WAS SACRED, drawn out for twelve days, the same every Christmas.

Sarah Lindeman looked out the smudged window of her cramped room at Greer Retirement Village, and already she could hear the music, feel her tired, old vocal chords coming together to sing again. The way they came together every thirteenth of December.

The box was opened, its contents spread across the worn bedspread. Twelve envelopes, yellowed and faded by the years, the way all of life was faded now. All except the memory of that single year, the year when heaven cracked open and spilled stardust and miracles into the life of a young woman who had given up hope.

She was that girl, and the year was 1941.

Patched together, the events of that time created a journey, a story she remembered still, every teardrop and smile, every exchange of words, every bit of laughter. Every impossible twist and turn down the alleys of a yesterday even time couldn't touch.

Sarah had broken the story into twelve parts, created twelve paper ornaments, each with a single word or words to remind her. Over the years it became the ritual it was today. Twelve ornaments, one each for the twelve days of Christmas, a chance each December to drift back through the decades, back to 1941, and remember it all again.

And there was the song, of course, playing in the background, standing like an anthem for all they'd known, all she missed now that he was gone. The notes, the melody, the haunting refrains pulled from the story of their lives. Always she would sing the song. She would hum it at first, and then as the days of December wore on, the words would come. They would come as they had at the beginning, born of despair, desperate for a second chance.

All of it, every word, every note, for Sam.

Sarah turned around, leaned hard into her aluminum walker, and shuffled to the bed. Distant voices filled the hallway outside her room, staff assistants talking to the elderly residents the way young people did these days, loud and condescending; someone going on about the cooking staff and its bland version of lasagna.

And somewhere above it all the piped-in refrains of "Silent Night."

Sarah eased herself down next to the envelopes. The bed seemed lower all the time. Her hips hurt worse this year, and each breath came slower, with more effort. No doubt her time was short. Death wasn't far off.

Not that Sarah minded. Dying, after all, would reunite her with Sam.

Had it been thirteen years since his death? Thirteen years since she'd shared this Christmas ritual with the man who had made it possible? Back then they'd gone through the twelve days together—taking out the ornaments, finding their way through the days and months and years back to 1941, remembering their story.

Singing the song.

She was eighty-six now, and if Sam had lived he'd be ninety-one. Instead, cancer had taken him—not slowly over a course of years, but in six months. That May he was traveling with her to Los Angeles to see the kids, to welcome the birth of a great-granddaughter. A sluggish few weeks, a bad blood test, and he was gone before Thanksgiving.

At first Sarah lived alone in the old house where they'd raised their two children and entertained grandchildren. The house was as much a part of the glorious past as anything else because it was walking distance to the park, the place where it had all come together.

But more years passed and she grew tired, too tired to dress in the morning or take a walk or shop for groceries. Heart failure, the doctor told her. Nothing imminent, just a slow and steady decline that would worsen over time.

After her diagnosis, the kids had taken a week off work and tried to talk her into moving to LA. Sarah was gracious, glad for their concern, but only one place could possibly serve as her final home, the place where she would live out her days.

The facility was built across from the park the summer after Sam died. Greer Retirement Village. Assisted living, they called it. An oversized bedroom with space enough for a recliner and television. Also a kitchenette with a sink, a microwave, and small refrigerator. The staff organized bingo on Tuesdays, Bible study on Wednesdays, low-impact aerobics on Thursdays, and old movies on Fridays. Meals were served on china and linen twice a day in the dining room, and on weekends they had live entertainment in the form of Mr. Johnson, the assistant manager who also played the piano.

Most of all, each room had emergency buttons near the bed and in the bathroom, and staff assistants who came by to remind residents about their medication—how much and when to take it.

And so, after a few days' discussion, the kids had come around and reserved Sarah a place at the village. A room on the first floor overlooking the park and the bench. The very same bench where Sarah had written the song in the first place.

"I'll never leave," she told the kids before they returned to LA. "This—" She waved toward the window and the park and the bench beyond. "—is where I'll feel your father every day." She hesitated. "I'll come see you; don't worry."

They understood, both Harry who was fifty-five that year, and Sharon, fifty-three. And at first Sarah kept her promise, heading for California two weeks each summer and two weeks in January. But her heart failure progressed, and three years back the doctor ordered her to stop flying. Sarah was moved to the third floor, to a wing that was more nursing home than assisted living.

But she kept her view of the park bench.

And she kept the ritual, the twelve days of Christmas.

Sarah rested her weathered fingers on the first envelope and a thrill worked its way through her. The story always did that to her, always moved her heart a few inches closer to her throat and made her mouth dry. No matter how many decades had passed, the memory of that year made her feel young and in love and awed by the miracle they'd shared.

She dusted her fingertips over the old envelopes one at a time, the numbers scrawled across the fronts reminding her, filling her spirit, readying her soul for the remembering that was to come. If this was the last time, the last Christmas, then she'd need a little help.

Her eyes narrowed and she lifted her face toward the window. "Dear God . . ." The words were a scratchy whisper. "Make the days come to life again, every moment. Please."

The quiet prayer hung in the room for a moment, and then slowly a thought began to form. If this was the last time she was going to remember, the last time she would sing her song, then someone had to hear it. Not just hear it but feel it—feel it in the fabric of their heart the way Sarah did.

God had promised her that much, hadn't He?

A stranger needing encouragement, a doctor or a nurse, one of the staff assistants. Someone at Greer Retirement Village who would be changed by "Sarah's Song," the way she had been changed by it so long ago.

She cleared her throat and struggled to her feet again. The walker seemed lighter, her bones filled with an energy that came every December. When she reached the window, with a clear view of the park bench, she finished her prayer.

"Send someone, God. Someone who needs hope." She could feel her eyes dancing despite the cataracts that clouded them. "Someone who could learn the song."

When she finished praying, a certainty filled her and made her long for tomorrow, the first of the twelve days. Something different was going to happen this time; she could feel it in her soul.

Now all she had to do was wait.

CHAPTER ONE

DECEMBER 13 DAWNED bright and sunny, unseasonably warm according to the morning nurse. Sarah didn't mind. Temperatures in South Carolina could change in an afternoon, and snow wasn't out of the question. Even for the week ahead. Snow had been a part of their first December; it was bound to come sometime in the next twelve days.

Beth Baldwin was in charge that morning. Beth was a young caregiver who never spoke more than the essentials. *Good morning. How are you? Nice December we're having.* That sort of thing. Beth was married, or at least Sarah suspected as much since Beth wore a wedding ring. She was a pretty girl, a gentle caregiver, but her eyes were wild and restless. They reminded Sarah of something she couldn't quite take hold of.

"Beth, dear, do you know what day it is?" Sarah leaned forward so Beth could ease her into her red Christmas sweater.

The young woman blew a wisp of dark hair off her forehead. Her voice was pleasant, but she didn't make eye contact. "Monday, December 13."

A soft chuckle came from Sarah's throat. "No, dear. I don't mean the date, I mean the day." Sarah waited until she had Beth's attention.

"The day?" Beth straightened, one hand on her hip. "I give up; what's special about today?"

"Why, it's the First Day of Christmas!"

Beth cocked her head. "You mean like the song? The partridge in a pear tree and all that Twelve Days of Christmas stuff?"

"Yes." Sarah tugged on the sides of her sweater, and when it lay smooth around her scant frame, she eased back against the pillow. "Today's the first day."

"Hmmm." Beth took hold of the water pitcher sitting on Sarah's bedside table. "I thought those were the twelve days after Christmas."

"Only in the history books, dear. My twelve days begin today."

"Oh." Beth stopped. "Okay. That's nice I guess." With purposeful steps, she went to the sink, rinsed the pitcher, filled it, and returned it to its place. "I guess that means one thing." She stopped and gave Sarah a lopsided smile. "Twelve shopping days until Christmas."

Sarah pursed her lips, the prayer from last night playing over in her mind. Beth wasn't the one; she wouldn't hold a conversation, never mind listen to a story that stretched over twelve days.

"You know the routine." Beth headed for the door with a glance over her shoulder. "Press the call button if you need anything."

"Thank you, Beth. I'll be okay for a few—"

She was gone. Sarah stared at the closed door and gave a gentle shrug of her shoulders. Just as well. If Beth wasn't the one she'd prayed for, better to be alone for the first day of the ritual. She'd been waiting for this moment since the leaves began turning orange back in October.

The envelopes lay fanned out on her nightstand in numerical order, the small plastic tree set up a few inches away, pressed against the wall. Sarah shifted to that side of the bed and let her legs hang over the side until her woolly socks rested on the cold linoleum floor.

The first envelope called out to her, begging to be

opened. She lifted the flap, removed the paper ornament, and studied the word scrawled across both sides.

Tomorrow.

That's what she had wanted that cold January day, wasn't it? Everything about tomorrow. Today, what she had in the moment, was never enough. Not Greer or her parents or their faith. Not even Sam. Everything she'd done back then was focused on tomorrow, that far-off day when she could go after everything country music had to offer. Everything a young woman with her looks and voice and determination deserved. Everything her small town of Greer couldn't offer. Every moment of it.

Tomorrow.

Sarah studied the word, the faded ink, and bit by bit the piped-in music, the conversations in the hall, the aches and pains of nearly nine decades, all grew dim. She closed her eyes, and in a rush she felt herself going back, pulled into a time that still existed, a time that had never really ended at all. She blinked her eyes open, and she was no longer perched on the edge of her bed at Greer Retirement Village.

She was twenty-three, in her parents' farmhouse across the street from the high school. Her mother was canning in the kitchen and the smell of warm apples and cinnamon filled the air. It was Christmas Eve 1940, and

Sam Lindeman was over. The way Sam always had been back then.

Sarah fingered the paper ornament in her hand and blinked. She felt the weathered skin above her eyebrows bunch up and she pulled herself from the memory. She couldn't start in 1940. No, she had to go back to her girl-hood days, when she dreamed day and night of catching Sam's attention, dating him, and one day marrying him.

Sam was five years older than her, the brother of Sarah's best friend, Mary. Though the Lindemans sometimes vacationed with Sarah's family, Sam never noticed Sarah in the early years. His age stood like an ocean, the span of time too far to consider bridging. But sometime after her twelfth birthday, despite their age difference, Sarah fell hard for him.

"He's so cute," she would tell Mary whenever the two were visiting. Back then, they spent hours listening to records in Mary's room, pretending they were famous singers.

"Nah," Mary would wrinkle her nose and turn up the music. "He's just my bossy brother."

Sam played football for Greer High and Sarah used to dream of aging four years overnight, waking one morning, showing up at the high school, and being Sam Lindeman's girl. They would graduate high school and head for some foreign land—Spain, maybe, or the South of France or the Bahamas. One of the places her teachers were always talking about.

In the dream, Sam would lead tourists on daring excursions and she would gain fame and fortune singing— not in a church choir the way her mother wanted her to sing, but in fancy dance halls and nightclubs, decked in beautiful gowns, with Sam sitting in the front row smiling at her.

The dream never panned out. Every morning Sarah woke up still twelve years old, and the next year Sam graduated from high school and went off to college without so much as a good-bye to his kid sister's little friend.

Years passed, and Sarah kept singing. By the time she turned seventeen everyone in Greer knew about her gift.

She'd been born with a voice that could silence a room; a voice her mama said would make angels cry with envy. Sarah proved it again and again, every Sunday when the church choir featured her as a soloist. Each week Sarah smiled and sang her heart out. But she hated singing in a choir robe. She kept a small calendar beneath her bed where she counted down the days until she could finish high school and take her singing somewhere exciting—Nashville or New York or Chicago. Anywhere but Greer.

One summer Sam returned home for an entire month. Four years had passed since Sam left for college, and he no longer figured into Sarah's dreams. Sarah would never forget the first time she saw him that July day. That morning at the Lindeman house, she was on her way up the stairs to find Mary when she heard a man's voice call to her from the dining room.

She turned and there he was. Sam Lindeman, twenty-two years old, taller, more filled out and more handsome than she had remembered. Sarah's breath caught in her throat and she froze near the bottom of the stairs. Visions of Spain and France and the Bahamas flashed in her mind.

"Sarah, look at you." He crossed the parlor to the place where she stood. His voice fell a notch and his eyes seemed to find her for the first time. "What happened to the little girl down the street?"

"Uh . . ." Heat rushed into Sarah's cheeks and she remembered to smile. "I grew up." She batted her eyelashes, willing herself to exhale.

"I guess so." He leaned against the wall, watching her. "You must be, what, seventeen now?"

"Yes." She was breathing again, but her racing heart threatened to give her away. "I'll be a senior in the fall."

"You're beautiful. I almost didn't recognize you."

"Gosh," Sarah lowered her chin, suddenly shy. "Thanks. I mean . . . I guess we both grew up, huh?"

"Yeah." He was quiet for a moment, a smile playing at the corners of his lips. "Can I ask you something, little Sarah all grown up?"

She giggled and felt some of her confidence return. "Ask."

"I'm taking my sister out for burgers tonight." His smile was as true as time, and her knees grew weak again. "Wanna come?"

Sarah didn't have to think about her answer. "Yes" was out of her mouth almost as soon as he finished asking. Her parents wouldn't mind; not if Mary was going along. Besides, Sarah chided herself, Sam wasn't interested in her. He was only being nice, probably wanting to catch up on the past four years.

That night they bowled before dinner and Sam entertained them with hilarious stories about his roommates back at college. Later, halfway through the meal, conversation turned to Sam's plans after college. Travel, Sarah expected him to say. Exploration and adventure and daring, the sort of life that long ago she had dreamed they'd share together.

Instead, he set his burger down and leaned forward.

"I'm getting my teaching certificate and coming back home." His eyes held a new sort of knowing as they found hers. "I'll marry a local girl, raise a family; and teach in Greer. Be the principal one day." He shifted his attention back to his sister. "That's all I've ever wanted. Sooner the better." Once more he looked at her. "How about you, Sarah? What are you doing after high school?"

Sarah's head was still spinning from his answer. "I'm leaving Greer, getting a recording contract."

"Really?" His expression held a hint of amusement. "Someone told me you could sing."

"She's amazing." Mary ate a French fry and nodded hard. "One day everyone will know Sarah."

"That's the plan." Sarah tried to find an appropriate laugh to help keep the conversation light, but none was available. Instead she excused herself.

Alone in the restroom she stared at the chipped mirror, her eyes wide. Marrying a local girl right out of college was one thing, but Sam Lindeman living and teaching in Greer? Forever in a town where the closest thing to entertainment was Al's Drive-In or family night at the library?

She shuddered and fear took a stab at her composure.

As a girl she'd dreamed of following Sam to the ends of the earth, and now that he was home, now that he'd finally noticed her, those feelings were coming to life again. But she never imagined the dream would take her no farther than the Greer city limit sign.

A mix of emotions competed for control inside her. She was in trouble. Not because of the way Sam had looked at her when he talked about his future, but because of the way her heart leapt within her when he did.

SARAH RAN HER THUMB over the first ornament and pressed her other hand into the small
of her back. The first day of the Christmas ritual was always the longest.

Two years passed before she saw Sam Lindeman again.

This time it was August, and Sam found her working at
The Mixer, a diner with cheap food, a jukebox, and more
teenagers than tables. Sarah was delivering a platter of
cheese pizza to a group of baseball players when Sam walked
through the door. A booth full of girls looked his way and
began whispering and giggling, trying to get his attention.

He ignored them, and from his spot near the door he

searched until he found her. "Hi." The word was silent, mouthed as he held up one hand and gave her a brief wave.

She served the food, wiped her hands, and met him near the door. "Sam!" Without thinking, she stood on her toes and hugged him. "You're back."

"I did it, Sarah." He grinned. "You're looking at Jackson Elementary's new fourth-grade teacher."

A warning bell sounded on the panel of Sarah's heart, but she spoke too fast to heed it. "That's great, Sam!" She felt her eyebrows raise, and she clasped her hands, happy for him. "Mary didn't tell me you'd be home this soon."

His smile softened. "I thought you'd be gone. Off to find that recording contract."

The reminder stung. "I'm saving up the money. Then I'm going to Nashville." She lifted her chin, proud of her efforts. "I work seven days most weeks."

"Well," Sam's eyes met hers and held them. "If you can spare a night this weekend, I'd love to take you out."

"Really?" Sarah glanced at her tables, making sure none of her customers needed her. Butterflies rose and fell in her stomach. A date? With Sam Lindeman? She looked at him again, suddenly shy and soft spoken. "That'd be nice."

"Okay." He leaned in and kissed her on the cheek. "See you at six o'clock Saturday."

The days that followed were painfully slow.

"Is it a date?" her mother wanted to know before he showed up in his new Rambler. "Because I'm not sure a girl of nineteen should be seeing a man in his twenties."

"Mama, it's Sam. Our neighbor, remember? We used to vacation with them and you never worried."

In the end, her mother relented, agreeing that Sam couldn't possibly be a threat. Sarah had to laugh about her mama's reaction. Sam never wanted to leave Greer. If her mother had known that, she'd have Sarah married to him by Christmas.

Of course, regardless of what she told her mother, that first night definitely felt like a date. Sam brought her flowers, opened doors for her, and made her laugh so hard at one point she had tears streaming down her face. Before he walked her up the steps to her house that night, he turned and the two of them locked eyes. "I had fun tonight."

The summer temperatures had cooled and a strong breeze sifted over the front yard and up onto the porch. Sarah moved closer, so that only a few inches separated them. She was five-foot-seven, but he was still much taller than her. She held her breath. "Can I ask you something?"

He stuck his hands in his jeans pockets and the moonlight shone in his eyes. "Anything."

"Okay." She tilted her head, trying to figure him out. "Was this a date?"

His expression changed and slowly, a fraction of an inch at a time, he took hold of her hands and drew her close. Then, in the sweetest single moment of Sarah's life to that point, he kissed her. Sarah was dizzy with the feelings swirling inside her, glad she had Sam to lean against. Otherwise her knees wouldn't have held her up.

When they pulled apart, Sam searched her eyes. "Does that answer your question?"

Sarah had a dozen things to say, a hundred questions, but she let the most pressing rise to the top. "How long, Sam?" She exhaled, trying to catch her breath. "When did you stop seeing me as Mary's little friend?"

A sigh eased from Sam's lips. He released one of Sarah's hands and wove his fingers through her hair. "You wanna know?" He leaned in and kissed her again. "That morning when I saw you at the foot of our stairs. You were seventeen, and I thought I'd seen a vision. This blonde, blue-eyed angel walks through the front door and all of a sudden I realize it's you. Mary's friend, Sarah."

"But you didn't call." Sarah swallowed. Maybe she

shouldn't be telling him this; maybe it would only make it harder to leave once she had the money to get away from Greer. "I thought . . ."

"I had school." He let his lips brush against her forehead, her cheekbones. "You had to grow up. But now, here we are." He drew back and gave her a crooked smile. "Maybe you're not supposed to leave Greer, Sarah. Ever think about that?"

She couldn't say anything. At that moment, all she wanted was to be lost in Sam's arms forever. Nothing could've pulled her from him. But later that night after he was gone, she reminded herself of the truth. No matter how much she enjoyed Sam's company, she had to move ahead with her plans. Leaving was something she'd spent a lifetime wanting, and not even Sam Lindeman could make her stay.

At least that was the idea.

In the end, Sarah did stay, for a while, anyway. For the next four years she dated Sam on and off. He took college courses toward his administrative credentials and hinted about marriage. She continued to sing at church, and without fail Sam sat in the second row, watching.

When Sam would call for a date, Sarah couldn't help but say yes. She loved him, didn't she? Besides, by then most of her friends were married and having babies. A night out with Sam was better than a night at home with her parents or an extra shift at The Mixer.

Every few months, Sarah counted her money and every few months she convinced herself she needed more if she wanted to do well in Nashville. In hindsight, she was only doing what was safe. Staying in Greer, dating the only man she'd ever desired, dreaming about a far-off future, but never actually packing her bags and making it happen.

Finally on Christmas Eve of 1940, Sam presented her with a ring. "Be my wife, Sarah." He dropped to one knee and the small diamond solitaire shone in the glow of the Christmas lights.

This was the part of the memory that matched most with the first ornament, the part that pained Sarah even now.

As if it had only just happened, Sarah could see herself. The way she stared at the ring as her head began to spin. How had she let their relationship get so serious? Why had it taken so long to save up the money to leave Greer, and how come she hadn't talked more often about her plans? There'd never been any question that she would leave as soon as she had the money.

Hadn't she made that clear?

With Sam still kneeling, still waiting for her answer, her words began tumbling out. "Sam, I'm sorry . . . I never . . ." She looked down, pinched the bridge of her nose, and gave a hard shake of her head. "I can't."

Slowly, as if he'd aged ten years in as many seconds, Sam stood. "Four years, Sarah." He hung his head so their foreheads touched. "You talked about moving away, but every month, every week you were still here. I thought . . ." He drew back and met her eyes. "I thought you stayed because of me; because you loved me."

"I do." She folded her arms tightly around her waist. "I care about you, Sam." Tears stung her eyes but she blinked them away. She hated the pain in his expression, hated the fact that she'd let him think she was ready to get married. "It's not about you. I have to get out of Greer. It'd kill me to stay here forever. I have to go, find a life outside of—"

"Stop." His voice was quiet, kind. "I understand." With that, Sam's expression changed once more. He no longer looked hurt and vulnerable, but resigned. He studied her for a long time, the desire from earlier that evening gone. In its place was the brotherly look he'd had for her back when she was a young girl. "It's over; no more explanation."

Sarah bit her lip, unable to stop the tears from spilling onto her cheeks. "I'm sorry, Sam."

"Shhh." He kissed her forehead. "Don't say it."

Then, without another word, he closed the small velvet ring box, slipped on his coat, and headed for the door. Before he left, his eyes met hers one last time and he whispered, "Good-bye, Sarah."

She watched him leave and over the next hour she packed her bags. She would go even if she didn't have enough money, go even if it meant never seeing Sam again. When the holidays were over, her parents drove her to the train station where she bid them good-bye, took hold of her two oversized suitcases—one of which held an envelope with every song she'd ever written—and boarded a passenger car that would make a handful of connections and eventually take her to Nashville.

The future lay out before her as the train pulled away. She was going to Nashville, going after the dream. She wanted more than a sweet, simple life with Sam Lindeman. She wanted a big stage and a packed house, a record contract and all the glitz and glamour that went with it. She didn't want a wedding and babies.

She wanted everything tomorrow had to offer.

And the entire train ride to Nashville she was absolutely convinced that's what she would find.

❦

Sarah lowered the paper ornament to her lap.

Her back and legs were sore from sitting on the edge of the bed for so long. She closed her eyes against a wave of tears. The ritual was not without pain, especially at the beginning. How could she have walked away?

She sniffed hard and sat a bit straighter. Enough. She would take the pieces one at a time. Her eyes opened and despite her trembling fingers, she hung the ornament on one of the lower tree branches. Then she pulled her legs back onto the bed and rested against a mound of pillows. Her eyes moved across the tree— only a few feet high, sparse and dime-store green—to the ornament.

Tomorrow indeed.

A long breath made its way through her clenched teeth and she looked toward the window. The song came next. Not the words, not until it was time. But the melody at least, the tune that had turned it all around. Notes forever etched in her mind.

The song couldn't come until she reached the window. Too tired to move just yet, she waited ten minutes, fifteen, twenty, until she was finally ready. Then, with a determination bigger than yesterday, she forced her legs over the edge, found her walker, and worked herself across the floor to the window. Ahh, yes. It was there still, and now that the twelve days had begun, she could almost see them, the two of them sitting there.

She and Sam.

The tune came, quietly at first and then louder until her humming filled the space around her. She leaned against the window and lowered her chin, searching the heavens, as the song rang out, trapped in her closed mouth. He was up there somewhere, her precious Sam. Could he see her now? Hear her?

The door opened behind her. "Sarah?"

She didn't turn. The song stopped for no one, because it couldn't. Sarah had to hum it all the way through before the first day would be complete. She hummed through the verse and the chorus. When it was over, she looked at the bench one last time and then turned around. "Yes?"

Beth had taken a seat at the end of Sarah's bed. "That was beautiful; someone told me you used to sing."

"Yes." Sarah smiled. The minutes spent in the past were never long enough. She pushed her walker back to the bed and allowed Beth to help her get under the covers.

"Did you sing professionally?" She tucked the sheet

beneath Sarah's arms. Her tone was tinged with intrigue. "I mean, you know, did you record anything?"

Sarah considered the young caregiver and felt the corners of her lips lift. "I did." She leaned into the pillows. "It's a long story."

Beth looked around until her eyes fell on the small artificial tree. "Just one ornament?"

Sarah followed her gaze. "For now."

"*Tomorrow.*" Beth narrowed her eyes and looked at Sarah. "Does it mean something?"

"Yes." Sarah folded her hands. "Much." She nodded to the envelopes spread across the nightstand at the foot of the tree. "One ornament for each of the twelve days of Christmas."

"I see." Beth smoothed out the wrinkles in the bedspread. "Does each ornament have a word?"

"A word . . . and a story." Something warm ignited inside Sarah's soul. "Stay longer tomorrow. I'll tell you the story behind the second ornament. And after the twelfth day, I'll tell you the secret."

"The secret?" Beth raised an eyebrow, her expression doubtful.

"The secret to love." Sarah managed a tired smile. "It's worth finding, Beth."

"Yes, well . . ." Beth gave a quiet nod, her eyes never leaving Sarah. "I might have to come back for something that special. The secret of love, and all."

Sarah bit her tongue. Beth thought she was a doddering old fool, eccentric and troubled by the ravages of old age. Nothing could be farther from the truth, but Sarah wouldn't say so. Beth would have to find out on her own.

The conversation ran out and Beth patted Sarah's hand. "Lunch'll be ready in a few minutes; just thought I'd warn you." She stood and headed for the door before stopping. "Sarah?"

"Yes?"

"Did you write the song, the one you were humming?"

"Yes." Sarah dropped her eyes and then looked at Beth again. "It's part of the story."

Beth nodded. "I thought so."

For a moment Sarah thought the young woman would ask more questions. But instead she reached for the door. "I'll get lunch."

The knowing came as soon as Beth left the room.

So she was the one after all. The one Sarah had prayed for. And God would bring her back. She would come tomorrow and hear the story, learn about the second ornament, find hope in the telling, even learn the words to the song.

And maybe, by the twelfth day, Beth would know it well enough to sing along.

CHAPTER THREE

THE SONG stayed with her.

Beth heard it in her head the entire drive home to Spartanburg. Sad, really, the old lady sitting in her room, singing some old song, reminding herself of a story that had been forgotten for decades.

The radio in Beth's Honda didn't work, so her mind wandered to the scene ahead. This was the night. Her planning and plotting and figuring out had finally come to this. She took one hand from the wheel and snagged a piece of gum from the side pocket of her purse. Without looking, she pushed the paper wrapping off, dropped it back into her purse, and popped the gum into her mouth.

Yes, tonight was the night.

She'd been talking with her mother about the separation for weeks, making promises that her time away from her husband would only be temporary. But she'd never told Bobby, never let on that the routine that passed for their marriage was making her crazy with boredom.

Bobby's face came to mind—simple, faithful, content. Uninteresting. How would he take the news? And what about their five-year-old daughter, Brianna? Beth pictured them, Bobby and Brianna. She would be watching TV with him now, same as every afternoon. Bobby worked maintenance at the local hospital, six to two. Brianna's preschool was on his way home.

What would happen to their routine after tonight? She squinted at the sun, bright and low in the sky. The good weather wouldn't last; not in December.

The song came to mind again.

Whatever the old lady's story, Beth was sure it involved a man. Sarah Lindeman might be pushing ninety, but she was a woman after all. And a woman in love couldn't hide the fact, nineteen or ninety-nine. It was that part that made Beth doubt she'd show up to hear the story. Not when she herself had spent a lifetime longing for that look, that kind of love.

Ahead of her, the two-lane road curved first right

then left, and she saw her turn-off. The low-income neighborhood where they lived spread out for eight blocks, the houses small and old and boxy. But for the paint and a few differences in the trim, it was hard to tell one from another.

She wasn't a praying woman, but if she were, this would've been a good time to ask for help. She'd dropped out of college to marry Bobby Baldwin, and in seven years, the man had learned nothing about her. What she was about to do that night was sure to catch him off guard. She parked, grabbed her purse, and headed inside.

"Hello?" The screen door slammed behind her and she dropped her bag on the kitchen table. She turned and faced the sofa where Bobby and Brianna were watching television. Beth dropped to her knees and sat back on her heels. "Where's my Brianna bug?"

"Mommy!" Their little daughter bounced off Bobby's lap and ran across the room, honey-blonde ponytail flying behind her. "Guess what?"

"What?" Beth tried to sound excited. She nuzzled her face against Brianna's and kissed the tip of her nose.

"I made you a Cwis'mas present at school! And it was the bestest one in the whole class."

Beth smiled. "Do I get it now?"

"No," Brianna gave a hard shake of her head, her eyes serious. "Only on Cwis'mas morning."

"Okay." She looked over her daughter's shoulders at Bobby. "Tell you what, sweetie. You and Daddy can finish watching TV later."

Bobby cast her a curious look, but Beth ignored it. She stood and led Brianna down the hallway toward her bedroom. "How 'bout you go color a picture for Daddy, alright?"

Brianna gave a small gasp. Her eyes lit up, glowing with enthusiasm and innocence. "Okay, Mommy! Then I'll have a present for Daddy, too!"

"Yes, honey." Beth scooped her daughter up, held her for a minute, and walked her down the hall. "That would be very nice."

When Brianna was in her room, Beth headed back to Bobby. She could feel his eyes on her the moment she came into view, but she didn't look at him until she was seated at the other end of the sofa.

"Something wrong?" Only his eyes were directed at her; his body, his face were still locked on the TV. He still had the television remote in his hand.

Beth studied him, the tufts of brown hair sticking out of his old Braves baseball cap, the blue flannel shirt he'd worn every winter for the past five years. "Turn off the TV, Bobby." She crossed her arms. "We need to talk."

He clicked the remote and the television went dark. Then he shifted his body in her direction. "Okay." His crooked smile was still cute. It reminded her of the reasons she'd fallen for him in the first place. "What's up?"

Amazement washed over her. *Look at him,* she thought. *He doesn't have a clue what's coming.* She drew a deep breath and let the words come. "I'm leaving you, Bobby. Brianna and I are moving in with my mother."

Bobby waited a few seconds, then chuckled. "What's this? Some sort of Christmas joke?"

"No." Beth didn't blink. "I'm already packed."

The laughter in Bobby's eyes faded and his lower jaw fell open. "You're serious?"

"Yes."

A frustrated anger filled his face. "Don't be crazy, Beth. We haven't fought in a month and now you're walking out on me? At Christmastime?" He let his head fall back and forced out a mouthful of air. "Whatever's eating you, don't blame it on me, okay?" His eyes met hers. "Maybe you had a bad day. So . . . take a nap or a walk around the block. But don't threaten to leave, Beth. That isn't going to make things better."

Calm, Beth told herself. *Stay calm.* She had expected his reaction. Her voice was gentle, quieter than his. "Nothing's eating me, and I didn't have a bad day." She ran her tongue along her lower lip, searching for the words. "Look, Bobby, I've made up my mind. This—" She looked across the room and waved her hand at their cramped kitchen and then at him. "The way we live . . . you and me, none of it's the way it was supposed to turn out."

"Oh, I get it." Fire flashed in Bobby's eyes. He was a gentle man; Beth had only seen him angry a few times. Once, when she'd talked about wanting more from life, he'd thrown his guitar through the bedroom wall. She hoped this wouldn't be one of those nights. "There's someone else, right?"

She sighed and it came from the basement of her heart. "No. This isn't about anyone but me. I . . ." she lifted her shoulders. "I can't do this anymore."

He gave her a sarcastic nod. "Nice, Beth." He huffed. "What happened to the whole faith thing, living for God and doing things His way?" Bobby stood up and glared at her. "I thought marriages made in heaven didn't die. Weren't those your words?"

"Yes." She was ready for this, too. "I was young. We

were both raised in the church, but so what? When's the last time you took us to a Sunday service? For that matter, when's the last time you took me anywhere?"

"I don't need this, Beth." He gestured toward the hallway. "Brianna will hear you."

Beth didn't care. She stood up and kicked the sofa, her eyes boring into his. "Every night it's the same thing. You sit here watching that stupid television, and then you fall asleep before your head hits the pillow. We don't laugh or talk or dance or date." She was louder than she meant to be. "I had dreams when I met you." A sound that was more cry than laugh came from her. "Now look at me. I can't take one more day of it, Bobby. Not one."

His mouth opened and for a moment it looked like he might shout at her. But then he gritted his teeth and looked away.

"You promised me more than this." She hesitated, and her voice lost some of its edge. "See. You can't deny it. What we have is meaningless—an existence, nothing more."

This time when he looked at her, the fight was gone. "Is that really how you see us?"

She sucked at the inside of her lip. "Yes." Her sniff

punctuated the word. "I'm not in love with you, Bobby. I can't . . . I can't make myself feel something that isn't there. I need time. Me and Brianna will be at my mother's until I decide what to do next."

A slow disgusted shock colored his features. "Twelve days before Christmas, Beth? Couldn't you wait a few weeks? Give me a chance to make things right?"

"No!" She barely let him finish his sentence. Anxiety grabbed hold of her and shook hard. "I don't want to try again. It's not in you, Bobby. We've had this talk a dozen times. Things seem better for a week or two, but then they're right back the way they were." She spread her hands out. "This . . . this life we live is enough for you. Pretending for my sake won't turn things around. It never has before."

"Fine." Something hard as steel filled his eyes and he took a step back. "If you don't love me, I won't ask you to change your mind. But consider our daughter. Leaving now, a few weeks before Christmas? How do you think she'll feel about that?" He paused. "Wait two weeks for Brianna and then go." His lips were pinched as he spat out the last part. "I won't try to stop you."

Beth stood frozen in place, her mouth open.

What had he said? That he wouldn't try to stop her if she left after Christmas? That's what she wanted, wasn't it? It's what she'd wanted for two years. She'd expected to feel new and alive if Bobby released her, as if she'd been given a second lease on life. So, why didn't she feel better about it?

Instead her heart was heavy, and an emptiness made it hard for her to breathe.

She sat back down on the edge of the sofa. "Stay through Christmas?"

"Not for me." His look was harder than before. "For Brianna."

Beth swallowed. If she was going to leave, better to go now, right? Wasn't that what she'd decided when she made the plan? That way the holidays might take the edge off any sorrow Brianna would feel—sort of a softening of the blow.

But now, with the facts on the table, Bobby's argument made sense.

Staying home would at least give Brianna a happy Christmas, even if her parents were separating. They could keep the truth from her until the end of the month so that whatever pain Brianna felt, it wouldn't darken Christmas, too.

"Beth?" Bobby shifted his weight and flexed the muscles in his jaw.

"Okay." She looked at the ceiling. "I'll stay until the end of the month, but then we're gone."

"And until then?" Bobby looked away. His tone was so cold it made her shiver from across the room.

"Look . . ." She thought about fighting with him, then changed her mind. Her lungs emptied slowly, emphasizing her sadness. "I don't hate you. I just don't . . . I don't love you like I used to, Bobby. But Brianna doesn't have to know that." She hesitated. She hadn't counted on having to share a house with him even after he knew her feelings. "I think we need to be civil. Otherwise I can leave tonight."

"Civil?" His eyes found hers once more and this time, despite his obvious effort at indifference, the pain shone through. "Telling me two weeks before Christmas that you're walking out, Beth? Is that civil?"

They went another two rounds of her reasons and his explanations and promises, but it got them nowhere. In the end they agreed to keep their distance and focus their attention on their daughter. On giving Brianna a wonderful Christmas despite what the New Year would bring.

Beth kept to herself that evening. Sometime after nine o'clock she crept into Brianna's room and laid down on the floor. Sleep didn't find her at first. Instead a slideshow of pictures played in her mind. Bobby and her on their first date; Bobby and her playing in the snow; Bobby and her teaching Brianna how to walk. The succession of images was relentless, and all of it played out to the same piece of music. The haunting simple tune from earlier that morning, the one the old lady had written.

Sarah's song.

CHAPTER FOUR

Now that the twelve days were underway, Sarah found the transition from present to past an easy one. The words *High Hopes* were scrawled across the ornament in the second envelope, and when Sarah was certain the young caregiver wasn't coming, she allowed the memory to move ahead.

❦

She arrived in Nashville that cold January evening with more high hopes than money, but that didn't matter. Her expectations would be met; she was sure of it. She would take her songs to the first music company she could find, sing a few of her favorites, and let the executives explain the steps to getting a contract.

Money wouldn't have to be much up front. Just enough to make a living, nothing more. But touring was important. Anyone in the industry knew touring was the way to find a following and get a song on the charts. The recording company would have to send her on a tour; she would insist.

Sarah took a hotel that first night and reviewed her plan. She had enough money to last a month or so, but it wouldn't take that long. Two weeks and she'd be on her way, connected with a label and moving forward with her singing career.

Her mother and father had prayed for her before she left. That first night, alone in a dark hotel room in a strange new city, the words to her parents' prayer came rushing back.

You know Sarah's heart, God, and the future You have for her. Keep her safe and let her find the place, the purpose, and the plans You've laid out for her.

Sarah repeated the prayer several times, adding her own requests. As she did, a thought came to her. This was the first time she'd gone to sleep without her parents nearby, and yet she felt at home, comfortable. Unafraid.

Not once that first night did Sam Lindeman even cross her mind.

When morning came she set out to find her record

deal, but by dusk she'd found just one thing. A reality check. Getting a label to back her might be harder than she'd thought.

The first week blurred into the second. She visited agents and production houses and the executive offices of recording studios. Once in a while someone would look her up and down and raise a curious eyebrow. Then they'd pass her off to a talent scout or an agent or someone on the other side of town.

"Come back when you get a demo, kid," they'd tell her.

By the end of the first month, Sarah's high hopes had dwindled to one: survival. She moved her things to a seedy hotel in what was obviously the worst part of town. Talking to God didn't seem to help, so Sarah stopped praying. It was one more break with the routine of her past, and it felt good, more independent. Whatever happened next would be her doing—good or bad.

Not the result of God.

Sarah was sure her parents would be shocked with her new attitude, so she didn't tell them.

"You're praying, right, Sarah?" her mother would ask.

"Of course, Mama," she lied. "All the time."

"Us, too. God will show you the way, honey. Just keep looking."

"I will, Mama."

Her father's question was the same each time. "Finding any work?"

"Still looking, Daddy, but don't worry. Any day now."

Sarah spoke with her parents once or twice a week, and always the phone calls ended the same. Yes, she had enough money; yes, she was fine; yes, her big break was just around the corner.

Never did they mention Sam, and Sarah didn't ask. She didn't want to know. She'd walked away from Sam and the church-girl life that had all but smothered her. She was a new person, and though she wasn't always honest with her parents, she truly believed what she said about her future.

Her break into the music industry was coming. Any day and she'd be on her way.

Six weeks after arriving in Nashville, Sarah had been to every industry location in Nashville twice. She would take a cab to the general area and canvas every address in a ten-block radius. The answer was always the same—she needed experience.

By then she had reduced her expenses to one meal a day—a buffet three blocks from her hotel. The food was bland and greasy and one dish tasted suspiciously like another, but she could eat as much as she wanted, and the meal kept her going. Late that week, she spread what was left of her money across her hotel bed and realized how dire her situation had become.

She was down to eleven dollars.

If she didn't find work the next morning, she would have to leave the hotel, and then what? Call her parents and tell them she'd failed? Ask for money and risk having them see her dreams as sheer foolery?

Sarah gritted her teeth and stared at her file of songs perched on top of the cheap dresser. No, she wouldn't let that happen; she wouldn't fail. The dirty walls of her lousy room closed in a little more each day, but they would have to crush her before she'd give up. She'd get a job tomorrow and she'd do it without anyone's help.

That night before she fell asleep she stared at the mirror. Her long blonde hair and church dresses made her look sixteen, not twenty-three. Maybe the industry officials would take her seriously if she changed her look. Tucked in her bag of personal items was a pair of scissors and a small sewing kit.

With a building excitement, she grabbed them both, returned to the mirror and began cutting. Fifteen minutes later she'd given herself an entirely new look. Her short bob wasn't the most professional she'd seen, but it took care of the girl-next-door look. Next she grabbed her most colorful church dress, laid it out on the bathroom counter and began cutting the skirt. When she was done, she hemmed it, slipped it on, and grinned. The dress had once fallen almost to her ankles, loose and modest around her hips and waist. Now it came to just above her knees. With the extra material, Sarah quickly fashioned a belt, fastened it around her waist, and undid the top buttons on the dress. She studied the mirror once more.

This time she made a slight gasp, her eyes wide. She looked like a different person. Her figure was stunning, something even she hadn't realized. And with her new haircut she could hardly wait for morning.

The next day she walked into Trailway Records, the first office she'd been to when she arrived nearly two months earlier. A young man was working the phones and when she came through the door and removed her coat, he did a double take and spilled his coffee. He smiled at her and held up a single finger, silently asking her to stay.

Sarah nodded and took a nearby chair. She held her portfolio of songs close to her chest and crossed her legs the way she'd seen showgirls cross them in the movies. Making sure the young man had a clear view of her curvy calves.

In two minutes he was off the phone and on his feet. "Hi." He walked around his desk and smiled. "Can I help you?"

"Yes." Sarah stood and gave him a look she'd been working on all morning. "I'm a singer." She flashed him a slow smile. "I need a job."

"I see." The man was nodding before she had the words out. "I think we can help you." He introduced himself as Mr. Hamilton, and in a hurry he called to a man in a nearby office. Before Sarah could grasp what was happening, she was standing on a small stage in front of four men. One of them was at the piano, the music to her songs spread out before him.

"Okay, Sarah," one of the men said. "Let's hear what you've got."

She sang three pieces, but after the first they no longer seemed to be listening. The three men brought their heads together and whispered. Sarah felt a thrill work its way through her body. They were talking over the details of her contract. Once in a while one of them waved at her to keep singing. Sarah was so happy she could barely remember the words.

When they were finished talking, Mr. Hamilton approached her and motioned for her to stop.

"So . . ." She was breathless. This was it, the moment

she'd been waiting for. They would present her with a contract and she'd be on her way. "Am I in?"

"Well," Mr. Hamilton smiled big. "Our office girl left yesterday." His tone suggested this was the best possible news. "We'd like to bring you in, train you on the phones, the filing, that sort of thing."

Blood rushed to Sarah's face and she felt faint. "Phones?" She blinked hard. "What about . . . what about my songs? My contract?"

"Uh . . ." Mr. Hamilton hesitated, then turned and looked at the three men waiting at the back of the room. When he met Sarah's eyes again his smile faded some. "We might be able to get you some studio work, singing backgrounds, demos, that sort of thing." A nervous laugh slipped. "Yeah, the uh . . . the contract, why, that comes later on. Down the road."

He explained the pay. Fifty dollars a week plus bonus money if they needed her for studio work.

Sarah wanted to spit at the man. How dare he give her a job answering phones and filing paperwork? But she stopped herself. This was the first job she'd been offered, and the manager at the hotel wanted his money. He'd made her a deal—a hundred dollars a month if she cleaned her own room. The job would leave her enough spending money to eat and eventually buy a new dress or two.

She thought about the alternative—calling home and asking for train money.

"Fine." She lifted her chin, too proud to smile. "When do I start?"

The men looked at each other again and Mr. Hamilton cleared his throat. "Right now if you're ready."

Sarah was, and by the end of the day she had the office system memorized. Before she left for the evening, Mr. Hamilton approached her. The others were already gone, and something more suggestive shone in the man's eyes.

"Want a ride?" He reached out and brushed his finger against her chin. "Maybe we could, you know, talk about that studio work you're wanting."

A chill passed over Sarah. She slipped her coat on and shook her head. "I'll take a cab, thank you. And it's not studio work I'm wanting, Mr. Hamilton." She snatched her packet of songs from the desk and glared at him. "It's a contract."

That night she checked the mirror again and admired her new look. If she had to answer a thousand phone calls on the way up, at least she had a job in Nashville. A job she'd gotten on her very own, without handouts or connections or any praying on her part. It was hers, fair and square, and despite the circumstances Sarah was bursting at the seams.

She had come to Nashville seeking a career in the music industry, and now she was on her way.

"It's just like I dreamed, Mama," Sarah didn't mention the phone work or filing when she reported home that night. "I'll be singing in Nashville."

"Baby, be careful." Her mother's tone was always reserved, anxious about the entire situation. "I'm still praying."

Her father was more upbeat. "You let us know when you'll be onstage, now. We'll come and see you sing, all right?"

"It should be sometime soon, Daddy. I'll let you know." Sarah bit her lip. The lie felt bitter on her tongue, but then, it wasn't a total lie. She would be on a stage singing sometime soon. The people at Trailway Records were bound to see the light, and then the offers would come. A contract, a tour, a traveling band. All of it would happen, especially now that she was in with a studio.

The weeks blended into months and Sarah found herself fielding more passes from Mr. Hamilton than phone calls or files. But every now and then he made good on his word and allowed her some studio work. Backgrounds for a small piece, or harmony on a demo tape.

Each time she stood before the microphone Sarah felt the same way. One step closer to her dream. All she needed was a break, one single break. And at the end of her third month with Trailway Records, Sarah found it.

CHAPTER FIVE

THE SECOND DAY of Sarah's Christmas ritual blended into the third, and the ornament read *Excitement*. Even now that was the only word that could've described the feeling Sarah had the day Mitch Mullins walked into Trailway Studios.

Mitch was a country music star, an overnight phenomenon, a man on his way to becoming an icon. He'd broken onto the scene two years earlier and already he had six number one songs. His dark looks and smooth voice made him a heartthrob, and for a nation looking for purpose, Mitch's soulful lyrics kept the industry hungry for more.

Sarah was aware of him. She loved his music, and she'd heard enough chatter working at Trailway Records to know his wild reputation. Mitch was the kind of man her parents had warned her against. Not that it mattered. Nashville was a big town and Sarah never expected to meet him.

But that month he was between contracts, looking for a new label when he came into the office for a meeting with the higher-ups. Electricity filled the air when Mitch and his agent arrived, though Sarah didn't talk with him. She was in the studio all day working on a demo.

Halfway through the day Sarah was trying to bring life to a worn-out song when Mitch walked through the studio doors, spotted her, and froze. Sarah's breath caught in her throat. He was even more striking in person. She felt her face flush under his gaze, but she kept her attention on the producer and his directions for the song.

When the music ended, a break was called and Mitch meandered his way toward her.

"Hello." An easy grin tugged at his mouth. His eyes made a lazy trip down the length of her and back up again. He was only a few feet away now and he held out his hand. "My name's Mitch."

"Hi." Sarah took hold of his fingers and the sensation sliced its way through her. She swallowed, searching for her voice. "I'm Sarah."

"Well, Sarah . . ." Mitch released her hand and took another step closer. A presence surrounded him, something powerful, stronger than anything Sarah had felt. "Since when does Trailway Records hire angels?"

She smiled and her cheeks grew hot again. This was Mitch Mullins talking to her, complimenting her. For a moment she broke eye contact and looked at the ground, not sure what to say. She reminded herself not to take the moment too seriously. If the stories about Mitch were true, he probably reacted this way to most women.

"I was in the office talking with the guys when I heard you." His tone was softer, genuine. "I had to see where that voice came from." He took her hand again and guided her along the edge of the stage and down three steps. "You're absolutely stunning, Sarah. Everything about you."

"Thank you." Sarah hoped her palms weren't sweaty. *Calm down,* she told herself. *He says the same thing to all the girls.* She scanned the back of the studio for the director. The break wouldn't last much longer, even if she was talking to Mitch Mullins.

"Sarah, look at me."

Her eyes found his again. "Yes?"

"Let me take you away from here." He caught her other hand and eased his thumbs over the tops of her knuckles. "Sing backup for me on my tour, and when we get back to Nashville I'll make you the biggest star this town's ever seen."

The floor felt suddenly liquid; Sarah had to brace her knees to keep from falling. Mitch Mullins wanted her to sing backup for him, tour with him? He wanted her to make it big, and he'd only known her for five minutes? "I . . . I don't know what to say."

Mitch chuckled and squeezed her fingers. Then, as if it was the most natural thing in all the world, he leaned in and kissed her cheek. "Say yes, Sarah. You'll never regret it for a minute."

That evening Mitch had a driver bring Sarah to his Nashville estate, where his staff served them steamed fish and wild rice. They drank sweet tea from crystal goblets and Sarah tried to convince herself she wasn't dreaming. When they finished eating, he explained the situation. His backup singer had quit the week before to be with her family. His tour would start the following Monday—a ten-week bus trip through the south.

"Hamilton tells me you write your own songs." Mitch had dropped the slick one-liners from earlier that afternoon. Outside the studio atmosphere, he didn't seem like the country's fastest-rising star. He was genuine and likeable, a man oozing charm and utter confidence.

"Yes." She made a face and took a sip of tea. "I'm surprised he remembers."

"He said they were good."

Sarah's heart skipped a beat. "Really?"

"Yes." Mitch tossed his napkin on his plate and slid back from the table. He was across from her and his gaze never wavered. "I'm serious about the offer, Sarah. Sing for me on the tour and we'll get those songs on the air before summertime."

He stood and made his way around the table. With a familiar ease, he reached for her hand, waited until she was on her feet, then directed her into a sitting room. Before they reached the sofa, he stopped and turned to her. "Sarah," he gave a gentle pull and she was inches from him before she knew what had happened. "You're beautiful."

For a single instant, Sarah remembered Sam telling her that. She refused the thought. Mitch was so close she could feel his breath, smell the hint of his intoxicating cologne. "Thank you, Mitch."

Without waiting another moment, he drew her into his arms and kissed her, and suddenly there was no turning back. She quit her job the next day and gave herself to Mitch Mullins, heart and mind, body and soul.

"I've made it; I got my break," she told her parents. "I'm touring with Mitch Mullins."

Her father had doubts from the beginning. "He has a wild reputation, Sarah."

"Dad." She'd practiced her response, perfected the lie. "He likes my voice; nothing more."

From the time she hit the road with Mitch, warnings screamed at her. Girls were crazy for him, throwing themselves at the stage and bursting into tears if he reached out and touched their fingertips. At each show, dozens of girls would toss him gifts—flowers or teddy bears or slips of paper bearing phone numbers and unmentionable promises. Sarah figured since she and Mitch were an item, he'd toss the numbers as soon as the show was over. Instead she walked into his dressing room one night and caught him with a phone in one hand, a slip of paper in the other. When she asked him about it, he shrugged. "A man's gotta have friends, baby."

But Mitch's escapades were beyond shady, even if Sarah didn't want to ask questions. Mitch would disappear after a show and return by cab the next morning just as the bus was ready to pull out. Other times he'd leave with a group of girls after a show, stay out until three or four in the morning, and still have the nerve to show up at her hotel door—shirt unbuttoned, lipstick on his cheek—looking for her affection.

Sarah wanted to be mad at him, but she couldn't. No matter how many girls he toyed with, she was the one he kept coming back to, the one he was in love with. Besides, what more could she ask for? She was singing backup for Mitch Mullins, performing for a packed house night after night, the way she'd always dreamed. Mitch was going to make her into a star, even though he hadn't talked much about it since they'd gone on tour.

"Mitch," she told him every few shows, "I haven't played my songs for you yet. Don't you want to hear them?"

"Yeah, sure, baby." He'd lean in and kiss her long enough to take her breath away. "Maybe at the next stop, okay?"

But at the next stop he'd say the same thing. *Next time, baby . . . we'll look at your songs next time.*

The routine was identical in nearly every city. After the shows, Mitch would spend the night with her. And in those moments she could barely remember what city she was in, let alone her parents' warning or the girl she used to be. Every now and then she thought about her forgotten faith and the promises she'd made as a young girl— promises to stay pure and set apart, to wait for her wedding day. But the longer she stayed on the road with Mitch Mullins the more distant that girl and those promises became.

A shudder passed over Sarah and gradually she pulled herself from the memory. The early days were the hardest to relive, but they were part of the story, part of the ritual all the same. Not because Sarah missed those days, but because without them there would've been no story at all.

That night she lay down on the pillow and struggled to get comfortable. Her breathing was shallow and stubborn, more so than before, and her tired heart beat slower than usual. When sleep finally found her, it wasn't with dreams of Mitch Mullins and the three ornaments already on the tree. It was with silent prayers and bits of her song, and a single thought she couldn't quite shake.

If God was going to let someone be changed by her story, her song, then where was her caregiver, Beth? The young woman had to be the right one, so why hadn't she come to hear the story?

The more Sarah thought about Beth, the more she became certain of something. Three days earlier, she had seen a look in Beth's eyes, something she couldn't quite identify. But now, now Sarah knew where she'd seen the look before, and that could only mean one thing. Beth was in trouble. Maybe with a child or a parent. Maybe with a spouse, but she was in trouble.

Because the look in her eyes was a rebellious defiance—the same type of look Sarah herself had carried back in 1941.

CHAPTER SIX

Bᴏʙʙʏ Bᴀʟᴅᴡɪɴ couldn't sleep.

Beth was on the sofa, probably snoring under a mound of blankets the way she'd slept most nights since her announcement. At first Bobby hadn't minded. He was mad at Beth, frustrated with her. How dare she make a decision that would so swiftly and totally end their family?

But that night Bobby felt sick to his stomach and his heart ached. Now that he'd had time to think about the situation, he knew the score. Beth was serious. She was going to leave him after Christmas and nothing was going to stop her. Because of that, lately he walked around in a state of shock and desperation—frantic to find a way to turn back the clock.

He might be upset with Beth; he might not like her demands or the way she made him feel inadequate as a husband. But he loved her; with all his heart he loved her. He couldn't imagine living without her and Brianna— not for a week, let alone a few months or a year. Maybe forever.

The prospect of giving up his family was more than he could take, worse than he'd ever imagined. Even now—late at night with an early work shift in a few hours—the idea of losing them sat on his chest like a cement truck.

Beth was going to take his Brianna away and he could do nothing to change her mind. Sweet Brianna, who adored climbing into bed between the two of them. Brianna, who clamored about in the kitchen every Saturday while he made her Mickey Mouse pancakes. Brianna with her Eskimo kisses and *Hold-me-forever-Daddy* hugs.

How would he survive without her? Without either of them?

Brianna would be asleep now, dreaming about Christmas, sprawled out beneath her fairy princess bedspread. He slipped his feet out from under the covers, grabbed a crumpled sweatshirt from the floor, and threw it on. The house was chilly, more so than usual. He shivered once and snuck out the bedroom door. Without stopping, he passed a sleeping Beth and tiptoed into Brianna's room.

For a moment he stood there, silent, barely breathing. The moonlight splashed through her window and across her face. She was so pretty, such a delight.

"Hi, Brianna." He walked to her bed, his voice softer than a whisper. He eased himself onto the edge of her mattress and stared at her. "Daddy loves you, honey."

Sitting there, looking at his only child, Bobby felt a lump rise in his throat. How many days like this did he have left? Times when Brianna would be sleeping under his roof? Life was bound to play out predictably from here, wasn't it? Divorce had a sameness about it, a brokenness that repeated itself no matter how many people chose it.

Beth would leave and at first he'd see Brianna often—several times a week at least. But life would get busy, and eventually Beth would grow tired of Spartanburg the way single people tire of small towns. She would move away, maybe back to Atlanta where her sisters lived, and then what?

Bobby closed his eyes and remembered something he hadn't thought of in years.

He'd been traveling late one August, going to

California to visit his mother before she died. Beth and Brianna had stayed home, since the visit would take place at a hospital and Brianna had only been a baby at the time.

His layover was in St. Louis, and once the gate attendant started the boarding call, Bobby noticed a man and a little boy fifteen feet away. The man was standing, and the child—maybe seven years old—was holding onto his legs, clinging to him as though he never wanted to let go.

That's when Bobby noticed the woman.

Sitting a few feet back, her expression hard, was a woman whose arms were crossed. The man dropped to one knee and spoke to the little boy, but the woman checked her watch and shifted her position.

Finally a gate attendant approached them, and the man stood. He nodded as the attendant relayed something Bobby couldn't make out. Then the man pulled the boy into one final hug, held on for several seconds, and bid him good-bye. The boy straightened himself and that's when Bobby got a clear view of him.

The child was crying, sobbing. His next words were loud enough for Bobby to hear. "I don't want to go, Dad."

The man hugged the boy once more, a desperate sort of hug. The two exchanged words and nods and one last embrace. Then the man stepped away and the boy—trying to be stoic—went with the gate attendant toward the jetway. Every few steps he craned his neck around and gave the man a little wave, and the man—his expression strong—made an attempt to smile back.

Not until the boy turned the corner and disappeared did the man break. He turned around, took a few slow steps past the woman, and hung his head against the wall. For a long while—through most of the boarding call— the man stayed there, his shoulders shaking as he cried for the boy.

Bobby watched the entire scene, watched how the woman left the man alone, how she looked pained for him, but indignant. She shared none of the man's brokenness. What, Bobby wondered, would have explained such a scene? A man saying good-bye to his son? A woman sitting nearby disinterested?

And then it hit him.

The situation was obvious; it was the end of summer, after all. The boy's parents obviously lived in separate cities—possibly separate states. After a summer with his father, the boy must have been returning home—wherever home was—to be with his mother.

The disinterested woman was probably the new wife.

All of it made sense. And for weeks the image stayed

with him—the broken man leaning on an airport wall, weeping, his head buried in the crook of his arm.

A portrait of divorce.

It was the same picture any time children were involved. Oh, sure, at first divorce promised freedom, an answer to every trouble marriage had a way of bringing. But divorce was a lie, a con-artist that moved into a family and stole the little moments, robbing every member blind. It was a hand grenade that shattered lives and destroyed dreams, taking no prisoners along the way.

At least that's the way Bobby remembered thinking about it at the time.

He never shared the image with Beth, never felt the need to share it. They were happy, right? Why talk about divorce? They'd promised each other forever, and forever was what Bobby expected. They went to church and prayed with Brianna before bedtime. And if their schedules and budgets didn't allow time for date nights or yellow roses, well then, at least they had Sunday mornings together.

Nothing had changed there, but over time Bobby forgot about the scene at the airport and divorce began to seem somehow more understandable. Not for him and Beth, maybe, but for some of the guys on the maintenance crew at work, guys with issues in their marriages. Not serious issues of abuse or unfaithfulness, but bickering and boredom and a spouse hardly worth going home to.

For them divorce meant the chance for new love, someone more exciting, more sympathetic. For years, despite everything he knew to be true, that's the way Bobby had viewed it.

Until now.

The nausea within him grew worse and he gave a hard shake of his head. Was Beth crazy? Couldn't she look ahead and see where leaving would get them? It was her fault, after all. She wanted to leave.

He studied Brianna, her little-girl lips and the soft way her chest rose and fell with each breath. It didn't matter if it was Beth's fault. Either way, a divorce would touch them all, change them from what they'd been to another statistic.

If Beth left with Brianna, one day he'd be the man in the airport, telling his daughter good-bye at summer's end, waiting until the following Christmas or maybe an entire year before seeing her again. Only he wouldn't fall against the airport wall in tears, he'd collapse right there at the jetway. Unable to breathe or move or exist with his daughter leaving him.

The ache in his heart grew stronger and Bobby hunched forward, one hand on Brianna's pillow.

How had they let it fall apart? He and Beth had been perfect for each other, hadn't they? In love and excited about a lifetime together? Wasn't that them? So what had gone wrong? Had Beth found someone else, someone with a better job, more money, and security?

Bobby exhaled and the sound of it rattled his soul. Whatever the reason, this whole mess was her fault. He hadn't done anything but put in his forty hours a week and show up each night at home. He didn't drink or gamble or hang out with the guys. He'd never once been interested in another woman, so what was her problem?

"God . . . what happened?" His words were barely audible. "Why isn't this enough for Beth?"

He heard nothing in response, no booming voice telling him how he might change Beth's mind. But a strong sense came over him, a sense that made him long for a look at their wedding pictures, the place where their lives had come together. He kissed Brianna on the cheek, and crept out the door, down the hall to the TV room.

Quietly, so he wouldn't wake Beth, he scanned the top bookshelf until he saw the brown leather-like cover. Their wedding album. He reached for the book and pulled it out. A layer of dust came down with it. He carried the album to their bedroom, sat at the end of the bed, and stared at the cover.

In golden letters the front read, "Robert and Elizabeth, forever." Their wedding date was centered beneath.

What was it they'd promised that summer, when the photographer presented them with the book? That they'd look at the pictures every year on their anniversary, wasn't that it? That they'd take an evening and remember the events and people who brought them together, so that their love would never have a chance to fade, right?

But two years later, Brianna came along and somehow the promise was forgotten.

Bobby ran his fingers over the dusty cover and figured it had been four years since either of them had even thought of the wedding pictures, let alone taken the time to look at it.

Still, he wasn't sure why he suddenly wanted to see them now, in the middle of the night. If Beth wasn't interested in staying, a bunch of photographs wouldn't do them much good.

He opened the first page and for a moment he couldn't breathe.

Beth looked beautiful. She was facing him, the two of them looking like the definition of love. She was beyond beautiful, and not just her face and hair and the dress she wore. But her expression, caught in his embrace, unaware of the camera. Hunger and longing filled their eyes, and a passion that went beyond physical desire.

But even that wasn't what made him struggle for the next breath. Instead it was the words scrawled at the bottom of the page, a Bible verse he'd used in his vows.

"Husbands, love your wives, just as Christ loved the church and gave himself up for her."

Since Beth's announcement that she was leaving, Bobby had insisted the trouble was her fault. Her fault for being unhappy, her fault for being self-centered, her fault for even thinking of taking Brianna away from him.

But here, now, those excuses were leaking from his airtight understanding like air from an untied balloon.

Sure, he went to work each day and came home every night. His job had kept them fed and clothed, but what had he done to keep their marriage alive? Slowly, he shut the book, too sad and tired to turn another page.

The book tucked up against his chest, he fell asleep, and for the first time that week it wasn't with condemning thoughts of Beth and her selfishness.

Rather, it was of his own.

He'd been wrong to let their marriage die. Tomorrow morning he would stop pointing fingers at Beth and start finding ways to love her, the way he'd long since stopped loving her. He had no idea how—in a few weeks' time—he could find a way to make things right again, but he had to try.

Most of all, he had to find a way to lay down his life for the only girl he'd ever loved.

Beth's first thought the next morning was that she must have been dreaming. She'd dreamed that Bobby had been creeping around the TV room while she was sleeping, and that he'd taken their wedding album down from the top shelf. It wasn't until she was fully awake that she realized she hadn't been dreaming at all. Where the book had been was now only an empty space.

She sat up and squinted, puzzled. What would he want with their wedding album, and why now? No answer came, and she turned her head one way and then the other, trying to stretch out the kinks in her neck. The Christmas season was proving to be unbearable. She was anxious and frustrated and sick of sleeping on the sofa.

She and Bobby had barely spoken to each other, and Brianna was getting suspicious. Later that morning, as she was eating Corn Flakes, she dropped her spoon into the bowl and turned to Beth.

"How come you don't like Daddy anymore?"

Beth set down her coffee and stared at Brianna. What had Bobby said? Something to poison their daughter's mind about who the bad parent was? Something to soften the blow in the battle that was about to be their lives? She leaned in, already angry. "Did Daddy tell you that?"

"No." Brianna gave an angry pout. "You keep sleeping in the TV room without Daddy and that means you don't like him."

Guilt hit Beth hard. Brianna was waiting for an answer, but Beth had none to give. How had Brianna found out about the sofa, and when had she grown so perceptive? "Well, honey . . ." She tapped her fingers on the table and tried to smile. "That's because Mommy isn't feeling good. It's almost Christmas and I don't want poor Daddy to get sick."

The excuse sounded ridiculous even to Beth. Brianna only rolled her eyes. "If you liked him you'd sleep in your own room, Mommy. You sleep with me when I'm sick, remember?"

They ate the rest of their breakfast in silence, and nothing felt quite right between them even after Beth dropped her off at day care.

Beth leaned hard into the seat of her car as she headed

for work. Suddenly she remembered the old woman at the retirement home. Sarah Lindeman, the woman with the beautiful voice and that melody, the one Beth hadn't been able to get out of her head. Great. She gritted her teeth as she parked her car in the back lot of Greer Retirement Village. How many more people would she let down before Christmas?

Beth locked her door and headed across the parking lot. What had the woman said? If Beth listened to the story, then she'd tell her the secret of love? Yes, that was it. The secret of love.

Fine. Today she'd go see the old woman. Her own life might be falling apart, but that didn't mean she had the right to ignore a sweet old dear like Sarah Lindeman. The woman was probably suffering from dementia, among other ailments, but that didn't matter. She had something important to say and the woman didn't get many visitors. Beth might be the only person who would listen.

Crazy or not, the old woman deserved at least that much.

That morning she made sure Sarah was on her list of residents, and after she helped the old woman finish breakfast and wash up, Beth took a spot at the end of the bed. She looked intently at her. "You think I've forgotten."

Sarah angled her head, unblinking. "Yes. I guess so." She shifted her attention to the crooked plastic Christmas tree perched on her bedside table. "Today's the sixth day."

"I know." Beth folded her hands on her lap. "I'm sorry. Things . . . well, things haven't been good at home." She hesitated. "Is it too late, Sarah? Could you catch me up so I could hear the story?"

"Yes." Sarah sat a little straighter in her bed. Her smile said she wasn't mad about Beth's absence these past few days. "Yes, that would be very nice."

Beth stood, closed the door, and pulled a chair up to the bed. "What have I missed, Sarah?"

The old woman looked at Beth again and cleared her throat. Then she began. She talked about her love for Sam Lindeman, but her greater love for a career in Nashville. She shared about her decision to leave Sam and Greer and everything familiar in order to follow her dream of finding a recording contract. Then she shared about her job at Trailway Records and meeting Mitch Mullins.

"Mitch Mullins?" Beth narrowed her eyes. "I've heard of him."

"Yes." Sarah's expression changed, and something sad haunted her eyes. "He was quite well known in his day. By the fans . . . and the women." She paused and looked out the window. When she spoke again, she was a million miles away. "I toured with him. He was going to make me famous." A sad laugh died on her lips. "I thought . . . I thought he loved me."

Beth waited, studying the woman spread out on the hospital bed before her. For the first time, she tried to picture her not as the old woman in Room 11, but as she was back in her day. No doubt a beautiful girl with a voice and a figure that stopped even celebrities in their tracks.

When Sarah didn't speak, Beth leaned forward. "Sarah?"

"Yes?" She cast a sideways glance at Beth.

"What happened? Did you and Mitch stay together?"

Sarah made a sad, tired sort of sound. "No, dear. That's the story behind the fourth and fifth ornaments." She pointed a bony finger at the little tree. "Four is **Rebellious** and five is **Exposed**." Her head moved up and down in a slow, trancelike manner. "Yes, indeed. I was rebellious. I knew what I was doing but I did it anyway."

She explained how the touring life grew crazier with each week. Always she would ask Mitch what was going on with the other girls, and he'd say the same thing. They needed his time, his attention. Hanging out with the fans was part of the act, part of making it big.

Was he sleeping with them, Sarah wanted to know. His answer was the same every time—definitely not. She was the only one he was interested in, the only one he cared about. And one day soon he would listen to her songs and make her a star. One day very soon. Meanwhile, he paid her less than she'd been making at Trailway Records, always with promise of raises and bonuses. Any day, he'd tell her, just a few stops down the road.

The extra money never came, but things definitely got wilder, Mitch's nights away more frequent. One night he sent one of his band members to her room when he was out with his groupies.

"It was past midnight and there was a knock at the door. I opened it, and there was Mitch's drummer. 'Mitch says you're up for a good time tonight, Sarah,' he told me. 'Whad'ya say?'"

Beth leaned closer, sucked in by the story. "No!"

"Yes." Sarah pursed her lips, as if talking about the memory left a terrible taste in her mouth.

"Wow." Beth tried not to look surprised. Sarah had said her story took place in 1941, a time when the American life was supposed to be wholesome and innocent. Beth had no idea such craziness went on so many decades back.

Sarah stared out the window again and finished the story.

When she realized Mitch's intentions, that she should offer them the same favors she'd been offering Mitch, she felt dirty and cheap and ugly.

"Like a rotting bag of leftovers," Sarah frowned. "Sitting too long on the curb."

Two nights later, Mitch took his own room instead of sharing hers. Suspicious, Sarah waited until the early hours of the morning, donned a bathrobe, and strode down the hall to his door. After ten minutes of incessant knocking, Mitch answered. He had a towel around his waist. Over his shoulder, in the hotel room, Sarah saw a young blonde in his bed, the sheet pulled up to her neck.

"The lie was out," Sarah turned her attention back to Beth. She pointed to the tree again. "See, there. The fifth ornament says *Exposed* because Mitch Mullins was never going to lie to me again."

Beth sat back in her chair, captured by the story. "So what happened?"

"What happened?" Sarah looked startled, as if the answer was obvious. "With Mitch, you mean?"

"Yes. Did you let him have it there in the hallway?" Beth willed her words to come more slowly. Sarah wasn't in a rush. If she'd planned twelve days to tell her story, the answers weren't bound to come in as many minutes.

Sarah said nothing in response. Instead she reached a shaky hand to the table by the bed and picked up an envelope with the number six on it. "That's today's story. The part that changed everything."

"Oh." Beth looked at the clock over Sarah's bed and winced. Her boss would never understand her spending so much time in one room. She started to stand, started to tell Sarah she'd have to catch up the next day. But something made her stay seated, riveted to her chair.

With slow, careful fingers, Sarah opened the envelope flap and pulled out the ornament. Like the others, it held just one word. A word Beth hadn't thought about for years, but one that obviously held special meaning for Sarah.

The word was *Dance*.

CHAPTER SEVEN

SARAH COULD FEEL HERSELF getting sicker, slipping away a little more each day. But her heart hadn't been so full in a long, long time.

Not even a visit from her children or grandchildren had brought her the purpose she felt sharing her story with Beth Baldwin. The woman had an edge, a sadness Sarah recognized. Something she'd said when she first arrived, about having trouble at home, explained some of it. But there was something else, something deeper.

And it still reminded Sarah of herself, the way she'd been the summer of 1941. Sarah wasn't sure how, but God was going to do something amazing for Beth Baldwin, something that could only happen as Beth listened to the story, as she heard the song.

It was Day Six, the day that represented the turning point, the moment when things changed for Sarah. With Beth sitting nearby listening, Sarah connected once more with a series of events that were over six decades old.

The epiphany took place the day after she found Mitch Mullins in a room with another girl. As shallow as his stories about groupies had been, Sarah had always believed him, always wanted to believe him. But after catching him in the act that night, she went back to her room and never fell asleep.

For the first time since leaving Greer, she missed Sam Lindeman, missed him with every fiber of her being. Strong, handsome, dependable Sam, a man who had loved her enough to let her follow her dreams. But now, after giving her virtue to a man who had cheated on her and lied to her from the beginning, Sarah was sure of something else.

Sam would never be interested in her.

She wasn't the same girl she'd been when she left home, and no matter how much she missed Sam, she wouldn't mess with his heart by calling him now. Instead she sat on her hotel bed and wept. What had she been thinking, taking up with a man like Mitch Mullins? So what if the whole world adored him; his nature had been obvious from the beginning.

Since when does Trailway Records hire angels?

Indeed. Mitch was master of the come-on lines; he'd had her following him around like a puppy dog after just one dinner.

Sarah paused and looked at Beth. "At that moment, the lights in my conscience came on again." She ran her tongue over her lower lip. "After weeks of living in darkness, I was suddenly able to see the horrifying mistakes I'd made—all of them spread out like a train wreck."

One by one her bad choices screamed at her that night. She'd turned her back on everything her parents had taught her, everything that had ever mattered to her. She had given up on God and His plans for her life, and her promise to remain pure until marriage was gone. Her virtue was forever lost.

But worst of all, she'd walked away from Sam.

Sarah stared at the tiny blue-bonnet wallpaper. The smell of the hotel's musty carpets filled her senses as she choked back quiet, desperate sobs. All of life was a dance, the steps measured out to the music of the days. But since she'd arrived in Nashville, she'd checked herself at the door and let an imposter take over.

Now, though . . . now it was her turn again. Time to find her way back to all she'd once been.

Mitch Mullins had no plans of making her into a star, no plans of hearing her songs or giving her a pay raise. He was using her, the way her parents had warned he would.

That night she packed her things, and the next morning, long before Mitch and his band members were awake, she took a cab to the train station and spent nearly all of her remaining money on a train back to Greer. Over the hours, the clickity-clack of the train became music, and her heart pounded out a rhythm she could live with, one she could dance to.

The next day, when she arrived home, she had one place to visit before taking a cab to her parents' house.

Greer Community Church.

"Wait for me, please." She gave the cab driver an extra quarter and ran lightly across the church lawn. It was Thursday, in the middle of the afternoon, but she was sure the doors to the sanctuary would be open. They were always open at Greer Community.

Once inside, she took slow steps toward the front and slid into the second row. She was the only one in the building, but she felt surrounded by love and peace and acceptance, the way she hadn't felt since meeting Mitch Mullins.

"God . . ." She closed her eyes. "I'm . . . I'm so sorry. I was wrong about everything. I walked away from You, from all I know to be good and true and right." A single tear slid down her cheek and she dabbed at it with the back of her hand. "But if You'll have me, I'm back, Jesus." She sniffed, and the sound of it echoed across the empty room. "I'm back for good. I promise."

Sarah exhaled, the sixth part of the story told.

She looked at the young woman sitting across from her and saw that she'd been right earlier. The story was touching something in Beth's soul, because the woman was crying. Not loud or with dramatics. But tears had formed two trails on both sides of her face and there was something broken in her expression.

Sarah reached her hand out to the woman and patted her arm. "Are you okay?"

"Yes." Beth snatched a tissue from the bedside table and wiped it beneath her nose. "That moment at the church . . . it sounds . . . it sounds very freeing."

Sarah smiled. "It was." She inhaled until her lungs were full. "It's time for me to move to the window."

"To the window?" Beth made a strange face. "You've been walking to the window by yourself?"

"Once in a while." She felt her smile creep a little higher. "But today I could use your help, if you don't mind."

"Not at all." Beth tossed her tissue in a nearby trash can and stood, easing Sarah up until she was on her feet and positioned over her aluminum walker. "Why the window, Sarah?"

Sarah focused on the path in front of her and shook her head. When she reached the windowsill, she turned to Beth and held up a single finger. "That will come."

She stared out the window at the park until her eyes found the bench—the park bench that meant the world to her. And with all the energy she had left, she began to hum the melody, the notes that would always fill her heart and soul.

The notes to *Sarah's Song*.

Throughout the humming, Beth remained at her side, quiet, respectful. When she'd hummed the last line, Sarah pulled her eyes from the park bench and nodded at Beth. "That's all. I can go back now."

Beth helped her, and when Sarah was too tired to swing her legs up onto the bed, Beth lifted them. Once the old woman was settled back beneath the covers, Beth hesitated and then gave a slight shrug of her shoulders. "The music is beautiful, haunting." She glanced at the window and then back. "But why no words, Sarah? Didn't the song have words?"

"Indeed." Sarah yawned and squeezed Beth's hand. "I'm tired, dear. I think I'll take a nap."

Beth nodded, but she wouldn't let the idea go. "What about the words?"

"Later." Sarah could feel her eyes beginning to close. The familiar peace surrounded her again—a peace that defied all understanding. God was doing something here, something in young Beth's heart. And that was knowledge enough for Sarah.

She was almost asleep when Beth asked her question one final time. "When, Sarah . . . when will the words come?"

Slowly Sarah opened her eyes. "Day Nine."

There. She let her eyes close again. That would

bring Beth back for sure. Not because she wouldn't survive without knowing the words to the song. But because God had placed a special truth deep inside Sarah's heart: A miracle was underway, a miracle for Beth Baldwin.

And God would bring her back if He had to move heaven and earth to do it.

CHAPTER EIGHT

It was Tuesday, December 21, and the good weather had finally given out.

That morning Beth woke to a six-inch blanket of snow spread across Spartanburg, and she mumbled under her breath as she headed for the shower. White Christmases were overrated. The city would take a week to dig out from beneath the snow, and until then the commute to Greer would be unbearable. Snow would turn to ice, leaving the roads slick and dangerous. Beth was scheduled to work every day that week, and the snow meant she'd have to get up an hour earlier each morning.

Her shower was quick, and as soon as she was dressed she hurried into Brianna's room. "Get up, sleepyhead. Time to eat."

Brianna moaned.

"Come on, honey. We gotta eat if we're going to be on time."

Brianna rolled over in her bed. "No! Don't wanna eat!"

"Mommy's not giving you a choice." Beth yanked the covers from her daughter and waited, arms crossed. "Get out of bed."

"Do I have to, Mommy?" Brianna's tone was more whine than words.

"Yes. One . . . two . . . three . . ."

Brianna spilled out of bed and stopped short of scowling at Beth. "Help me get dressed."

Beth hesitated, then went to the closet and sorted through the clothes. Her daughter's accusations regarding Bobby had dropped off, but she was grumpy or pensive most of the time. Earlier that week, Bobby had asked about it. "Did you say something to Brianna—something about us separating?"

"No." Beth's answer was short, the way she felt most of the time toward her husband. "Did you?"

"Of course not." He scowled at her. "We agreed."

"Right."

"So why's she asking about us, telling me I don't like you all of a sudden?"

Beth shrugged. "She's telling me the same thing. Maybe she feels it."

"Feels it?"

"Yes. That her parents don't love each other anymore."

"Listen . . ." Anger flashed in Bobby's eyes as he pointed a finger at Beth. "I never said I didn't love you. Those were your words." Then, as if he somehow caught himself, his expression eased and his voice grew calmer. "I'm sorry. I didn't mean to yell. All I'm saying, Beth, is I still love you. For whatever that's worth."

The conversation had stayed with her because it seemed so unlike Bobby. Sure, he had tried initially to change her mind about leaving. But when things didn't go his way, he was usually quick on the defensive. That time, though, he had backed off, even told her he was sorry and he loved her. Not just once, but several times after their initial confrontation, he'd pulled her aside in an effort to talk to her or apologize. Beth tried not to look too deeply into it. Probably last-minute remorse over their failed marriage, or maybe the Christmas season getting to him.

Either way, their conversation had done nothing to ease Brianna's mood. The carefree child with bright eyes and bouncing pigtails had disappeared, and in her place was a little girl both moody and melancholy.

Beth kept the morning routine at a fast pace, and managed to get Brianna in the car eight minutes earlier than usual. Sure enough, the commute was stop and go, with an occasional car sliding off the road and others spinning into oncoming traffic. The speed was slow, so none of the mishaps was serious, and Beth pulled up in front of Brianna's day care just a few minutes later than usual.

Dana Goode—one of Beth's friends from high school—ran the day care from her house. Beth felt good leaving Brianna with her, and sometimes, if she was early, she and Dana would talk about the old days, high school and dating and how Bobby was always the only one for Beth.

"Everyone always said it," Dana would say as she punished a piece of gum, "Bobby Baldwin only had eyes for you, Beth. As far back as time he only had eyes for you."

Beth had still not told Dana about her decision to leave; she was sure the idea wouldn't go over well.

Just as well she had no time to talk that morning. She led Brianna up the walk, careful not to slip in the snow, and shouldered her way into the house. She was about to kiss Brianna good-bye when she looked up and saw Dana standing there, both eyebrows raised halfway up her forehead.

Beth went ahead with her kiss and patted Brianna's back. "Go on, honey, the kids are waiting for you."

Brianna looked from her mother to Dana and back again. "Bye." She shuffled off, a blank look on her face.

The moment she was out of earshot, Dana leaned in and hissed at Beth. "You and Bobby are splitting up? What, Beth, are you crazy?"

Beth refused to react. She put her hands on her hips and gave a slight roll of her eyes. "Who told you?"

"Who do you think?" She huffed hard and paced two steps away, then two steps back. "Bobby called, asked me to pray for you guys."

"He what?" Beth was amused at the idea. Bobby hadn't talked about prayer in years, other than an occasional dinner when he remembered to pray over the meal. They went to church once in a rare while, but that was the extent of it. "Now I know you're making it up. Come on, who told you? Really . . ."

Dana stopped, her mouth open. "I can't believe you, Beth. What's happened?" She straightened, the shock wearing off. "Wasn't that you driving me to church every Sunday during our college years? Weren't you the one telling me to trust God, that someone right would come along if I put God first?"

Beth's gaze fell. "That was a long time ago." She looked up. "For all of us."

"Meaning?"

"Meaning Bobby and I haven't prayed together in years. Don't tell me he asked you to pray for our marriage."

"Well." Another huff. "That's exactly what he did. Now listen, Beth. It's my job as a friend to tell you this." Dana was a fast talker; she paused only long enough to snatch another breath. "No one will ever love you the way Bobby loves you. He might've slipped lately, forgotten what was important, but that doesn't change the facts."

"Slipped?" Beth looked at her watch and gave a chuckle that sounded more sarcastic than humorous. "I haven't seen a yellow rose in three years, Dana. When Bobby and I were dating, he brought me yellow roses every week. Yellow roses and homemade key lime pie— the only thing he knew how to cook."

"So you grew up. So what?"

"So?" Beth tossed her hands up. "So now I'm old hat, and you know what?" She lowered her voice so Brianna wouldn't hear her in the next room. "I'm sick of it. Sick of coming home each afternoon to a husband parked in front of the television. Sick of competing with Sports

Center for my husband's attention. If he had to choose between me and the TV remote, he'd take the remote. Hands down." She tossed her hair over her shoulder, fuming. "I'm sick of not mattering, Dana, sick of wishing he'd bring me roses or look at me the way he used to. I don't love him anymore. I don't." She straightened her sweater, grabbing at her composure. "I'm getting out before I forget how living feels."

A mix of emotions worked their way into Dana's expression. Shock became horror, and that became hurt and disappointment. Finally she shook her head. "Love's about more than yellow roses and key lime pie."

"Yeah." Beth took a few backward steps toward the door. "It's about more than the sports channel, too."

She was out the door and halfway to work before she realized how terrible she'd acted. Dana was only trying to help, trying to influence Beth not to leave.

But what about Bobby? What right did he have calling her friend and asking for prayer? He might as well have come right out and asked her to intervene.

Beth tightened her grip on the steering wheel.

It didn't matter; the ordeal would be over soon enough, as soon as Christmas was behind them. Bobby could say whatever he wanted, he could ask people to pray and tell her he still loved her. The truth was he wanted her to leave as badly as she wanted to go. Otherwise he would've spent more time with her, talked to her more often. Turned off the television once in a while.

No, it was over, and nothing would change the fact now.

She pulled into the parking lot of the Greer Retirement Village and headed to the third floor. That's when she remembered. It was Day Nine. She'd missed days seven and eight because they were her days off. But Day Nine was the big day, wasn't it? The day the sweet old woman would add words to her ritual?

For a moment she considered working the opposite side of the floor. The drawn-out story couldn't possibly help her, so why was she listening to it? Then it dawned on her: Because this was Christmas, and even if her entire life was falling apart, spending time with Sarah Lindeman was the least she could do—her way of giving something back to a lonely old lady.

She entered Sarah's room and found the woman sitting up, smiling at her. "You came."

"Yes." Beth stepped inside, not sure what she was feeling. "I want to hear the words to the song."

Last time she was here, listening to the story, the details had made her cry. But now—in light of the events that morning—she didn't feel a bit tenderhearted. She wanted to put in a mindless eight hours and move one day closer to December 26. For a beat, she considered turning around, but then she changed her mind. She returned Sarah's smile and set about finding fresh clothes for the woman. Over the next hour she prepared Sarah's bath and made sure she got her meal down.

When they were finished, Beth took her place in the familiar chair. "I've missed a few days."

"You weren't at work." Sarah shot her a thoughtful look. "Home with your family, no doubt."

"Yes." Beth couldn't force a smile. Enough about her family. She leaned forward in her seat. "Okay, catch me up."

"You have to promise something."

Promise something? Beth bit her lip. She barely knew the old woman. "What?"

"Promise you'll be here for the last three days."

Beth calculated the dates in her head. The twelfth day would take place on Friday, her last day of work before Christmas. She nodded at Sarah. "I promise." But the words felt hollow, even to her. She was about to walk away from her husband, after all. If she couldn't keep the most important promise she'd ever made, how could she expect to keep this one?

Still, Sarah seemed satisfied. She pulled herself up some and settled into a stack of pillows propped against the headboard. "You remember where we were?"

"The dance." Beth felt herself relax. Her time with Sarah did that to her. Now that she was back again, the story drew her, made her anxious for the next piece. And not only the next piece, but also for the special meaning Sarah had spoken about. Because in the midst of this crazy, hectic, hurtful Christmas season, between divorce plans and arguing with Bobby, Beth had an almost desperate need to understand the bigger picture.

It was possible Sarah knew what she was talking about, right? If she did, then in just a few days Beth might actually learn something she'd wanted to know for the past several years.

The secret of love.

CHAPTER NINE

Sᴀʀᴀʜ ᴛᴜᴄᴋᴇᴅ ᴛʜᴇ ᴄᴏᴠᴇʀs ɪɴ tight around her waist. Her heart glowed at the return of Beth Baldwin. The miracle was coming; Sarah could feel it.

"Yes, dear. That's where we were. The dance."

"You were at the church when we finished Day Six."

"Right. After stopping at the church I went straight home, to my parents' house." Sarah smiled, and her eyes grew watery. "My parents were great people; such love for God and me."

Sarah didn't comment on the irony, but it was there. In less than a week, Beth also was going back to her parents' house; Sarah had heard one of the nurses talking about it. She found her place in time.

"It was summer by then." Her eyes found the window, the place where she looked when her memories were the strongest. "Late July. The summer of forty-one."

Sarah's parents were at the doorstep the moment they saw her pull up. Without a single question, they took her in their arms and welcomed her inside. For the next hour—sparing them any of the shocking details—she told them how she had trusted Mitch Mullins, how he'd led her to believe he was interested in her music, and how he'd betrayed her in the end.

"I thought he loved me, Daddy." She lifted her eyes to her father, glad she hadn't told him how serious her mistakes had been. He was a kind, gentle man. The detailed truth would be more than he could handle.

"And now?" Sarah's mother was quiet, probably afraid of her answer. "How do you feel about him now?"

Sarah shook her head. "I never knew him. I made . . ." She hung her head. "I made a fool of myself."

"No, you didn't." Her father was on his feet, his arms outstretched. "You're here, aren't you? You had the sense to come home, to know that we were waiting for you." He gave her a hug. "Nothing foolish about that."

"Thanks, Daddy." Sarah held her breath. She'd been dying to ask the question since the night she found out about Mitch, but now the moment had come. "Have you heard from Sam?"

Her parents exchanged a look, and then her father sat back down in his chair, his elbows planted on his knees. "Sam left, sweetheart. Took a job somewhere up north. New York, maybe, or New Jersey."

Sarah's mouth went dry. What? Sam left? He took a job and didn't tell her parents whether it was in New York or New Jersey? Her head began to spin and she sat in the nearest chair, digging her fingernails into the palms of her hand in order to concentrate. "What . . . sort of job?"

"He's a principal, honey." Sarah's mother gave her a sad smile. "The last time we saw him, he said something about getting on with his life." She dropped her chin, her gaze gentle but unwavering. "I think he was referring to you, dear."

Sarah was drowning. As if she had a steel cable around her waist and no matter how hard she kicked and swam she couldn't get to the surface, couldn't grab another mouthful of air. "Where . . ." She gave a few short exhales and rubbed her fingers into her brow. "Where did he apply? Do you know?"

"To tell you the truth, honey, I don't think he wanted us to know. His parents moved away a few years ago— you know that. And when he came by the house his visit had a sense of finality to it." He looked at Sarah's mother. "Wouldn't you say so?"

"Yes." She bit her lower lip and gave a sad shake of her head. "I'm sorry, Sarah. I somehow guessed you'd come looking for him one day."

Sarah didn't have to finish the thought. The truth hung out there in the open for all three of them to gawk at. She'd waited too long for Sam Lindeman. He'd given years of his life to courting Sarah, and now he'd moved away, given up. The way he should've given up a long time ago.

In the next few days, Sarah tried everything to find him. She called the principal at his previous school, but the man was adamant. "We don't discuss former employees," he told her. "The files of our teachers—past and present—are highly confidential."

Sarah had another idea. She called the operator in the town where his parents had moved and asked for their number. After nearly a minute of checking, the operator came back on the line and apologized. "Apparently they've moved. There's no one in that town by the name Lindeman—listed or unlisted."

At the end of the week, she had to admit her situation. Sam was gone, and there wasn't a thing she could do about it.

❧

Sarah broke her stare at the window, peered at Beth Baldwin, and nodded her chin toward the little Christmas tree. "That's why the seventh ornament says *Gone.*" She kept her eyes on the tree. "And number eight, see it there?"

Beth slid to the edge of the padded chair and looked on the backside of the tree. "*Longing?* Is that the one?"

"It is." Sarah relaxed her neck and allowed herself a view of the window once more. She would've liked to tell the whole story perched along her walker, staring down at the bench. But this would have to do, this knowing that the bench was there, just outside the window.

She drew a full breath and continued.

❧

When her efforts turned up nothing, she had to admit the truth. Sam was gone. With every hour that passed,

Sarah longed for him, and became more certain that he had been exactly right for her, the man she'd always wanted. She'd left him to chase paper dreams and lost more than her high hopes along the way. Yes, Sam was gone, but she could no more stop longing for him than she could stop the sun from rising.

Not that Sarah expected much to come of her feelings.

Sam deserved someone whole and pure; he was too good for a girl like her. She was yesterday's news, dead broke without a plan in the world, her singing career over almost as soon as it had started.

For the next month she held that opinion, certain that though God had forgiven her, it must've been a struggle for Him to do so. And Sam—if she ever saw him again—couldn't possibly see her the same as before. Not if he knew the truth.

But something changed at the end of that month." Sarah's voice sounded distant, dreamy, even. "People kept seeing me and asking about Sam, and finally one Sunday I took the situation to God."

Beth's eyes were wide; she looked like she wouldn't have moved from her chair for anything in the world. "And?"

Sarah smiled, slow and full. "He gave me my song."

"And that's Number Nine?"

"Yes, dear." She pointed at the four envelopes remaining. "Could you hand me the one with the nine, Beth. Please?"

The envelopes looked ancient, cracked and faded. Beth took Number Nine and handed it to her. "I'm dying to know what happened."

"The most amazing thing, really." Sarah paused. "Sit back, Beth. You won't want to miss it. Not the story . . . or the part that comes afterwards. Remember, I told you?"

Beth grinned, and her eyes didn't look as pained as before. "The secret to love?"

"Exactly." Sarah pointed her finger in the air to make her point. "The secret to love."

Sarah took the ornament from the envelope and said the word out loud. "The word is **Opportunity**." She placed it on the tree. "Let me explain."

The more time passed that summer, the more Sarah had longed for Sam. All she needed was a way to find him, to let him know she was thinking about him. An opportunity.

"And so I did the only thing I could think to do." She angled her head, her eyes on the window once more. "I wrote a song."

"The one you've been humming?"

"That very one."

❦

Every day Sarah would walk to Greer Park and sit on the bench at the edge of the grassy field, allowing God to mold the words and lyrics to her song. That fall, sitting on the bench, she finally finished it. And then she begged God for a miracle, for His help in finding Sam. Even if only for a few minutes, so he could hear her song.

Another month went by. Then, one Monday morning in late September, Mr. Hamilton, her boss from Trailway Records, called. Someone had fallen for her voice. Not a Mitch Mullins. This time the person interested was the head of the company. The president of Trailway Records.

Sarah couldn't believe it, not even as she waited for Mr. Hamilton's explanation. While working in Nashville, she'd never met the president of the recording company, and now—now that she'd given up her dream and crawled home with her tail between her legs—now her voice had caught the attention of someone at the top of the industry.

"We'd like to bring you back out, Sarah." Mr. Hamilton's voice was brimming with excitement. "You can sing some of your other songs, and maybe something new. Would that be a problem?"

Sarah was thrilled, but not at the idea of living in Nashville. "I can come out, but I won't stay. My home is here in Greer."

"That's fine. We'll only need you for a week or so."

She thought of something. "I'm . . . I'm not sure I have the money to get there."

Mr. Hamilton gave a soft laugh. "Sarah, we'll pay for the train ticket, your meals, and your hotel. You'll be staying in the Trailway Records suite at the big hotel just down the street from our offices."

Sarah had to stifle a scream. She was getting her break after all! And without compromising anything! Her excitement was dimmed only by the fact that Sam would never know. He had prayed for her, wished her well, and let her go. But now he wouldn't be a part of whatever God was about to do. And she knew it was God, as surely as she knew what day it was. She'd given all of it—her life, her singing, her heart—back to God. And now, in all His mercy, He was giving her the chance to sing her own songs on her own terms, living at her own address.

She accepted the offer to come, and that afternoon

she promised her parents that this time was different, legitimate. Among the musical pieces she slipped into her satchel before she left for Nashville was "Sarah's Song." She wasn't a bit surprised, when she sang for the president of Trailway Records later that week, that it was "Sarah's Song" he fell in love with.

Six weeks later it debuted in the number one spot on the country charts, and suddenly Sarah had the answer to her prayer. The opportunity she'd needed all along. The words she wanted to tell Sam were out there for all the country to hear. Absolutely everywhere.

Sarah stopped and looked at Beth. "It's time for the words. The first verse and the chorus."

Nothing more needed to be said.

Beth helped Sarah to the window, and there, for the first time since starting the simple ritual, Sarah opened her mouth and sang the words to her song—the one she'd written for Sam Lindeman back when she'd thought all hope of finding him was gone forever. Despite the years, her voice was sweet and clear, and the words were marked by feelings that had never dimmed.

It's not too late for faith to find us.
Not too late for right to win.
Not too late, let love remind us.
Not too late to try again.

The tune changed, and Sarah stared at the park bench, willing him to be there beside her one more time—one more day when they could sit together and marvel at the miracle of 1941.

She uttered a quick sigh; it was time for the first verse—the only one she wanted to sing that day. From the corner of her eyes, she glanced at Beth. The woman wasn't only listening, she was hanging on every word. Sarah kept singing, but she closed her eyes so nothing would interfere with the memory.

In my life the straight and narrow had a face, and
it was yours.
I took crooked paths around you, shut you out, and
locked the doors.
Long I wandered tired and aimless, seeking all the
world might hold.
There you waited, true and blameless, soul of good-
ness, heart of gold.

They were both silent, and Beth swallowed hard. Sobs built within her, sobs she couldn't explain. What was it about the story that touched her so? And how come whenever Sarah spoke, the story seemed to be about Beth and Bobby instead? Not the details maybe, but the heartache behind them.

Or maybe it was the song. The words played again in Beth's mind. *It's not too late for faith to find us. Not too late for right to win. Not too late, let love remind us. Not too late to try again.*

Wasn't that what Bobby had been trying to tell her ever since her decision to leave?

Beth choked back the sobs and cleared her throat.

"I'm tired." Sarah made a backwards shuffling motion. "Help me, Beth, will you?"

When Sarah was in bed again, when she'd caught her breath, Beth searched the old woman's tired eyes. "Sam must've heard the song eventually. Right, Sarah?"

"Now, now." Sarah's eyelids lowered, as if she might fall asleep in the midst of her sentence. "You said you'd come tomorrow."

"I'll be here." Beth took her chair again.

"The answers are coming, Beth. I promise you."

"When, though? Which day?"

"Some will come tomorrow."

Beth didn't push beyond that. She refilled Sarah's water pitcher, tucked the blanket in around her again, and bid her good-bye. The story of Sarah and Sam couldn't be rushed, and maybe that was the richness of it.

Beautiful stories took longer to tell.

For a moment, as she hurried into the hall and off to the next resident's room, Beth let that thought simmer in her heart. If beautiful stories took longer, then why was she in such a rush to leave Bobby, to move Brianna away from her father and give up on their marriage?

The thought was fleeting, gone almost as soon as it came. The reasons were all too obvious. A story like theirs wouldn't get better over time; it would get worse. Unbearably worse, right?

But somehow, even with all the justifications she could muster, her decision to leave felt weak and wrought with poor excuses.

Several times over the next few hours Beth caught herself remembering the early days with Bobby, the silly little somethings only the two of them understood, the rich rainy Sunday afternoons before Brianna was born, the quiet intimacy that had lasted long after they left the bedroom.

Why had they let time barge its way between them? And how could they rewind the clock now that they'd reached this point? She'd already made up her mind, hadn't she? Willing things to be better wouldn't make that happen between them. Beth mulled that over and wondered: What would it take to find their way back to a marriage marked by love and laughter?

By the time she drove home late that afternoon, one line of "Sarah's Song" had etched itself firmly in her mind. She had hummed it and sung it to herself a hundred times that day, and every time the first four words caught in her throat and made her feel like crying.

It's not too late . . .

They were words that screamed of hope and forgiveness and new life. But the sound of them on her own tongue made her heart heavy with sorrow because Beth was pretty sure about one thing.

Precious words like those would never apply to her.

CHAPTER TEN

Panic shot through Sarah, and she couldn't catch her breath.

She struggled to sit up, to wedge a pillow beneath her, but she couldn't do either. Instead, she sucked in with all her might. For her efforts, a single raspy bit of air toyed with her lungs, hardly enough to bring relief to her screaming body.

"Help me!" The words hung on the edge of her tongue, not loud enough for even Sarah to hear. She was dying; that had to be what was happening. Dying before she had a chance to finish her story, before she had the chance to tell Beth how everything had come together.

Before she'd gotten to the secret of love.

God, no! Don't let me die now. Not yet. She winced at the pain in her chest and made another desperate attempt at a breath. This one brought in less air than the last and she could feel herself waning away, feel her heart slowing within her.

Her eyes darted around the room, looking for an escape, a way to pull herself higher on the pillows. If only she could sit, she could catch her breath, and she chided herself for not taking the doctor's suggestion earlier that month.

"It would help if you'd sleep sitting up, Sarah. People at the end stages of heart failure find it much more comfortable."

"Doctor," Sarah had smiled at him. "I can't sleep sitting up. You know that."

She reached her hands over her head and wrapped her fingers around the top of the headboard. *Pull, Sarah. Come on, pull.* She strained until every muscle in her arms ached, but her efforts did nothing to lift her torso, nothing to relieve the pressure in her chest.

Just yesterday she could sit up on her own, so that meant something was wrong. Something that might send her home to heaven before lunchtime if she didn't find a way to get the staff's attention.

Suddenly she remembered the bell. Of course. Why hadn't she thought of it before? Her eyes darted to the wall beside her bed and there it was, bright red, screaming for her to notice it.

She started to lift her hand, but her body demanded another breath. Squinting, closing her eyes from the effort, Sarah sucked in everything she could, but still her body cried for more. Her eyes opened and she stared at the buzzer. Now! She had to press it now or it would be too late.

With all her remaining energy, she raised her hand up and jabbed her finger into the button. A buzzer sounded, and Sarah let her hand fall back to the bed, limp and trembling.

God, help me. I can't go home yet; that would ruin everything.

She concentrated on using as little air as possible, but just as she heard fast steps outside her door she felt herself slipping. Farther and farther away she fell, black spots dancing before her eyes, connecting, blocking out the faces of the people entering her room.

"Help . . ."

"Oh, dear! Someone get an ambulance," Sarah heard. But the sound was so faint she wasn't sure if she was dreaming. "We need oxygen in here, stat."

Don't let me sleep, God . . . don't take me home. Not yet. Not . . .

The thought faded from her consciousness and she was surrounded by a peaceful quiet and a darkness so heavy she couldn't think or move or even try to draw a breath.

Just when the darkness began to frighten her, a warm glow appeared, soft and gentle and drawing her near. Her soul was filled with a longing, a desire to go after the light as if this was the thing she'd been born to do, the thing she'd waited for all her life.

But something just as strong stopped her, made her turn and search the darkness for a way out. Sarah was no longer sure why, or what mattered so strongly on the other side. Only that she was desperate to go back. *God . . . please . . . please.*

And in that instant her eyes opened and she could see a host of people working on her. Beth Baldwin was standing in the back of the room, her fingers over her mouth. One of the men held something over Sarah's mouth and she realized she was sitting up. She could take a breath now, and the terrible weak feeling was going away. She pushed the soft plastic piece away from her mouth, her eyes wide. "What . . ." She gasped, filling her throat with sweet air. "What happened?"

"Ma'am, you need the oxygen mask." A paramedic slipped it back over her mouth, his eyes kind but firm.

Once she was breathing steadily again, he leaned closer. "I'll explain this as simply as I can, ma'am. Your congestive heart failure is getting worse. Last night while you slept, your lungs began filling with fluid. You almost drowned."

Another medical technician stepped in beside him. "You'll need to stay propped up from now on."

From now on . . .

The words filtered through Sarah's mind and immediately she understood what was happening. This was the end her Doctor Cleary had told her about two years ago, when he first made the diagnosis of heart failure.

"Eventually, your lungs will fill up with fluid," the doctor had said. "We'll move you to a permanently upright position, but after that the end could come quickly."

Sarah hadn't been afraid. "How quickly?"

"Days." He gave her a sad sort of knowing look. "Sometimes only a few days."

Now here she was, three days left in her story, and the time had come. Dr. Cleary had explained it this way: Congestive heart failure was like lying down in a pool that was slowly filling with water. When the water began to cover a person's mouth and nose, the person with heart failure could sit up, but they wouldn't have the energy to swim or stand. The water, meanwhile, would keep rising, and eventually it would drown the victim. Slowly, painfully, but as surely as one day followed the other.

"We're going to transport you to the hospital, Sarah." The medic leaned in and smiled at her. Behind him someone else was moving a stretcher into the room.

Sarah shook her head and pushed the oxygen mask away from her face. "No! My . . . doctor gave me permission . . . to stay." She stared at them, tired from the effort of talking, and just short of angry. "I have a right . . . to stay; I know what's happening."

A tension hung in the room as the staff members and medical team stopped and stared at her. Out of the corner of her eye Sarah saw Beth quickly leave the room. Sarah coughed twice and waved off the attempts to return the mask to her face. "I'm fine. I need to talk." She drew a few quick breaths and looked each of them in the eyes. "I'm dying; I know that. But I refuse to . . . die in a hospital when this . . . this is my home."

The medic took a step back and looked at his peers.

Just then Beth burst back into the room with what looked like a patient chart. She took hold of the medic's arm, her voice passionate. "She's telling the truth." Beth held the chart up and read the notes written there. "Dr. Cleary listed her as a D.N.R. Do not resuscitate. She's been given permission to die here, without a trip to the hospital as long as her symptoms are caused by heart failure." Beth looked up at the man. "They are, right?"

"She's very sick, ma'am. We only want to give her the best possible care."

Mr. Johnson, the manager on duty, stepped forward. "Let's honor her wishes. We'll keep her on oxygen. If there's anything else we can do, please let us know."

A look of resignation crossed the medic's face. "She could be on intravenous fluids, but as long as she can sip from a straw, the IV isn't absolutely necessary." He lowered his voice. "Her lungs are very wet; to be honest, she may not have more than a few days."

Sarah felt a sense of elation flash through her. She still had a few days! Just like Dr. Cleary had said! And at this point in her life, that was all that mattered, because a few more days was all she needed.

God was giving her enough time to finish telling her story to Beth Baldwin.

CHAPTER ELEVEN

THE GROUP OF PEOPLE standing near Sarah's bed talked for another few minutes but the decision had been made, they would follow the plan outlined in Sarah's chart.

She could stay.

Sarah wanted to shout for joy, but she was too tired. Instead she held out her hand to Beth and mouthed the words, "Thank you."

The others left the room, but Beth stayed. She squeezed Sarah's hand, her eyes watery with tears. "Sarah, I'm . . . I'm sorry. I wish you weren't so sick."

Sarah held tight to Beth's fingers. The medic had removed the oxygen mask and placed two small air tubes into either side of her nose so she could talk. Her words came slower than she would've liked, but at least they came. "Don't be . . . sorry. I'm ready to go." A smile tugged at the corners of her mouth. "I have just . . . one thing left to do."

Beth pulled up a chair and stroked Sarah's hand. Two small tears fell from her eyes and splashed across her cheeks. "Is it what I think?"

"Yes." Sarah hesitated, waiting until she caught her breath. The waters were rising; she could feel them even now. "I must finish the story."

"Finish it today, Sarah." Beth wiped at her cheek. "Please."

"No." A feeling of peace and knowing settled over Sarah's soul. "Today is the tenth day . . . I will tell you . . . only that part."

Beth exhaled and fearful uncertainty colored her expression. "But what if . . ."

Sarah shook her head. She could feel the light shining in her eyes. "God will give me three days." She pressed her hand against her heart. "I know it in here." She made a gentle motion toward the nightstand. "But I'll need . . . your help, Beth."

Beth bit her lip, her expression determined. "I'm here, Sarah. Whatever you need I'm here."

"Very well." Sarah relaxed against her pillows and found the window once more. "Let's get started."

Beth was filled with dread, and nothing Sarah said about being ready or having three more days did anything to relieve the feeling. In the days of December, she'd come to rely on Sarah in some way she couldn't quite define. In a world turned upside down, a world where divorce and defeat and discouragement reigned, "Sarah's Song" had given her hope again.

And now Sarah was dying.

Even the medics had said so; Sarah Lindeman was going to die, and then what? Who would remember her song or her story? And what if she didn't live long enough to finish it?

The questions haunted her even as Sarah asked her to take the ornament from the tenth envelope. The frail piece of paper inside read *Victory,* and Beth found a place for it on the small tree. Bit by bit, the story began to spill from Sarah's lips in soft breathy bursts. As it did, Beth felt her anxiety grow dim, felt herself forget about the panic that had been welling up inside her since she'd arrived at work and saw the ambulance and fire truck parked outside.

Sarah's words soothed her soul, allowed her to be carried back, back in time to the fall of 1941, to the next part of the story.

Sarah explained how Trailway Records released

"Sarah's Song" as a single and placed it on a fast track. It came out in mid-November, and immediately hit number one on the country charts. Sarah was an overnight sensation.

"You were a celebrity, Sarah!" Beth narrowed her eyes, surprised. One of the girls on staff had mentioned something about Sarah being a professional singer in her day, but a number one single? "No wonder Sam heard the song."

"He didn't . . . hear it right away." Sarah inhaled through her nose and waited a moment. When she'd caught her breath, she picked up the story again.

Offers poured in and dates were set for Sarah to cut her first album. Everywhere she went people congratulated her on her success, praising her voice and the impact the song was making in the lives of the listeners. But it wasn't enough for Sarah.

"Victory would only come if Sam heard the song." She chuckled softly and it became a series of short coughs. "In the end, he didn't hear the song at all, but an interview. A radio interview."

Sam Lindeman had been at home in his New Jersey apartment on Saturday morning, about to enjoy a two-week break from school, when he flipped on the radio. Instantly, he recognized the voice of the woman speaking. It was Sarah; he would know her voice after a hundred years of missing her.

He turned up the volume and heard what she had to say.

Sarah's eyes drew distant. "The announcer asked me what had inspired 'Sarah's Song,' and I told him. I'd loved just one man in my life, and I'd lost him. I would do anything to have him back again, but it was too late. The announcer asked me his name and I told him. Sam. Sam Lindeman. Then I took it a step further. 'Sam,' I said over the air. 'If you're out there, I'm sorry for leaving. I love you; I always will.' "

Sarah's words were slow with frequent stops but that didn't matter. Beth hung onto every line, imagining a young man sitting near the radio, hearing the woman he still loved declaring her feelings for him.

When the interview was over, the station played "Sarah's Song." Sam allowed every word to work its way into his heart. His career gave him little time for listening to music, so that was the first time he'd heard it. But long before the song was over he knew what he had to do.

That afternoon he called the school's superintendent and explained that something had come up; he wouldn't be able to finish out the semester because he had to get home. The next day he packed his things and boarded a train back to South Carolina.

"And that's the tenth part of the story." Sarah closed her eyes for a moment and then blinked them open. "I'm tired, Beth. Too tired to sing."

Beth's throat felt thick, and she swallowed back her sorrow. "That's okay. You can sing the song tomorrow."

Sarah nodded, but she was already asleep.

That night after she tucked Brianna in, Beth found Bobby sitting in the TV room, the television off. "Hey." She sat down beside him and waited until he looked at her. "I'm sorry if I've been mean these past few weeks."

The lines on his forehead softened. He eased his arm around her shoulders and pulled her close. They stayed that way a long while before he spoke. "I understand. Leaving isn't easy."

She wanted to say something more, something about working things out or finding a way to fall in love again. But she couldn't. Leaving was still the right choice, wasn't it? The only way either of them would ever be happy again?

After a while, they both stood and found their separate sleeping areas.

"Sarah's Song" rang in Beth's mind again that night, especially those four words that had stayed with her. *It's not too late . . . It's not too late . . .*

The next day, she could hardly wait to get to work and find out what happened next—what Sam had done once he arrived back in Greer with his things.

Sarah's breathing was more labored that morning, but her spirits were high. This was the eleventh day of her ritual, which meant she was almost at the end. The prospect gave her an energy she hadn't had since the first day, and it made Beth certain that somehow Sarah was right.

She would live long enough to finish the story.

Not for herself, but for Beth. For whatever was happening in Beth's heart and soul and mind. And because only at the end would she hear the rest of "Sarah's Song" and learn the secret of love.

The secret only Sarah could share.

CHAPTER TWELVE

THE ELEVENTH ORNAMENT read *Embrace,* and again Beth hung it on the tree for Sarah.

Only one envelope remained now. When the newest ornament was in its proper place, Sarah drew a slow breath and began.

Sam arrived in Greer on Monday, December 22, and immediately took a cab to Sarah's house. Her parents were thrilled to see him, but they explained that Sarah wasn't there. She was writing again, something she liked to do at Greer Park, on the far bench near the big grassy field.

Sam knew the place; he and Sarah had met there before. He hugged Sarah's parents and headed for the park.

"Actually, I wasn't writing a song that day," Sarah smiled, her eyes suddenly watery. "I was writing in my journal, asking God about Sam. I looked up and—" Her mouth hung open, but she couldn't speak. The soft folds of her chin trembled and a tear made its way down her leathery cheek. She shook her head. "I'm sorry. This is my favorite part." She gazed out the window. "I looked up and there he was. Sam Lindeman, walking toward me. I thought . . . I thought I was seeing things until he walked right up and held out his hands."

Sarah closed her eyes and a smile worked its way up her cheeks. More tears splashed onto her face, but the smile remained. "I can hear him now, see him. Standing there, arms outstretched. I went to him and the feel of his arms . . ." She opened her eyes and looked at Beth. "Has stayed with me a lifetime. I don't need the twelve days or the ornaments to feel his arms around me. I was born for that moment, and the memory of that embrace will stay until I draw my last breath."

Beth swallowed hard and realized there were tears on her own cheeks.

"I'll finish the story tomorrow." Sarah folded her hands, simple and demure.

Reluctantly, Beth bent over and kissed Sarah on the forehead. "I'll be here."

That night, again, Beth's heart felt softer than before. She caught herself making conversation with Bobby, even laughing at something he said. But the morning couldn't come soon enough, and when it did, she hurried to Sarah's room, desperately hoping the woman was still alive.

It was Christmas Eve, the twenty-fourth of December. The Twelfth Day of Christmas. Sarah was awake, gray and tired, but her eyes sparkled. "Are you ready for the rest of the story, Beth?"

She dropped to the chair, and gave Sarah's hand a gentle squeeze. "Yes. Please . . . go ahead."

"Today, the ornament comes last."

"Okay."

Sarah breathed in and coughed several times. Then— in a way that even her failing health couldn't stop—the story came.

That day at the park, Sam held onto her for what felt like forever. When he pulled back he asked her nothing about the past or Nashville or what had happened to bring her home again.

Instead he held out a ring and asked her to be his wife.

"We sat on that park bench," Sarah stared out the window, "the rest of the afternoon. Kissing, talking . . .

amazed we'd found each other. Until he died we returned to that bench again and again and again." She closed her eyes and when she opened them, her lashes were damp. "I feel him there, with me, every time I see that old bench. Even now that he's been gone so many years."

Beth nodded. If only Sarah could make it over to the window one more time. Maybe when the story was finished.

Sarah went on, explaining how she and Sam told her parents about their engagement and how her mother pulled her aside. She paused, weary from the effort, but clearly determined to press on.

"My mother gave me something that night. Look under my bed, Beth. Please."

Beth hesitated, but only for a moment. She didn't want to look under the bed; she wanted the story. But Sarah's expression pleaded with her, and Beth nodded. She dropped to her knees and there, under the bed, was a small white box. "This?" She pulled it out and held it up for Sarah to see.

"Yes." Sarah looked at the box as if it were a long lost friend. "Open it. I don't bring it out until the twelfth day."

Beth sat back in her chair and lifted the top from the box, her movements slow and reverent. Inside lay a pair of red gloves, worn and slightly faded. She looked up at Sarah, puzzled. "Your mother gave you gloves?"

"Red gloves." Sarah's eyes sharpened, and a knowing look filled her expression. "I'm giving them to you, Beth. Put them on."

Beth was overcome with a sense of awe. Sarah had obviously cherished the gloves for sixty years, but now . . . now she was giving them away. "Sarah, I can't take—" She stopped when she saw the certainty in Sarah's eyes. "You really want me to have them?"

"Yes." Sarah's eyes glistened.

Beth hesitated, looking down at the gloves. With great care she slid them on, first one hand, then the other.

Only then did she see the white stitching, the embroidery that made a pattern across the palms of both gloves. She was about to ask what it meant when she realized it wasn't a pattern at all, but words.

Her eyes found Sarah. "There's . . . a message here, isn't there?"

"There is." Sarah was teary again. "Hold your hands up toward heaven. That's the only way to read it."

Beth did as she was told, holding her outstretched

hands heavenward. As she did, the words sprang to life. The palm of the left red glove read, *"Above all else . . ."* And the palm of the right glove read, *"guard your heart."*

Above all else, guard your heart.

Sarah smiled through her tears and made a small shrug with her tired shoulders. "There it is, Beth. The secret of love. Above all else, guard your heart. It's a Bible verse, Proverbs 4:23."

Beth stared at the words and felt them penetrating her soul, probing about and challenging her in a way nothing ever had. "I . . . I've never heard that before."

"You see," Sarah sniffed and adjusted the oxygen tubes in her nose. "If I would've guarded my heart, Beth, I never would've given myself to Mitch Mullins. I would have realized Sam's worth long before I ever left Greer."

Beth stared at the gloves for a long time. "Sarah . . . I can't take these. They're . . . they're too precious. Your children should have them."

"No." Sarah's eyes shone. "God wants you to have them, dear. He told me you need that message this Christmas."

The gloves were soft on her fingers, and Beth held them to her face. They smelled of old love and days gone by, and they were warm. Not so much against her cheeks as they were warm against her heart. "Thank you, Sarah. I'll treasure them."

Eventually she let her hands fall to her lap and she looked at Sarah. "What happened then, with you and Sam?"

"We didn't want to wait, so we got married." She looked toward the window again, lost once more to the past.

The couple gathered their closest friends and family and the preacher from Greer Community married them on Christmas Eve at the park, right in front of the bench where Sarah had written the song, the place where Sam had found her when he returned to Greer.

"You can open the last envelope now, Beth."

The gloves remained as Beth reached for the envelope and pulled out the final ornament. The word read *Still*, and Beth felt the sting of tears as she placed it on the plastic tree.

"We married on Christmas Eve." Sarah's eyes were dreamy, her smile that of a girl sixty years younger. "I wore a white dress and the red gloves. The ceremony was short, and halfway through it started to snow. Our preacher pronounced us husband and wife and then Sam turned to me and started to sing." She hesitated, still amazed. "He knew all the words."

And then, the way Sam had sung to her that magical Christmas Eve, Sarah began to sing.

" 'It's not too late for faith to find us . . . Not too late for right to win.' " The words came crisp, clear despite Sarah's struggle to breathe. " 'Not too late, let love remind us. Not too late to try again.' "

Sarah closed her eyes, squeezing out two small streams of tears. "I took over from there, singing the entire song to him, all three verses. When I finished, the pastor said he had just one prayer for the two of us. That fifty years from then, we would still know the words to the song, still make time to sing it the way we were singing it that night."

Still.

The word on the twelfth ornament. Beth looked at the tree, at the words scattered amidst the branches. It was the greatest love story Beth had ever heard, but the best part of all was the lesson in the red gloves. *Above all else, guard your heart.*

Sarah lifted her tired hands and pulled them across her cheeks. "I still love him, Beth." Their eyes met. "I still love him, and I still remember the song. Just the way the pastor prayed that Christmas Eve." Sarah settled back some, her eyes never leaving Beth's. "You know why I only remember the details of our story once a year?"

"No." The question had come up several times, but Beth had never voiced it. "How come?"

"Because going back makes me miss him, and—" Her voice cracked, and for the first time since the story's beginning Sarah was overcome with emotion. Sobs shook her, stopping her from speaking and causing her shoulders to shake. The pain in the old woman's face was so gut-wrenching Beth considered calling for help. But then gradually, it began to ease. Her weathered hands came up and covered her face and the sounds of her soft cries filled the room. "God, how I miss him."

Beth stared at her hands, at the red gloves and the message written across the palms. After a while, Sarah stopped crying. She sat a little straighter and exhaled long and slow. "I'll be going home soon; I'm ready now." She smiled through her tears. "Sam's been waiting a long time for me to join him."

There were a hundred things Beth wanted to say, things she wanted to ask. What happened next, and how long before they had children. How did they keep their love alive and how—after more than six decades—did she still feel the same way about Sam Lindeman.

But Sarah's eyes were closing. "I . . . I'm finished, Beth."

"Sarah, wait . . ." Beth leaned forward and gave Sarah's arm a light shake.

Sarah opened her eyes. Her gaze was so direct, so sincere it took her breath away. "I believe you have something to do, Beth." She hesitated. "It's Christmas Eve. Do it now; before it's too late."

Before Beth could respond, Sarah nodded and fell asleep.

But that was okay, because Sarah was right. Beth had something to do, and nothing was going to stop her. Tucking her gloved hands into her pockets, she slipped downstairs and outside and crossed the street to the park.

She found the bench instantly and the moment she sat down, she started to cry. Her tears came with an intensity similar to Sarah's, but for different reasons. She didn't miss a man long dead, but she'd very nearly missed the truth. If not for Sarah's story, her song, Beth would've walked out on the man God Himself had given her, a love she was suddenly desperate to fight for.

The words embroidered across the palms of the red gloves shouted at her now. She didn't need to talk to Sarah about how she and Sam had kept their love alive. The secret was right there, plain as day.

Above all else, guard your heart.

It was five o'clock when Beth finally got home that evening.

The red gloves still on her hands, she took the bulky package from the back seat of her car and was halfway up the walkway when Bobby opened the door. "Beth, I . . ." He stopped, his mouth open, eyes wide.

In her hands were four dozen yellow roses.

The tears blurred her vision, and she blinked so she could see his reaction. She stopped walking, stood there in the glow of the Christmas Eve moon, and before he could say another word, she started to sing.

"It's not too late for faith to find us. Not too late for right to win." Tears came but she sang anyway. Never mind the freezing night air or the fact that her voice was not smooth and rich like Sarah's. It was sincere. And the words came straight from her heart as she sang them to the man she still loved, the man she almost lost.

"It's not too late, let love remind us. Not too late to try again."

She began walking toward him, her eyes locked on his. "I'm sorry, Bobby." Before she reached the front porch she saw that he, too, was holding something. The smell hit her just as she realized what it was.

A fresh-baked key lime pie.

"Merry Christmas, Beth." His eyes were red and wet as he led her into the house.

A sweet, tart smell warmed the air, and suddenly Beth realized what she was seeing. There, on every available surface in the kitchen, were key lime pies. She stared at them, and slowly, in a way that would've made old Sarah proud, she set the flowers down and melted into her husband's embrace.

"Don't ever let go, Beth." He whispered the words against her hair, trembling from desire and desperation and the decision they'd almost made to end it all. "Please, don't let go."

Brianna came running into the kitchen, her eyes dancing. "Mommy, guess what? Me and Daddy baked you a hundred pies!" She joined the hug, her little arms tight around both of them.

Beth smiled at their daughter, the feel of Bobby's embrace still warming her from the inside out.

"Ten, to be exact." Bobby met her gaze and looked straight to the center of her heart. "I stopped trying, Beth. I'm sorry." He kissed her, ignoring Brianna's giggles. "I'll never stop again."

For a moment, Beth looked down at the red gloves. Bobby did the same and he made a curious face. "Are those new?"

Beth lifted her hands and framed his face with the furry red wool. "Yes. They're from a good friend."

"It's going to be the bestest Christmas." Brianna jumped up and down as she trailed away from them across the living room. "We have enough pie for a million weeks. Plus tomorrow is Christmas and . . ."

Their daughter's happy voice faded as Beth kissed Bobby, long and slow and with a lifetime of feeling. The way she hadn't kissed him in years.

"I guess . . ." He came up for air and grinned at her. "I guess this means you're not moving out."

Beth worked her gloved fingers through his hair and buried her head into his shoulder. "Not now or ever." She thought about Sarah. "Wait till I tell you what happened."

EPILOGUE

THE IMAGE CAME OUT OF NOWHERE.

Sarah was sitting straight up in bed, struggling to breathe, when suddenly she saw it as clearly as if it were happening there in the room before her. Only there was a problem. Sarah's eyes were closed; she couldn't possibly be seeing people standing before her.

The image was of Beth and a young man and a little girl, locked in an embrace not far from a Christmas tree. They were smiling and the look on their faces said much about the strength of their feelings for each other.

The picture was so strong, she opened her eyes and looked about the room. *God?* She couldn't voice the words so she said them in her head. *Is it true? Are things okay with Beth? Did the story change her?*

The answer resonated deep within her, and she knew what had happened. God had granted her the miracle she'd asked for. He'd allowed her to live long enough to tell her story, to pass on the miracle of "Sarah's Song." And in the process, the love between her and Sam would continue even after they were both dead and forgotten.

Sarah saw the image once more, Beth with her family, and she smiled. Then, in a sudden rush, she realized she could no longer draw a single breath. Again she tried, and again, until she realized what was happening. Her life was draining away, but she felt no urgency, no desire to press the panic button.

It was time to go home, and what better day than Christmas Eve.

The night of the greatest miracle of all.

🍂

The service was small, attended by Sarah's children and several grandchildren.

Beth stood at the back next to Bobby, and when it was over, she found her way to Sarah's daughter and introduced herself. "Here." She held out the red gloves. "Your mother gave me these because I needed them."

The woman recognized the gloves immediately, and took them, clearly grateful. "I wondered what happened to them. I found the tree and the ornaments, but not the gloves."

"Yes." Beth nodded. "She thought I needed them, and I did." She glanced back at Bobby and shot him a sad smile over the small crowd. She looked at Sarah's daughter again and sniffed. "I don't need them; I understand the message now." She paused, her throat thick. "I thought you'd want to keep them in the family."

The woman had Sarah's clear blue eyes. She hesitated for a moment. "Did she teach you the song?"

"Yes."

A knowing look dawned in the woman's expression. "Then . . . you're the one."

Beth lowered her brow, confused, and waited for the woman to explain herself.

"Last year at this time, I spent Christmas with Mother. She told me God was going to give her one more year, one more time to go through the twelve days and remember the story she and Dad had shared." Sarah's daughter blinked back tears, her chin quivering. "I asked her why she thought that and she told me someone out there needed a miracle. She was sure that if only that person would listen to the story, the miracle would happen, and a life would be changed forever."

Beth was too choked up to speak. She hugged Sarah's

daughter and took a final look at the white casket and the spray of roses that covered it. On the way home she stared out the window. How good was God to give Sarah a reason to live an extra year? To let the miracle be hers, a miracle she had needed more than she'd known?

Suddenly an idea hit her.

She turned to Bobby and grinned. "Hey, let's go home and make something."

He raised an eyebrow and gave her a welcoming smile. "Make something?"

A giggle slipped from her lips and she gave him a playful shove. "Not that, silly." She loved this, the way it felt to be with Bobby now. The two of them had found their way back to the beginning. She had shared Sarah's story with him, and taught him the song. What had happened between them in four short days was beyond explanation, and together they were determined to hold on forever to what they'd found.

Bobby angled his head, his eyes on the road. "Okay, then what should we make?"

"Well . . ." Beth bit her lip, and in the corner of her mind she could almost see Sarah smiling from heaven. "How about a dozen ornaments?"

During the Christmas season of 2002, many of you journeyed with me through the pages of my first Warner story, *Gideon's Gift*. In that book, I shared with you the miracle of a sick little girl and an angry homeless man, and the gift that changed both their lives forever. And in honor of Gideon's precious gift, at the back of that book I suggested several Red Gloves Projects for you and your friends and families.

In the hundreds of letters you've written me since then, I've heard one theme resonate loudly: You love the idea of the red gloves. Red for Christmas, red for a heart full of love and hope and Christmas miracles.

Red, the color of giving.

And because of that, I've decided to let the red gloves of *Gideon's Gift* play a cameo role in each of my Warner Christmas stories. The Red Gloves Series, we're calling it, and each book will have a new list of Red Glove Projects. Last year I gave you *Maggie's Miracle,* the second book in the Red Gloves Series. The Red Gloves Projects in that book dealt with helping orphaned or foster children.

As one of you told me last year, "I bought fifty copies of *Gideon's Gift* to give to everyone I know. My prayer is that we'd see red gloves all around us in the coming years, that they'd grace the hands of the homeless and widowed, the children without parents and parents without hope. So that red gloves would forever be the symbol of Christ's love at Christmas."

Sarah's Song is the third in my series of Red Gloves books, and it has become especially dear to me. The reason is simple: It deals with an old woman whose message literally brings about a miracle. A Christmas miracle.

There's something special about older people, people who've talked the talk and walked the walk. Take a trip through a retirement center some time, or visit a nursing hospital. What you'll see are frail, white-haired folks whose words don't come easily or quickly.

But don't let that fool you.

Every one of them, people in their seventies, eighties,

and nineties, has a story to tell. A tale of God's faithfulness, of love won and lost, or of a truth that took years to come to life.

But here's the tragedy.

Too often older people have no one to share their stories with. They sit in retirement homes playing their bingo and shuffling their way to their twice-daily meals, counting the days until heaven. And no one thinks to ask the questions.

In *Sarah's Song,* Beth Baldwin hears Sarah singing and asks, "What song is it? What does it mean?"

And because she asked, God cracked open heaven and gave Beth a miracle that changed her life. All she had to do was listen.

In that light, I bring you this year's Red Gloves Projects.

RED GLOVES PROJECTS

🐝 Take a trip to a retirement center. Most cities have these facilities now, and the residents are often well enough to realize their loneliness. Call the facility and set a date. Then gather your friends and family, and ask everyone to bring a pair of red gloves. Go as dinner is just ending, and fan out through the dining room. Have each person in your group find a resident, introduce themselves, and ask a few questions. Why is Christmas special, for instance, or in all your life what year was most special to you? Ask God to teach you something in the course of the conversation. Then give your set of red gloves to that resident.

🌿 Go caroling. If you and your family, or you and your group of friends can't sing well, don't let that stop you. Older people make a very forgiving audience. Simply locate a nursing home or retirement center, contact the facility, and set up a date. Then put together a few Christmas carols, wear Santa hats, and bring a box of red gloves to pass out. The hardest part will be trying to make it through "Silent Night" with twenty teary-eyed seniors soaking in every word. A note of caution: Don't bring baked goods. Most people in assisted living can't have sugar. The red gloves and your song will be gift enough.

🌿 Adopt an older person. Contact your local nursing home or retirement center and ask if they have a resident who doesn't receive visits very often. Maybe never. Then make it a point to visit that person at least once a week throughout the Christmas season. Bring that person a pair of red gloves, and get to know him or her. Your life just might be changed in the process.

🌸 Invite a lonely older person to dinner. This should be done with contacts through your church. Check if there are former members who are now residing in assisted living facilities. If they have no family in the area, offer to arrange a time when he or she can join you for dinner or a Christmas party. In the process, give that person a pair of red gloves and ask them to share their favorite story. It might be one you decide to keep in your family for decades to come.

I pray this finds you and your family doing well this Christmas, determined to seek the riches our seniors can offer. In doing so, I pray you make time to mend broken relationships and let fall the walls that have come between you and those you love. In Jesus, God gave us the greatest gift of all that first Christmas Day. How much richer we—like Beth Baldwin—are when we seek all He has to offer us, even now.

Please check out my Web site at www.KarenKingsbury.com for more information about the Red Gloves Projects that have happened since last year. And leave me a note in my guestbook. As always, I'd love to hear from you, and if you have a Red Gloves Project idea you'd like to share with me, please do. I'll add it to my website and perhaps suggest it in my Warner Christmas story next year.

Until next time, may God's light and life be yours in the coming year.

In His love,
Karen Kingsbury
Web site: www.KarenKingsbury.com
E-mail: Karen@KarenKingsbury.com

P.S. Did you figure out the hidden meaning in the words on Sarah's Christmas ornaments? If not, take a look:

T omorrow
H igh hopes
E xcitement

R ebellious
E xposed
D ance

G one
L onging
O pportunity
V ictory
E mbrace
S till

Remember? The secret to love was in the red gloves. *Above all else, guard your heart.* The secret was in the words on Sarah's tree, as well. Now you know.

Hannah's
Hope

Hannah's Hope

A NOVEL

KAREN KINGSBURY

WARNER
Faith

NEW YORK BOSTON NASHVILLE

Warner Faith
Time Warner Book Group
1271 Avenue of the Americas, New York, NY 10020
Visit our Web site at www.warnerfaith.com

The Warner Faith name and logo are registered trademarks of the
Time Warner Book Group.

Book design by Fearn Cutler de Vicq
Printed in the United States of America
First Warner Faith printing: October 2005
10 9 8 7 6 5 4 3 2 1

Library of Congress Cataloging-in-Publication Data
Kingsbury, Karen.
    Hannah's hope / Karen Kingsbury.— 1st Warner Books ed.
        p. cm. — (Red gloves series)
    Summary: "A fifteen-year-old girl longs for the father she never
knew"—Provided by the publisher.
    ISBN 0-446-53236-3
    1. Teenage girls—Fiction. 2. Fatherless families—Fiction.
3. Paternal deprivation—Fiction. I. Title.
    PS3561.I4873H36   2005
    813'.54—dc22   2005014900

To . . .

Donald, my Prince Charming

Kelsey, my precious daughter

Tyler, my beautiful song

Sean, my wonder boy

Josh, my tender tough guy

EJ, my chosen one

Austin, my miracle child

And God Almighty, the author of life, who has—for now—blessed me with these.

ACKNOWLEDGMENTS

A special thanks to Rolf Zettersten, Leslie Peterson, Andrea Davis, Lori Quinn, Jennette Merwin, Preston Cannon, and everyone at Warner Faith who helped make this Red Gloves novel possible.

Also, thanks to my agent, Rick Christian, president of Alive Communications. Rick, you continue to amaze me, leaving me blessed beyond words. Thank you for keeping my family life and my faith as your utmost concern.

I couldn't complete a book without help from my husband and kids, who know what it is to eat tuna sandwiches and cheese quesadillas when I'm on deadline. Thanks for always understanding! I cherish every minute of our family time!

The work of putting together a book doesn't take place without other people picking up the slack in my life. A heartfelt thanks goes to my mother and assistant, Anne Kingsbury, and to assistants Katie Johnson and Nicole Chapman. Also thanks to Aaron Hisel for your work with Tyler, and to the Shaffers and Heads and Weils, and to Kira Elam and Tricia Kingsbury for helping out with rides when I'm on deadline.

Prayer is a crucial part of taking a book from its original idea to the written page. So, thanks to my prayer warriors—Ann Hudson, Sylvia and Walt Walgren, Sonya Fitzpatrick, Teresa Thacker, Kathy Santschi, the Chapmans, the Dillons, the Graves, and countless readers, friends, and family who lift my writing ministry to our Lord on a daily basis. I couldn't bring you these books without that type of support. Thank you!

Thanks also to those who keep me surrounded by love and encouragement. These include my extended family, my church friends, the parents on our various soccer, baseball, and basketball teams, and the wonderful friends who make up our Bible study group and closest relationships. You know who you are—you are wonderful! I love you all!

Finally, a humble thanks to the men and women of the U.S. Armed Forces, especially Air Force reservist Jonathan Vansandt. My family and I completely support your work overseas across the world—particularly the efforts in Iraq and Afghanistan. If you are one of these, please let me know. I love hearing from my readers, but especially I love hearing how these stories are encouraging you. Your sacrifice is immeasurable. You remain in our prayers and thoughts as you carry out your mission. Because of you, I have the freedom to write books that give glory to Jesus Christ.

Thank you isn't nearly enough.

Hannah's Hope

*H*annah Roberts was late for lunch. Again. Her backpack was on a roller board, and she pulled it as she darted down the hallway of the music wing at TJ Prep, a private school for kids in Washington, D.C.'s politically elite. Hannah had gone here since sixth grade. As a freshman, she knew her way through the halls as well as she knew her own house. She tore into the commons area and bolted by the glass-walled administrative offices, past the storied brick fountain at the front entrance. A bronze plaque read, *"Bethesda, Maryland Welcomes You to Thomas Jefferson College Preparatory School for the Leaders of Tomorrow."*

No doubt about that. A number of politicians, lawyers, and international ambassadors had made their way through TJ Prep. Hannah didn't care much about that. Right now all she wanted was lunch. If she hurried, she might still make it.

She burst through the lunchroom doors, her backpack flying along behind her. Several hundred students milled about, eating cheeseburgers and fries or sipping on pop cans while they caught up on the latest gossip. Most of the guys were gathered around a baseball game playing on the eight-foot flat-screen television at the center of the room. There was a line at the automatic teller machine in the corner, same as always, and a few stragglers remained at each of the food court windows.

There was still time.

Hannah tugged on her blue-plaid skirt and adjusted her white blouse as she rushed toward the Salad Sensation line. If she didn't eat now, she wouldn't have another chance until late that evening. Cheerleading practice went until five, and after that yearbook had a committee meeting until seven. By the time her driver picked her up, she'd barely have a minute for dinner before her dance instructor came at eight.

On her way to the salad window, two of her cheerleading friends approached her. "Hannah, you're so bomb!" Millie tapped her shoulder with her fingertips. "Where did you get that blouse? Bloomingdale's?"

"Saks." Hannah kept walking, but she smiled at her friends over her shoulder. "Save me a spot at the table."

"Save you a spot?" Kathryn put her hands on her hips. "Lunch is over in nine minutes. You'll never get here on time."

"I know." Hannah was next up. "Save me a spot anyway."

The girls looked put out. They hated when Hannah stayed late in choir and missed most of lunch. But they shrugged off their frustration and returned to their table.

It took Hannah three minutes to get her salad, and then, still rushing, she joined her friends. "Okay," she was out of breath. "What's up?"

"You won't believe it." Millie leaned low over the table, her voice little more than a whisper. "Brian—you know Brian, the senior in my algebra class—he came by my house the other day." She squealed. "Hannah, he wants to go out!"

"Really?" Hannah took a huge bite of salad. It didn't keep her from talking. "I thought you couldn't date a senior."

"I can't." Millie grinned. "My parents think he's a junior."

"Yikes." Hannah took another bite. "When they find out you'll be grounded until summer."

"So?" Millie made a brushing gesture with her hands. "My dad's gone till then, anyway. He'll never know." She raised her shoulders a few times and glanced at the others. "Besides, nothing ever happens when I'm grounded. My parents always forget about it."

Kathryn finished her pop and pushed her can to the middle of the table. "My parents took my cell away, which stinks. Just because I'm getting a D in English." She exhaled hard, and her frown became the beginning of a grin. "But at least I don't get grounded."

"Yeah." Hannah took another two bites. She lived with her grandmother in The Colony, the enclave for D.C.'s wealthiest families. Whatever she wanted, she got. She could stay out late, date whomever, and she never lost her cell or her privileges. Not that she took advantage of the situation. She was too busy to get in trouble.

"You're blowing me off tonight." Kathryn plopped her elbows on the table and stared at Hannah. "You have yearbook." She made a face. "Frank Givens in Biology told me."

"Uh-oh." Hannah downed another bite of salad and grabbed her Palm Pilot from her Coach purse. A few key taps and she had her schedule up. "Yep. Yearbook five to seven." She would call for a ride after that. Her grandmother had a full-time driver, Buddy Bingo, a retired Navy guy. Buddy was available whenever Hannah needed him. She took another bite of salad and then scrolled down. "You're right." She looked up at Kathryn. "We were supposed to study."

"That's what I'm saying." Kathryn gave an exaggerated sigh. "We planned it a week ago."

"I remember." Hannah raked her hand through her thick, dark hair. "Give me a minute." A few more taps on her Palm. "Okay, how about six-thirty tomorrow after cheer practice? Dance classes are at eight this week." She found Kathryn's eyes again. "That gives us ninety minutes."

Before Kathryn could answer, two guys—a blond and a freckle-faced brunet—walked up. Both were juniors on the debate team, sons of senators. The blond took a step closer. He wore his usual cocky smile, the one that convinced so many of her friends to fall at his feet. "How's TJ's finest freshmen?"

"Well," Hannah lowered her chin and raised her brow at the boy. She wasn't interested, so why not have a little fun? "We're *fantastic*." She raised her voice above the conversations and clanking lunch trays in the cafeteria. In a school marked by money and madness, Hannah Roberts was one of the wealthiest, most prestigious girls on campus. There was no shortage of interested guys. "The question isn't how are the finest freshmen, but why the jerky juniors care?"

"Nice." The blond was unfazed. His grin crept a little higher into his cheeks. "Nothing gets to you, does it, Hannah Roberts?"

"Not much." She gave a practiced little wave to the guys. "See you around."

The bell rang before they could answer. The blond cocked his head. "Give me a call when you want a real man, Hannah."

"Okay." She took a long sip of water. "If I run across any, you'll be the first to know."

They walked away, Freckle Face laughing at Blondie.

Hannah chuckled, took the last two bites of her salad, stood, and tossed the plate into the nearest trashcan. Millie and Kathryn took up their places on either side of her.

"I can't believe you did that!" Millie's eyes were wide. "That was Jaden Lanning!"

"So?" Hannah picked up her pace. "I can't stand him." She rolled her eyes. "He thinks he's every girl's gift. Besides, I don't have time for guys."

"You don't have time for us, either." Kathryn hugged her books to her chest. She was doing her best to keep up as they maneuvered their way through the halls to their next class—a speech course, the only one they all shared. Kathryn blew at a wisp of her bangs. "Ever think about slowing down?"

"Never." Hannah's answer was even quicker than her pace. "I like staying busy."

"All right." They reached the classroom door and Kathryn lowered her voice to a whisper. "I just wish I knew what you were running from."

Hannah didn't answer. Already the conversation was too close for comfort. She gave her friend a smile that said she was finished talking. Then she made her way to her desk.

Her speech today was on the challenges of international politics—a topic normally reserved for juniors and seniors. But Hannah handled it like a master, no trouble. She could've given the talk without a bit of research. International politics was her parents' life.

❧

*A*fter school she led the cheerleaders in a new dance routine, one the cheer coach had asked her to create. "You're a better dancer than me, Hannah. Would you mind?"

"Not at all," Hannah had told her. Every challenge was a reason to keep going.

By five o'clock the squad had the dance down. Hannah grabbed her duffel bag and her roller backpack and sprinted across campus to the yearbook room. It was seven-thirty before she called Buddy for a ride. She must've looked exhausted because when he pulled up he gave her a worried frown.

"Runnin' on empty again, Miss Hannah?" He caught her look in the rearview mirror.

"A little." She smiled back.

Some days she spent more time talking to Buddy Bingo than anyone in her family. That wasn't saying much. Most of the year, the mansion she lived in was empty, home to just her and her grandmother.

Her father was the U.S. ambassador to Sweden, a former senator well known in the highest political circles. Her mother kept his social calendar, but for the past year she'd worked some at the embassy, serving as liaison between Swedish bankers and various politicians on several key projects.

There was talk that sometime in the next five years,

her parents might return home so her mother could run for senate in Virginia. "Then I'll take over the social calendar," her father had quipped more than once during their last visit that summer.

The ride home was quiet. Hannah wondered if Buddy was praying. Buddy was a man who talked to God, and most nights he'd tell her he was praying for her— something she didn't quite understand. God—if there was a God—seemed far away and uninvolved. Hannah wasn't sure if He had time to know who the real Hannah Roberts was, the reason she ran from one event to another without ever taking a day off.

"Things okay at school?" Buddy took a slow left turn onto the hilly road that led to The Colony.

"Great." Hannah yawned. "Aced my speech on the challenges of international politics, tore up in cheerleading, and designed the layouts for a third of the yearbook."

"You mean you didn't solve world hunger between classes?" Buddy's voice was upbeat, teasing her.

"Not today." She pressed her head back into the leather seat. "Maybe tomorrow."

"You'll probably try." Buddy chuckled. "Busy, busy girl. You sound like a twenty-five-year-old grad student. Not a high school freshman."

"My teachers say that." She breathed out. This was her resting time, and she made the most of it. She could've fallen asleep in the backseat of the new Lincoln.

"I guess it comes from hanging out with adults. That and staying busy."

"But you're a kid first, Miss Hannah. Don't forget that."

"I'm all right, Buddy. Staying busy keeps me sane." Her feet were sore, and she wiggled her toes as she stretched them out in front of her. That was the nice thing about Town Cars. Lots of leg room. "I have to be moving."

"That's because you're a butterfly, Miss Hannah. Nothing could ground you."

Hannah smiled. She liked that. A butterfly. Dear, sweet Buddy Bingo. He was a single man, the age of a grandfather. Blue eyes with a shock of white hair on his head and his face. Her friends thought he looked like Santa Claus, and when Hannah was little she used to wonder herself. He'd been a faithful driver for the Roberts family since Hannah was in third grade.

They pulled into the spacious entrance to The Colony and stopped at the guard station. Buddy waved to the man in the booth, and the man raised the gate. Buddy was beyond passwords at this point; all the guards knew him. When they pulled up at her house, he stopped the car and turned around, the way he always did. "How can I pray for you, Miss Hannah?"

Buddy asked her this every time he drove her. Usually she shrugged and told her it didn't matter; he could pray however he liked. But this time she thought a little longer.

"I know: pray for a miracle." She could feel her expression warm at the idea. "A Christmas miracle."

"Okay." Buddy gave a thoughtful nod of his head. "But Christmas miracles are the biggest, most amazing ones of all." He squinted. "Any certain kind of Christmas miracle?"

"I'm not sure yet." She grabbed her bags and waited for Buddy to open her door. One of her friends had talked about Christmas miracles during the yearbook meeting. The idea sounded good. Christmas miracles. Whatever that meant. And since Buddy was willing to pray, she might as well ask.

He got out, walked to her door, and opened it. "Well, Miss Hannah, you let me know if you decide. Meanwhile, I'll pray just like you asked. For a Christmas miracle."

It was a nice thought, one that settled her racing spirit and gave her peace even as her dance instructor forced ten minutes of pirouettes at the end of practice that evening.

She didn't see her grandmother until ten o'clock as she trudged up to her suite. "Hannah." The elderly woman stood, proud and stiff, outside the double doors of her own bedchamber. "How was your day?"

"Very well, Grandmother." It was always *Grandmother.* She stopped three steps short of the landing. "Thank you for asking."

"Have you brought up the B in Spanish?"

It was Hannah's only low mark. She bit the inside of her cheek. "Yes, Grandmother. It's an A-minus now."

"Very well." The woman smiled, and in it was a hint of warmth. "You'll have it up to a solid A soon, I imagine."

"Yes." Hannah took another step. "Soon."

"I assume you finished your work in class today?" Her grandmother raised her chin. "It's very late for extra attention to your studies at this hour."

"I'm finished, thank you." Hannah looked at her grandmother and felt the corners of her lips push up into her cheeks. The woman was too formal, too taken with her parents' world, their money. But still, she was all Hannah had, the only family she shared her daily life with.

The conversation stalled, and her grandmother bid her goodnight.

Not until Hannah was alone in her room did she let the truth she'd found out earlier today set in—a truth she couldn't share with anyone yet, not even Buddy Bingo.

Her parents wouldn't be coming home for Christmas this year.

They'd sent her an E-mail that morning before school. Usually they visited in summer and at Christmas—both times for a few weeks. But this year the schedule at the embassy was too busy.

"The social calendar is full, my dear," her mother wrote. "I'm afraid we'll be Christmas'ing in Sweden this year."

And like that, Hannah's Christmas had gone down the drain. Without her parents, there would be no Christmas parties or trips into the city to see the Living Christmas Tree and the annual pageant performances in the theater district. No one to exchange presents with or share a cup of cocoa with on Christmas Eve.

Her parents were even busier than she was, so she wouldn't miss out on any deep conversation or sentimentality or warm, cozy traditions—the things that made up Millie's and Kathryn's Christmas holidays. But without her parents home, the time would be quiet and lonely, just her and her grandmother—a woman who didn't believe in wasting resources every twenty-fifth of December simply because the calendar read, "Christmas."

She pulled off her dance clothes, tossed them into the hamper, and laid her blazer and skirt on the back of the sofa. The housekeepers preferred she didn't hang up her own clothing. Their method was better, easier to work with.

When the lights were off she lay there, considering her friend Kathryn's comment from earlier in the day again. *I just wish I knew what you were running from.*

The idea bounced around her brain like a pinball. She was running from a dozen things, wasn't she? From her empty mansion and her grandmother's unsmiling face, from quiet dinners and a forgotten childhood. And now she was running from Christmas. At least when her parents came home for the holidays she could convince herself they cared. They might not talk to her much or show a genuine interest in her life the way other parents did, but at least they came.

Now, though, there was no denying the obvious. Her parents had chosen their friends and social obligations over spending Christmas with their daughter. She felt a stinging in the corners of her eyes.

Of course she was running.

Every time she thought about the E-mail a sad sort of ache started in her belly. An ache that hurt all the way to her heart. If she didn't keep busy, running from one obligation to another, the hurt would eat her alive. It shouted at her now, reminding her that no one really cared, no one knew the private places in her heart.

They especially didn't know about the memories.

Now, in the dark, they came to her again. Memories that crept through the window and kept her company on cold November nights like this one. She remembered herself as a little girl, three or four years old, sitting in a small living room—a space no bigger than her walk-in closet. She was looking at her mother—a much younger version of her mother—and in the memory she was sitting near the feet of a handsome, strapping man, and the man was playing a guitar.

The song ended and the man pulled her into his arms. He nuzzled his face against hers and the two of them rubbed noses and she felt like the luckiest little girl in the world. In the memory, her daddy loved her. Both her parents did. There were other memories, all from about the same time, and in each one her parents were happy and laughing. Talking to her and holding her and reading to her and getting down on the floor to play with her.

She opened her eyes and stared at the ceiling ten feet overhead. In the darkness she could barely make out the molding along the perimeter of the room. Here was the problem: if that was the memory, where had it come from? And why had her parents changed?

Even when they did come home, they were busy entertaining dignitaries stateside, busy throwing parties for political friends they hadn't seen since their last visit. Almost none of their time was set aside for her. The family chauffeur cared more about her life.

She thought of Buddy Bingo and the notion of a Christmas miracle and a chill ran down her arms. She knew what she wanted now, what he could pray for. She would tell him the details tomorrow; that way, if he was putting in an order with God in the near future he could be more specific.

What she wanted more than anything in the world would take divine help to pull off. Nothing simple like a new handbag or a trip to France. What she wanted was bigger than that: she wanted her parents to come home for Christmas. When she'd received the E-mail that morning, Hannah had written back. "How completely understandable that my parents would choose parties in Sweden over Christmas with me. Love you, too."

Her mother's response was quick and to the point.

"It's impossible this year, Hannah. We'll see you during summer vacation."

And that was that. In fact, at this point—with her mother's social calendar booked through the holidays and her father entertaining princes at the embassy—it would take more than wishful thinking to get her parents home.

It would take a miracle.

A Christmas miracle.

$\mathcal{M}$otherhood never slowed Carol Roberts. Not when she'd first had Hannah fifteen years ago, and not now.

Back when Hannah was born, her father took care of her. He was smitten by the dark-haired, blue-eyed baby from the moment she came home. Hannah was a good girl. When she was old enough for kindergarten she was easily top of the class, and she held that distinction up until her current year as freshman at Thomas Jefferson College Preparatory. Carol was proud of her. But Hannah was still a child, and ambitious career plans didn't mix with children. Even the nicest children.

That's why Carol didn't mind living half a world away from Hannah. The two kept in touch through E-mail and phone calls, and twice a year—summer and Christmas—Carol and her husband found their way back to the States for a visit. Hannah wouldn't have had any normal sort of life living overseas, and it wasn't as if they had any choice.

Carol's husband was ambassador to Sweden.

The role of ambassador came with a host of responsibilities—some political, some practical, and some purely social in the name of goodwill. That November numerous dignitaries had passed through the office, and plans had been made for a round of holiday parties that would involve key international politicians—all of whom deserved the attention of Jack Nelson Roberts Jr.

Carol loved being in the middle of it all. Whether the day's work included a luncheon with visiting influentials or a party at a nearby ballroom, she thrived in her husband's arena, being a part of what he did—not only to help him look good, but because she had political aspirations of her own.

Maybe when Jack was finished with his work at the Swedish embassy, they could return to Maryland and she could try her hand at an office—something small to start with—and eventually work her way to being a representative, or a senator, even. She would be closer to Hannah that way. By then her daughter would be older—old enough that Carol could hire her as an intern and the two could get to know each other better.

For now, though, that type of day-in, day-out relationship would have to wait. Life at the embassy was simply too busy, too important, to take a chance on missing a key party or business dinner. Never had there been so many people to connect with, so valuable a host of politicians to get acquainted with. They were doing the United States a favor by giving the job their complete attention as winter approached. That was the reason they'd made their decision about the holidays.

This Christmas—for the first time—there would be no trip home. The holiday social demands on the embassy were too great to leave behind. Late the night before, Carol had alerted Hannah about the conflict. There would be a change of plans, she told her daughter. "Your father and I won't be coming home for Christmas after all," she wrote. "Not this year."

She'd hoped Hannah would understand. Christmas was just another day, after all. Another day in a round of parties and celebrating and merriment that went from September to January, and January to June, one year into the next for the Roberts family. Certainly Hannah could get through one Christmas without being dragged to a round of adult parties in Washington, D.C. In fact, Carol had expected Hannah might be relieved. The revised plan meant Hannah could spend the holidays relaxing with her grandmother or visiting her school friends.

But Hannah's response had been short, almost jaded.

"Fine, Mother," she'd shot back in an E-mail that morning. "How completely understandable that my parents would choose parties in Sweden over Christmas with me. Love you, too."

Love you, too? Carol had stared at those words, puzzled.

What sort of response was that? The letter made Carol wonder if she'd made a gargantuan mistake with Hannah all these years, if she'd grossly underestimated Hannah's acceptance of her lifestyle.

Ever since returning to the D.C. area, Carol had assumed her daughter understood her position. The Roberts family wasn't like regular families. There was a price to pay for Jack's title, both when he was a senator, and now as an ambassador. It wasn't so unusual, really. Nearly all of Hannah's school friends had parents whose lives involved political obligations. Senators stationed in Washington, D.C., spent half their time with their constituents in offices across the country. And those involved with international politics spent most of the year overseas.

It was a way of life.

So why the attitude from Hannah? As if Christmas wouldn't be the same if she and Jack didn't come? Carol fixed herself a salad for lunch and mulled over the situation. Hannah was beyond the sentimentality of the working class, wasn't she? The girl understood their lifestyle, how power and position came with a certain type of independence, one that didn't have room for hurt feelings or needy pairings between parents and children.

She loved Hannah, of course—loved her the way mothers in her social strata best loved their children. Not with gushy hugs or kisses or flowery words, but with actions. The proper way. Carol and Jack paid for the house in The Colony and tuition at TJ Prep, the best education a child could ask for. Beyond that they provided Hannah private instruction in dance, voice, and piano, and finishing school. In a few short years, Carol had plans for her daughter to work with her.

That was love, wasn't it?

But as Carol finished her salad, as she made her way to the back door and studied the meticulous gardens around the cobblestone patio, she thought of something she hadn't before: maybe Hannah was lonely. She was still young, after all. Maybe her schoolwork and lessons and practices had worn her out, and left her wanting adult company more than a quiet grandmother could give.

The clock ticked out a steady rhythm in the background and a pleasant lemony smell wafted through the kitchen, the result of something the housekeeper was working on in the next room. Carol squinted at the sun-sprayed shrubs in the back of the yard. Yes, that had to be the problem. Hannah simply wanted a little life in the old house.

So who could spend Christmas with Hannah? She and Jack were out of the question, at least for now. But there had to be someone in their circle, someone besides Grandmother Paul, who could spend a few days with Hannah over the Christmas break.

Then, for the first time in years, a thought came to Carol.

Maybe it was time to tell her about Mike Conner. Mike, who had been Carol's first love, the man she lived with for nearly four years after Hannah was born. The man Hannah knew nothing about.

Her biological father.

Carol had hoped to wait until Hannah was eighteen to tell her, but she was fifteen now. That was old enough, wasn't it? She held her breath as she made her way through the kitchen and into her office. The box was still tucked away under the desk, in the corner of the room. The box held everything that reminded Carol of her old life, the one she'd lived before she married Jack.

She remembered to exhale. Then, with quiet steps, she crossed the room, pulled the box into the middle of the floor, and removed the lid. The first thing inside was a manila envelope with a single name written in black permanent ink across the top: *Mike*.

A rush of feelings came over her and she could see the vast stretch of Pacific Ocean, hear the steady rush of waves against the shore, feel the warm sand between her toes as she sat on the beach watching him surf. She'd met him there, and from the beginning he'd had a surfboard tucked under one arm.

Carol closed her eyes and allowed the memory to have its way with her. She had been a dreamer back then, and Mike her blond, blue-eyed dream boy. Her parents had taught her about prestige and propriety and marrying well, but Carol ignored their advice. She'd been a hopeless romantic who had her own ideas about love, and all of them centered around Mike Conner.

"He's a drifter," her mother had told her. "With him you'll never amount to anything."

"He loves me, Mother," Carol insisted. "We'll find our own way."

"He's not the marrying type." Despair rang in her mother's voice. "You'll find nothing but heartbreak."

In the end, she'd been right—after four years of scrimping and barely getting by, Carol and Mike began fighting. The magic was long worn off by then, and Carol had to admit the truth in her mother's prediction. Mike wasn't the marrying type. He'd never even asked her, not until she first brought up leaving. But by then it was over. Mike had enlisted in the Army and gone to Fort Seal in Oklahoma for training. Three weeks later, alone and anxious for her old life, Carol and Hannah left one rainy April morning and never looked back.

Knowing she couldn't marry him, Carol hadn't put Mike's name on Hannah's birth certificate, and he hadn't argued about the fact. Not at first, anyway. Probably because he'd figured Carol would come around eventually, and the two of them would marry. Then he could easily add his name to Hannah's birth records.

In the months before he enlisted, he'd been anxious for it all—marriage, a proper place on Hannah's birth certificate, a family life together. But by then, Carol was ready to go home, ready for the life her parents had wanted for her. When she and Hannah said good-bye to the small beach house, Carol left behind no information or letters or forwarding address. She returned to Maryland and picked up with Jack Roberts—high-society politician and former playboy. The two were married within a year, and Carol's mother moved into Jack's guesthouse while she and Jack and Hannah took the main house—a veritable mansion.

Life improved overnight for everyone except Hannah. For two years Hannah had talked about her daddy, asking where he was and crying for him. Sometimes Jack would hold her and rock her, telling her that he was her father now. Always, though, they had known Hannah would be fine—and she was. In time she forgot about the daddy they'd left behind, believing that Jack was, indeed, her father.

But she deserved to know about Mike, and now was as good a time as any.

Carol held the envelope to her face and breathed in. It smelled old and musty and faintly like the sea, the scent of forgotten days and bygones. She opened the flap and pulled out the first picture. It was a photo of Mike and Hannah, just around the time when Hannah was starting to walk. The two were cuddled in a worn-out recliner, and Mike was reading to her. He'd always been reading to her. Hannah had one pudgy arm draped along the back of his neck, her grin reached from one ear to the other.

Carol set the picture aside and sorted through the rest of the envelope. After a few minutes she chose two photographs—the first one, and one of Mike with his surfboard, his blond hair cut short per the instructions of his Army enlisting officer. She sifted through the bag again and found a metal lapel pin—a pair of wings Mike bought in the days before he left for training.

"Daddy's gonna be a pilot one day, Hannah. An Army pilot. Then I'll have a real pair of wings." She could hear him still, full of confidence and hope that he'd make good on his dreams and give Carol the life he thought she wanted.

By the time Mike had plans to leave for training, he was worried Carol would bolt, that she'd pick up her things one day, leave with Hannah, and never look back. Before he left he'd pulled her aside and given her the wings, the ones he'd bought. Sincerity rang in his words. *"I want Hannah to have these. Make sure, okay?"*

A gust of guilt blew over Carol. She'd forgotten his request until now. Forgotten it as if he'd never even asked. She blinked and set the wings in the pile with the two photographs. At least she was taking care of it now. It wasn't too late. Besides, if Hannah were any younger she wouldn't have appreciated this—not the pictures nor the wings nor the information about Mike.

Carol sorted through the envelope and pulled out a list of details scribbled on an old, yellowed piece of notebook paper. The list represented all the information she'd had on Mike Conner back then.

She studied the sheet: his name, an old address and phone number in Pismo Beach, California. His age back then—twenty-three—and his birth date. And the fact that he'd joined the Army in early spring 1994.

That was it—all she had to remember him by.

For nearly a minute Carol studied the sheet and wondered. Was this the right thing for Hannah? The right timing? Would she be angry that she hadn't been told sooner? She hesitated and stared at the photo. It had been her decision to keep the information from Hannah. If Hannah was upset, they'd work through it, the same way they'd work through spending a Christmas apart.

Parenting wasn't much different from a business arrangement where most of the time the details ran smoothly, but some days brought disturbing news and hard work.

Carol made a copy of the detailed information and slipped it with the photos into a new envelope. Then she typed a quick letter of explanation. She was sorry about the past, but there was nothing she could do about it. Hannah needed to know. Maybe if the girl spent the holidays looking up Mike Conner, the distraction would keep her from being lonely.

Carol sealed the envelope, addressed it, and set it in the outgoing mail tray. She glanced at her watch. It was time to put together the invite list for the black-tie Christmas party.

CHAPTER TWO

he mission would be the most dangerous Mike Conner Meade had ever faced. At least that's what his commander had told him.

He dropped into a dusty canvas chair and kicked his feet up on his rumpled cot. Another week of gusty wind and blinding sand, no relief in sight. Baghdad gave new meaning to the word *desert*—even when things were cooling down. It was sky and sand, sometimes the same color, and a hot grittiness that ground itself into the spaces between his teeth and his socks and the layers of his sleeping bag. It was a parched dry heat that seemed to age him ten years in as many days.

The meeting with his commander, Colonel Jared Whalin, was set to take place in five minutes, three tents down in the shanty barracks where they lived. The meeting was private. No one knew about the mission, not yet.

If Colonel Whalin had his way, only a handful ever would.

Two minutes ticked past and then another two. Mike stretched out his legs and wondered how long it had been since he'd sat on a surfboard, his legs dangling into the ocean while he waited for the perfect wave. After three years of tours in Iraq he'd never look at sand again the same way. His surfer days felt like they belonged to another person, someone he didn't even try to remember.

He checked his watch. It was time.

He stood, shook his pants legs down around his boots, pressed his lips together, and slipped out through the flap in his tent. A burst of wind and sand hit him in the face and he squinted hard. Every step felt like a countdown to destiny—a destiny he had avoided every year, every mission, until now. He breathed in through his nose. Days like this he wished he hadn't given up smoking.

"Meade, that you?"

Meade. That was the name they knew him by—his legal last name. Conner, his middle name and the name he'd actually used all his civilian life, wasn't something that had followed him into the Army. Mike Meade. That was who he was now. No surfer-boy nicknames for the U.S. military.

Mike grabbed the canvas flap and stepped inside. "Yes, sir." He straightened and gave a sharp salute. He had to talk over the sound of the wind and the flapping tent. "You wanted to talk about the mission, sir?"

"Yes." Colonel Whalin sat behind his desk, one elbow anchored amid a slew of documents. He gestured in Mike's direction. "At ease." He sounded tired, defeated. "Listen, Meade, we don't want you to run this mission. Assign it to someone else."

Mike spread his legs apart and allowed his spine and shoulders to relax. He had expected this. "Can you run through the details, sir? I'm a little unclear."

The colonel sorted through the paperwork in front of him. "One of these days we'll pack up our tents and go home, you know that?" He rested his forearms on the desk. "But we're not quite there, not yet."

"Sir." Mike wouldn't say more. Not until the man got more specific.

A long sigh passed through the colonel's gray teeth. "We found the headquarters for a group of insurgents just outside Baghdad, you know that much, right?"

"Yes, sir."

"Well," the colonel narrowed his eyes. "They're set up in an old, abandoned grade school." He waved his hand in the air, disgusted. "Living quarters, training compound, the whole works. Hiding where kids used to play."

"The goal, sir?"

The colonel leveled his gaze at Mike. "The mission is two-fold." He pulled a pack of Camels from his pocket, tapped it twice, and slipped a cigarette between his lips. "Fly six Rangers in at night, rappel onto the roof of the building adjacent to their dorm area. The

Rangers break in through the windows, capture the insurgents, and get back out. A ground crew will be waiting to pick up the men. But you'll provide air cover. We're looking at ten, eleven minutes tops."

Mike swallowed. *Eleven minutes?* The chopper would be the biggest target in the area, stationary long enough for an insurgent to grab a rocket-propelled grenade and bring the bird down three times over. No wonder Colonel Whalin had told him it was dangerous. He looked straight ahead. "The second part?"

"Reconnaissance." He pulled a lighter from the top drawer of his desk and lit his cigarette. "We have a feeling they're holding prisoners there. You and your copilot will have night-vision goggles, of course. We want as much information as you can get."

"Will we use a gunner, sir?" Not all missions included a gunner at the open door of the chopper. But if the chopper was going to hang in the air for eleven minutes, it would be a must.

"Definitely." The colonel rubbed his eyes. His throat was thick. "There'll be nine men altogether. Pilot, copilot, the gunner, and six Rangers." He took a long drag from his cigarette. "A lot rides on it, Meade. We need someone capable. But let's use the young guys. A dispensable crew."

"Beg your pardon, sir." Mike clenched his jaw. "I don't have a crew like that."

"I know." Colonel Whalin pinned the cigarette between his lips and tossed up his hands. His tone was gravelly. "You get what I mean. The mission's dangerous. It's crazy dangerous."

Mike unclenched his jaw. "I figured it was something like that, sir. I'm not worried; I can handle it."

"Of course you can handle it." His commander let the cigarette dangle from his lower lip. "Your crew's the best we've got, Meade. I want you to think about the other crews, all five of them." He inhaled sharply and let the smoke filter out through his nose. "I need an answer by tomorrow. Your top two choices."

"Sir, what if I want to go?" Mike didn't flinch. It wasn't a matter of hiding his fear. He simply had none. His copilot was single, a guy everyone called CJ. The two of them were legend in wartime missions. Legend getting in and out of situations like the one the colonel had just described.

They would handle the mission better than anyone.

"At this point, we want someone else. You and Ceej are my ace crew. The best we've got." Colonel Whalin pinched his cigarette between his second and third fingers and brought it down to desk level. "Give it some thought. We want the insurgents gone before the next Iraqi election."

"January, sir?"

"Yes. January." The colonel checked a document on his desk. Outside the wind howled against the tent. "December 12." His tone was flat. "That's D-Day." He took another drag and held it. After a few seconds he brushed his hand out in front of him. The smoke curled up from his lips. "Get back to your quarters. We'll talk tomorrow."

"Thank you, sir."

The colonel dismissed him, and two minutes later Mike was back in his tent, sitting on the edge of his cot. He linked his fingers at the base of his neck and stared at his boots.

Someone dispensable?

He went down the list. Joe and Sage and Larry and Gumbo were the two crews with the least experience, and eleven children between them. Tito and Fossie were fresh off their honeymoons. Andy and Stoker, and Jimbo and Junior all had kids on the way. He worked his fingers into the muscles at the base of his neck and turned his head first one way, then the other.

All five of the other crews were made up of men with a reason to live.

But what about him and CJ? No wives, no family. Nothing to lose. It was part of what made the two of them such good chopper pilots. They took risks other pilots wouldn't, but they always came out on top. No fear, no failure. Wasn't that what they told each other?

The fact that he and Ceej had more experience didn't make them less dispensable. It made them more likely to come out alive. If anyone could handle the mission, they could. With CJ by his side, he could hover a chopper twenty minutes if he had to. They would spot an insurgent with an RPG and duck out for a few minutes if they had to. They could have the gunner fire on anyone aiming anything in their direction. Never mind the odds; they could handle the mission better than any of the crews. With CJ, Mike could take the cockpit and fly with nerves of steel, no reservations, nothing in his rearview mirror.

He reached under his cot and felt the worn brown paper sack.

Nothing but this.

CHAPTER THREE

$\mathcal{M}$ike scanned the rest of the cots in his tent—the men spread out, snoring beneath their dusty sheets. A single light hung above him, bright enough to see the contents of the bag if he wanted to. And tonight he did. He slid it out and stared at it. It wasn't much, the bag. Just a little bigger than an average lunch sack. The top was scrunched closed and worn around the edges, proof that Mike had carried it with him for eleven years. Wherever his cot was set up, the bag was beneath it.

He opened the mouth of the bag, and with careful hands he took out the contents. He spread them on his sheet and looked at the items one at a time. There was a photo of Hannah in his arms when she was an infant, and another taken three years later that showed the two of them building a sandcastle on the beach. Scattered among the items were the broken clay pieces of a miniature playhouse she'd made for him with modeling clay she'd gotten for her third birthday.

"You and me, Daddy." Her little girl singsong voice sounded in his heart every time he saw the broken pieces. *"This'll be our house someday."*

Funny how even back then she hadn't mentioned her mother. Daddy and me this, and daddy and me that. Hannah had liked her mother, but Carol had been more of a kindhearted roommate than a caring, involved parent.

"She needs you," Mike could hear himself telling Carol. "Spend a little time with her, why don't you?"

"I already told you." Carol would toss her brown hair and scowl at him. "I wasn't ready to be a mother. That sort of thing doesn't just happen when the baby comes. It takes time."

Lots of things didn't happen when the baby came. He had convinced her to have Hannah in the first place, and once that part was decided, he'd done his best to make them both happy. Three years later, when she hinted at leaving, he brought home a wedding ring and asked her to be his wife. But by then she had school and careers on her mind. "We can get married later," she told him.

Mike moved his fingers over the broken clay pieces from the bag. His eyes fell on something else—a folded piece of lined paper. The creases were yellowed from age; a few of them had worn through the page, leaving long, narrow slits in the paper. He opened it and felt himself smile, the way he always smiled when he looked at the crayoned drawing.

Hannah had made it for him two weeks before he left for basic training. It was a little girl consisting of a big head, short stick legs, and round blue eyes. Stick arms stuck out straight on either side, and one appeared to be attached to an equally straight stick arm belonging to a man. Both of them had oversized U-shaped smiles, and a not-quite-round yellow sun took up the left side of the sky above them. On the right side she had written her first sentence: *Hannah loves Daddy.*

That was it—all he had to remember her by, all he had to push him on the days when he thought he'd never leave the desert alive. Whenever he felt himself getting down, he checked the bag. The clay pieces and photographs, the folded drawing, were enough to remind him of the most important thing:

He had to come home alive so he could find her.

Back when they all lived together in his father's house a block from the beach, Mike had felt things falling apart. Carol came from money. At first she found Mike and his simple existence refreshing and daring, but eventually the novelty wore off. By the time Hannah was two, Carol complained about their living conditions.

"Lifeguards are drifters, Mike." She would put her hands on her hips. "I love you, but I need more than this. There must be something else you can do."

He hadn't known what, but one day he heard two of

the other guards talking about the Air Force. Four years. Free education and career training. Maybe something like that would make Carol happy. He went with his buddies to the recruiting office and smiled big at the man behind the desk.

"I want to be a pilot, sir. Is this the right place?"

The man sized him up. "You got a four-year degree, son?"

Mike felt his shoulders slump a little. "No, sir. I figured I'd get that in the Air Force—while I was learning how to fly planes."

"Right." The man smiled. "It doesn't work that way in the Air Force, son. But I tell you what. You go next door and go through a door marked 'Army,' and you can sign up to be a chopper pilot." He smiled again. "How's that sound?"

A chopper pilot? Mike took only a few seconds to mull over the idea. Flying choppers wouldn't be bad. He remembered a comment Carol had made—that she'd always figured she'd marry a politician or an officer, someone of stature. He cleared his throat. "Could I be an officer if I flew choppers in the Army?"

"Definitely." The man gave a firm nod. He pointed to the door. "You learn how to fly a chopper and you'll be an Army warrant officer, son."

Doubt flashed in his mind. "How long, sir? How long for training?" Carol would only be patient so long.

"Eight weeks for basic," the man stroked his chin.

"Maybe another eight to twelve weeks for tech training. Then you'd be off to a base where you'd spend the next eighteen months learning to fly choppers."

Eight weeks of basic and another eight plus weeks of tech training? Mike did the math in his head. That meant at least four months away from Carol and Hannah. But after that they could be together on the base while he went to pilot school. A surge of ambition welled up within him. The plan was all he had, the only way he could become the sort of man Carol wanted him to be.

He nodded at the man behind the desk. "Thank you, sir." He gave a quick salute and a smile. "I'll be heading next door now."

In a matter of hours he was no longer a carefree surfer, a lifeguard at the beach. He was an Army man, a person with a potential and a future. When Carol came home from school that night, Mike was ready with the news. He grinned at her and held up the Army folder. "I figured everything out," he told her. "Wait'll you hear."

Carol waited, but she had one foot out the door almost before he was finished with the details. "Army? Mike, are you crazy?" She huffed and tossed her designer bag on the scuffed tabletop. "I don't want to marry an Army man! I wanna be the wife of a lawyer or a professor or a politician. Something..." She waved her hands about in front of her face, frustrated. "Something with a little class and prestige."

"I'll be an officer, Carol. That has to count for something."

"An Army officer, Mike? Are you serious?"

Her words were like bullets, ripping holes in the fragile plans he'd laid out for himself. Training would take him away for sixteen weeks, but it took only days to figure out Carol's course of action.

"I need time, Mike. I need to be with my parents."

"It's not like I'm leaving you, Carol." He clenched his jaw. "I'll be gone four months, that's all."

"So maybe I spend that time back at home, and then we can talk."

"Talk, Carol?"

"Yes." Her voice was frantic, anxious. She exhaled and made an obvious attempt to calm herself. "Talk about whether we'll still have a reason to be together."

Mike could tell by looking at her that she was going to leave. There was nothing he could do to stop her. "What about Hannah?"

"You can see her. With or without me." Carol touched his shoulder, her eyes more tender than before. "Get through training and then you can look us up."

Mike should've known better, should've realized the dangerous situation he was in when it came to Hannah. But even in his most uncharitable moments, he never once imagined that Carol would leave with his daughter, disappear without a trace or a trail. It never occurred to him that he would spend the next eleven years searching for the dark-haired little girl who had worked her way into the fabric of his soul.

He started his training and convinced himself Carol would move to the base, that she'd marry him and they could live together while he was in pilot training. Surely she would realize his potential and jump at the chance for the three of them to be a family again. They talked three times in the early weeks before she and Hannah left for her parents' house.

"I'll go for a month, that's all. Don't call me, Mike. I'll call you." Carol told him before she moved. "My parents need time to adjust."

Carol called him once from her parents' house. At the end of the call she put Hannah on the line.

"Hi, Daddy."

"Hi, sugar." Mike's heart beat so hard he expected it to burst through his chest and bounce around on the floor. "I miss you."

"Miss you, too." Her singsong voice sounded sad, flat. "Come home, Daddy. Mommy doesn't read to me."

"Where is home, baby?" Mike wasn't testing her. He only wondered what Carol had told her.

"I'm with Grandmother and Grandfather." Hannah thought for a moment. "But home is where you are, Daddy. So come, okay?"

Mike could barely speak by the time Hannah handed the phone back to Carol. After that the phone calls stopped. When he finished training, the only information he had for her wound up being a bad address and a wrong phone number.

At first Mike drove himself crazy looking for her.

He checked phonebooks and called schools and churches in the Virginia and Washington, D.C., area, desperate to find her. He was sure he'd find them in a matter of weeks. His little Hannah needed him, and Carol had promised. She wouldn't keep him from her.

But the weeks slipped into months as his training continued. Every chance he had he looked for them, and even when five years became seven and then nine he held out hope. She was out there somewhere. Carol had married, of course. That was the reason he couldn't find anyone by her last name. But still they were somewhere.

It wasn't until his recent deployment, the past year in the desert that his hope began to erode. She would be fifteen now, far too old to remember him even if he could find her. If he survived Iraq, it was time to move on, to find another life. Time to let go of the one he'd imagined in his heart and mind every time he climbed into a fighter jet.

He looked at the scattered remains of the dream, the broken pottery and aging artifacts. One at a time he placed them back in the bag and crumpled the neck closed again. He would always keep the bag, but only as a reminder of what used to be. His fingers tightened around the bag and he held his breath.

It was over. The hoping and searching and believing

that he'd find his Hannah again . . . all of it was over. It had been over a lot longer than he cared to admit. No wonder he could look his commander in the face and tell him the truth straight up. The mission belonged to him. He was perfect for the job. Not so much because of his experience, but because of his lack of connection. He had no family, no wife, no dark-haired daughter to come home to. No one to grieve his loss if he never made it out alive. CJ was no different.

He clenched his jaw and slid the bag back beneath his bed. His commander was right. Maybe some men were dispensable.

And if that were true, maybe he was one of them.

CHAPTER FOUR

*T*he house was dark like always.

Hannah stepped out of the Town Car, waved good-bye to Buddy Bingo, and crept through the front door. The lights were off, same as outside. A chill ran down Hannah's arms, a combination of the quiet darkness and a draft that always marked the entryway of their home.

"Grandmother?"

There was no answer, and Hannah frowned. Sometimes she went days without seeing her grandmother, since the older woman went to bed early and woke up late. It was more like living alone all the time. She sighed and the sound rattled in the foyer. She closed the door behind her and dropped her gym bag. Cheerleading had been brutal and she had only half an hour until dance.

A light switch near the door lit up much of the downstairs. Hannah walked past the marble fountain that separated the entrance from the formal living room. She was about to head up to her bedroom when something on the dining room table caught her attention. She stopped and peeked around the corner. It was a package of some kind, a manila envelope.

Strange. Hannah walked closer, curious. Her grandmother took care of the mail, so what was this? She peered at it. *Miss Hannah Roberts,* it read. She opened her mouth and a soft gasp came out. The package was from her mother. After days of silence, not even an E-mail, her mother had sent her something.

She tore open the package and spread the contents on the table. A bulky white envelope, and next to it a single sheet of note paper and a hand-written letter. Hannah picked it up. Her mother's handwriting was familiar, but only vaguely so. She rarely sent packages from Sweden. Hannah let her eyes find the top of the note.

Dear Hannah,

You might not understand what I'm about to tell you, but I think it's time. I wanted to wait until you were eighteen, old enough to check into this information and make some decisions for yourself. Having Christmas all alone, you'll have time to think this through.

This is it: Jack isn't your biological father.

Hannah's knees trembled and she grabbed hold of the back of the closest chair. *What?* She moved her eyes over the line again, but the words wouldn't come together, wouldn't form into a logical sentence. Her mother must be crazy, sending her a note like this. She tried again and this time the words slammed at her like a series of rough waves, each one knocking a little more wind from her.

Jack Roberts isn't my biological father? A sharp stinging started in the corners of her eyes. This couldn't be right. Of course Jack was her father. Her parents wouldn't have lied about that all these years . . . would they? She swallowed hard, pulled out the chair, and sat down. Her vision was blurred, and she blinked, finding her place on the note.

> *Your father's name is Mike Conner. I've enclosed some details about him, but I know very little. I haven't spoken to him since we parted. But what information I do have is on a sheet of paper in the envelope, also.*

Hannah took three quick breaths and gave a sharp shake of her head. This wasn't happening, it couldn't be. She'd never heard the name *Mike Conner* before, so how could it be true? How could he be her father? Her heart thumped hard within her, a little more convinced than her mind and soul. Her mother wasn't a liar; though she wanted to rip up the letter, throw it in the trash, and pretend she'd never opened the package, that single truth kept her reading.

Hannah, there was a time when I loved Mike very much. But he wasn't the sort of man I could marry; I hope you understand, darling. We were together until your fourth birthday and then our lives took us in different directions. There are more details, information I'll share with you some day when we're together. For now, this is all you need to know. Inside the envelope are some photographs and a pair of wings he bought before he joined the Army. It was something Mike wanted you to have.

I suppose I should've told you this face to face. But for some reason I felt this was the time. Don't hold it against me, Hannah. Jack will always consider you his daughter, and he will be no less a father to you simply because you know the truth. Instead try to be adult about it. I know you will be. You're a good girl. Talk to you soon,

Mother

Hannah stared at the page. The only sounds were her heartbeat and the rustling of the note, still clutched in her trembling hand. She couldn't take it all in, couldn't rationalize about whether the information was or wasn't true. But her mother obviously thought it was true, and that meant . . .

She set the note down and reached for the stuffed white envelope. Carefully, as if it contained something too terrifying, too sacred, to examine, she slid her finger under the flap and slit open the top. Her heartbeat was louder than the envelope shaking in her hands. Her mind screamed at her, willing her to put it down. But she continued, moving slowly, trancelike.

The first thing she pulled from it was a photograph.

Hannah's breathing wasn't right, and she couldn't blink as she stared at the image in the picture. It was her—a little-girl version of herself—cuddled on the lap of a handsome blond man. The man was reading to her.

Again Hannah's mouth fell open. Gradually, like the changing colors in fall, the picture of her past began to come into focus. If the little girl was her—and she knew it was because of other baby pictures she'd seen—then the blond man would be Mike Conner. And if he was Mike . . .

A series of dots inside her mind connected at lightning speed. The lines in her memory came into crisp focus. If he was her father, and he liked to read to her, then maybe Mike Conner was the man in her memories. The one who sang with his guitar and got down on the floor to play with her.

Her hands shook harder, and she worked to steady the image. Something about his eyes looked familiar, and after a minute she figured it out. His eyes were the same ones she looked at in the mirror every day. Hers couldn't have been more like his—the shape, the color. Even the arch of her eyebrows.

The tears were back, spilling from the confused corners of her soul straight into her eyes, clouding her vision again and making her wonder at the feelings coming over her. Anger at her mother, of course. Because how could she lie about something so important? And for so many years? And maybe more anger because if her memories—the good memories—were about Mike Conner, then . . . how could her mother have left him?

But there were other feelings, too. So many others.

Confusion because this new truth still felt like a joke or a trick. Fear because her world was tumbling off center, wobbling and falling and threatening to break into a million tiny pieces. And curiosity because if it really was true, then she wanted to meet him. As soon as possible, so she could ask him if he was the one. The daddy in her dreams.

And over all of it was sadness. Because it had to be true; the picture in her hand told her so. Only now she was almost grown up and she'd lost ten years, a decade, with the man in the picture. Sadness because maybe he'd forgotten about her the way she had forgotten about him.

She laid the photograph down carefully on the table in front of her. Then she reached back into the envelope and pulled out another one. This picture was of the same man standing on the beach in shorts and a T-shirt. A surfboard was tucked under his arm.

Her mother's voice came to mind, faded by the years: *"Don't go near the water, Hannah. Stay here on the towel with Daddy."*

That was it. Nothing more came to mind. But her

mother's warning was as real as if she were standing upstairs shouting down at her. It was another clue, further proof that the photographs weren't a figment of her imagination. When she was little, her mother had warned her about the water—the ocean, probably. And Mike Conner was a surfer.

Another few dots connected.

The next item in the envelope was a sheet with Mike's name and birth date and the fact that he'd lived in Pismo Beach. A few other bits of information. And last inside was the lapel pin, the wings her mother had mentioned in the note. Hannah ran her thumb gently over the metal surface and held it up, noting the gray-and-black detail. Had he become a pilot, then? Someone flying for the Army?

A knock sounded at the door and she jumped. Her dance teacher! She set the pin and the photos back in the envelope and put the envelope back inside the bigger manila packaging. Whatever truth lay in her mother's note, she'd have to sort through it later.

Hannah let her dance teacher in and apologized for not being ready. Then she raced to her room, threw on her tights and leotard, and met the teacher in the dance room downstairs. For the next hour she practiced pirouettes and jazz leaps, but all the while she barely heard the music or the teacher chiding her to land lighter or jump higher.

Jack wasn't her father?

The blond man in the pictures overtook every other thought until finally the lesson was over and she scurried the manila package to her room. There she read her mother's note again and pulled out the photos from the envelope. Before she fell asleep that night she stared at the photos for a long time. That's when she realized another feeling had been added to the mix.

Happiness.

Because maybe it wasn't too late. Maybe, if Mike Conner was the daddy in her memories, she could find him again and they could start up loving each other where they left off all those years ago. Maybe the blond man would be her father, and Jack would be nothing more than a nice man who had married her mother.

Which was all he'd ever been, anyway.

She fell asleep and this time the memories of her long-ago daddy sprang to life in her dreams. In them she was chasing him down a sandy beach, giggling like mad when he turned around and caught her up over his shoulder.

The next morning she dressed in her favorite jeans and denim jacket, and on the lapel she pinned the wings. The wings Mike Conner had told her mother to give her.

Normally she didn't wake her grandmother before going to school, but this was an emergency. She would know if her mother's note was right, or if the information about Mike Conner was some sort of trick or mistake.

She was completely ready for school when she gave a light knock on the door into her grandmother's suite. "Hello?"

For a moment, there was only silence. Then she heard movement from behind the door. "Hannah? Is that you?"

"Yes. Can we speak for a minute, please?"

Her grandmother opened the door, a slight scowl creasing her forehead. "*May* we speak for a minute, you mean."

Hannah exhaled quietly. Propriety always came before purpose. That was her grandmother's rule, no matter what the situation. "May we speak for a minute, please?"

"Certainly." Her grandmother wore her long blue-velvet robe, the one she'd had for the past year. She stepped aside, and the robe swished around her ankles. "Come in."

"Thank you." Hannah hated this—the formality. But it was all they'd ever known. She followed her grandmother into the spacious room. The words were on her tongue, rehearsed. But before she could speak them, her grandmother's scowl deepened and her eyes grew wide. She was looking at the wings.

"What—" She pointed to the pin. "—is that?"

Hannah blinked. "Well, Grandmother. That's what I'd like to talk to you about."

Her grandmother's face looked paler than before,

almost as white as her linen bedspread. "They're pilot wings."

"Yes." Hannah gulped. Without realizing it, she fingered the pin. "My mother sent them."

"She . . ." Her grandmother's eyes lifted. "Did she say why she'd do such a thing?"

Hannah twisted her fingers together and shifted from one foot to the other. "Jack Roberts isn't my father, is he?"

For a long moment her grandmother stared at her, surprised. Then indignant. She took a step back. "Young lady, that's something for you and your mother."

"But he isn't, right?"

Her grandmother straightened herself and turned her back to Hannah. "Where did you hear that?"

"My mother." Hannah came closer. Her stomach twisted. "She sent me the wings and two photos and a note."

Her grandmother whirled around. "Photos?"

Hannah hesitated. "Pictures of Mike Conner." Her mouth was dry. "He's my real father, right, Grandmother?"

For a long minute her grandmother only stared at her, unmoving. Then she cleared her throat and lifted her chin. "Your mother would never lie to you, Hannah. You know that."

The thick carpet beneath her feet felt suddenly liquid. "So, it's true." Her words were breathy, a whisper, all she could force.

"Yes." Her grandmother turned toward the window again. "But I have nothing to say about him. I warned your mother not to go to California." She glanced over her shoulder at Hannah. "I taught myself to forget she ever actually did."

Hannah hugged herself. She felt faint, the way she sometimes felt when she'd gone too long without eating. Her grandmother had known about Mike all this time, and never said anything. Her entire family was in on the conspiracy. "Did you . . . did you know Mike?"

"Hannah . . ." Her grandmother spun toward her once more, and for the first time she looked less than controlled. Fear creased the skin at the corners of her eyes, and her voice was higher than before. "You need to get to school. Buddy will be waiting for you."

Anger hit Hannah then. She tightened her hands and wiggled her toes in her black dress loafers. "Grandmother, I asked you a question."

Her grandmother's voice rose another notch. "It was your mother's mistake." She pointed to the door and gave a terse nod at Hannah. "Ask her."

At first Hannah couldn't move. Two thoughts fought for position in her mind: the fact that her grandmother obviously knew something about Mike Conner, but refused to talk about him. And the possibility that maybe this was why her grandmother kept her distance—because she wasn't the child of the great Jack Roberts. Rather, she was the daughter of a California surfer.

That had to be it, the reason her grandmother had always seemed to barely tolerate her.

Hannah resisted the urge to say something spiteful to the old woman. Instead she turned around, flew down the stairs, grabbed her backpack, and ran out the front door. Tears stung at her eyes again, but she held them off. Even so, she didn't fool Buddy Bingo.

"Something wrong, Miss Hannah?" He glanced at her in the rearview mirror. "You look a little flustered."

Hannah situated herself and buckled her seat belt. She was breathing hard, keeping herself from crying. "I'm fine."

Buddy gave a slow nod and let the conversation stall until they were on the main highway to the school. Hannah's mind raced faster than her heart. How had she missed it all these years? Of course Jack Roberts wasn't her father. He never looked at her or hugged her or spent time with her the way she'd seen her friends' fathers do. The strange memories were a sign, one that had been there all along. In the soil of her heart, the truth had always lay buried, hadn't it? That the daddy in the dreams wasn't Jack Roberts, but someone else.

They were almost at school when Hannah remembered the Christmas miracle. She leaned forward and grabbed the back of Buddy's seat. "Can I ask you something?"

In the mirror, Buddy's eyes sparkled. "I've been waiting."

Hannah smiled. She should've told him the minute she climbed in. "Remember that Christmas miracle you're praying for—the one for me?"

"Sure do." He gave a firm nod of his head. "Praying every day about it."

"Good." Hannah held her breath. Fresh new possibility sat in the seat beside her. If there was a God, He wouldn't mind her being more specific, would He? She gripped the back of Buddy's seat a little more tightly. "Could you add a few more details to the prayer?"

"You bet." Buddy's smile faded. "What're the details?"

"Well . . ." She took another few deep breaths. "Pray that I can spend Christmas with my parents."

Cars whizzed on either side, and Buddy moved the Town Car over two lanes so he could turn into the school parking lot. When he was stopped, he turned and made eye contact with her. "They're not coming?"

Hannah thought about telling him the whole truth—that they weren't coming and, worse than that, Jack wasn't even her father. Instead she forced a sad smile. "No, Buddy. They're not."

He nodded, and his eyes looked watery. "Then that's what I'll pray for. That you and your parents would be together for Christmas." He paused. "But don't forget something."

"What?"

"Miracles happen to folks who believe. You gotta believe, Miss Hannah."

Believe? It was something she hadn't thought about before. "Okay. I guess I could do that." She grabbed her roller bag and patted the back of Buddy's seat. "See you later. Thanks, Buddy."

Not until she was halfway to her first class did she realize that she'd been walking with her fingers on her lapel pin, on the wings. She stopped before she reached the building and stared up at the clear blue sky.

Was he a pilot now? Had he stayed with the Army all these years? Hannah rubbed her thumb over the wings one more time.

She would wear them as long as Buddy Bingo was praying. And maybe one day she'd have more than the wings of the daddy in the memory. Maybe one day—if she believed really hard—she'd have the daddy.

The one in her dreams.

ongressman James McKenna had things to do. But the conversation with the girl wouldn't let him go.

He'd met her a time or two at political dinners. She was Hannah Roberts, daughter of the ambassador to Sweden, the powerful Jack Nelson Roberts Jr. And now apparently there was a family relative missing, someone the girl had only just found out about. McKenna remembered the conversation with the girl like it had just happened.

"Please, sir, my parents are busy and I can't find him by myself." She'd sounded on the verge of tears. "My mother gave me all the information she has, and . . . well, sir, it isn't enough."

Near as he could tell, the missing man—a Mike Conner—was the girl's uncle, someone she'd been very close to as a little girl. "I'll see what I can do," he told her. And now he felt stymied in every other way until he could at least point her in the right direction. It wasn't so much that she was Jack Roberts' daughter. It was the catch in her voice when she'd finished her request:

"If I can't find him, I'll spend the rest of my life looking."

McKenna sighed loud and hard. He shoved the paperwork on his desk to the side and grabbed a notebook. The details weren't much. Mike Conner from Pismo Beach, joined the Army in 1994.

He picked up the phone and called one of the top officers in the Army. He had contacts all over the country, and this was one of them. "Jennings, McKenna here. I need you to run a check on an Army man for me."

The sound of rustling paperwork came over the line. "Okay, shoot."

"Mike Conner. Joined in '94."

It took less than a minute for Jennings' answer. "We got a couple of Mike Conners. One joined in '65, and another one in 1973. Two last year. Nothing even close to '94."

"Any of them from Pismo Beach?"

"Uh . . . the one in '73 was from San Francisco. That's the closest I've got."

McKenna pinched the bridge of his nose. "You sure about the date?"

"Yes." Jennings sounded rushed. "The guy got a discharge. Hurt his leg, it looks like."

"Hmmm." McKenna doodled the name *Mike Conner* at the top of his notepad. "Okay, thanks. Maybe the information's bad." The phone call ended and McKenna tried every other branch of the service before tossing his pencil on the desk. He'd put in one more call—to a reporter contact at the *Washington Post.* Then he'd let it go. He wasn't a miracle worker, after all.

That territory belonged to Someone else altogether.

❧

*H*annah hung up the phone with the congressman and stared at the piece of notebook paper she'd ripped from her binder. The congressman had a few details, the first one enough to take her breath away. There was no sign of a Mike Conner in the Army, just a few other men with the same name, including someone who'd left with an injury.

So why couldn't the congressman find her father? He had to have been there at one time or another; her mother had been sure about that detail.

It was the congressman's last bit of information that gave her hope. Apparently he had a connection at a national country music television channel. Through the holidays they were running messages to soldiers serving in the war efforts in Iraq and Afghanistan.

Hannah might've been at the top of her class, and she might've had a better vocabulary than most adults, but even she wasn't sure what a "war effort" was. War, yes. That she understood. And if her dad was in the war, then she had no time to waste. She had to get word out that she was looking for him.

Assuming he was still in the Army.

But here was the best part of all. Even if he wasn't in the Army or anywhere overseas, he still might watch the country music channel. And if he did, then there was a chance he'd see her message.

She took a deep breath, picked up the phone, and called the channel. She wouldn't tell the man about her connection to Congressman McKenna or to Jack Roberts. No need. He was the one who took requests, and this was one request she didn't want linked to her political ties.

"Do you have a loved one in the service, miss?" The man was friendly.

Hannah felt herself relax. He wouldn't know who she was. And with all the people who watched the station's music videos, her father might just see her message. "Yes." She closed her eyes. "My dad."

"I'm sorry." He hesitated. "I'm sure you miss him a lot."

"I do."

"Well, then, what do you want to tell him?"

"You mean . . ." Hannah opened her eyes and stared out the window. It was raining, and the temperatures were colder than they'd been all winter. Snow was forecast before the end of the week. "You'll put it on the air? For sure?"

"Absolutely." There was a smile in the man's voice. "If your dad's watching, he'll see your message."

"All right, then." She'd written out what she wanted to tell him. Now she pulled that piece of paper closer and studied it. "Tell him this:

"Daddy, this is Hannah. Mom showed me the pictures, the one with you and me reading and the other one, with you and your surfboard. I'm trying to find you. So if you see this, call the station, and they'll tell you how to reach me. I love you, Daddy. I never forgot you."

She took a slow breath. "Is that good?"

The man didn't say anything at first. Then he made a coughing sound. "Honey, you mean you don't know where your daddy is?"

"No, sir." Her throat was thick. She touched the wings pinned to her sweater. "I haven't seen him since I was four. My mother said he's in the Army."

"Well, then let's get this message on the air today."

She left her phone number with the man, and he promised to get back to her if he heard anything from her father. The message she'd left was still playing in her mind when the phone rang.

Without checking Caller ID, Hannah answered it on the first ring. "Hello?"

"Hannah Roberts, please. This is Kara Dillon from the *Washington Post.*"

The *Washington Post*? Hannah pulled up a bar stool and leaned hard onto the kitchen counter. "This is she."

"Okay, then . . ." The reporter hesitated, and in the background Hannah could hear voices and the tapping of computer keyboards. "Congressman McKenna told us you were trying to find a long-lost relative."

"I am." Hannah was up off her seat. This was exactly what she needed; help from the media. "I haven't seen my dad in eleven years and now I have his name and his picture but no—"

"I'm sorry." The woman didn't let her finish. "Your father? I thought your father was Jack Roberts, the politician."

Fear grabbed her around the throat and for a moment she couldn't speak. Could she do this? Could she go public with something no one else knew? In the time it took her heart to thump out a handful of beats, she remembered her mother's note. It said nothing about keeping quiet on the issue.

So what if Jack Roberts wasn't her biological father? She swallowed and forced the words in a single breath. "Jack Roberts married my mother when I was four, and he raised me as his daughter, but my real dad is Mike Conner from Pismo Beach, California, and now he's in the Army, but there's no record of him." She grabbed a quick gulp of air. "He's the one I'm looking for."

"I see." The reporter took a minute, maybe writing down this new information. "Does your . . . mother know you've gone public with your search?"

Hannah bit her lip. "Not really." What's the worst thing the paper could print? And whatever headline might run, the fallout would be worth the possibility that her dad would see it and find her. She walked out of the kitchen and dropped into a suede recliner in the den. "But I don't think she'll mind. She's the one who told me about Mike Conner."

"Well, then." The reporter sounded overly happy. "I think it'll make a perfect Christmas story. Let's go ahead with the interview."

The questions went on for nearly an hour—questions about her childhood and the memories she held of her early years with Mike Conner. Once Hannah started opening up to the woman, the answers came easily. Not until she was brushing her teeth that night, after cheer and dance and a long conversation with Kathryn about which guys might be worth going to the prom with, did she feel a hint of remorse about agreeing to the interview.

Her mother wouldn't mind, would she? Whatever the paper printed, it was bound to help her find her father, right? Besides, her mother hadn't exactly told her no. But only then, hours after the fact, did it occur to her that maybe—just maybe—she hadn't only answered the reporter's questions because of her deep need to see her dad.

But because of her need to see her mother, as well.

CHAPTER SIX

$\mathscr{M}$ike Conner trudged through the tent to the food line, took a plate of hot chicken and gravy and a slab of bread, and found a folding chair near the television set, ten yards away. Usually he sat at one of the tables, sharing talk with the guys. But tonight he had nothing to say to anyone.

The mission was in twelve hours.

An old western played above the distant conversations—John Wayne telling somebody where to get off and why. Mike settled into his chair. The television was set up in the dining tent, as far away from the blowing sand as possible. This tent was bigger than the others, a makeshift cafeteria tucked away at the back of their temporary base. In it were a couple dozen folding chairs and rows of aluminum tables, usually filled with weary soldiers and chopper crews catching a quick meal between assignments.

Mike took a bite of the chicken and shifted it around in his mouth. Too hot, like always. After a few seconds he swallowed it and stared at the television. He rarely watched it. Life on the outside was no longer real to him, no longer something he wanted to see or be a part of.

All existence centered around the sandy base, the endless desert, and the enemy. Wherever he might be. Bombing missions came up every few days, some that never made the papers back in the states. Insurgents acting up or strategic military sites belonging to start-up terrorist groups. The Air Force handled strikes, but the choppers came in before and after, dropping supplies or men to aid in the attack. Air attacks made up a routine part of their work.

Always there were dangerous missions. And that Sunday, December 11, two weeks before Christmas, the mission that lay ahead was the most dangerous of all.

In the end, the conversation had been short. He had gone in to see his commanding officer, determined that he wouldn't leave the man's presence until he'd been granted permission to man the mission—the one that would have him hovering over an insurgent compound for eleven insane minutes.

"Sir," Mike had stood at attention, his hands at his sides, chin up. "I request permission along with CJ to crew the chopper for the mission."

His superior had mumbled something profane and leaned back in his seat. "I can't afford to lose you, Meade."

"You won't, sir." Mike kept his shoulders straight, his voice even. "Ceej and I can get the job done."

"What about the others? Wouldn't one of them work?"

Mike had held his breath. Some men were dispensable, right? "Sir, the others have much more to lose. CJ and I, we don't have family, sir."

"Fine, Meade." The colonel swore again. He grabbed his pack of cigarettes from the desk and tapped it. "Listen. I didn't ask for this mission, and I can't say I agree with it. The command came from higher up, so someone's got to do it." He snatched a cigarette, slipped it between his lips, and stared at Mike. "But no unnecessary bravery, got it? If you have to pull out and come back, do it. Just get the job done and get out."

Mike could still feel the fire inside his gut at the victory. He stifled a smile. "Yes, sir."

"And follow orders." The man's voice was louder, gruff. He lit the cigarette and inhaled deep. The smoke curled out from the corners of his lips. "The first order most of all."

"The first order, sir?"

"Yes, Meade." He lowered the cigarette. "Come back alive."

Now Mike took another bite of chicken. It was cooler. He studied the picture on the TV screen. The Duke was on horseback, charging ahead, rifle at his side. The movie was just starting to look familiar when one of the chopper pilots walked up and flipped the channel.

"Hey." A soldier jumped up. His coffee spilled, soaking into the dirt. "I was watching that."

"Tough." The man at the set pointed to the man's coffee and laughed out loud. "Looks like you got enough trouble all by your lonesome."

The soldier kicked his coffee cup and stormed off. Mike looked at the airman again. He was still flipping channels. Mike thought about saying something. The Duke was about to do in a few bad guys, after all. But he stared at his chicken instead. TV didn't matter. He needed a clear head if he was going to get the mission underway and come out breathing.

"Country videos?" The soldier was back with a new cup. He sat down and kicked his feet out. "What'd you go wussy on us, man? Come on! You turned off the Duke!"

"Look," the pilot raised his hand in the air. "None of yer bellyaching now, y'hear? I'm country folk myself, and my sweet little wife back in Alabama has a message comin' to me on one of these videos." He grinned, and a few of the guys seated around the television chuckled and muttered under their breath, guessing at the content of the message. The pilot waved off the comments. "We're watchin' country videos until I see the message. Period."

The soldier made a face and sipped his drink. "Wussies, all of you."

Another round of laughter as the pilot found the right channel. He turned the volume up and took the chair closest to the set, arms crossed, expectant.

Mike laughed to himself. Stations running those sorts of messages had hundreds on every day. He took another bite and shoved a chunk of bread into his mouth. Probably the last full meal he'd have for twenty-four hours, by the time they debriefed after the mission.

Across the tent the pilot was talking to the television. "No, not that message, man! Come on! My wife's got the best message of all. Now, please . . . put hers on the stupid screen, y'hear?"

The videos were numbing. Tim McGraw crooning something about a bull ride, and Rascal Flatts singing about today. The songs blended together and Mike helped himself to a second bowl of chicken. He was halfway done when Lonestar kicked in with their classic, *Already There*.

At that exact moment something caught his eye.

The pilot was shouting at the TV again, telling the screen to get it right, get his wife's message up. But this message was from a child. That much was obvious because it started out, "Daddy . . ."

The next part made his heart slip all the way down to his dirty boots.

In plain text along the right side of the video, the message read:

> *Daddy, this is Hannah. Mom showed me the pictures, the one with me and you reading and the other one, with you and your surfboard. I'm trying to find you. So if you*

see this, call the station and they'll tell you how to reach me. I love you, Daddy. I never forgot you. Hannah.

Mike lifted slowly from his chair and stared at the television. *Hannah?* His Hannah? Could it really be? He read the message again, the part about the girl's mother showing her pictures, and how they read books, and the surfboard. The video ended then, and without taking his eyes from the screen, Mike tossed his plate. He reached the pilot near the television in three giant strides. "What station is it?"

"Huh?"

"The station," Mike pointed at the TV. "What station is it?"

The pilot rattled off the name. Mike was gone before the last word was out.

Hannah remembered him.

He had to call. Colonel Whalin was at his desk when Mike walked in, breathless. "Colonel . . ." He straightened, at attention. "I need a favor."

The man was between cigarettes. "Don't tell me." He gave a wry grin. "You want out of the mission?"

Mike hesitated. If it was his Hannah and she was looking for him, then . . . He pressed his shoulders back some more. The mission was his, no matter what. "No, sir. I need to make a couple of calls to the States."

His commander was lenient with stateside calls. The regularly scheduled ones came often—especially for the family guys. He slid the phone across the desk. "You know the codes?"

"Yes, sir." Mike only knew them from checking on his house in Pismo Beach. Personal calls didn't happen.

"Go ahead." The officer stood, stretched, and headed out the tent door. "I need fresh air, anyway."

"Thank you, sir."

Mike worked fast, his first call to a buddy back at the base stateside. He'd need to use that number if Hannah was to call him. She'd call the base, talk to his buddy, and be patched in to the colonel's office in Baghdad.

Next he found the television station's number. It had to be her, didn't it? How many Hannahs had a lost father who surfed? His palms were sweating by the time a person finally answered at the station. "Hi . . ." He was short of breath. "I'm looking for the person who takes the messages, the ones for servicemen."

"Just a minute, please."

Mike gripped the phone, his posture stiff. Was he crazy? Had the desert heat and sand finally gotten to him? Or was it the mission? He'd looked for Hannah all those years. What were the odds he'd get his first clue the night before the most dangerous job he'd ever taken?

He braced himself against the desk. *Come on . . . Someone pick up . . .*

His commander was talking to a few men just outside the tent. He didn't have long by himself. Mike tapped his foot. *Come on and—*

"Hello . . . this is the message department, can I help you?" The woman on the other end sounded busy.

"Yes, ma'am." He raked his fingers across his short cut hair. How did he say this? "Okay . . . I'm an Army chopper pilot in Iraq, and I just saw a message on one of your videos."

"Good." Her voice softened. "You're the reason we have the messages. How are things in Iraq?"

Details of the next day's mission flashed in his mind. "Fine. Just fine." He worked the muscles in his jaw. "Listen, ma'am, a minute ago the message . . . It was from a girl named Hannah. She's looking for her dad." He paused. There was no turning back now. "I think she might be looking for me."

"Really? Let me write this down."

"Yes, if you could." He only had a few minutes of privacy left. "My name's Mike Meade. I'm stationed outside Baghdad in Iraq, and I've been looking for my daughter, Hannah, for eleven years." He waited. There was no sound of typing in the background. He turned around and rested against the desk. Was she scribbling it on a scrap piece of paper? "Got that, ma'am?"

"Yes." She sounded distracted. "How can she reach you?"

Mike gave her the base number, the one that would put her in to his buddy. "Ask her to have them patch her in to Colonel Jared Whalin's office in Baghdad."

"Okay." A few seconds passed. "There. You're Mike

Meade, you've been looking for a daughter named Hannah for eleven years, and you're in Baghdad."

"Right." He searched his mind. "One more thing." He hesitated. "I used to surf."

"Surf?"

"Yes, ma'am. It was part of the message on the video. She has a picture of her father with a surfboard."

"Well," the woman's tone was hopeful. "Maybe you're the one."

"I hope so. You'll make sure she gets the message?"

"I will. I'll look up her information and give her a call within the hour. So if I give her the number you gave me, she'll be patched through to you?"

"Yes, ma'am." Mike had no doubts. Colonel Whalin would walk through fire to give him the message if his daughter called for him.

"Very good, then. I'll do my best."

"Thank you, ma'am."

The conversation ended just as his commanding officer returned to his desk. "Take care of everything?"

"Yes, sir." Mike stood at attention again. "Something personal."

The man motioned to him. "At ease, Meade."

Mike relaxed. "I'm ready, sir. Everything's in order."

"Good." He looked down, took hold of the ashtray on his desk, and gave it a light shake. The soft gray ashes inside fell to an even layer. "Look, Meade, we've done everything we can to minimize the danger." He glanced up. "But it's still a risk. You'll be hanging in the air a long time."

"I know, sir." Mike tried to concentrate, but he kept hearing her voice. *"You and me, Daddy. This'll be our house someday . . ."*

Colonel Whalin anchored his forearms on his desk. "Your guard has to be up every minute, every second."

"Yes, sir." She was drawing him the picture with the big yellow sun, writing her first sentence. *Hannah loves Daddy.* He squinted. "Every second."

"Take no chances, Meade. Everything by the book."

"Of course, sir." And she was in his arms, cuddling with him while he read *The Cat in the Hat Comes Back* and giggling when the cat ate pink cake in the tub and . . .

"No chances at all, Meade, you understand?"

"Yes, sir." And now there was the slightest small chance that she remembered him, that she was looking for him the same way he'd been looking for her. That he might see her again. "No chances at all."

Colonel Whalin rapped the desk and pushed his chair back. "I'll be out there tomorrow to see you off. And one more thing . . ." He searched Mike's eyes. "We'll have Air Force medevac on standby. Just in case."

"Yes, sir." The news was good, but it underlined the obvious. A mission like this came with an expected number of wounded men. Possibly even casualties. "Thank you, sir."

"Go get some sleep."

Mike started to go, but he hesitated. "Sir . . . I might get a phone call tonight. It's, well," he scratched his head. "It's important, sir."

The colonel looked at him for a long moment. "I'll get you, Meade. Whatever the hour, I'll get you."

As soon as he was back at his bunk, Mike pulled out the bag. It was still early, and he was alone in his area of the tent. He eased the contents out onto his bed and let his fingers move slowly over them. The broken clay pieces, the delicate folded paper, the photo of him and Hannah building a sandcastle on the beach.

"Hannah . . ." He let her name settle on his lips, the way it had so often back when she was his. Her eyes seemed to look straight to his soul, and he moved his finger over her hair, her face. "Hannah girl, I love you."

He looked at the items for a long time, and put them away just before the other men filed into the tent a few at a time and prepared for bed.

CJ approached him first. He sat on the edge of his cot and gave his socked foot a squeeze. "We'll be okay. I have a good feeling about it."

Mike nodded, fear far from him. "Definitely. No fear, no failure."

"Right." He grinned. CJ was long and lanky with an easy smile, even in the most tense situations. "I figure eleven minutes in the air isn't too bad. Remember the Gulf War? What'd we hang there for, half an hour that one time?"

A smile tugged at the corners of Mike's mouth. "I think it was eight minutes."

"Ah, you know . . ." CJ leaned back on his elbows. "Eight minutes, thirty minutes. Same thing, right?"

Mike thought about the brown bag beneath his cot. "All in a day's work."

"Right." CJ winked at him and jumped up, headed off to his own cot and whatever he still needed to get in order for the mission.

Jimbo and Fossie took turns talking to him after that, laughing about some joke they'd heard in the food tent.

"Hey, man, be careful out there." Jimbo gave him a light punch in the shoulder. "We need you."

"You know it." Mike still had the bag in front of him, his fingers tight around the neck. "Don't give my bed away. CJ's, either."

"You'll be back tomorrow night."

"But if I'm not." He gave Jimbo an easy smile. A mission like this came with the possibility of capture. "You know. Just don't give my bed away."

"Never."

Fossie was next, handling his good-bye the same, keeping things light. He patted Mike's stomach with the back of his hand. "Nerves of steal, Meade. Same as back in your surfing days, right? Catch a wave and ride it home."

Mike chuckled. "Hadn't thought of that."

"See . . ." He grinned. "That's why they call me Fossie the Optimist."

The other guys made a point of saying something, both to him and to CJ. Wishing him luck or the best or whatever it is guys say when they know there's a chance they won't see each other again. Only Stoker mentioned prayer.

"You a praying kind of guy, Mike?" Stoker pulled up a chair and turned it around, sitting so that his arms rested on the back.

Mike shrugged. "Sometimes more than others."

"Me, too." Stoker shrugged. "I guess it's never a perfect science."

"No." Mike glanced at his watch. It had been an hour and still she hadn't called. *Come on, Hannah . . . pick up the phone and dial the number.*

"Anyway, I want to promise you something."

"What?"

"I'll pray for you, Meade. The whole time you're gone."

"Okay." Was it the danger ahead or the video message from a girl named Hannah? Mike wasn't sure, but the idea of Stoker praying for him made something inside him relax a little. He smiled at his friend. "Don't forget."

Stoker stood and turned the chair back around. "I won't."

It took another hour for the guys in his tent to fall asleep. All but him. She still hadn't called, and that could only mean a few possibilities. Either she wasn't home, or she wasn't the right Hannah.

And as the night wore on, as ten o'clock became midnight and midnight became two, and the mission drew closer, Mike forced himself to fall asleep. Because he couldn't be on his guard unless he got some rest, and if he wasn't on his guard he wouldn't come back alive.

Which was something he had to do. Not just because it was Colonel Whalin's order, but because Hannah might be looking for him, because she might still remember him. That fact and the image of a little girl who still lived in his memory would be enough to keep him alert and ready at all times.

Even on the most dangerous mission of all.

***

At eleven o'clock that night in Nashville, Tennessee, an evening janitor made his way into the studio of the nation's biggest country western music television station and began cleaning around a bank of computers. The room was empty except for a few producers working on feature pieces.

As was his routine every night, he sprayed a fine mist of industrial cleaner on the desktop around the computers and rubbed away the day's grime and germs. The producers and staff assistants at the station knew to keep loose notes and scrap papers in their desk drawers and normally he could clean around whatever stacks of information or files or documents might be shoved up against the computer screens.

But this night—as was the case on occasion—when the janitor rubbed his rag across the desktop, a single piece of notepaper drifted to the floor. The janitor stopped, straightened, and pressed his fist into the small of his back. He'd been cleaning offices for twenty-two years. His body was feeling the effects.

He set the rag down, bent over, picked up the piece of notepaper, and stared at it. The words were scribbled and hard to read. Something about Mike Meade and surfing and someone named Hannah. A phone number was written across the bottom. The janitor studied it a moment longer and turned back to the row of computer stations.

Where had the paper fallen from? Had it been near the computer on the end, or the one in from that? Or possibly the computer four stations down? The janitor shrugged, opened the desk drawer closest to him, and tossed the paper inside.

Someone would find it eventually.

CHAPTER SEVEN

*C*arol Roberts boarded a plane bound for Washington, D.C., late Tuesday night, December 13. Her frustration was at an all-time high. She hadn't wanted to come home during the holiday season, but now she had no choice. Four days had passed since bedlam broke loose in the States, since the *Washington Post* ran an article under the headline, "Daughter of Former Senator Searches for Biological Father."

The plane was crowded, but Carol barely noticed. From her seat in first class, she stared out the window, closed her eyes, and pressed her forehead against the cool glass. What was Hannah thinking? The letter hadn't been for anyone's eyes but hers. She was supposed to read it, take in the information, and squirrel it away somewhere. It was supposed to occupy her mind and make the holidays less lonely.

Since then the story had run in every major newspaper in the United States, including *USA Today*. None of the reporters were pointing fingers at Carol or Jack. Instead it had become a human interest story: "Will Ambassador's Daughter Find Birth Father in Time for Christmas?" One paper wrote an emotional plea for the man to surface under the headline: "Hannah's Hope—will Christmas Include a Visit from Her Father?"

The media circus had made its way to Sweden, doubling the calls that normally came from the U.S. to the embassy. Reporters wanted to know what was being done from the ambassador's office to help find Mike Conner. And what was the reason Hannah was only finding out about him now? And how come Carol had left him when he joined the Army? And had he really joined the Army, since no record had been found indicating the truth in that?

Finally Jack had given her an order. "Get home and take care of this mess. We can't afford the distraction."

Carol clenched her fists. Jack was right, and that's why she was on a plane headed for Washington, D.C. A dull ache pounded in her temples. If Hannah wanted help finding Mike Conner, why hadn't she simply called? Carol might not have had all the answers, but she could've put Hannah in touch with someone who did. Instead the girl had shown the independence that had marked her recent years.

Calling Congressman McKenna? What fifteen-year-old did things like that? And granting an interview with the *Washington Post*? Carol repositioned herself, settling against the headrest. She kept her eyes closed. The next two weeks were supposed to be spent planning parties and receptions and dinners for dignitaries.

Since the news had broke, the conversations with Hannah had been short. The last one, two days earlier, was what finally convinced her to board the plane. She needed to get back to the States and cool things off. For everyone's sake. Carol let the words play in her mind again . . .

"The *Washington Post*? How could you, Hannah?"

"You're repeating yourself, Mother."

"I'll repeat myself as much as I like." Carol had been pacing across the Italian stone floor in her spacious kitchen. "The *Washington Post*? Do you realize what you've done?"

"What, Mother? What have I done?" Hannah's voice rang out, shrill and sincere. "You mean by telling the truth?" She exhaled hard and fast. "Well, maybe I'm not much of a liar. Can you imagine that? Maybe I think it's better to be honest."

"Your father is a very important man." Carol hissed the words. "He doesn't need our name plastered over every newspaper in the country."

"My father is missing. Isn't that the point?"

"Our family life is no one's business but ours." Carol heard the lack of compassion in her voice. "The world doesn't need to know about Mike Conner."

"Yes." The fight left Hannah. "But *he* needs to know." She made a sniffing sound. "Otherwise I'll never find him."

"What's the rush, Hannah?" A calm came over Carol. She was angry at Hannah, but she hadn't meant to make her daughter cry. "He's been out of your life for more than a decade. Why do you have to find him now?"

"Because." She coughed twice, her words thick. "Because I want to spend Christmas with him."

That was when Carol knew she'd have to go home. Her plan had backfired. She had hoped the information about Mike would distract Hannah, keep her mind occupied so she wouldn't be bored during the holidays. But she never should've said anything, never should've told her. Not until she was older. Because now the whole world knew about Mike Conner.

As the flight got underway, Carol tried to sleep, but all she could think about was a blond, blue-eyed surfer and whether right now, somewhere in the world, he knew that Hannah's single hope was to find him before December 25. Like gathering storm clouds, other details about her time with Mike built along her heart's horizon. She held them off while they crossed the Atlantic and as they landed at Dulles International Airport just before noon Wednesday. She kept them at bay on the limo ride to her house and even as she came through the front door and greeted her mother.

There was no need to talk about the subject. Obviously she'd come home to clear up the media disaster. Her mother only raised her brow and gave the slightest shake of her head. "Why did you tell her?"

Carol looked away. "She had to know sometime."

"Yes, in person, maybe. When she would have been old enough to sort through the news."

Carol's anger bubbled closer to the surface. "Thank you, Mother. I'll handle it from here."

And that was all there was. After a few minutes, her mother returned to her room. Two hours later when she appeared downstairs again, she was stiff and distant, her chin tilted upward, eyes narrow. "Have you called Hannah?"

"Not yet."

"Call her. I'll have lunch for us in the dining room."

Carol studied her mother, watched as she turned, back straight, and headed for the kitchen. When had things between them grown so shallow and cold? A functional ability to exist in the same room was all they had together, all they shared. But even as she pondered the lack of depth between her and her mother, a question slammed into her soul.

Was this how Hannah saw her? An imposing figure who visited a few times a year? Suddenly the cost of living overseas felt overwhelming. What had she missed with Hannah? Walks in the park and bedtime stories? Endless conversations about school and boys and maybe even Mike Conner? Certainly his place in her life would've come up sooner if she and Hannah lived together.

Carol dismissed the thoughts. She spun, walked down the hall and into their home office, and shut the double doors. Hannah's cell phone would be off during school hours. She went to the phone and dialed the school's number.

"Thomas Jefferson Prep, how can I help you?"

"This is Carol Roberts." Carol leaned against the desk and felt the tension at the base of her neck. Maybe Hannah wouldn't care if she was home; maybe she'd disregard her request and stay at school all afternoon. Carol summoned her strength. The clouds in her memory were about to break wide open. "I need to get a message to my daughter, Hannah. She's a freshman."

❧❀❧

*H*annah was in advanced placement history that afternoon sitting next to the jerky junior, the one with blond hair, when an office attendant came through the door and whispered something to the teacher. After a few seconds the teacher nodded his head and took a note from the attendant.

As the woman left, the teacher looked at Hannah. "Ms. Roberts, I have a note for you."

A note? Hannah felt her back tense. Could it be from Mike Conner? Had he seen the story and found her at TJ Prep? Who else would be sending her a note in the middle of the school day? She gulped and straightened herself in her chair, her eyes on the paper in the teacher's hand.

"Hey, Hannah." The blond next to her leaned in. "Secret admirers in the office, too?" His tone was ripe with teasing. "So what's wrong with me, Hannah? I could help you find your dad."

"You—" She made a face at him, her voice louder than she intended. "—are pathetic. You couldn't help me find my way out of the room."

The teacher rapped his hand on the closest wall. "Classroom visitors," his voice boomed across the room, "are no excuse for childish behavior." He gave a sharp look at the junior and then at Hannah. "Miss Roberts, you will refrain from any further outbursts."

Hannah's hands trembled as she took the note from the teacher. She gave the blond one last glare. Everyone knew about her father now, but she didn't care. He had to be out there somewhere, seeing the stories, watching the music video with her message. Any day now he was bound to get in touch with her.

She opened the paper slowly, like it was a bad report card. Her eyes skipped to the bottom of the wording, and what she read there made the blood drain from her face. What was this? The note wasn't from her father at all. It was from her mother: *Darling . . . I'm at home waiting for you. Cancel your afternoon appointments. We need to talk. Mother.*

Hannah stared at the words. She read them two more

times, folded the note, and slipped it into her backpack. The jerky junior was staring at her, and she didn't want to tip him off, didn't want him to know that the note had upset her.

Her mother was home? All the way from Sweden? For a fraction of an instant, Hannah wanted to believe she'd come because of her request—that she be home for Christmas. After all, Buddy Bingo was praying every day for a Christmas miracle, so that Hannah could spend the holidays with her mom and dad.

But that wasn't why her mother had come. Of course not. She'd come because of the newspaper stories, because her own reputation was on the line. Hannah quietly seethed. Her mother cared nothing about being together for the holidays, but when her own public image was threatened, she'd get on a plane practically without notice and fly all day if she had to.

Three hours later—after talking with her cheer coach and her dance instructor—Hannah walked out the doors of TJ Prep. She'd told Buddy Bingo about the change in plans. He'd be there by now.

But instead, as she headed down the brick-lined walkway toward the circular drive and parent pick-up area, she saw her mother's sporty silver Jag. Hannah's steps slowed. Her mother had come? Were they headed straight for the office of the *Washington Post*?

She bit her lip and kept walking. Whatever her mother wanted from her, she wasn't about to cooperate. Not until her mother helped her find her dad. Hannah reached the car, opened the door, and slid inside. Without looking at her mom she said, "Hello, Mother. Thank you for picking me up." Formalities came first in the Roberts family. She set her backpack on the floor of the car and turned to meet her mother's eyes. "Can I ask why you're here?"

Her mother leaned back against the headrest, her gaze locked on Hannah's. Something in her eyes was different, softer. Instead of rattling off a list of things they were going to accomplish, instead of slipping the car into gear and driving away without so much as a glance in Hannah's direction, her mother gave her a sad sort of look.

"I'm here—" She reached out and touched Hannah's shoulder. "—because I want to tell you about Mike Conner."

CHAPTER EIGHT

$\mathcal{W}$ith every moment, every step, Carol could feel the years slipping away.

They went to a coffee shop, a dimly lit place tucked between the Yarn Barn and a Geoffrey Allen hair salon in an older section of Bethesda. At three-thirty in the afternoon they were the only customers. They ordered—a nonfat, sugar-free vanilla latte for Carol, a caramel macchiato for Hannah—and took their drinks to a booth at the back of the room.

The entire time, Carol watched Hannah with new eyes. A long time ago, she'd been just like her, hadn't she? Independent, indifferent to the political importance of her parents, articulate beyond her years. Her father had been a congressman, and her mother had planned out Carol's life long before she entered high school.

They sat across from each other and Carol stirred her

drink. "Mike was everything I couldn't have," she said without explanation.

"Really?" Hannah's eyes were wide. She looked nervous, expectant, like she was afraid to breathe for fear Carol would change her mind.

Carol sipped her coffee. Her eyes found a place at the center of her drink. "After high school I went to Pismo Beach with my best friend, Clara. Her aunt and uncle lived there." Carol's vision blurred and she could see Clara again, feel the excitement of getting away from Washington, D.C., going somewhere as foreign and exotic as California. She looked up at Hannah. "I met Mike on the beach the second day of summer."

"What was he like?"

Carol smiled. "He was the most handsome boy on the beach. Tan and blond, muscled from years of surfing." Carol looked at the table, the past clearer still. "He saw Clara and me on our towels and came over. His hair was wet." She touched her eyebrows. "Drops of salt water hung on his eyelashes and from the tip of his nose. He had a beat-up surfboard under one arm." She uttered a single chuckle at the image in her memory. "He said he was giving surfing lessons if we wanted to learn."

"That's so cool."

Carol smiled and found Hannah's eyes again. "It was."

A spark lit in Hannah's eyes. She was engaged now, fully caught up in the story. Carol settled against the back of the booth and allowed the story to come in rich detail, the way it had felt all those years ago . . .

✳✳✳

*W*ith Mike standing on the hot sand a few feet from them, hand outstretched, Carol looked at Clara and shrugged. Then she took Mike's hand, let him pull her to her feet, and ran after him toward the surf.

She'd never stepped foot in the Pacific Ocean, let alone been on a surfboard. But Mike was tall and confident, strong in a way that felt safe and dangerous all at the same time.

"So," he looked over his shoulder at her as they hopped the surf and headed out to waist-deep water, "where you from?"

"D.C."

He stopped, the surfboard still under his arm, and gave her a slight grin. "Washington, D.C.?"

"Right." She felt uneasy, as if being from the East Coast meant she somehow didn't measure up.

But he only studied her and said, "I'm Mike Conner."

"I'm Carol. Carol Paul."

"Hi, Carol." He grinned again and gave her hand a quick squeeze. Then he said something that stuck with her for the next few years. "People from Washington, D.C., are too serious."

"Oh, yeah?" She felt her eyes dance, felt them catch a splash of sunshine in the reflection off the water.

"Yeah." He took a few more steps forward, his eyes still on hers. "Way too serious."

"Okay." With her free hand she made a quick skimming motion over the surf, spraying water at his face. "How's that for serious?"

He laughed again, shaking the wetness off his face. "Not bad." He dropped his surfboard in the water and high stepped it through the shallow water until he caught her. Then he gripped her waist, picked her up, and tossed her toward the deeper water.

"Mike!" She was breathless when she came up for air, not so much because of the cold water, but because Mike was standing a few feet away grinning, his chest heaving.

"More?"

"No!" She held her hands out, trying to keep him away. "I thought you were teaching me how to surf!"

He held his arms out and laughed again. "But then Miss Serious went and splashed me!" Mike turned and snagged his surfboard, which was drifting away. They were the only ones in that area of the water. "You want a lesson or not?"

***

*C*arol blinked and took another sip of her coffee. "I felt free and happy and alive, Hannah." She looked at her daughter. "It was the first time I could remember feeling that way."

Hannah was quiet, waiting for the rest.

"We surfed together the rest of the day." Carol stared at the empty seat beside Hannah. She could see Mike pressing the surfboard down below the water and climbing on top of it, hear him explaining it to her that first time . . .

❧

*Y*ou get on like this, then you paddle to where the waves are breaking." He pointed to an area of the ocean a few dozen yards out. "The wave builds up and you paddle like crazy. When you feel the wave catch the board, you pull yourself up onto your feet."

Carol must've looked lost, because Mike chuckled and shook his head. "Scratch that. First time just stay on your stomach and ride it in."

He showed her a few times, and on the third time he slipped his feet beneath him and stood up, easily maneuvering the board through the wave. Before the surf evened out, he saluted her and fell off.

"Your turn." He was dripping wet as he moved gracefully through the water, carrying the surfboard to her. She took the board and he looped his arm around her waist, holding the board steady while she climbed on. Her heart pounded within her; she was terrified that a shark would snatch her feet or that a big wave would pull her out to deep water, never to be seen or heard from again.

But Mike shouted at her from his place in the shallow surf, telling her when to turn around, when to paddle hard, and she caught the first wave that came her way. The speed gave her a rush she hadn't expected. She flew on the board across the water, not stopping until the wave died and the board spilled her into the knee-deep tide.

She hooted and raised her fist, pumping it in the air. Out where he stood in the water, Mike did the same. And in that moment, she forgot completely about her parents' politics or the expectations her mother had for her.

All that mattered was Mike Conner and the way he made her feel.

They spent the day in the water. Every now and then Clara would come close to the water, sometimes close enough to get her toes wet. "Carol," she'd holler across the sound of the surf. "You're gonna get sunburned."

"I'm fine," Carol would shout back.

And in that way she stayed out in the water with Mike until the afternoon sun was heading fast for the horizon. Mike walked with her back to the towel, looking at her the whole time. "How old are you?"

She was glad for the sunshine, glad he couldn't see the heat in her cheeks from his nearness and the bold way he had with her. "Nineteen this fall," she told him. "You?"

"Twenty-one." He seemed to anticipate her next question. He spread his hand out and gestured to the sandy beach. "This is my office."

"Your office?" She giggled.

"I'm a lifeguard." The two of them still made their

way up the sand toward where Clara was reading. He winked at her. "Today's my day off."

Carol didn't let her surprise show. Every boy that age back home—the ones in her circle, anyway—were working on their bachelor's degree, making plans to intern in someone's office or for someone's campaign. She couldn't imagine spending every day on a beach.

Just before they reached Clara and the towels, Mike turned to her and took her hand. "Go out with me tonight. We'll get some ice cream, maybe, and come back here, okay?" He gazed out to sea. "It's beautiful at night."

She'd been wondering if she would see him again. And in that moment, his words came back to her. *"People from Washington, D.C., are too serious."* She swallowed her fears and nodded big. "Clara won't mind."

Clara didn't, but her parents did. They asked Mike to come in when he stopped by to pick her up that night. After chatting with him for ten minutes they gave a nod in Carol's direction. It was okay; she could go out with him.

That night, when their ice cream was gone, Mike took her to a pier not far from the beach where they'd played earlier that day. They walked to the end and leaned against the old wooden railing.

"See?" He faced her, his elbow looped casually over the rail. "Isn't it beautiful?"

It was. Carol had never felt so free and alive and . . . and something else. She was trying to figure it out when he leaned in and kissed her.

School and political functions and vacations to the eastern seaboard had made up Carol's entire life until that point. She had never been kissed, and the feel of it—sweet and full and brief—made her wonder if she could ever go back.

She paced herself after that, spending half her time with Clara, and half with Mike. He had a friend, and several times a week the four of them would double date.

Partway through summer, her mother confronted her about the situation.

"Clara's mother tells me you've found a boy."

"Yes." Carol cringed. The way her mother said it, *boy* sounded like a contagious disease. "Yes." She tried to salvage the situation. "His name is Mike. He's very nice."

"He's a . . . surfer, is that it?"

"He protects people at the beach. It's a very honorable job, Mother."

"Carol, what would you know about honorable." Her mother was disgusted, the pretense gone. "Lifeguards are drifters."

"He's not a drifter. He's kind and funny and he makes me smile."

"This conversation is over." Her mother was hissing now, furious. "You won't see the boy again, is that understood? You have college and half a dozen wonderful young men waiting for you here at home. People like us don't date surfers, Carol." She huffed for emphasis. "Am I understood?"

Carol had nothing to say to her. She hung up before her mother could finish. She had no intention of following orders this time. She couldn't follow them if she wanted to. Because by then she'd fallen for Mike—fallen hard, the same way he had.

"Summer's almost over," he told her one night as they walked along the beach. He turned and searched her eyes. "Stay with me, Carol. Marry me. No one's ever made me feel this way."

Two thoughts hit Carol at the same instant: first, she would stay. How could she do anything else? But the other thought caught her off guard. She didn't want to marry him. Marriage meant a wedding, the sort that involved a year of planning and a beautiful gown and a dinner party with hundreds of important people. Those were the only weddings she knew, and if she ever got married, that would be the type she would have.

But if she married Mike Conner, she might as well elope. Her parents wouldn't come to the wedding. They'd hardly throw her a party.

"Well . . ." He slipped his hands in his pocket and gave a shrug of his shoulders. He had never looked more irresistible. Then he pulled a ring from his pocket, a slender solitaire with a small diamond at the center. He held it out to her, his eyes damp. "Will you marry me, Carol?"

"Mike . . . yes!" A soft gasp came from her and she let him slip the ring on her finger. Her brain was shouting at her, telling her it could never work with her parents so set against it. But in that moment she wanted only to be in Mike's arms, lost in his embrace, his kiss.

✻✻✻

Carol stopped talking and looked at her coffee. It was half full, too cold to drink. She looked at Hannah. "I never had time to think it through." She gave a light shrug. "When Mike gave me the ring, I figured it didn't matter. The world could fall apart and I'd be okay as long as I had him in my life."

"So . . . you did marry him?"

"No." Carol looked down at her fingers, at the ring on her left hand, the ring from Jack Roberts. She drew in a slow breath and met Hannah's curious eyes once more. "I called my parents the next day to tell them the news. They said if that was my decision, they would wash their hands of me."

Hannah took another swig from her drink. "I can picture Grandmother doing that."

The remark cut at Carol. Wasn't it the same thing she would've done if Hannah had called with a similar pronouncement? She leaned back, missing Mike for the first time in years. "I moved in with him." She pursed her lips and shrugged. "Not very smart, but that's what I did. I enrolled in a local college and every month or so I promised him we'd get married soon." She anchored her elbows on the table and gave Hannah a sad smile. "Instead, I wound up pregnant with you."

"What did . . . what did Mike think?"

"He was thrilled. He said it was the perfect reason to get married, now that we were going to be a family."

"Did Grandmother and Grandfather know?"

"I called and told them." Carol remembered their voices, the disappointment. "They told me they'd be waiting for me in Washington, D.C., if I ever got smart and decided to come home." She paused, the memories alive again. "Mike was a wonderful father." She looked at Hannah. "Better at parenting than I was, I'm afraid."

Hannah stirred the straw in her drink. "I remember him." She squinted, and it looked like she was fighting tears. "Did I ever tell you that?"

"No." Carol felt her heart skip a beat. Hannah remembered? No wonder the package had set her off, caused her to go on a frantic search for him. "What do you remember?"

Hannah looked up at nothing in particular. "I remember sitting and playing on the floor with him." Her eyes met Carol's. "I remember him playing the guitar."

"Yes." Carol's throat was thick. "He was quite good."

"So what happened?" Hannah's voice was thick. Tears filled her eyes. "Why did you leave?"

Carol squirmed, but there was no comfortable way to say it. "I grew ambitious, dreaming about the sort of life I'd lived as a kid. The successful politicians, the savvy businessmen, the wealth and privilege, I began to crave it all. Mike wasn't . . . He wasn't enough after awhile." Her heart wanted her to regret the decision, but she couldn't. The truth was she'd leave him again if she had it to do over.

She clenched her teeth, not sure how to go on. But after a few seconds she summed up the ending. Mike had wanted to give Carol the life she hungered after, but he wasn't able. He was a lifeguard—a happy, kind man who would never be invited to high-powered political parties, never provide a six-figure income for his family.

By the time Hannah was three, Mike became insistent that they get married. "This is no life for a little girl, Carol," he would tell her. "We need to give her security, a real life. I don't want her to think of me as her mother's boyfriend."

Carol refused, insisting that she couldn't commit a lifetime to him unless he had some other direction for his future, something other than guarding Pismo Beach.

"That's lousy, Mother." Hannah's voice was just short of condemning.

"I know it." Carol deserved this, deserved the pain in her heart that came from talking about the past, from admitting her part in it all. "It was very lousy."

Hannah played with her straw some more, her eyes never leaving Carol's. "So what happened?"

"He enlisted with the Army. He wanted to fly planes, but he didn't have a college degree. So he joined the Army. That way he could be a helicopter pilot. A warrant officer. Something he thought would carry the prestige and future I wanted." Carol pressed her fingertips to her eyes, warding off the headache that was starting near her temples. "He absolutely enlisted. I'm sure of it."

"They can't find his records. I had them check every branch for Mike Conner."

"Wait." Carol's eyes narrowed. "*Conner* wasn't his given name. It might've been his middle name, actually." She closed her eyes, willing herself to remember. Suddenly it came to her. "His legal name was Mike Meade. Mike Conner Meade. I'll bet he's enlisted under that name."

Life sprang to Hannah's eyes. "Really?"

"Yes." Carol was catching Hannah's enthusiasm. "On the beach he went by Conner. It was his middle name. The guys called him Mike Conner. Almost no one knew him by his last name."

"It's worth checking." Hannah's expression came to life again. "Maybe when we get home, okay?"

"Okay." Carol's stomach tightened. Was it possible? Would they really find Mike, and if a visit was arranged, would she be able to look him in the eyes after so many years?

Hannah leaned in, her eyes sad. "Was it hard? Saying good-bye to my dad?"

Carol felt her chin quiver. "I loved him, Hannah. I didn't know how much until I left him." She hesitated. The headache was getting worse. "But it was harder on you."

A memory drifted back. Mike had his things in order for basic training, the period that would take him away for as much as four months . . .

*W*ait for me, Carol." He'd found her outside staring at the sky that night. He positioned himself in front of her and put his hands on her shoulders. "Please. You and Hannah. Let me get through training, then we'll live on base and after a few years we'll make our way back here, to the beach."

But she shook her head. By then her mind was made up. Her mother was right; her kind was in Washington, D.C. She'd been tricking herself all those years, but no more. "I can't stay here, Mike. Hannah and I are going home. At least for now."

In the end there was nothing Mike could do. He begged her to stay in the beach house, begged her every day. But she left one morning after he left for Oklahoma. There were a few more conversations, and lots of questions from Hannah. But neither of them ever saw Mike Conner Meade again.

*C*arol took a breath. The story was over, there were no more details to share, no more anecdotes to remember.

"What about me?" Hannah's voice cracked, fresh tears on her cheeks.

Carol reached across the table and took hold of her daughter's hands, which after so much time apart didn't feel even a little bit familiar. "You . . . you cried for days, weeks." It hurt worse now, remembering how it felt to leave Mike, how it had been to watch Hannah fall apart.

Now that the truth was out, tension made the air between them thick. Why had she done it? So she could find a man with money? With political power and connections in the nation's capital? Mike had been so different. He'd taught her how to laugh and spend quiet nights around the fireplace while he played the guitar. He taught her to run carefree down a sandy beach and, for a little while at least, to live free of the expectations of others.

But even so, she was sure of the thought that had struck her earlier in the conversation: if she had it to do over again, she would still leave him. Her life with Mike would never have been enough. She belonged in politics, in powerful circles. She'd been wrong to leave her parents' house, wrong to take up with Mike in the first place. And in that sense, no one could ever be more right for her than Jack Roberts.

"Mother," Hannah didn't blink. "How long before I stopped talking about him. Before I forgot him?"

The answers were harder with every question. "Two years." Guilt hung around Carol's neck like a necklace of bricks. It was all she could do to look at her daughter. "When you turned six, you seemed to forget."

Hannah hung her head. Then slowly she folded her

arms up on the table and buried her face in the crook of her elbow. She made no crying sounds, no noise at all. But her shoulders began to tremble and after a minute, her back shook from the force of her silent sobs.

And that was when Carol knew with absolute certainty that she'd been wrong. Hannah had never forgotten, never stopped caring. She'd never for a moment gotten over the loss of her father. For the first time in eleven years, Carol could see that. Her selfish decision had given her the life she truly wanted, the one she loved. But it had hurt other people—her parents, for sure, and of course Mike. But now she knew the worst part.

She'd hurt Hannah most of all.

CHAPTER NINE

*T*he mission had been postponed.

An intelligence report confirmed that the insurgents had left the compound for what appeared to be a short trip into the city. When they returned, there would be little warning. Mike and CJ, the gunner, and the Rangers had to be ready to go at a moment's notice.

In the days that had passed, there'd been no call from Hannah, and Mike had convinced himself. It was a lark, a fluke, a mistake. Somewhere in the world there was another Hannah with a father serving overseas, a father who used to surf and read to his little girl. Mike had made peace with the reality and he was ready to get the mission underway, ready to eliminate the insurgents.

They knew more about the bad guys now. These weren't only insurgents, but terrorists in training. The most elite and organized of the opposition to freedom in

Iraq. Men who were dangerous and cunning, responsible for the deaths of numerous American and Allied forces. A group who needed to be removed from the theater of war as soon as possible.

And so it came as no shock early on the morning of Thursday, December 15, when Mike woke from a light sleep to see Colonel Whalin standing over him. Mike sat up immediately, working to clear his head. "Sir?"

"Meade, it's time. The others are getting ready."

"Yes, sir."

Mike was up and dressed for flight in a few minutes. When they were ready, Colonel Whalin lined them up for a briefing.

"The insurgents have returned to the compound as of yesterday afternoon. They're tired and asleep—sleeping hard, we believe." He was smoking again, pulling hard on the end of a Camel. He paced a few steps and looked at Mike first. "There won't be a better time than now."

Mike was standing at attention alongside Ceej. The gunner was on CJ's other side, and the Rangers were lined up beside him. It was two o'clock in the morning. Their window was a small one.

Colonel Whalin stopped and put his hands on his hips. "The chopper's ready, men. Any questions?"

Mike gave a slight nod. "Yes, sir. Total time for the mission?"

"It's a thirty-minute flight, ten of it over the enemy lines into the area of insurgents. Add ten or eleven minutes for the mission, and I'd expect you back here in seventy-five minutes. Ninety tops. Nothing more."

"Yes, sir." Mike knew the answer, but he wanted to hear it again. That way he could will himself to believe his commander was right. That in an hour and a half they'd be back in their tents, facing Colonel Whalin, debriefing the events of the mission. Thanking Stoker for praying.

The colonel went over a few other details, items they'd discussed before. Then he flicked his cigarette out through the tent flap and stared at the men. "Are we ready?"

Mike was the captain, the one with the most seniority. He saluted his commander. "Ready, sir."

They were ushered out onto a makeshift tarmac where the helicopter was going through last-minute checks. By the time Mike and CJ took the cockpit, it was fueled and ready to go. The Rangers were armed to the teeth, packing M-16 machine guns and M-9 pistols, along with enough ammo to fight their way out of any firestorm. They had protective chest gear and bulletproof helmets.

The gunner was a guy named Fish, with big eyes and few words. He took the jump seat closest to the open door. Mike went through a series of checks with CJ, and then—with the target insurgent compound keyed in on the radar, they lifted.

Choppers were the best way to pull off a mission like this one. They could hover a few feet above a target, waiting while the ground crew handled the job. But noise was always a factor. There was no way to move a military helicopter into an area without noise.

Mike stayed focused as he moved across the enemy lines. The camps below looked quiet, almost completely dark. They were bound to hear the chopper, but by the time they crawled out of bed Mike and his men would be too far gone to bother with.

"Closing in." CJ stared out the window and checked the points on the radar. A few minutes and we'll be overhead."

"Roger that." Mike narrowed his eyes. The men in the cargo area behind him were quiet, no doubt going through the motions of their assignments. Intelligence reports had helped a great deal. Mike knew exactly which part of the roof to hover above, and the Rangers knew which window to break through. The course on the inside had been marked out also.

If everything went well, they might finish in as few as nine minutes. That's what Mike was pulling for.

"Okay, we're coming up on it." CJ still had the trace of a smile, but his voice was tense, the way it always was in situations like this. He was a great copilot because he left no detail to chance. "See it there . . . just ahead."

Mike could see it, but there was something wrong. They'd been told that the compound would be dark. Tired insurgents, sleeping hard after a several day outing into the city for supplies and weapons. Instead, a fire burned in the center courtyard, and a group of people stood around it. Far more people than the fifteen insurgents they'd been sent in to capture.

"It's an ambush." Mike said the words even as the realization was hitting him. The information must've leaked somehow. Or maybe it wasn't an ambush. Maybe the insurgents weren't sleeping because they were debriefing, planning an attack of their own. Either way, it didn't matter. They weren't only in trouble, they were in danger. "Let's get out of here."

Mike was circling, turning the chopper around, when the first grenade ripped through the side of the aircraft, narrowly missing CJ. The control panel was partially destroyed, but before Ceej could survey the damage, a second grenade tore into the rear blades.

"We're hit! We're hit!" CJ shouted the obvious, doing his job, keeping Mike informed.

"Roger, heading back to camp." Mike shouted the affirmation, but it was wishful thinking. The chopper was mortally wounded, losing air speed and altitude. Mike could hear the Rangers' voices, sharp and intense, making plans for the crash landing that was coming.

"We're in trouble!" CJ stared at the crowd of men running toward the wounded chopper.

"Come on, baby, get us over the line." Mike could feel sweat break out across his forehead and his heart raced. He'd been in more firestorms than he could count, but he'd never been hit like this.

"We're losing speed." CJ's face was pale even in the dark. His eyes darted from what was left of the control panel to Mike, and back to the controls. "We need a landing spot."

The chopper was stuck in a circling motion, unable to move ahead because of the damaged rear blades. Mike fought with the machine but it was no use. Ceej was right. They'd have to land the chopper in enemy territory, in plain sight of the insurgents who had fired the rocket-propelled grenades, full sight of every one of the enemy men gathered around the fire at the compound.

The crash came quickly.

Mike and CJ spotted the field at the same time, a small patch of tumbleweeds and sand with buildings on either side. It was their only choice. He let up on the engine and the chopper sputtered toward the ground. "Prepare for landing," he shouted at the men in the back.

Ceej checked the radar once more. "When we touch down, run north," he craned his neck, yelling at the others. "Run away from the compound."

They were details all of them knew, but in the final minute before the chopper hit the ground, the instructions were all Mike or CJ could do. Mike forced his arms to go limp, something he'd learned in flight school. Relaxed pilots survived more often. *Stay relaxed.*

"Don't tense up!" He screamed at Ceej, and in the last seconds before they hit the ground he wondered if this was it, the end of the road for all of them. His eyes met

CJ's just as the chopper leaned hard to the right and made contact with the field.

The fuselage fell apart, ripping right across the place where CJ sat. His head took most of the force of the crash, and by the time the chopper's engines fell silent, Mike didn't have to ask.

Ceej was dead. Just like that, life one second, death the next.

"No!" Mike unbuckled himself, grabbed the name-and-rank patch off CJ's flight suit, and placed his hand on his friend's damaged head. "No, Ceej . . . I'm sorry. I'm so sorry." He hung his head, hesitating only for a heartbeat. Then he pushed his way into the broken cargo area. The gunner and every Ranger had survived. "Let's go!"

Mike was first out of the open door, but already it was too late. The chopper was surrounded by armed insurgents—angry, shouting profanities, mocking the soldiers. Mike stood in front of the others, guarding them. He raised his hands and made eye contact with the insurgents. "Don't shoot!"

One of the insurgents laughed, and then the mob came at them. They were grabbed and pulled from the scene of the crash, six of their guys to every one of the men in the chopper. The fight was over before it began. In the chaos, Mike heard a few English sentences. The one that came across the clearest told him that the end was near:

"Wait," one of the insurgents shouted. "Don't kill them until they're inside."

But the beatings began long before that. With sticks and clubs and rifle butts, the insurgents attacked Mike and the others, hitting them again and again, forgetting the instructions about waiting until they were inside. Mike closed his eyes and one single thought ran through his head.

Hannah . . . Wherever you are, Hannah, I love you. He could feel her in his arms, feel her head cradled against his chest as he read *Cat in the Hat* to her and—

"You!" someone screamed at him. "Open your eyes!"

He did as he was told, blinking back the blood that was streaming down his forehead into his eyes. The door to the compound was still fifty yards away, and at that instant, Mike saw one of the insurgents run through the crowd and swing a boot toward his face.

Then there was nothing but gritty sand and hot-blinding pain and darkness.

CHAPTER TEN

*T*he clue that Mike Conner's real last name was Meade turned out to be all they needed, and now Hannah had a feeling they were hours away from finding her dad.

Her mother had called Congressman McKenna when they returned home from coffee, but he was out for the day. Now it was Thursday afternoon and she had him on the line.

"You've probably read about Hannah's search." Carol managed a polite laugh. "We didn't mean for it to be a media event, but, well . . . the fact is we need to find him." She explained that they had more information now. Mike Meade, she told him. Could he please check the Army for a Mike Meade?

Hannah barely remembered to breathe as her mother put the call on speaker phone. The congressman was checking. After a minute he returned to the phone.

"That's it," he sounded excited. "Mike Meade, born May 7, 1970."

Hannah's mother hung her head, relief filling in the lines on her forehead. "That's him."

"He's a chopper pilot, a captain." The man hesitated. "Looks like he's been in since 1994. He's stationed over in Baghdad, piloting one of the crews designated to fight insurgents."

Hannah wasn't sure what that meant, but it sounded dangerous. She clutched at her stomach and crossed the room to the bank of windows that looked out over their stately neighborhood. *Daddy, we found you.* Tears stung her eyes. *We found you.*

But what if he was in trouble? Insurgents? Those were the bad guys, right? She pressed her head against the window frame and willed herself to think clearly. It was dangerous, but it would be okay. He'd been doing this for years.

She turned and listened to the conversation. Congressman McKenna was talking.

"I'll contact his commander, get a message to him right away so he can call Hannah. If anything comes up, I'll give you a call."

Her mother rattled off a list of cell phones and contact numbers, in case the congressman couldn't get through on the house line. Then she thanked him and hung up.

Hannah had never felt close to her mother, not as far

back as she could remember. But now—with her father found—she walked back to the place where her mother stood, and without saying a word she fell into her arms. The moment was awkward, but Hannah needed it, anyway.

They were still hugging a minute later when the phone rang. Hannah pulled back, confused. Had the congressman located her father's commander that quickly? She wrapped her arms around her middle again and watched as her mother took the call.

After a few seconds her mother handed the phone over. "It's for you," she mouthed silently. "It's the country music station."

Hannah's breath caught in her throat. So much information at once, she could hardly take it in. She held the phone to her ear. "Hello, this is Hannah."

"Hi, this is Megan, I'm one of the producers working with the video messages for soldiers overseas."

"Hello." Hannah braced herself against the back of the sofa. "Have you heard from my dad?"

"I think so." The woman sighed. "It looks like one of the editorial assistants took a message from a Mike Meade a few days ago. The message was misplaced until today. I'm sorry."

"That's okay." Hannah wanted to rush the woman, get to the good part. "Really, you heard from him?"

"Yes. The man who called said to tell you he has similar pictures." She paused. "Oh, and that he was a surfer at Pismo Beach eleven years ago."

Hannah's head was spinning. Her father had called. It had to be him. He'd seen the video and tried to reach her! She wanted to jump through the roof and fly around the neighborhood. How could it be happening? It was all she could do to stay standing, but the woman was rattling off numbers and she took down the information, thanked her, and hung up the phone.

Then, with only a glance at her mother, she dialed the number she'd been given. A woman answered, and Hannah did as the instructions told. "Could you patch me in to Colonel Jared Whalin, please."

"Yes, just a minute." She was silent for a moment. "It's after midnight there. Maybe you could try tomorrow."

"Please!" Hannah heard the panic in her voice. "It's urgent, ma'am. Could you please try? Someone might be awake, right?"

"Well," the woman hesitated. "All right. If it's urgent, I'll give it a try."

She put Hannah on hold and after a few seconds the phone rang and a man picked up. "Colonel Whalin." His voice was terse.

"Yes . . ." Hannah was shaking. She could be minutes from talking to her father. The entire scene felt unreal, like something from a dream. She steadied herself. "My name's Hannah Roberts, and my father—" She let her eyes meet her mother's. "My father is Mike Meade. He's one of your chopper pilots, I believe."

For a few beats the man said nothing. Then he exhaled slowly. "Hannah . . ." His tone was kinder, but it was heavy. "Your father told me you might call."

"Yes, well . . ." Hannah could barely speak. Was this really happening? After so many years of dreaming about her daddy, had she finally found him? Her words were breathless, stuck in her throat. She forced herself to exhale. "Could I talk to him, sir?"

"Hannah, is your mother there? I have some things I need to tell her."

The colonel's words came at her like some sort of disconnect. What did her mother have to do with the conversation? She wanted to speak to her father. Why didn't the colonel go find him and put him on the phone? "Sir? My mother, sir?"

"Yes." The commander sighed again, but it sounded more like a groan. "Please, Hannah."

"Fine, sir." Hannah held the phone to her mother. She felt faint, her mind swirling with the information. What was wrong? Was there a problem, something the colonel couldn't share with her? She gripped the edge of the sofa back and studied her mother.

"Hello?" Her mother knit her brow together, clearly confused. "This is Carol Roberts, Hannah's mother."

Whatever the colonel told her next, Hannah knew it wasn't good. Her mother's face grew pinched, her eyes watery. She gave the commander their phone number and address, but otherwise she said very little, and then the conversation ended. When she hung up the phone, it took a while before she lifted her eyes to Hannah's.

"What's wrong? Why couldn't he come to the phone? How come the colonel didn't tell me?" Hannah's questions ran together. "What's wrong? Tell me, please."

Her mother reached for her hands and eased her around the edge of the sofa and onto the cushion. Then she crouched down and searched Hannah's eyes. "He's a prisoner, Hannah. His helicopter was shot down earlier today. They're trying to find a way to rescue him."

The words ripped into her, tearing at her dreams and breaking her heart. She slid off the sofa onto her knees and let her head fall against her mother's knees. "No, Mother . . . No, it can't be true. He was fine when he left me the message."

"The colonel talked about that." Her mother's voice was thick. "Your dad called you on Sunday, a few days before the mission."

Hannah grabbed her mother's arms. She was desperate, frantic. She had to find a way to get to him, to tell him she'd gotten his message. "They have to rescue him now, right now! Before something happens."

"Honey, they're trying." Her mother's eyes filled with tears. "The colonel said they're putting together a plan."

"But how can I reach him?" She was trembling, sick to her stomach, searching for an answer where none existed. The truth was more than she could take in. *My dad is a prisoner of war? What if someone's hurting him?* She shook her head, trying to clear her thoughts. "I have to talk to him."

"Shhh." Her mother ran her hand along the back of her head. "All we can do is wait. I'm sorry." Her voice cracked, and this was something else new: her mother allowing a show of emotion. She sniffed and held Hannah closer. "All we can do is wait."

✳✳✳

There was no word from the colonel by the next morning, so Hannah went to school. It was the only way she could make the time pass, the only way to keep running—the way that was familiar to her. But she couldn't concentrate on her classes or the lectures or anything but her father. There had to be something she could do, some way she could help him.

The idea came to her just after school let out. Her mother had a meeting with the congressman, looking for a way to speed up the rescue of her father and the men who had been with him on the mission. Hannah was skipping cheerleading, so she met Buddy Bingo out front near the flagpole at three o'clock. The temperatures hovered around freezing, and an icy wind hit her in the face as she flew out the school doors. More snow was in the forecast.

As soon as she climbed in the Town Car she leaned forward and craned her neck over the seat. "Buddy, I need help."

"What is it, Miss Hannah?" His eyes were instantly concerned.

She tugged on her sweater sleeves and explained the situation—how she had a different dad, one that she'd known as a little girl. And yesterday she'd found him, only he was overseas in Baghdad and now he was a prisoner of war. "He's in danger, Buddy." She gulped, terrified, too afraid to picture where he might be even at that minute. "You're praying for a Christmas miracle for me, right?"

"Right." Buddy's tone was gravely serious. "But Hannah, if he's a prisoner of war . . . has anyone heard from him?"

"That's just it." Her words came out fast, clipped. "His commander says they're putting together a rescue. So how about if we change the prayer and ask for a different miracle. That they'd find my dad and get him out of there before he gets hurt."

Buddy looked down and rubbed the back of his neck, slow and deliberate. When he looked up, he searched deep into her eyes. "Miss Hannah, can I ask you something?"

"Anything?" Hannah was out of breath. Her heart hadn't stopped racing since she saw the Town Car. If Buddy's miracle thing worked, then this might be her dad's only chance.

"Miracles aren't a given, Hannah. Do you know that?" Buddy's voice was serious.

"What do you mean?" She blinked; her heart skipped a beat. She needed a miracle now, more than ever.

"It takes belief, Hannah. Belief and prayer. Even so, sometimes God has another plan." He lowered his chin. "But either way, I can't be the only one believing and praying."

The notion hit Hannah square in the face. Buddy couldn't be the only one praying . . . of course not. She sat back and stared out the window. Why hadn't she thought of that before? Buddy was right. She could hardly ask him to pray for her Christmas miracle if she wasn't also willing to pray. She leaned up again and looked at him. "I do believe, Buddy. I've believed for a while now, I think. So . . ." She ran her tongue over her lower lip. "How do I pray?"

"There's no formula." Buddy gave her a familiar, tender smile, the one that made him look like Santa Claus. "You talk to God the same way you'd talk to your best friend."

"Can I try it?" Hannah tapped her toes on the floorboard of the car, the way she did when she was nervous. She looked around. They were still parked up against the curb in front of the school, but most of the other cars had already gone. "Right here?"

"Go ahead." Buddy bowed his head. "Give it a try."

Hannah followed his lead. She bowed her head and closed her eyes, more because it felt natural than because she was sure it was the right way to pray. She cleared her throat.

"Hi, God, it's me, Hannah." Her voice was shaky,

caught somewhere between scared-to-death for her father and uncertainty about what to say. She sucked in a quick breath. "God, my dad's in trouble. I haven't seen him in—" Her voice broke, and tears stung at her eyes.

"It's okay, Hannah." Buddy's voice was soft, low. "Take your time."

"Thanks." She swallowed a few times so she could find the words. She opened her eyes for a moment, and a trail of tears slid down both her cheeks. She sniffed and closed her eyes once more. "Anyway, God, I haven't seen my dad in a long time. And now he's a prisoner in Baghdad, and he needs your help. Remember the Christmas miracle Buddy's been praying for? That I would have Christmas with my mom and dad? Well—" The prayer was coming easier now. Buddy was right; it was just like talking. "—we'd like to add something. Please, God, just help Colonel Whalin and his men rescue my dad. That really would be the biggest, most amazing miracle of all. Thank You."

When she opened her eyes, Buddy was smiling at her. He held her gaze for a moment, then turned and pulled something out of a box on the seat next to him. It was a beautiful pair of red gloves—homemade, maybe. He held them out to her. "These are for you."

"Buddy . . ." She took them and turned them over, amazed at how soft they were. "Where did they come from?"

He turned so that he could see her straight on, see the

way the gloves fit her hands perfectly. "A long time ago, my mother gave me those." He pointed at the cuff on the gloves. "Look inside."

Hanna turned the cuff back and there, stitched on the inside in white, was the single word: *Believe*. She eased them onto her hands, one at a time, bringing them to her cheeks. "They're perfect."

"I've had them with me for a week or so." His eyes were bright, a mix of sadness and hope. "They're your Christmas present. But somehow"—he motioned to the gloves—"this seemed like the right time."

Hannah made her hands into fists and held her gloved fingers together. "Because of the message."

"Yes." Buddy patted her hands. "Because you need to believe. More now than ever."

"Thank you, Buddy." She felt warm all the way to her insides. "You always know what to say, what to do."

He took her home then, and she went inside to her room, to the quietest corner. There she took the gloves off and pressed them against her face. They smelled old, of cedar chests and cinnamon and long-ago Christmases. Already she treasured them. They would be a symbol, she decided. A reminder. She would wear them every time she left the house. That way she'd remember how important it was to pray.

And, when it came to miracles, how important it was to believe.

CHAPTER ELEVEN

$\mathcal{T}$he call Carol was dreading came Monday morning.

From the moment she'd heard that Mike was a prisoner of war, she'd been sick to her stomach. She was well aware of the treatment prisoners received in Iraq. Some were tortured and kept in cages, others were beaten and placed in pitch-dark solitary confinement. But ultimately, most of them were killed.

Hannah, meanwhile, walked around the house talking about prayer and belief and miracles, wearing a pair of red gloves the chauffeur had given her.

Carol had nothing against faith. If her daughter wanted to believe in something, fine. But believing in a miracle for her father couldn't possibly be wise. Not when he might already be dead.

Now, Hannah was at school when the phone rang. The knot in Carol's gut tightened as she took the call. "Hello?"

"Ms. Roberts?" It was Colonel Whalin's voice.

"Yes." Her heart rate doubled. "Do you have information about Hannah's father?"

The man was silent, and in that silence Carol knew. She knew that whatever news the commander was about to deliver would be bad—devastating, even. He cleared his voice. "We received an envelope from the insurgents."

Envelopes were never a good thing. Carol closed her eyes and waited.

"Inside were Mike's dog tags, the patches from his uniform—his name and rank—and a photo of a corpse." His voice was heavy. "I'm sorry, Ms. Roberts, as far as we can tell, the photo is of Hannah's father."

The bottom of Carol's heart fell away and she felt herself floating. *What will I tell Hannah?* How would her daughter ever forgive her for waiting so long to tell her about her dad? She pinched the bridge of her nose and forced herself to concentrate. "Are there identifying features, something that makes you sure it's him?"

"The body's dressed in a flight suit—one that appears to belong to Mike Meade."

Carol opened her eyes and stared out at the winter clouds. For a moment she saw him standing there, drenched in California sunshine, the surfboard beneath his arm. *"Come on, Carol, race you to the water!"* Her eyes stung. He was so strong, so vibrant and alive. She never should've kept Hannah from him, and now it was too late. She gave a shake of her head, searching for something to say. "Colonel Whalin . . ." How could he be gone? She massaged her throat. "What about the rescue?"

"It'll happen any day. From what we can tell nine men went down in the chopper and eight survived the crash, including Mike." He exhaled, his voice weary. "As many as seven of them may still be alive, trapped inside the insurgents' compound."

"Very well." She straightened herself, willing air to fill her lungs despite the panic suffocating her. "Please contact us afterward. Just in case."

"Yes." He paused, but in that pause there wasn't even a glimmer of hope. "Just in case."

※※※

*H*annah flew through the door just after three, the red gloves on her hands.

"Mother . . ." She was about to ask whether the colonel had called or not when she saw her mother's face. All her life, when she pictured her mother, Hannah had seen a dark-haired woman, beautiful and neatly put together. The image Carol Roberts gave to the world was not one that allowed shows of emotion or anything short of perfection.

That's how Hannah knew something was wrong.

As she rounded the corner into the living room, her mother was sitting on the sofa, her legs tucked beneath her. When she heard Hannah, she turned. Her face was streaked with mascara, her eyes swollen from crying. Her hair was flat and tucked behind her ears, as though she'd never even attempted to curl it.

"Mom?" Hannah stopped a few feet from her. She crossed her arms, cupping her elbows with her gloved hands. "What's wrong?"

"Hannah . . ." Her mother stood and shook her head. "I'm so sorry." Her eyes fell to the floor. "I should have told you about him sooner."

The thoughts in Hannah's head swirled and skipped around, and she struggled to make sense of her mother's statement. "Did . . ." She couldn't finish, couldn't bring herself to ask it. But she had no choice, because she had to know. Moving slow, carefully, she sat on the sofa arm, her eyes never left her mother's face. "Did the colonel call?"

Her mother lifted her head, her expression frozen, mouth drawn. "Yes." Her voice was so quiet, Hannah could hardly understand her. "They think your father's dead."

"No." Hannah shook her head, refusing to allow the words entrance to her mind. "No, Mother, he's a prisoner. He's not dead."

"Hannah," her mother stood and came to her. She looked tired and old and defeated. "His commander received an envelope with his things, his tags and patches, and a—" Her voice caught and she brought her hands to her face.

"What, Mother?" Hannah stood and went to her, taking hold of her wrists and lowering her hands so she could see her mother's face. But all the while she felt like a robot, as if her heart had been removed from her chest and she was merely operating on instinct. "What else?"

Her mother twisted her face, pain marking every crease and angle. She searched Hannah's eyes. "There was a photo of a dead man. They think . . . they think it's your father."

Hannah dropped her mother's hands. Her mouth hung open for a few moments, her mind racing. What had her mother said? They *thought* it was her father, right? Wasn't that it? They could be wrong, couldn't they? She swallowed, but her throat was too dry and the words wouldn't come.

Her knees shook and suddenly she couldn't stay on her feet another second. She dropped slowly to the ground, and somewhere in the distant places of her brain she heard herself begin to moan. "No . . . no, he can't be gone!"

"Hannah . . ." Her mother dropped to her knees next to her and put a hand on her back. "I'm so sorry."

"No!" She only shook her head, and this time the moan became louder, a desperate shout against everything that was happening around her, against the details that hung in the air like daggers over the two of them. She looked up and found her mother's eyes. "He could be wrong, couldn't he? The photo might not be my dad, right?"

It was her last hope, the last possibility that maybe—*maybe*—he was still alive, that the information was all some sort of terrible mistake. Her breathing was faster now, and she couldn't get enough air, couldn't seem to take a deep breath. Her chest heaved and she stared, wide eyed at her mother. "Right, Mom? Tell me I'm right!"

"Hannah . . ." Her mother shook her head, but that was all. There were no promises, no possibilities, nothing that would make her think for a moment that her mother held out any hope.

The red gloves felt like they were strangling her. Was this what she got for believing in miracles? A missed opportunity? A loss so great she couldn't fathom it? A father who never even knew how much she'd missed him? Was this what praying had brought about in her life?

She turned her hands palms up and was starting to tug on the fingers of the left glove when she spotted the word embroidered into the cuff: *Believe*. She stared at it and realized in a rush that already she'd stopped believing. In fact, she'd been about to throw the gloves across the room. Now, though, she froze, her eyes still on the word.

Next to her, her mother was saying something else, something about a rescue for whatever men might still be alive and how Colonel Whalin would call if there was any news, and suddenly Hannah gasped. "What did you say?"

Her mother slid over, closer. "Hannah, don't get your hopes up. Colonel Whalin saw the picture. It . . . it looked like your father."

"But they're doing a rescue, right?" She was on her feet, unable to contain the feelings welling within her. The gloves were only partway on her hands, and now she pushed her fingers hard back into them. No matter what, now, the gloves would stay. She lowered herself so her eyes were at the same level as her mother's. "A rescue, Mother, don't you see. The insurgents could've sent a bad picture. We won't know until they get all of the men out."

"I don't think it's smart to—"

"Please . . ." Hannah stood and touched her mother's shoulder with one red-gloved hand. "Give me this, Mother. I have to believe."

It was a truth she clung to the remainder of the day and through the night, when images of his capture and mistreatment threatened to suffocate her. Instead she prayed, just the way she'd done in Buddy Bingo's car.

Believing God could hear her, and that even now her father might still be alive. Believing it as though her next breath depended on it.

CHAPTER TWELVE

*T*he cell where they had him locked was more of a cage, a four-by-four box with metal bars. Twice a day they opened the door, jerked him onto the floor outside the cell, blindfolded him, and took him outside. He could tell because of the wind and sand, and because of the sun that shone through even the thick cloth over his eyes.

It was the middle of the night, and near as Mike could tell, he'd been a prisoner for nearly a week.

The initial blows from his captors had knocked him out, but only for a few minutes. He came to as they were shoving him into the cell, and even then he pretended to be unconscious. Peering through swollen eyes he could see he was alone with his captors, no sign of the Rangers or his gunner. The moment he moved, the insurgents were on him, grabbing him from the cell, placing him in crude handcuffs and chaining him to a table. The questions came like machine-gun fire, in a sort of broken English that was common among the people of Iraq.

"What you name?"

Mike had set his jaw and spit out the information. He was allowed to tell his name, rank, and serial number. Nothing else.

In a matter of seconds, the questions got harder. "What you mission?"

The air in the room was stifling hot, dank and suffocating. There were no windows, and Mike had the feeling they were underground. He remained silent and looked away from the man who asked the question.

A chorus of angry shouts came at him in Iraqi. The man asking the questions took a step closer, grabbed Mike's chin, and jerked his face forward again. "You watch me," he said, his breath hot and stale. "Understand?"

Mike had no choice, not with his hands tied. He glared at his captor, studying him. His hair was longer than the others, and a scar ran across his right cheek.

"I ask again." His lips curled in a sneer. "What you mission?"

Whatever the consequence, Mike would never answer such a question. He'd given the insurgents all the information they would ever receive from him. He jerked hard enough so his chin broke free from the man's grip, and he was able to turn his head sharply left once more.

This time the man slapped him, sending his head forward with a jolt. He spit at Mike and when the men behind him chuckled, he shouted something in Iraqi at them. Then he looked at Mike once more. "I say tell me you mission."

The session had lasted for what felt like an hour. When they saw they could get no more information from him, the insurgents took turns kicking him. Finally the leader unchained him and pulled him to his feet. "You finished," he shouted at Mike. Then he yanked off every patch on Mike's flight suit. He leaned in so his nose was touching Mike's. His voice dropped to a whisper. "You dead soldier."

The man's tone had left no doubt. Mike closed his eyes, but instead of imagining the bullet that would certainly slice through him any moment, he put himself in another place—the place he'd put himself for the past eleven years. On Pismo Beach with Hannah at his side, the smell of salt water filling his senses, the sun hot on his back as they worked on a sandcastle.

He could hear her little-girl laughter, feel her hand on his arm as she clamored for his attention every few minutes. *"Look, Daddy . . . a new shell!"* or *"See, Daddy . . . it has a door now!"*

But the bullet never came.

Instead, the leader grabbed his arm and shoved him onto the floor. "Crawl, soldier!"

And Mike did. He shuffled forward on his knees and when he was near the cell door, the man kicked him hard enough to send him crashing into the backside of the metal bars. The man locked the door, shouted something Mike didn't understand, and then the group of them left him alone.

Mike hadn't taken a full breath until they were gone. He was handcuffed, but he brought his fingers to his face and covered his eyes, unable to believe they'd let him live.

That was six days ago. The men—with different ones acting as the leader—had repeated the questioning every few hours since then, always with death threats. Once they showed him a photo of a headless corpse, and the leader from the first day gave him an evil smile. "That will be you, soldier. Soon."

Mike still believed it was true, but after surviving the first day, he began to do something he hadn't done in years. He began to pray. Back at the base, Stoker was praying for him. He had no doubts. He might as well pray for himself. The confinement was tight and cramped and lonely, and if nothing else, praying gave him someone to talk to. He believed in God, believed there was a purpose to life and the people who came and left from it.

At least that's the way he saw it that first night. But trapped in the cell, his body cramping from the heat and lack of water, certain that death was hours away, talking to God became a life rope, a desperate cry from the depths of darkness. And all because he wanted the one thing he'd wanted since he'd enlisted.

The chance to see Hannah again.

Mike brought his cuffed hands to the cell bars and

gripped them. He could hear the scurrying of a mouse—or what he figured were mice, but what might've also been cockroaches. The sound had been constant since they locked him up. But now, no matter how hard he tried to peer into the darkness, he couldn't see a thing. Nothing.

"God . . . I know You can see me, even here." He whispered the prayer out loud this time. Hearing his own voice on occasion helped him stay focused. Because even though the situation seemed dismal, he had to believe he was getting out, that his captors would forget him outside one of these times or leave him at the interrogating table unwatched. Something so that he could get away.

He tried again. "I know You're here, God. Talk to me, be with me." He tightened his grip on the bars. "Get me out of here. Please. Let me find Hannah."

No audible voice answered him in return, but something strange happened. The scurrying in the background stopped. It stopped for the next few minutes, and there was only the sound of his heartbeat. He relaxed his hands some. "God?"

He waited another few minutes and still the silence remained, and something more. A sense of peace, a knowledge that he wasn't in control but that God certainly was. No other way to explain it. He settled back onto the floor of the cage and leaned against the bars.

Whether he was there for ten minutes or two hours, he couldn't tell, but suddenly there was a shattering sound and the rapid explosion of gunfire. Before he could process what was happening, the room filled with light and three Army Rangers tore into it.

"Identify yourself," one of them shouted.

"Captain Mike Meade, U.S. Army."

"You're alive!" The lead Ranger snapped the lock on the small cell. "We have to move fast."

"I'll keep up." Mike could barely breathe. He was being rescued? Was that what was happening? Or was he dreaming, barely holding onto his sanity?

"There's no time." The first Ranger helped him out of the cell. "You all right?"

He ducked until he was clear of the bars, and then stood up. "Fine." Questions could come later. "Let's go."

They raced across the dirt floor and up a flight of stairs. As they were running another round of shouts rang out, followed by a quick string of bullets. Mike's heart pounded in his throat, but he had no time to think, no time to analyze whether it was all a dream or not.

When they reached the outside, he tore around the corner, close behind the Rangers. The loud pulsing of a helicopter made it impossible to hear anything. Where were the others, his gunner and the Rangers who'd been on his chopper? From the corner of his eye he saw bodies on the ground and for half a second he turned to look. The insurgents—it must have been them. All dead. His men must've already been rescued. Mike gulped, faced straight ahead again, and picked up his pace.

"Hurry!" One of the Rangers shouted above the sound of the helicopter.

Mike moved faster, keeping up with the soldiers even though his muscles were cramping, his lungs burning inside his chest. He had barely moved in a week. Now he was running on adrenaline, step after step, closer to escape. *God . . . is this real? Did You hear me?*

He blinked and gave a few shakes of his head. Whatever it was, he had to keep moving. Four more steps, five, six, and there she was. Hannah, standing in front of him, twirling in her first princess nightgown. *"You're my best friend, Daddy. Right?"*

"Faster, move it!" The Ranger's voice snapped him to attention.

Mike pushed his feet through the sand, one after the other, again and again. Ahead of him, an Army helicopter hovered over the roof of the building, not far from the place where he had attempted to hover a week earlier. A rope dangled from an open door, and the first Ranger grabbed it and shimmied up. Mike was next, but he didn't need help. He was in the chopper in record time, his sides heaving.

"I'll contact Colonel Whalin," one of the rangers said to another.

And only then did Mike know one thing without a doubt.

He wasn't dreaming.

✳︎

*T*he chopper flew to Baghdad International Airport and after an hour of debriefing with military personnel in a private area, Colonel Whalin entered the room. He stopped short when he saw Mike. His steps slowed, and their eyes locked.

When his commander reached him, Mike stood at attention. "Sir, the mission . . ." Emotions that Mike hadn't known before swelled in his chest. *Where are my men?* He coughed, working the words free. "The mission failed."

"Yes, Meade." Colonel Whalin's eyes were steely, but they glistened. "At ease."

Mike exhaled and let himself fall against a wall. They'd fed him and given him a sports drink to help hydrate him faster. But still he felt weak, overwhelmed. "I'm . . . sorry, sir."

"Meade, it wasn't your fault." The colonel looked Mike straight in the eyes. "You've gotta believe that."

He didn't want to ask the next question. "The others? They must've gotten out first?"

"No." An angry sigh came from the colonel. He raked his hand across the back of his head and let out an angry sigh. "Meade, I don't know how to tell you this."

Somewhere above his ankles, Mike felt himself begin to tremble. *No . . . It can't be . . .* "They did get out, sir." He searched his commander's face. "Tell me they got out."

Colonel Whalin pursed his lips, stared up at the ceiling, and gave a quick few shakes of his head. When he looked at Mike, there was no mistaking this time. His eyes were full of unshed tears. "We lost them all, Meade. All of them. Insurgents shot them before they ever made it into the building." He cursed under his breath. "It was a setup, Meade. A bad tip. No one should've made it out alive."

Mike felt faint, his head dizzy. They were gone? All the men on the mission? Why would their captors kill everyone but him? Then slowly it began to make sense. He was in charge; he had the information they wanted. The insurgents would've viewed the others as . . . dispensable.

He bent at his waist and gripped his knees. His breathing was different, more shallow. He couldn't get enough air no matter what he tried. *Deep breaths,* he told himself. *Slow, deep breaths.* He craned his neck back and looked at the colonel again. "I should've died with them, sir. The way it ended . . . it isn't right."

"You're wrong, Meade." Colonel Whalin searched Mike's face. "You followed orders."

"Sir?" Mike blinked. His head was still cloudy, his mind unclear. He could see his team in the chopper as they crossed enemy lines, CJ at his side, the gunner and the Rangers ready for action. Now they were gone, all of them. He blinked the memory back. "What orders, sir?"

"My orders, Meade. I told you to come back alive."

The colonel coughed, but his chin quivered. "You did what I asked."

Mike's throat was too thick to speak. There was nothing more to say, nothing he could add. The reasons weren't clear, they'd never be clear, but he was here, alive. His commander was right.

The debriefing lasted another few hours. When they were finished, Colonel Whalin lit a Camel and lifted a piece of paper from the desk in the room. "We have a plan for you, Meade. We're getting you home as quick as possible."

"Thank you, sir." Mike gripped his knees and tried to make sense of everything that was happening. His co-pilot was dead, the gunner, the Rangers, everyone else on the chopper. But here he was getting special treatment, a quicker trip back to the U.S. Probably so he could be home for Christmas. As if he might have any reason to be home.

Colonel Whalin was going on about the trip home, explaining that he would be placed on a C-130 Hercules cargo plane for a five-hour flight to Ramestein Air Base in Frankfurt, Germany. From there he'd fly on a C-17, a bigger cargo aircraft, back to the States.

"I pulled some strings." The colonel's face was still shadowed by the seriousness of the situation. "You got a nonstop to Andrews Air Force Base."

"Andrews?" That airport was more than a day's drive from his base. "I'm flying to Maryland?"

The colonel took a long drag from his cigarette. "It's Christmas, Meade." The smoke eased out between his words as he spoke. "I figured you'd want to be with your daughter."

It took several heartbeats before he could fully process the statement. His daughter? *Hannah?* What would Colonel Whalin know about her? He rubbed the back of his head and stood, gripping the edge of the desk. "Colonel," I haven't seen my daughter in eleven years."

"You said you were expecting her call?" The colonel cocked his head, curious. "That's the same daughter, right?"

Mike breathed out. He hadn't told anyone in the service about Hannah, not ever. "I have one daughter, sir. Her mother took her from me when I enlisted. I haven't heard from her or seen her since."

The colonel leaned forward and slammed his elbows on the desk. "How'd you know she might call?"

"A video. It's a long story." This time Mike's heart stopped. "Wait . . . she called?" He straightened, his mouth open. By the time his heart kicked in he found his voice again. "Hannah called? At your office?"

"She lives in the outskirts of Washington, D.C. I have all the information." For the first time that day, the colonel smiled.

"That's why I'm flying to Andrews, sir?"

"Now you're getting it, Meade. I thought you'd like to

spend Christmas with your daughter. The way the flights worked out, you should be there Christmas Eve."

Mike felt something strange and unfamiliar, a bursting in his heart, a giddiness that spread through him, along his limbs all the way to his hands and feet. Hannah had called? She'd talked with his commander? How was it even possible? Hours earlier he was locked in a cage, death raging around him, and now here he was. Every dream he'd ever had, about to come true.

He closed his eyes. *God . . . You did this, didn't You?*

In light of the future that lay ahead of him, the horror of the past week faded a little. And suddenly he realized what he was feeling, the amazing sensation making its way through him. It was something he hadn't felt for years.

Pure, uninhibited joy.

EPILOGUE

$\mathcal{H}$annah still wore the gloves.

She had nothing if she didn't have hope, and somehow the red gloves reminded her she could still pray, still believe. It was Christmas Eve, and she hadn't moved too far from the phone all day. Her mother had given up. She was busy in the office making calls to Sweden. Whenever she passed by, she would pat Hannah on the shoulder and give her a sad smile, as if to say everything would be okay, the sorrow would pass in time.

Hannah would only shake her head. "Mother, don't look at me like that. He's okay, I can feel it. I won't quit believing that until he comes home."

Her mother would hesitate and move on to some other order of business. There was always an order of business, and for her the order of finding Mike Meade was over.

But it wasn't over. Hannah refused to believe it. She'd

prayed, and Buddy Bingo had told her that God heard everything. And if God had heard her, then somehow she'd get to see her dad again, right?

Hannah walked into the front room and stared out the window. It was snowing again, the way it had been all day. The fireplace was alive, the flames dancing merrily, unaware of the trouble her father was in. She moved closer and turned one of the chairs so it faced the fire.

What else had Buddy said? That miracles weren't a given?

That idea was the one she couldn't allow to take root, because then she'd have to believe it was possible—after not knowing about him for so many years, now he might really be gone.

She sat down and faced the fire. "God . . . where is he?"

Her cheeks were cold, and she lifted her gloved hands to her face. The question floated in the air like the clouds outside. In the flames she could see him, his face the way it looked in the picture, the way it looked in her long ago memories. She was still thinking about him, still remembering, when she heard a knock at the door.

The house staff was off for the day, and her mother and grandmother were upstairs. She stood, stretched, and went to the foyer. They weren't expecting anyone, so maybe it was a delivery. They delivered on Christmas Eve, didn't they? If presents needed to get somewhere, right?

She opened the door. "Hello?"

On the step stood a man dressed in Army gear. In his hand he held a worn-looking paper sack. Something about him was familiar, and for half a second she wondered if he was her father. But that was impossible. He might be alive, but he was in Iraq, not Washington, D.C. Whoever the man was, his cheeks were red and he stared at her like he was seeing a ghost.

Just then she had a sudden fear and she took two steps backward. What if he'd come on official Army business, to tell her that her father was dead? Would the Army do that to her? On Christmas Eve? She took another step back. "Can . . . can I help you?"

He didn't look at her, he looked through her. And the "something familiar" was more so all the time. Then he swallowed and said, "Hannah?"

Her heart beat faster than before. "Yes?" Why did he look at her that way? Was this how it happened? How families found out that someone they loved was gone? She wanted to close her eyes and make him go away, but it was too late. The conversation had already begun. Now she'd have to see it through.

Then, the Army man's eyes welled with tears. He swallowed and took a step forward. "Hannah . . . I'm your father."

Her body shook and she felt dizzy, so dizzy she had to grab the doorframe to keep from falling. "Dad?" How could he be here? He was supposed to be in Iraq, a prisoner of war. His commander thought he was dead, right?

She blinked, trying to make sense of what she was seeing. "How could . . . I can't believe it." Her voice faded to nothing before she finished the sentence.

"Look at you, Hannah." A tear rolled down one of his cheeks. "You're all grown up."

And suddenly she knew it was him, knew it because the eyes were the same as the ones in the photographs. But more than that, they were the eyes from her memory. In a rush she ran to him. Her red-gloved hands went around his waist and she pressed her cheek to his chest. "I never forgot you, Daddy."

He shook against her, and Hannah could tell he was crying. They stayed that way for a while, holding on as if by doing so they could somehow find the years they'd lost. When he finally drew back a little, he searched her eyes. "I looked for you every chance I had." He held out the brown paper sack. "I kept this with me."

Hannah took the fragile bag and opened it. From inside she pulled out a folded piece of paper. She handed the bag back to her dad and opened the sheet. It was tattered and creased, but clearly it was a picture she'd drawn for her father. Across the top she'd written *Hannah loves Daddy*.

In an instant the memory came back. She was sitting at a small table, her father across from her. They were both coloring, weren't they? And hers had been a drawing of the two of them, her and her father, complete with their oversized silly grins and the big sun ball in the sky.

A picture of everything life had been for the two of them. Smiles and sunshine and togetherness.

She folded it carefully, handed it to her father, and met his eyes. "I remember making it for you."

"Really?" He slipped the paper back into the bag. "You really remember me?"

Hannah sniffed and tried to find her voice. Her tears were becoming sobs as the moment became more real. This was him, her father. The man she'd been missing for eleven years. "Yes." She grabbed a quick breath. "I remember you playing with me on the floor and . . . and reading to me." She took hold of his hands, feeling the warmth of his fingers through the red gloves. "I remember you playing the guitar." She put her arms around him again and pressed her cheek against his chest. "You must've seen my message."

"I did." He stroked her hair. "I couldn't believe it was you. After so many years of looking."

"They told us . . ." She swallowed a series of sobs. "They told us you were dead."

He tightened his hold on her. "I should be."

She drew back and studied his face. Whatever he'd been through, it must've been horrible. "Look at this." She held up her gloved hands, and turned the cuff down so he could read the embroidered word written on the inside of each.

"Believe." His voice was quiet, amazed.

She thought of Buddy Bingo, praying every day for her

Christmas miracle. Her tears subsided, and she caught her breath. "A friend gave them to me." She looked at the inside of the cuffs, and then up to her dad. "I wore them because I believed you'd be okay, that they'd rescue you, and you'd call." She made a sound that was mostly laughter. "I never thought you'd show up on my doorstep!"

He peered around her. "Can I come in?"

The question was a serious one; Hannah could see that in her father's eyes. After all, her mother had left without a forwarding address. He wouldn't know whether she'd want him in their house, even after so many years.

"Of course." Hannah hurried back a few steps and ushered him inside. "Mother's been helping me find you. She'll be so glad you're okay."

They made their way inside by the fire and sat in opposite chairs, their hands joined in the middle. Hannah told him about her life, how her mother had married a politician and how she rarely saw either of them.

"I'm sorry, Hannah." His shoulders slumped. "That's not right."

She shrugged. "It's all I know."

"Not after today." He flexed the muscles in his jaw. "I'm never leaving you."

There were steps in the foyer and then in the hallway, and she could hear her mother's voice. "Hannah? Is someone here?"

The look of perfection was back, and as her mother stepped into the room she was the picture of poise and position. Her eyes moved from Hannah to her father, and she came to a slow stop. "Mike?"

He stood and went to her, stopping short of a hug. She reached out her hands and he took them as their eyes locked onto each other. "Carol. You're still beautiful." He smiled, but Hannah could see the pain in his eyes.

"They told us you were dead." She looked at Hannah. "Did you tell him?"

"Yes, Mother." She stood, amazed at what she was seeing.

Her dad said something else then, something about being rescued and getting a rushed trip back home, but Hannah wasn't really listening. Her heart was in her throat. She'd found her daddy, the man in her memories. And now, whatever happened after this, she wasn't letting him go. He would be a part of her life forever more. Wasn't that what he'd said?

God had brought him home to her on Christmas Eve. She could hardly wait to tell Buddy. And what would her grandmother say? What would her daddy and her mother have to say to each other, once they got past these first few minutes?

That's when Hannah realized what had happened. Not only because her father was standing before her, but because her mother was, too. The thing she'd wanted most of all was her father's rescue, and that she might spend Christmas with her parents. Now, against any reason or commonsense, she was going to do just that.

A smile lifted the corners of her mouth and she studied her father, proud of him. He was a captain, a chopper pilot. And there he was, tall and strong and bigger than life! A song rang out from the depths of her soul. Because she could imagine getting to know her dad again, and maybe living with him when her mother was out of the country. Maybe singing while he played the guitar, or taking a trip to Pismo Beach with him so he could teach her to surf. She could imagine all of it, a life with her dad the way she'd always known it could be.

And that was something so big, so amazing, Buddy Bingo was right.

It could only be a Christmas miracle.

AUTHOR'S NOTE

*H*ello friends!

Merry Christmas, and thanks for traveling with me through the pages of yet another Red Gloves novel. It's become part of my pre–Christmas tradition, writing these stories and bringing them to you, knowing that for many of you they are now a part of your traditions as well.

If this is your first Red Gloves novel, let me give you a little background. In the book *Gideon's Gift* I told the story of a sick little girl and an angry homeless man and the gift that changes both their lives forever. That gift was a pair of red gloves. In the back of that book, I listed service project ideas—Red Gloves Projects. The goal was that you would travel from the pages of the story to the streets of your community, where you and your family or friends or coworkers might do something to help the homeless.

Next came *Maggie's Miracle*, with Red Gloves Projects

for needy children, and *Sarah's Song,* with Red Gloves Projects for the elderly. Always the red gloves play a cameo role in the story, bringing to mind again the gift Gideon gave to old, angry Earl in the first Red Gloves novel.

Hannah's Hope, of course, is a story centered around an earnest teenager who wants desperately to be reunited with her military father. The fact is around our country today there are thousands of children who feel the same way Hannah did. Not because they've been separated from their parents by thoughtlessness, the way Hannah was. Rather, because war has separated them.

Because of this, and to bring honor to the men and women who serve this country through the U.S. Armed Services, this year's Red Gloves Projects will center around the military. Our family started a Red Gloves Project for the military a few years ago. When we're in an airport, whenever we see a uniformed soldier, we slip him or her a twenty-dollar bill. Then we tell him or her, "Thank you for defending our freedom. Have lunch on us."

My kids and I did that last January at O'Hare International Airport. One of the uniformed soldiers was a tentative-looking young man standing in a food line with an older man who appeared to be his father. We gave him the money and the thank you and returned to our table.

A few minutes later, the young man's father approached us. He had tears in his eyes. "My son is going back for a second tour in Iraq." He held out his chest, clearly proud of his boy. "We would've been tempted to feel pretty low today." He paused. "You will never know how much your gift meant to us."

My kids and I were left with a joy that is indescribable. The simple joy of giving the gift of hope and appreciation to someone who deserves it.

With that in mind, I bring you this year's Red Gloves Projects:

RED GLOVES PROJECTS

By networking through your church or school or workplace, identify two to four soldiers currently serving overseas. Make a plan to bring them as much joy and appreciation as possible this Christmas. Round up as many people as you can, and have them write thank-you letters to the soldiers. You might contact your local school or organize this through your place of employment. Letters from both children and adults would be best. Next, purchase something special to go with the letters. Soldiers tell me that chewing gum and jelly beans are especially nice in the dusty desert areas. Finally, pack the letters and gifts in a box and top it off with a pair of Red Gloves and a copy of *Hannah's Hope* or another Christmas story whose message you enjoy. You might consider multiple copies so the soldier can pass them out to his or her friends. Reading material is hard to come by.

❧ Contact your local Armed Services recruiting office and ask if there are any soldiers who will not have the finances to come home for Christmas. Organize a group of people willing to help in this matter. Stage a fundraiser, or have these people donate money to the cause. Then arrange with the local office to purchase airfare for that soldier. Make sure you know the date and time he or she will be returning. Plan for your group to be at the airport with signs that read, "Welcome Home," and "Thank you!"

❧ Some soldiers will not have time off during Christmas. This will be an emotional burden on their families, but it can also be a financial strain. Talk to the local Armed Services office again, and ask if there are soldiers whose families could benefit from donated gifts. If so, get a group together and purchase those gifts. Deliver them with letters to the families, thanking them for sacrificing time with their loved ones so that we can remain a free country.

❧ Using the method in the first idea, locate a soldier who has family in your area. Next contact the soldier and express an interest in letting his or her entire unit know how grateful you are for their service. In our area, third-grade teacher Kathy Santschi arranged a campaign called "Jelly Bellies for Jonathan." Jonathan Vansandt is a friend of ours, and he had expressed a general wish in his unit for Jelly Bellies. All told, Kathy Santschi's third graders collected well over a hundred pounds of Jelly Bellies. Jonathan was the recipient, but he shared Jelly Bellies with dozens of soldiers serving in Iraq alongside him. The candy came with letters from the children, and Jonathan says it lifted the spirits of the entire unit for weeks. You could do this sort of thing with chewing gum or inspirational novels or whatever you think might change the course of a few weeks for an entire unit of soldiers.

❦ Of course, the one thing we can all do for our men and women serving overseas is pray. Make a prayer calendar with your family or group, and choose to deliberately pray for those serving in all branches of the Armed Forces. Pray for our president and the decisions he must make in the fight for freedom. And pray that God's mighty hand of protection be over everyone fighting for freedom across the world.

❦ You may not have twenty dollars for every soldier you see in an airport or at a supermarket this Christmas. But make a point of going up and shaking his or her hand. Look that soldier in the eyes and be clear about how thankful you are. You never know. Your words of thanks might make all the difference.

✳✳✳

I pray you have a wonderful, joyous Christmas season, finding time with friends and family, and making special note of the moments together. The years fly quickly, and what we celebrate today will tomorrow be but a memory. Please contact me at my E-mail address, rtnbykk@aol.com, and tell me about your Red Gloves Projects. They are happening around the world now. If we all do our part to experience the joy of giving, together we truly can put Christ back into our Christmas celebration.

Until next time, in His light and love,

Karen Kingsbury

P.S. I'd love to hear from you, as always.
www.KarenKingsbury.com

Life-Changing Fiction by Karen Kingsbury

Gideon's Gift

Maggie's Miracle

Sarah's Song

A Thousand Tomorrows

One Tuesday Morning

Ocean's Apart

Redemption

Remember

Return

Rejoice

Waiting for Morning

A Moment of Weakness

Halfway to Forever

When Joy Came to Stay

Where Yesterday Lives

On Every Side

A Time to Dance

A Time to Embrace

The Treasury of Miracles Series by Karen Kingsbury

A Treasury of Christmas Miracles

A Treasury of Miracles for Women

A Treasury of Miracles for Teens

A Treasury of Miracles for Friends